Angela Carter and Folk Music

Bloomsbury Studies in Global Women's Writing

A major scholarly series focusing on women's writing from around the world across the centuries and up to the present day, *Bloomsbury Studies in Global Women's Writing* will celebrate the diversity of women's writing throughout various genres, including the novel, poetry, drama, journals, diaries and letters etc. It is distinctive in not being restricted to any particular time-period, by traditional models of periodization, nor by any geographical boundaries. As such the series provides the space for greater fluidity and points of transition, whilst challenging pre-conceived ideas of cultural difference by exploring diverse understandings of women's writing, gendered identities, and the potential for literature to create bridges across international and historical divides.

Series Editors

Jennifer Gustar (Associate Professor, University of British Columbia, Canada)
Marie Mulvey-Roberts (University of the West of England, Bristol, UK)

Series Board

Eleanor Ty (Wilfred Laurier, Canada)
Claire Chambers (University of York, UK)
Ping Zhu (University of Oklahoma, USA)
Elleke Boehmer FRSL FRHistS FEA (University of Oxford, UK)
Rose Casey (West Virginia University, USA)
Indrani Karmakar (Chemnitz University of Technology, Germany)
Danai Mupotsa (University of Witwatersand, South Africa)
Brinda Bose (Jawaharlal Nehu University, India)
Grace Musila (University of Witwatersand, South Africa)

Angela Carter and Folk Music

'Invisible Music', Prose and the Art of Canorography

Polly Paulusma

BLOOMSBURY ACADEMIC
LONDON • NEW YORK • OXFORD • NEW DELHI • SYDNEY

BLOOMSBURY ACADEMIC
Bloomsbury Publishing Plc
50 Bedford Square, London, WC1B 3DP, UK
1385 Broadway, New York, NY 10018, USA
29 Earlsfort Terrace, Dublin 2, Ireland

BLOOMSBURY, BLOOMSBURY ACADEMIC and the Diana logo are trademarks of
Bloomsbury Publishing Plc

First published in Great Britain 2023
Paperback edition published 2024

Copyright © Polly Paulusma, 2023

Polly Paulusma has asserted her right under the Copyright, Designs and Patents
Act, 1988, to be identified as Author of this work.

For legal purposes the Acknowledgements on p. xv constitute an
extension of this copyright page.

Series design by Rebecca Heselton
Cover image: Ink and wash drawing from memory of Angela Carter
performing at 'Folksong and Ballad' in 1967 by Christine Molan

All rights reserved. No part of this publication may be reproduced or transmitted in any
form or by any means, electronic or mechanical, including photocopying, recording,
or any information storage or retrieval system, without prior permission in writing
from the publishers.

Bloomsbury Publishing Plc does not have any control over, or responsibility for, any
third-party websites referred to or in this book. All internet addresses given in
this book were correct at the time of going to press. The author and publisher regret any
inconvenience caused if addresses have changed or sites have ceased to exist,
but can accept no responsibility for any such changes.

A catalogue record for this book is available from the British Library.

Library of Congress Cataloging-in-Publication Data
Names: Paulusma, Polly, author.
Title: Angela Carter and folk music : "invisible music", prose, and the art of canorography /
Polly Paulusma.
Description: London ; New York : Bloomsbury Academic, 2022. | Series: Bloomsbury
studies in global women's writing | Includes bibliographical references and index.
Identifiers: LCCN 2022018607 | ISBN 9781350296282 (hardback) |
ISBN 9781350296329 (paperback) | ISBN 9781350296299 (ebook) |
ISBN 9781350296305 (epub) | ISBN 9781350296312
Subjects: LCSH: Carter, Angela, 1940–1992–Criticism and interpretation. |
Folk songs in literature. | Music and literature.
Classification: LCC ML3849 .P374 2022 | DDC 780/.08—dc23/eng/20220801
LC record available at https://lccn.loc.gov/2022018607

ISBN: HB: 978-1-3502-9628-2
PB: 978-1-3502-9632-9
ePDF: 978-1-3502-9629-9
eBook: 978-1-3502-9630-5

Series: Bloomsbury Studies in Global Women's Writing

Typeset by RefineCatch Limited, Bungay, Suffolk

To find out more about our authors and books visit www.bloomsbury.com
and sign up for our newsletters.

*In memory of my much-missed father
Professor Jonathan Riley-Smith
who died just as I began writing this book,
and for Mick, Vee and Coren,
without whose unfaltering support
I could not have completed it.*

Contents

List of figures	viii
List of folk songs and links	xi
List of abbreviations	xiv
Acknowledgements	xv
Preface	xvii

1	Songful influences	1
2	'a singer's swagger': Angela Carter, the folk singer	19
3	'me and not-me': folk songs, narrative perspectives and the gender imaginary in *Shadow Dance*	41
4	'an invented distance': folk songs, sonic geographies and the Erl-King's greenwood	61
5	'moving through time': folk songs, journeys and the picaresque in 'Reflections' and *The Infernal Desire Machines of Doctor Hoffman*	87
6	'only a bird in a gilded cage': folk songs, avianthropes and the canorographic voice in 'The Erl-King' and *Nights at the Circus*	113
7	'continued threads': Angela Carter and the folk singer Emily Portman	131
8	Sympathetic resonances	151

Appendices	157
Notes	163
Bibliography and Discography	209
Index	227

Figures

1. Photo detail of hand-written inscription on inside cover of James Reeves, *The Everlasting Circle* (1960), from Paul and Angela Carter's Folk Music Archive. Copyright © Christine Molan. Reproduced with kind permission of Christine Molan — 21
2. Peggy Seeger, *Troubled Love* EP, back cover (Topic Records TOP72, 1962). Copyright © Topic Records. Reproduced with kind permission of Topic Records — 23
3. Peggy Seeger, *Early in the Spring* EP, back cover (Topic Records TOP73, 1962). Copyright © Topic Records. Reproduced with kind permission of Topic Records — 24
4. Photo detail of 'Lucy Wan' notated by Angela Carter, from Paul and Angela Carter's Folk Music Archive. Copyright © Christine Molan. Reproduced with kind permission of Christine Molan — 32
5. Photo detail of 'Higher Germany' from Paul and Angela Carter's Folk Music Archive. Copyright © Christine Molan. Reproduced with kind permission of Christine Molan — 32
6. Photo of a page in Angela Carter's *1963–64 Journal*. Copyright © The Estate of Angela Carter. Reproduced with kind permission of the Estate c/o Rogers, Coleridge & White Ltd., 20 Powis Mews, London W11 1JN — 33
7. Photo detail of 'Three Pretty Maids' notated by Angela Carter, from Paul and Angela Carter's Folk Music Archive. Copyright © Christine Molan. Reproduced with kind permission of Christine Molan — 53
8. Photo detail of B. H. Bronson's 'modestar' diagram. Republished with permission of Princeton University Press from B. H. Bronson, *The Traditional Tunes of the Child Ballads* (Princeton, NJ: Princeton University Press, 1959), p. xlii; permission conveyed through Copyright Clearance Center, Inc. — 77
9. Photo detail of Paul Carter's 'modestar', from Paul and Angela Carter's Folk Music Archive. Copyright © Christine Molan. Reproduced with kind permission of Christine Molan — 77
10. Photo detail of Charlotte Sophia Burne's tune for 'Cold Blows the Wind' (a variant of 'The Unquiet Grave'). Republished with permission of Princeton University Press from B. H. Bronson, *The Singing Tradition of Child's Popular Ballads* (Princeton, NJ: Princeton University Press, 1976), pp. 203–5 (p. 205); permission conveyed through Copyright Clearance Center, Inc. — 78

11	Detail from 'Tam Lin' in James Johnson's *Scots Musical Museum* (1803). Image taken from the National Library of Scotland website <https://digital.nls.uk/special-collections-of-printed-music/archive/87802922> [accessed 18 February 2022]. Image reproduced with the permission of the National Library of Scotland	79
12	Photo detail of 'George Collins' notated by Angela Carter, from Paul and Angela Carter's Folk Music Archive. Copyright © Christine Molan. Reproduced with kind permission of Christine Molan	79
13	Anne Briggs, *Anne Briggs* LP, front cover (Topic Records 12T207, 1971). Copyright © Topic Records. Reproduced with kind permission of Topic Records	92
14 and 15	The Willett Family, *The Roving Journeymen: English Traditional Songs* LP, front cover, inner label (Topic Records 12T84, 1962). Copyright © Topic Records. Reproduced with kind permission of Topic Records	97
16	Photograph of a page in Angela Carter's *1960 Journal*, BL Add MS 88899/1/100. Copyright © The Estate of Angela Carter. Reproduced with kind permission of the Estate c/o Rogers, Coleridge & White Ltd., 20 Powis Mews, London W11 1JN	99
17	Image of *The Arundel Psalter* (1075). Copyright © British Library Board (Arundel MS 60, f.52v). British Library Online Gallery <http://www.bl.uk/onlinegallery/onlineex/illmanus/arunmancoll/c/011aru000000060u00052v00.html> [accessed 2 March 2022]	107
18	Photo detail of 'The Swan' notated by Angela Carter, from Paul and Angela Carter's Folk Music Archive. Copyright © Christine Molan. Reproduced with kind permission of Christine Molan	119
19	Photograph of a page in Angela Carter's *1972 Journal*, BL Add MS 88899/1/94. Copyright © The Estate of Angela Carter. Reproduced with kind permission of the Estate c/o Rogers, Coleridge & White Ltd., 20 Powis Mews, London W11 1JN	123
20 and 21	Jean-Louis Barrault, *Baudelaire et Rimbaud: Les Poètes Maudits* LP, front and back covers (Decca Records 105.011, 1953). Copyright © Decca Records. Reproduced with kind permission of Decca Records	152
22	Paul and Angela Carter, 'Folksong and Ballad, Bristol Manifesto', from Paul and Angela Carter's Folk Music Archive. Copyright © Christine Molan. Reproduced with kind permission of Christine Molan	157
23 and 24	Photos of archive books and journals, from Paul and Angela Carter's Folk Music Archive. Copyright © Christine Molan. Reproduced with kind permission of Christine Molan	158
25	Photo of archive LPs from Paul and Angela Carter's Folk Music Archive. Copyright © Christine Molan. Reproduced with kind permission of Christine Molan	159

26 and 27   Photos of Cheltenham Folk Club log book pages from January 1967 and May 1966. Copyright © Christine Molan. Reproduced with kind permission of Christine Molan and Ken Langsbury at the Cheltenham Folk Club   160

Folk songs and links

Folk songs as audio play an important role in this book. I have placed a number in square brackets in the body text of the book which corresponds to an audio reference, listed below, so that the reader can hope to hear the song being discussed. I have provided online listening links where possible.

[1] Angela Carter, 'The Flower of Sweet Strabane', recorded live at the Cheltenham Folk Club, 15 January 1967, copyright © Denis Olding.
[2] Angela Carter, 'Saint Mary's & Church Street Medley', recorded live at the Cheltenham Folk Club, 15 January 1967, copyright © Denis Olding.
[3] Shirley Collins, 'The Unquiet Grave', from *False True Lovers* (Folkways Records FG3564, 1959). Link https://youtu.be/wEjDsOhYCYM
[4] Karine Polwart, 'The Dowie Dens of Yarrow', from *Fairest Floo'er* (Hegri Music HEGRICD03, 2007). Link: https://youtu.be/MCM66RWZXoM
[5] Polly Paulusma, 'The Streams of Lovely Nancy', from *Invisible Music: folk songs that influenced Angela Carter* (Wild Sound/One Little Independent WLDSND008, 2021). Link: https://pollypaulusma.bandcamp.com/track/the-streams-of-lovely-nancy
[6] Jeannie Robertson, 'My Son David', from *Scottish Ballads and Folk Songs by Jeannie Robertson World's Greatest Folk Singer* (Prestige International INT13006, 1961). Link: https://youtu.be/ykOBpsVMN1s
[7] Joe Heaney, 'The Bonny Bunch of Roses', singing live. Link: https://www.joeheaney.org/en/bonny-bunch-of-roses-the/ (jump to 1.02). Heaney released a recording of this song in 1960 (Collector Records JEI7, 1960); Paul Carter was the music supervisor, and Angela Carter drew the bee illustration on the cover.
[8] Patti Smith, 'Gloria', from *Horses* (Arista Records AL 4066, 1975). Link: https://youtu.be/bPO0bTaWcFQ
[9] The White Stripes, 'Jolene', live music video. Link: https://youtu.be/yXlULkwhgrc
[10] Sarah Makem, 'The Banks of Red Roses', from *Ulster Ballad Singer* (Topic Records 12T182, 1968) Link: https://open.spotify.com/track/28XgytxSBJHBnty-g3tqfk
[11] Sandy Denny, 'The False Bride' (variant of 'The Week Before Easter'), from *Alex Campbell and his Friends* (Saga Eros ERO8021, 1967). Link: https://youtu.be/Jf7dIATrtNc
[12] A. L. Lloyd, 'Reynardine', from *First Person* (Topic Records 12T118, 1966). Link: https://youtu.be/PSrJIwgshijA
[13] Enos White, 'George Collins', from *The Folksongs of Britain, Vol. 4: The Child Ballads Vol. 1* (Caedmon Records TC1145, 1961).

[14] A. L. Lloyd, 'Jackie Munro', from *English Street Songs* (Riverside RLP 12-614, 1956).
[15] Polly Paulusma, 'Lucy Wan', from *Invisible Music: folk songs that influenced Angela Carter* (Wild Sound/One Little Independent WLDSND008, 2021). Link: https://pollypaulusma.bandcamp.com/track/lucy-wan
[16] Ruth Perry, 'Bold Wolfe', posted by MIT Literature Section. Link: https://youtu.be/EbG-Z2ap9Cw
[17] Tom Willett, 'Died for Love', from The Willett Family, *The Roving Journeymen: English Traditional Songs* (Topic Records 12T84, 1962).
[18] Jimmy Gilhaney, 'Blow the Candle Out', from *The Folksongs of Britain, Vol 2: Songs of Seduction* (Caedmon Records TC1143, 1962).
[19] Diane Taraz, 'The Game of Cards', from *Songs of the Revolution* (Raisin Pie Music, 2010). Link: https://youtu.be/dwDvxUgZt3U
[20] Lisa Theriot, 'Lady Isabel and the Elf-Knight', from *A Turning of Seasons* (Raven Boy Music, 2001). Link: https://youtu.be/OipbPM_NK7w
[21] Fred Jordan, 'The Outlandish Knight', from *The Folksongs of Britain, Vol 4: The Child Ballads Vol 1* (Caedmon TC1145, 1961).
[22] Bob and Ron Copper, 'Babes in the Wood', from *Traditional Songs from Rottingdean* (EFDSS LP1002, 1963). Link: https://youtu.be/ylgGK_sk86o
[23] Anne Briggs, 'Young Tambling' (a variant of 'Tam Lin'), from *Anne Briggs* (Topic Records 12T207, 1971). Link: https://youtu.be/h6x2S8comEU
[24] Jim Moray, 'Hind Etin', from *Skulk* (Niblick Is A Giraffe Records NIBL013, 2012). Link: https://youtu.be/NYKdf4aYX7U
[25] John Stickle, 'King Orfeo' (fragment), from *The Folksongs of Britain, Vol 4: The Child Ballads Vol 1* (Caedmon TC 1145, 1961).
[26] Shirley Collins, 'The Cruel Mother', from *False True Lovers* (Folkways Records FG3564, 1959). Link: https://youtu.be/W8_d88dl9kw
[27] Emily Portman, 'Two Sisters', from *Coracle* (Furrow Records FURR008, 2015). Link: https://youtu.be/CljGmmd3Zrc
[28] Josienne Clarke and Ben Walker, 'The Banks of Sweet Primroses', recorded 2015 for *fRoots Magazine* digital download album *fRoots 53*, physically released on Various Artists, *Vision and Revision: The First 80 Years of Topic Records* (Topic Records TXCD597, 2019). Link: https://youtu.be/BCWTHwUlyRw
[29] Shirley and Dolly Collins, 'The Young Girl Cut Down In Her Prime', on *Love, Death and the Lady* (EMI/Harvest SHVL771, 1970). Link: https://youtu.be/5P46j5kSAFk
[30] Joe Heaney, 'As I Roved Out', on *The Road from Connemara: Songs and Stories told and sung to Ewan MacColl and Peggy Seeger* (Topic Records TSCD518D, 2000).
[31] Jean Ritchie, 'One Morning in May' (a variant of 'Grenadier and Lady'), from *Jean Ritchie Singing The Traditional Songs of Her Kentucky Mountain Family* (Elektra EKLP-2, 1953). Link: https://youtu.be/J0oBE7RhJIM
[32] Charlie Carver, 'Cupid the Ploughboy', recorded at The Gardener's Arms, Tostock, Suffolk, from *The Desmond and Shelagh Herring Collection*, British

[33] Library. Link: https://sounds.bl.uk/World-and-traditional-music/Desmond-and-Shelagh-Herring-Collection/025M-C0999X0002XX-0300V0

[33] Norma Waterson, 'The Leaves of Life' / 'Seven Virgins', from The Watersons, *Frost and Fire: A Calendar of Ritual and Magical Songs* (Topic 12T136,1965). Link: https://youtu.be/kk6c8keJ2sA?t=509

[34] Anne Briggs, 'Polly Vaughan', from *The Hazards of Love* (Topic Records TOP94, 1964). Link: https://youtu.be/EOi6t_3zICE

[35] Emily Portman, 'Hinge of the Year', from *Hatchling* (Furrow Records FURR006, 2012). Link: https://emilyportman.bandcamp.com/track/hinge-of-the-year-2

[36] Emily Portman, 'Ash Girl', from *Hatching* (Furrow Records FURR006, 2012). Link: https://emilyportman.bandcamp.com/track/ash-girl

[37] Emily Portman, 'Little Longing', from *The Glamoury* (Furrow Records FUR002, 2010). Link: https://emilyportman.bandcamp.com/track/little-longing

[38] Emily Portman, 'Stick Stock', from *The Glamoury* (Furrow Records FUR002, 2010). Link: https://emilyportman.bandcamp.com/track/stick-stock

[39] Emily Portman, 'Mossy Coat', from *The Glamoury* (Furrow Records FUR002, 2010). Link: https://emilyportman.bandcamp.com/track/mossy-coat

[40] Emily Portman, 'Tongue Tied', from *The Glamoury* (Furrow Records FUR002, 2010). Link: https://emilyportman.bandcamp.com/track/tongue-tied

[41] Emily Portman, 'Eye of Tree', from *Coracle* (Furrow Records FURR008, 2015).

Abbreviations

AYL MS   Aylesford Mss, Lilly Library, Indiana University, Bloomington, Indiana

BL Add MS   London British Library Additional Manuscript

BYB   Angela Carter, *Burning Your Boats: Collected Stories* (London: Vintage, 1996)

SAL   Angela Carter, *Shaking a Leg: Collected Journalism and Writings* (London: Vintage, 2013)

Acknowledgements

This book could not have been written without help from the following individuals and organizations. Firstly and most importantly I want to thank my generous and patient supervisor Dr Stephen Benson, whose belief in this project from the outset secured its completion, and the School of Literature, Drama and Creative Writing at the University of East Anglia for support and encouragement. The Consortium for the Humanities and the Arts South-East England (CHASE) provided the generous funding which allowed me to undertake this research.

I am grateful to Dr Rachel Carroll, Dr Nonia Williams, Prof Marie Mulvey-Roberts, Prof Jennifer Gustar, Dr Julia Bishop and Prof Martine Hennard Dutheil de la Rochère for their editorial advice and scholarly encouragement, and to Dr Sebastian Franklin, Dr Jane Elliott and Edmund Gordon at King's College, London whose guidance and kindness got my research on a firm footing in its early stages.

I am indebted to Christine Molan for her careful custodianship of Paul and Angela Carter's folk music archive and her unlimited generosity in granting me access, for her art and her friendship. I thank Denis Olding for his serendipitous recordings and his permission to use them. I thank Emily Portman from the bottom of my heart for sharing so many insights about her work, and Edward Horesh and Christopher Frayling who gave me time, tea and crumpets. Thanks to Peggy Seeger and to Reg Hall who shared thoughts and memories with me over the phone. My thanks extend too to Susannah Clapp and the Angela Carter Literary Estate for my queries always answered with good grace, and to Dr Charlotte Crofts at the University of the West of England, whose kindness in allowing me at the last minute to participate in a conference in the early days of my research informed much of its development. Prof Natsumi Ikoma has also furnished me with both academic and moral support, and I am immensely grateful to her.

I am indebted to the staff of the Manuscripts Room at the British Library, London, and to Alison Zammer and Kat Davies at the University Library, Cambridge; Seth Michael James at The Lilly Library, University of Indiana; Laura Smyth, Nick Wall and Malcolm Barr-Hamilton at the Vaughan Williams Memorial Library, London; Claire Berliner at the London Library; Katy Spicer and the English Folk Dance and Song Society (EFDSS) at Cecil Sharp House, London; Neil Pearson and the EFDSS Creative Bursary scheme that afforded me time and space to develop this project as a musician; Maz O'Connor, Jack Harris, John Parker and Jed Bevington, who brought the music to life; Stuart Lyon and the University of East Anglia Music Centre, whose awards allowed me to buy equipment to record; Steve Roud, for his endless knowledge; Anne Briggs; David Suff and Topic Records; Rod Stradling and Musical Traditions; Derek Birkett, Sue Birkett, PJ Johannes, Ben Knight and Sam Birkett at One Little Independent Records; Dr Anna Watz; Prof Werner Wolf and Prof Walter Bernhart at the Words and

Music Association, University of Graz; Dr Emily Petermann, Words and Music Association Forum; Dr Rachael Durkin; Dr Leo Mellor and Prof Heather Glen at my alma mater, Murray Edwards College, Cambridge; Dr Corinna Russell and Dr Gavin Alexander, the Cambridge University Song Seminar; Dr Jenny Bavidge and the Institute for Continuing Education (ICE), Cambridge; Dr Simon Barber and the Songwriting Studies Research Group; Sophie Daniels and the Institute for Contemporary Music Performance; Dr Micha Lazarus; Dr Emma Dillon; Dr Katherine Baxter and Dr Adam Hansen; Dr Holly Laird; Dr Christin Hoene and Dr Avital Rol; Patrick Wildgust and the Laurence Sterne Trust; Ly Bell; Kathryn Williams; Annie Dressner; Suzy Bell, Fiona McDougall and Lucy van Beek.

I wish finally to express my gratitude to my mother Louise Riley-Smith, and my siblings Toby Riley-Smith and Tammy Riley-Smith, for their ceaseless encouragement. But most of all, I want to thank my late father Prof Jonathan Riley-Smith who, while dying of cancer, read early drafts and engaged with me in lively discussions that helped me to shape my arguments, and my loving husband Mick and dear children Valentine and Corentine, who every day give me the motivation to do my best for their sake.

Preface

This book has been written backwards.

It started with a feeling of profound recognition which I then spent six years trying to explain. In 2013, I was attending a folk music conference; proceedings were set to go late into the night, and musicians from the contemporary folk scene[1] were performing traditional British (mostly Scottish and English) folk songs in the hotel bar – songs of bloody murder, betrayal and supernatural horror such as 'The Twa Sisters', 'Tam Lin' and 'Barbara Allen'. I had recently been contracted to supervise a student writing an Angela Carter dissertation, and I had a pile of Carter novels by the bed upstairs in my hotel room. Because of this serendipitous alignment, and perhaps because of my own fifteen years of experience as a performing singer-songwriter, I was suddenly overcome with what Melissa Gregg and Gregory J. Seigworth describe as the 'enjoyment-joy at the prospect of an undiscovered set of connections'[2] – I 'felt', very strongly, that Carter not only knew the songs I was hearing, but that she also knew what it felt like to sing them. My somatic, affective response in this moment of recognition was visceral: the hairs on the backs of my arms stood on end.

The approach I have subsequently developed, of identifying a 'canorographic' or 'songful' quality of prose writing through syntax and grammar is 'intermedial', in the sense Werner Wolf describes it, for it presents 'the participation of more than one medium of expression in the signification of a human artefact'.[3] Emily Petermann also highlights features of what she calls 'the musical novel' in these terms, noticing

> temporal shifts, [...] shifting points of view or narrative voices, or a different use of repetition, rhythm, or other patterns that is frequently found in prose texts. Accepting such postmodern narrative surprises is one thing, understanding their purpose is yet another.[4]

But I query Wolf's assertion that 'fiction, after all, cannot simply become music',[5] that 'an actual "translation" of music into fiction is impossible',[6] that a 'story is never regarded primarily as sound' and that the prose reader experiences a 'habitual disregard of sound'.[7] Petermann, too, claims that 'the typical signs of the foreign medium of music are not materially present, but are only imitated by the text'.[8] For the most part they prioritize salient features of instrumental music and limit their attention to song as a discrete subset. They do not appear obviously to distinguish between the music one hears and the music one makes oneself.

The evidence of Carter's physical performance of folk songs, not just her familiarity with them, is of utmost importance to my argument for, as Roland Barthes explains, there are 'two musics (at least so I have always thought): the music one listens to, the music one plays. These two musics are two totally different arts'.[9] It is my singer's sensibility which hums in sympathetic resonance with Carter's singing-memory-in-prose, the 'grain' of her voice, 'the body in the voice as it sings, the hand as it writes',[10] suggesting a 'musical remainder'[11] immanent in her writing, infused within her prose constructions, a performed sonority learned and remembered from her singing performances.

I do not mean to suggest that Carter's writing is 'performative',[12] nor that it is *like* a performance; but rather that it *is* a performance, an iterative, evanescent event occurring in real time between author-subject and reader-object (like a kind of grammar) – a sounded-out, voiced-out, played-out performance which is folded-in, absorbed-in and transformed through the living reader's 'auditory imagination',[13] in which interpretations, understandings, confusions and subversions are newly forged each time. Because, as Walter Ong explains, 'reading a text oralizes it',[14] author and reader create a unique collaboration which resonates sympathetically with 'oral residue',[15] sounded meaning through the beguiling medium of that seemingly silent page.

This book therefore works its way backwards, because it started with the ending: it started with the answer: an intuitive, speculative, subjectivist moment of embodied awareness. It charts a journey, via the discovery of a previously unknown archive of Carter's folk notes and recordings, the anecdotal evidence of Carter's folk-singing days still thankfully evident in Bristol, and the text-trail left by Carter herself, towards an attempt to systematize exactly what it is in Carter's prose that alerted me to her physical understanding, her muscle memory, of singing British traditional folk songs – and her ability to perform that physical understanding through her prose to me.

To this end, I perform archival and musico-literary analyses of Carter's prose against the folk songs with which she was familiar and performed, drawing on a range of qualitative methodologies borrowed from literary theory, musicology, affect theory, performance theory, and voice theory. This intervention aims to ascertain which folk-song features Carter transcoded into her prose that allowed her to create such a sounded, engaging, canorous reading experience, a musico-literary performance of the singing voice that I will endeavour to frame as 'canorography', song-infused prose, and what its identification might bring to emerging interdisciplinary enquiries and pedagogies that explore the porous boundaries between prose literature and song.

1

Songful influences

> *... the richness and allusiveness of imagery in folk poetry, which reaches one[1] through singing almost on a subliminal level, means one's appreciation of the mode grows with one's knowledge. And so, naturally, does one's imagination, one's ability to think in images oneself, one's sensibility and one's perceptions, because folk song is an art, and these are the things all the arts do.*
>
> Angela Carter, 'Now is the Time for Singing', 1964

In 1964, the young Angela Carter – English undergraduate, aspiring first-time novelist, sporadic journalist, wife, folk singer and folk club co-founder – published an article in her student magazine called 'Now is the Time for Singing' (hereafter 'Now'), in which she describes in detail what she perceives to be the cultural importance of singing traditional folk songs, and the osmotic, pervasive power of the form's praxis upon her own creative development.

Carter penned 'Now' in 1964 while she was writing *Shadow Dance*, her debut novel which would be published two years later.[2] In this essay, she discusses the symbiotic relationship between her own artistic evolution and her somatic experience of singing British traditional folk songs, songs whose 'richness and allusiveness' enter her imaginative life 'subliminally' through the act of singing, heightening her 'ability to think in images'. Her physical folk singing praxis, she announces here, is transforming her capacity for imaginative and creative thought.

The revelation that Carter was a folk singer is unequivocally proved by the discovery of a new archive, at the time of writing in private hands in Bristol, which includes Carter's own folk song scholarship and two recordings of her performing live: on one she sings unaccompanied, and on the other she plays a medley on the English concertina. These discoveries throw open new interdisciplinary musico-literary doors of enquiry within existing critical debates surrounding Carter's myriad influences from popular culture.

Critical silence on Carter and folk song

Carter's relationship with folk song has not yet been critiqued because it has, until now, remained largely unknown. Some commentators have come close to uncovering folk song's pivotal role in Carter's early life, but they only mention it in passing. Marina

Warner touches on the minor influence of folk song and folk music as part of Carter's journey towards her apparently more satisfying relationship with fairy tales, claiming how Carter 'first began developing her interest in folklore, discovering with her husband the folk and jazz music scenes of the 1960s'.[3] However, Warner makes no connection between the modes of *faery* fantasy present in fairy tales and the magically gothic universes of folk song narratives contained within, say, the Child ballads ('Tam Lin' or 'Lady Isabel and the Elf Knight', for example), or the folk song collections of Frank Purslow or James Reeves, with which Carter was so intimate.[4]

Charlotte Crofts notes in passing Carter's 'involvement with the folk movement in the early 1960s'[5] while analyzing Carter's connections between the medium of radio and the subversive potential of fairy tale; she links the orality of radio and Carter's interest in oral traditions in general, observing that writing for radio

> allowed her to partake in a specifically oral story-telling culture. Radio also enabled Carter to explore the processes at work in the transmission of oral narratives and their audiences – the active relationship between the teller of the tale and the listener – which foregrounds the potential for renegotiating the patriarchal structures of the literary versions.[6]

But Crofts does not then forge links between Carter's engagement with the 'atavistic' orality of radio, its connections to 'the most antique tellers of tales', and Carter's deep investment in the ancient and oral traditions of folk song performance, both sung and heard, and the intricate relationships between Carter's prose production and her own singing voice. Like Crofts and Warner, Jack Zipes briefly mentions that 'Carter became part of folk music circles with her husband and toured the festivals of Great Britain'[7] but he does not link her folk singing praxis with any later fairy tale scholarship.

Lorna Sage claims that the 1970s was the decade in which Carter became 'more explicitly and systematically interested in narrative models that pre-date the novel: fairy tales, folk tales, and other forms that develop by accretion and retelling'.[8] Sage too, it seems, may not have realized the depth of Carter's investment in folk song praxis and scholarship during the 1960s, an investment evidenced by: trips to see performances with Paul Carter and Reg Hall documented as early as 1959,[9] her early journalism,[10] her 1964 article 'Now is the Time for Singing', her 1965 undergraduate dissertation on folk song's links with medieval poetry,[11] her private journal entries,[12] the book of folk music notations she left with Paul,[13] the album sleeve notes she authored for the important folk label Topic Records,[14] and the recently discovered folk club recordings made in 1967[15] before the Carters separated in 1969, events and documents I shall present in more detail in Chapter 2. Folk song belongs to that family of forms which evolves through exactly the processes of 'accretion and retelling' Sage describes, which Cecil Sharp characterizes in 1907 as 'continuity, variation, and selection';[16] although Carter's interest in the folk song form, a full decade before Sage's estimation, was both systematic and explicit, Sage does not mention it in her critiques.

Sage does, however, point out that Carter revelled in the sound of her own performing voice, and that the 'fairytale idea enabled her to *read* in public with a new appropriateness and panache, as though she was *telling* these stories'.[17] Sage describes a Carter who enjoys reading her own work aloud and who 'laments that prose writers are seldom asked to'.[18] The presence of her own voice in a physical sense, as an acoustic event, is an important aspect of Carter's authorial methodology, Sage suggests. Susannah Clapp has also observed that Carter's 'prose, like her own speaking voice, was allusive, parodic and playful. [...] she wanted to write works that could be performed'.[19] I will elaborate on this celebration of 'voice' and argue that it can be enriched with an understanding that Carter not just enjoyed to speak, but to sing.[20]

In his 2016 biography, Edmund Gordon provides some details of Carter's 'interest in the English folk revival'[21] and uncovers some of her early journalism on the subject, from which we can glean her admiration for 'our great and still living heritage of rough and ready poetry';[22] but he does not link Carter's singing experiences with her subsequent artistic development. However, Gordon has been extremely instrumental in this book: it was through his generosity and the sharing of a contact that I was able to locate some of original members of the Carters' folk club, and to unearth the archive of notes and recordings that have been so pivotal to my research.

None of these critics ponders on the possible implications of Carter's active participation in the 1960s folk song revival on her subsequent output, and this is an omission in the critical conversation which needs correcting, for Carter's scholarly interest in the textual material of folk song's imagery and topographies, and her non-verbal understanding, entrained through iterative performance, of the musical materiality of folk song's repetitive melodic shapes and rhythmic characteristics, can be seen to have profoundly influenced her literary imagination; so far, these influences have been overlooked.

Carter and fairy tales

In contrast, the extent of Carter's influences from European folk and fairy tale heritage has been explored extensively during more than two decades of detailed scholarship by critics such as Cristina Bacchilega, Stephen Benson, Sarah Gamble, Danielle Roemer, Martine Hennard Dutheil de la Rochère, Sage and Warner to name but a few, who have each contributed to our growing understanding of the depths of Carter's influences from these ancient traditional forms. They have exposed the power of her extractions through fiction of the forms' 'latent content'[23] to illuminate contemporary life, and the significant onward impact of her appropriation of them upon subsequent cultural production.

A burgeoning critical conversation surrounding Carter's relationship with traditional tales envelops and sometimes threatens to overwhelm her oeuvre,[24] yet Carter was the first to initiate this conversation. In her editor's introduction to the *Virago Book of Fairy Tales*, she revels in the opportunities for subversion afforded by these ancient forms:

> So fairy tales, folk tales, stories from the oral tradition, are all of them the most vital connection we have with the imaginations of the ordinary men and women whose labour created our world. [...] The history, sociology and psychology transmitted to us by fairy tales is unofficial [...]. They are also anonymous and genderless.[25]

With new knowledge afforded by the archive that Carter sang folk songs herself (and especially considering her subtle dedication in the same document to A. L. Lloyd, one of the folk song revival's most important figures), the absence of traditional folk songs and ballads from this list of traditional forms becomes a significant omission – why would she *not* include in this list the very form with which she was so intimate? It seems that Carter deliberately remained silent about her relationship with folk songs, pointed her critical readership towards tales, and the debates surrounding her appropriation of folk and fairy tales subsequently exploded.

Danielle Roemer and Cristina Bacchilega frame Carter's appropriation of the fairy tale form not just as a response to the writings of Charles Perrault but as a continuation of a specifically female discourse appropriated by seventeenth-century French aristocratic women such as Marie-Catherine d'Aulnoy in the *contes des fées*. They suggest that Carter's literary fairy tales are not to be seen 'as departures from some simpler fairy-tale tradition but as intensifications and modifications of previously instituted and sophisticated narrative modes'.[26] Stephen Benson suggests that, in her 'double-edged relation to tradition' Carter both borrows from and re-informs fairy tales, so that we witness 'the seeping of one into the other' in a never-ending cycle of cause and effect; he argues that, in so doing, questions are raised about how the texts' relations with ancient sources 'affect our notions of the contemporary'.[27] Anny Crunelle-Vanrigh traces the fairy tale 'Beauty and the Beast' over Carter's short story 'The Courtship of Mr Lyon' to find that the 'never-never land shot through with contemporary references works out a schizophrenic vision paralyzing the reader's willingness to suspend disbelief and forget the text's "otherness"'. By pivoting fairy tale against new telling, Crunelle-Vanrigh highlights 'the "betweenness" that is so much part of this text',[28] and identifies a creative space Carter finds to play between the two.

Warner, in her wider analysis of the fairy tale's cultural history, identifies that it was Carter's 'quest for eros' which drew her to fairy tales, and declares that she is responsible for 'recuperation of the form' which was to influence subsequent writers such as Margaret Atwood, Salman Rushdie and Robert Coover.[29] Sarah Gamble situates Carter's more biographical essays within an imaginary fairy tale matrix, noticing how Carter conducts gendered socio-historical experiments on her own past; Carter claimed to 'write about the conditions of my life, as everyone does. You write from your own history'[30] and so Gamble suggests that 'The Mother Lode':

> is not so much concerned with describing the actual circumstances of its author's life as with mapping the fault line between the actual and the imagined from which all of Carter's stories spring. Her grandmother functions as the text's matriarchal origin, for like the fairy and folk-tales to which all of Carter's narratives are, to a greater or lesser extent, indebted, this is a narrative which has women at its centre and as its source.[31]

There are some aspects of Gamble's argument which attempt to paper over this 'fault line' through a notion of 'shared' history: for example, Gamble argues that these 'exercises in autobiography, whether they deal in facts or imaginative reconstruction, are [...] a way to develop a history through which the past can be known and also shared';[32] I would suggest rather that the very power of 'the curious abyss'[33] for Carter lies in the deliberate persistence of the enigma: the power and relevance of tradition over modernity, Carter seems to say, positively relies on the gaping fissures between them. None of these critics mentions the importance of traditional folk song in Carter's past.

Warner and Laura Mulvey (among others) have examined Carter's influences from cinema, and in particular the oral aspects of cinema as they intersect with cultural aspects of folk and fairy tale mediation. Mulvey posits cinema as a magical safe haven for 'old monsters and their oral culture [which] were being exorcised by the modern world',[34] while Warner argues that 'film is essentially an oral medium and shares many characteristics with traditional storytelling. The camera acts as an anonymous narrator'.[35] Carter's exploration of cinema culture in *The Passion of New Eve* and *Wise Children* can be seen not just as a celebration of the visual ephemerality of film, but also as an extension of an appropriation of the sounded, oral features of story-telling culture more widely.

Crofts and Guido Almansi discuss the fairy tale tradition and orality in Carter's radio plays, where 'by necessity, four-fifths of the five senses are sacrificed. There are no smells, no touches, no tastes, no sights, in radio drama: only hearing, with an intensive exploitation of the sole sense located in the ear'.[36] Following Carter's assertion that her writing for radio is 'a kind of three-dimensional story-telling',[37] Almansi explores the significance of the catalogue of sounds in her foley instructions and her habit of 'accepting and increasing and expanding the real world' to create 'an overloading of the frequencies of life'.[38] Crofts identifies links between Carter's writing for radio[39] and her wider appropriation of fairy tale, allowing her to 'literally recreate the voice of fairy tale'.[40] Crofts notices, for example, how in the radio play Carter gives Red Riding Hood an agency she does not enjoy in the story:

> The real radical potential of the voice in Carter's radio, therefore, stems not from a straightforward privileging of the female voice, nor from a simple recognition of the role of women in processes of acculturation, but from the negotiation between these two configurations of the female voice.[41]

Radio's dependency on sound as the only conveyor of meaning allies it with other oral traditions such as folk and fairy tale heritage, which historically were passed orally from teller to teller. Carter herself explains: 'For most of human history, "literature", both fiction and poetry, has been narrated, not written – heard, not read.'[42] No mention is made of the links between the orality of the radio medium and Carter's folk singing past.

Carter's diverse musical influences have been the focus of critics such as Stephen Benson and Julie Sauvage. Benson demonstrates how Carter's allusions to Debussy and Wagner in the story 'The Bloody Chamber' form a 'tissue of coded references',[43] while

Sauvage presents music's influence in the text as 'a polyphonic score meant for the readers to perform'.[44] Sauvage even links the songful refrain in Carter's prose constructions to oral forms of folk and fairy tales, but does not connect them to the folk songs Carter knew how to sing.

Why folk song differs from folk and fairy tale forms

With all this work already performed on Carter's influences from oral traditions and narratives as they manifest themselves through the prisms of folk and fairy tales, at first it might not appear obvious what differentiates the folk song form enough from these others to justify a separate intervention, nor what an examination of Carter's specific influences from folk song, and folk singing praxis, might bring to the debate. The pivotal differences between folk song and other forms of folk culture need outlining in order to reveal why a discrete examination of their influence on Carter's critical development is so necessary. What are folk and fairy tales, what is folk song, and how do they differ from one another?

Folk tales and fairy tales have proved problematic forms to define because of their mongrel origins and promiscuous modes of cultural dissemination which, as Roemer and Bacchilega suggest, are 'neither monolithic nor the product of a single branching of literary history'.[45] Zipes contextualizes the difficulties of genre specificity: 'Almost all endeavours by scholars to explain the fairy tale as a genre have failed. Their failure is predictable because the genre is so volatile and fluid.'[46] Carter attempts a broad-brush definition, commenting on the misnomer of the term 'fairy tale':

> fairies, as such, are thin on the ground, for the term 'fairy tale' is a figure of speech and we use it loosely, to describe the great mass of infinitely various narrative that was, once upon a time and still is, sometimes, passed on and disseminated through the world by word of mouth – stories without known originators that can be remade again and again by every person who tells them, the perennially refreshed entertainment of the poor.[47]

Stith Thompson attempts to taxonomize the 'fairy tale', or the '*Märchen*', as a subcategory of the umbrella term 'folk tale', presenting 'an unreal world without definite locality or definite characters [...] filled with the marvellous'; other 'folk tale' forms he identifies are the novella, the hero tale, the *Sagen*, the explanatory tale, the myth, and the animal tale (which becomes a fable when accompanied by a moral) but, as he confesses, these various forms continue to bleed into and mingle with one other:

> We shall find these forms not so rigid as the theoretician might wish, for they will be blending into each other with amazing facility. Fairy tales become myths, or animal tales, or local legends. As stories transcend differences of age or of place and move from the ancient world to ours, or from ours to a primitive society, they often undergo protean transformations in style and narrative purpose. For the plot structure of the tale is much more stable and more persistent than its form.[48]

Steven Swann Jones concurs with Thompson to a degree, suggesting that fairy tales are 'narratives that have been shaped over centuries of retelling and that have achieved a basic narrative form that is a distillation of human experience'. He too regards fairy tales as a subset of folk tales but, in contrast to Thompson, finds something more quotidian at work in them – they all 'use *common, ordinary people* as protagonists to reveal the desires and foibles of human nature'.[49] Using a psychoanalytical framework, Bruno Bettelheim defines fairy tales as didactic tools for child development, whereby 'the form and structure of fairy tales suggest images to the child by which he can structure his daydreams and with them give better direction to his life'.[50] Zipes too finds society has cultivated the fairy tale 'as a socially symbolic act within an institutionalized discourse of the Western civilizing process to comment on norms, mores and values'[51] but paradoxically, while folk and fairy tales on the one hand appear to reinforce prescriptive social codes surrounding conduct, propriety and morality, at the same time they act as anarchical influences to challenge hegemonic structures. Zipes argues that they

> have often been considered subversive, or, to put it more positively, they have provided the critical measure of how far we are from taking history into our own hands and creating more just societies. Folk and fairy tales have always spread word through their fantastic images about the feasibility of utopian alternatives, and this is exactly why the dominant social classes have been vexed by them.[52]

Andrew Teverson observes a similar duality at work: while depictions of social dissent in folk tales have 'operated as fantasies of vengeance and empowerment on the part of the poor', they operate only 'as a consolation and compensation for lack of real power'[53] and are therefore ultimately toothless.

While folk and fairy tales originated (and in some parts of the world still continue to propagate) in oral traditions, and therefore display the qualities of evanescence, mutability, plurality and anonymity of authorship which all oral traditions enjoy, in modernity they have also created a rich parallel literary tradition through the curatorial activities of famous collectors such as the Grimm Brothers and Andrew Lang. These collecting and publishing activities, while guaranteeing the preservation of tales for posterity, have proved problematic when viewed as disruptive agents in the organic flow of tales through the oral tradition, for these activities produce the unintended consequences of creating seemingly fixed 'original' or 'definitive' versions, and forcing traditional materials to pass through what Dollerup, Reventlow and Hansen describe as 'editorial "filters"', namely, 'the changes, "orientations", which editors deliberately impose on a tale because they want to reach a specific audience'.[54] The accumulative effects of these various disruptions become almost impossible to measure.

So far, these qualities of folk and fairy tales could quite comfortably be applied to folk songs, for songs too are 'without known originators', and are also 'passed on by word of mouth', with origins in oral traditions but with an extensive and equally problematic parallel history of recording, collecting, collating, transcribing and publishing.

Like the folk and fairy tale form, the folk song form has also proved notoriously hard to define. The famous collector Cecil Sharp's label, 'The Song Created by the Common People',[55] has come under repeated attack in subsequent debates. Maud Karpeles recounts how, at 'the Annual Conference of the International Folk Music Council held in London two years ago we attempted to define folk music, but were unable to devise a definition which completely satisfied all the members'.[56] Raymond Williams notes the complexities between terms 'folk' and 'popular', noticing that they 'remain uncertain and variable'.[57] As contemporary folklorist Steve Roud laments the, 'definition of "folk song" is fraught with difficulty, and many researchers even avoid the term altogether'.[58]

Folk songs share many of the narrative elements, characters, imagery and motifs with which folk and fairy tales are populated (see, for example, the shared attributes of the tale 'Thomas the Rhymer' and its equivalent folk song, Child ballad 37 'Thomas Rymer'),[59] and also some of their social functions. Folk song's diverse narrative subject-matters fall into many of the differing categories Thompson suggests for tales: songs involving magical events such as 'Tam Lin' or 'Lady Isabel and the Elf Knight'; songs involving ordinary people such as 'The Banks of Red Roses' or 'Barbara Allen'; songs with didactic social messages of the dangers of civil disobedience such as 'The Wild Colonial Boy', filial disobedience as in 'The Dowie Dens of Yarrow', or sexual impropriety such as 'The Cruel Mother' (although Carter herself questions their effectiveness);[60] sometimes conversely they can present more subversive messages and positively encourage social mobility, such as in 'The Gipsy Countess', 'Cupid The Ploughboy', or 'Jackie Munro'. The English Folk Dance and Song Society suggests many different types of folk song, including ballads, sea shanties, hunting and poaching songs, industrial songs, and a thematic category (intriguingly for Carter fans) entitled 'heroes and villains'.[61]

The tensions between published literary sources and oral sources are as evident in the history of folk song collection as they are in tale collection, and troubling questions repeatedly arise about the authenticity of traditional materials, the motives of editors and the consequences of their interventions. The song collectors, it has been observed, cannot help but exert their own influences on the materials they collect, sometimes despite their own best efforts. Sharp, for example, expresses protectionist feelings of responsibility as a song collector not only to record his findings accurately, 'just what he hears, no more and no less,' but also quickly, 'while there is yet the time and opportunity' – the songs, he argues, 'form part and parcel of a great tradition that stretches back into the mists of the past in one long, unbroken chain, of which the last link is now, alas, being forged'.[62] He wants to save songs from extinction, and to do so authentically. But, by transcribing them in his notebooks, while he is saving them from obscurity, he is also ossifying a living form. Even field sound recordists may be seen from anthropological standpoints to be disrupting fatally folk song's organic trajectory. The folklorist Reg Hall hinted to me in interview that, later in life, Paul Carter had begun to rethink his folk song field recording activities in these terms: 'I got the feeling he was in some way wanting to cut his links from recording traditional music, as if he felt that recording it had somehow been not in the spirit of the music'.[63] While the intention of collectors and field recordists may have been to preserve for posterity the lyrics, melody, voice and/or performance of folk song, at the same time an otherwise transient performance has become fixed at the price of evanescence.

As well as fixing songs, collectors unintentionally impose their own social niceties, constraints and prejudices through their practices. Sharp sometimes describes what he perceives to be errors in the folk songs he collected, which found themselves 'corrupt and due to the imperfect recollection of the singers,' which he feels an obligation to correct.[64] But Trish Winter and Simon Keegan-Phipps argue that Sharp's turn-of-the-century conceptualization of 'the folk' was a fantasy, and that critical 'deconstruction of this myth has been the main focus of much late-twentieth-century socio-historical scholarship'.[65] Dave Harker, assessing the influential American collector Francis J. Child's curatorship, has suggested that through processes of selection and omission, Child sought 'to impose onto cultural history his own class's concept of linear cultural development leading to what was worthy from a bourgeois-literary point of view'.[66] The problems surrounding collection and transmission abound in the folk song tradition just as they colour debates in fairy tale studies.

So what makes folk songs different enough from their folk tale cousins to warrant a separate intervention?

Firstly, folk songs are not just words; they also have tunes. These tunes have sometimes been neglected by literary-minded collectors; as Roud observes,

> Before the invention of recorded sound, very few people, apart from the folk-song collectors, bothered to tell us what ordinary people were singing, and the majority of the widely available, cheap printed sources, such as broadside song-sheets, chapbooks and songsters, do not include the music.[67]

Roud blames this unequal attention in part on the interchangeability of texts and tunes, whereby the 'same text could be sung to any number of tunes, and the same tune to many texts', which has allowed for the connection between the two to be perceived as 'weak'.[68] Victor Zuckerkandl also uses this interchangeability as proof of the existence of a hierarchy of lyrics over melody:

> A folk song is primarily a poem, that is, a verbal structure. It tells a story, evokes a situation, expresses feelings. There can be no doubt that the words of the song are all-important: the tune takes second place. The title of the song refers to what the words say, not the melody: indeed, different songs are often sung to the same tune.[69]

However, Zuckerkandl also states a folk song without a melody would be 'utterly unnatural' and concludes that 'what the musical tones contribute to the folk song is essential'.[70] Sharp identifies the 'two elements of the folk-song, the words and the melody' which 'should be considered as inseparable. They are so closely interwoven, one with the other, that both suffer by dismemberment'.[71] Roud's claim that a 'tune itself has no identifiable *meaning* in the way the words have', that the tune receives meaning by proxy, that it 'gets this, along with its subject matter, solely from its associative text',[72] arguably oversimplifies a wealth of critical discourse surrounding complexities of musical meaning, from Theodor Adorno's 'Music, that most eloquent of all languages'[73] to Lawrence Kramer's proposition that music 'adds something to other things by adding itself, but loses nothing when it takes itself away' and its 'potentiality for bearing ascribed meanings, meanings grounded in shared, socially mediated experience'.[74] Carter herself makes musicological observations in 'Now' that 'the texts are nothing without the tunes', illustrated with a description of the 'enormously virile tune' of the folk song 'Blow The Candle Out' which 'strides up and down the scale like a man in big boots'.[75] Through this vivid simile, Carter shows that melody brings more meaning to the lyrics than lyrics would have alone; symbiotic lyric-and-melody deliver more-meaning to the listener; together they comprise the song. In folk song then, melody interacts with lyric and lyric interacts with melody to form symbiotic and reciprocal layers of interactive meaning.

Kramer identifies as the 'musical remainder' the affect created when music is added to another cultural artefact:

> The remainder appears only in relation to the content it exceeds and by which it is in that sense produced. In the meshes of this relationship, the remainder comes to act both as the material medium and the fantasy space or screen through which the subjective content may be enfranchised and played out.[76]

The musical remainder in folk song emerges where lyrical meaning is transformed by its melodic counterpart and *vice versa*, and becomes manifest in the emergent gap between the two. Learned from her folk singing praxis, Carter toys with this gap created by the 'remainder' in her prose production: she borrows folk song's imagery, its figures, tropes and motifs to intensify lexical meaning, while simultaneously using its melodic and rhythmic features either to undermine and contradict or reinforce those meanings, creating a kind of semantic riptide, because 'these are the things all the arts do'.[77] Her manipulation of the 'remainder' in her prose allows her to write on two levels, the lexical and the musical, attuning us as readers to the interactions and contradictions of semantics and prosody.

Secondly, in folk song, the song needs to be *heard*, sounded out, performed. Folk song scholars mostly agree that a page-bound rendering of a lyric, even with its musical notation, leaves us wanting. Carter's declarations that the 'whole – the song – does not exist except in performance' and that 'the texts are nothing without the tunes',[78] gather authority from her own singing experience; Zuckerkandl agrees, stating that 'only in so far as it is sung does the folk song really exist'.[79] The poet Robert Frost recognizes that the 'voice and ear are left at a loss what to do with the ballad till supplied with the tune it was written to go with. That might be the definition of a true ballad to distinguish it from a true poem'.[80] George Herzog emphasizes folk song's living, performance-based praxis: 'Folk songs are best defined as songs which are current in the repertory of a folk group'.[81] Roud's pragmatic, ecumenical description also pivots around performance: 'A folk song is a song sung by a folk singer, and a folk singer is someone who sings folk songs'.[82] During performance in heard/lived/breathed space-time, perceived boundaries between lyric and melody melt away, for there is melody innately present in the resonant prosody of the lyric, and there is a semantically laden emotional recognition in the turn of the tune.

Could one argue that folk song retains some of those elements of orality that folk and fairy tales have lost? European folk and fairy tales appear now to occupy a territory situated somewhere between orality and textuality. Thompson remains non-committal about their ambivalent nature, which 'may be purely oral [or] may be literary';[83] Francis Lee Utley concedes that 'all or most of the evidence is of versions which cannot be trusted as clear cases of oral transmission'.[84] Hilda Ellis Davidson and Anna Chaudhri outline tensions between oral and literary traditions prevalent in fairy tales, citing Warner's simile of the suspension bridge between the two[85] to imagine 'a vigorous two-way traffic' between traditions, rendering it 'impossible to describe the fairy tale, within the broader context of the folktale, as an exclusively literary or an exclusively oral phenomenon'.[86] It becomes impossible, in other words, to disentangle orally transmitted elements of folk and fairy tales (if indeed any remain) from those which may have at one point been transcribed. They must be transmitted, passed along, and it might be argued that the dominant (though not exclusive) mode of transmission of tales in European culture has now migrated from oral to textual methods, and that tales are now communicated less through telling-from-memory and more through the reading from compendia such as those of the Grimm Brothers or Andrew Lang, or even the two-volume *Virago Book of Fairy Tales* which Carter herself edited.

But to assert that folk song is conversely a purely oral form in late modernity would be disingenuous; as Roud explains, 'There has not been a pure oral tradition for at least 500 years, and most folk songs owe their continued existence to their regular appearance in print'.[87] Critically, while seminal textual collations such as Child's *English and Scottish Popular Ballads* or Sharp's *English Folk Songs from the Southern Appalachians* are important in the history of folk song's continued dissemination, and despite the steady decline of singing rural communities, folk songs in print are only ever really considered a partial representation of the artefact, because of the absent 'voice' of the performing singer.

And this 'voice' is the third, crucial element of a folk song which differentiates it from folk and fairy tales – the medium, the vehicle which delivers the song, the singer's voice, which might carry an aching tenderness or a terrifying candour in its crack and timbre. Roland Barthes recognized the presence of performed, sung, semantic meaning in the 'grain of the voice', identifying within it a fundamental corporeal presence, 'the body in the voice as it sings, the hand as it writes, the limb as it performs'.[88] The singing voice resonates with musico-lexical meaning, a resonance which is transferred from the singer's body to the listener's, and which 'collapses the sense of distance' so that the 'resulting sense of intimacy tends to feel like bodily self-presence, the intimacy of oneself with one's own embodiment'.[89] The song resonates within the body of the singer *and* the body of the listener.

Folk song therefore, unlike folk and fairy tales, must be sung and must be heard. To sing a folk song is at once to be occupied by the song, to become possessed by 'so many ghosts of so many pasts',[90] and at the same time to find a gap in the song in which to insert oneself. Contemporary singer Peggy Seeger recognizes this embedding of the self within the song, an assimilation of past into present in the moment of performance:

every time you sing 'em you're going home! Every time you sing 'em you remember the way you heard them sung and you try not to sing them too differently even though you're not singing them standing on the porch of an Appalachian cabin ... they are deep into you, as deep as language.[91]

But paradoxically, the self is simultaneously obliterated in folk song performance. While presenting the problematic nature of the anonymity of folk songs, Child explains:

> The fundamental characteristic of popular ballads is therefore the absence of subjectivity and self-consciousness. Though they do not 'write themselves', as William Grimm has said, though a man and not a people has composed them, still the author counts for nothing, and it is not by mere accident, but with the best reason, that they have come down to us anonymous.[92]

Time, place, politics, gender, race and history are all erased and reforged in performance, held in exquisite tension through the triangulated amalgam of lyric, melody and voice. Milla Tiainen frames spatial ideas for kinetic singing bodies as 'open materiality', describing singers as those who are

> encouraged to open up to the acoustic space they are in, to the air that has to be sucked into the body in order to utter sounds, and so forth. As open materiality the spatial character of vocal bodies is hence comprised of continuous foldings-in of physical and affective particles and simultaneously, unfoldings-out of sonic-bodily forces. Singing bodies are spatial formations that exist, emerge and change in time.[93]

Tiainen unpacks the circular, mutually reciprocal relationship between discursive corporeal materiality and its target body in a physical space and, in doing so, highlights what Brian Massumi dubs the 'essential "gap of non-resemblance" between these registers of reality';[94] this is Carter's 'curious abyss',[95] the gulf between us across which 'invisible music'[96] can carry, across which meanings can resonate sympathetically.

Folk song needs to be performed, and a performance occurs before an audience; Richard Schechner defines the 'self-awareness, the awareness of the awareness, reflexivity' of an audience watching a performance, and notices how the space must be 'uniquely organized so that a large group can watch a small group – and become aware of itself at the same time'.[97] Folk song is therefore as much a participatory, spectatorial activity as a demonstrative one, requiring embodied presence, acoustic delivery, and the attention and participation of both performer and listener. While fairy tales and folk tales are still performed, both in public spaces (such as the folk festival, the pantomime, or the cinema) and in domestic arenas (such as story-time between parent and child), they do not rely on performance to exist, and have propagated and proliferated in textual formats perhaps more successfully than folk songs. But it is the ontological necessity of the sounded performance of the folk song, the necessity of the combination of lyric, melody and voice rendered together in real time in order to bring forth folk song's innate 'songfulness', unlike the form of the folk tale or fairy tale as we find it in modernity, which becomes the crucial factor in justifying this discrete intervention.

'Songfulness'

The musicologist Lawrence Kramer uses various examples to illustrate the nature of 'songfulness' as an energy situated in the voice which exceeds the song's individual components so that vocal delivery subsumes its parts. He identifies 'songfulness' as

> a fusion of vocal and musical utterance judged to be both pleasurable and suitable independent of verbal content. It is the positive quality of singing-in-itself: just singing.[98]

He describes a woman remembering her mother's singing in George Eliot's *Daniel Deronda*: 'because I never knew the meaning of the words they seemed full of nothing but our love and happiness'. He suggests this is an example of 'the experience of song as enveloping voice', where the text is irrelevant, where meaning is inserted, representing a relationship between desired object and desiring subject, in which desire is forever unattainable. Kramer suggests that 'one way to understand songfulness is as the medium or support for the fantasy of attaining this unattainable bliss'. Secondly, he analyzes Schubert's song setting of Goethe's poem 'Heidenröslein', where the sinister subject-matter of a rape is thinly veiled in a beautifully light-hearted, ludic melody; emphasis is distracted from the song's darker meaning by the playful tune and transferred to its 'seemingly artless and naive songfulness',[99] a distraction intended to 'convert the imaginary space unoccupied by meaning into the site of unfettered fantasy'.[100] However, there is 'a catch in the throat': the underlying terror exposes itself in an uncomfortable high note simulating a cry. Kramer identifies this tension as meaning loss within song: 'Songfulness projects meaning loss as the outcome of a relative indifference to meaning, a kind of higher carelessness or forgetfulness that simply does not avail itself of the symbolic, allows the symbolic to lie unused even if its words may still be heard clearly.'[101] For Kramer, it is the meaningful conjunction of words and music within song that creates the potential for the casting-off of meaning in favour of sheer pleasure, 'just singing'.

Carter's prose, when one listens to it, is potentially 'noisy' as her radio plays, and one can argue she is always presenting 'three-dimensional' prose, prose optimized for sounded performance.[102] It crackles with the cacophony of acoustic phenomena. Warner draws our attention to

> a crucial element in Angela Carter's writing: its acoustic weave of voice and sound effects. In her writings, her voice speaks from the page, addressing you, talking to you. The voice isn't on its own, ringing in a hollow space. Open any page and a full score rises from its word-notes, of winds howling, teardrops falling, diamond earrings tinkling, snapping teeth, sneezing and wheezing. Storytelling for Angela Carter was an island full of noises and sweet airs, and like Caliban, who heard a

thousand twangling instruments hum about his ears, she was tuned to an ethereal universe packed with sensations, to which she was alive with every organ.[103]

The notion of implicit prosody, and the manifestation of a reader's capacity to experience and interpret imagined sound when reading, is well-documented: from T. S. Eliot's 'auditory imagination'[104] and Jacques Derrida's 'interior holy voice'[105] to Jeremy Prynne's 'mental ears'[106] and Kramer's observation of 'reading as a silent recitation, listening as inner performance'.[107] When we read, we sound out in our minds all the 'noises and sweet airs' Carter buried in her prose ready for us to re-imagine and re-perform.

Other critics have observed the strength of the 'voice' across Carter's works; indeed the manner in which her characters 'speak' can at times tell us more than the semantic content of what they say. Ghislaine's voice in *Shadow Dance* performs her own disconnectedness: 'She used to speak with the electronic, irresistible sing-song of a ravished automaton; now her voice gave the final, unnerving resemblance of a horror-movie woman to her.'[108] Fevvers' voice jumps feverishly between registers, harnessing the attention of the world in *Nights at the Circus*: 'her cavernous, sombre voice, a voice made for shouting about the tempest, her voice of a celestial fishwife'.[109] The bathos evoked by Dora's all-pervasive 'colloquial discourse' in *Wise Children* pivots 'on the tendency to plummet from an elevated tenor to a prosaic or even bawdy voice'.[110] The absent voice of the elective mute Auntie Margaret in *The Magic Toyshop* paradoxically serves as an act of defiance against the tyranny of Uncle Philip; when his reign is over, she finds with her voice 'her strength, a frail but constant courage like spun silk'.[111] The voice withheld is a trope repeated throughout Carter's oeuvre, one I will discuss in more detail in subsequent chapters.

Warner's claim that Carter's 'voice speaks from the page, addressing you, talking to you' echoes Sage's recollection of Carter enjoying reading aloud. Carter celebrated the voice's inseparable relationship to the word, defying its assumed 'silence' in the scopic age, and asserting that for 'most of human history, "literature", both fiction and poetry, has been narrated, not written – heard, not read'.[112] Crofts notes how writing for radio 'enabled her to get even closer to that pre-literate source, with its reliance on the spoken word'.[113] The sounded female voice, resonating throughout Carter's prose, continually performs this negotiation between the assertion of privilege and the assumption of social and cultural responsibility.

But more than a general voiced soundedness, there is an awareness amongst critics of an innate musicality at work in Carter's prose. Warner celebrates Carter's 'word-notes';[114] Rushdie describes her 'smoky, opium-eater's cadences interrupted by harsh or comic discords'.[115] Her performing role in the folk music scene of the 1960s explains, at least in part, why this might be so; Carter was a singer and a musician, so it would therefore be unsurprising if her musicianship had seeped into her writing. More specific still, Don Ihde observes that 'sometimes there is a "singing" of voice in writing', and I propose that it is at the site of the specifically musical singing voice that Carter conflates all the qualities of 'songfulness' into her prose. In direct contrast to Roud's assertion that lyrical content subordinates any melodic meaning, Kramer proposes that melody is deliberately pitched to render subject-matter submissive to it, and yet at moments in its construction reveals tensions between innocence and artfulness. He explains,

> song harbours a powerful contrary tendency that can take the fore at any moment, either through the agency of a singer or by the invitation of a composer. The very techniques by which song becomes meaningful utterance often lead to at least a partial loss of meaning; songfulness makes meaning extraneous, if not downright superfluous.[116]

This creative tension, borne of the mutual interference between melody, lyric and voice, points to the site of an oscillating and powerful energy: a 'remainder', a 'songfulness', a 'curious chasm', which emerges at once as the product of the fusion of these elements and yet at the same time sits outside them, beyond them. It is this energy, borne of performance, which Carter seeks to harness and exploit when she appropriates the folk song tradition.

Carter's prose exudes this 'songfulness', a quality informed by the pleasure of her own somatic experience of folk singing which emerges from the complex, symbiotic intersection between the syntax and semantics of her written prose and its sounded potential in performance, the tension created by the presence of the potential of her own singing voice innately embedded within her prose production. Through the emergence of this songfulness, Carter recreates in her readers a multimodal experience through prose, reminiscent of Friedrich Kittler's 'powers of hallucination',[117] transcoding into her prose those vital elements of folk song of which I can now prove she had first-hand experience (melody, rhythm, lyrics, voice, performance) to elicit a series of physical recognitions in us. Carter deploys the disruptive energy of songfulness in her prose to initiate a powerful creative oscillation spinning at the heart of her writing, a 'curious abyss' between semantics and syntax designed to unsettle and undermine what we think we know and understand and hear and experience about/within her universes, and therefore our own.

A holistic critical approach

This book necessarily draws on different disciplines and research methodologies, combining archival, literary and musicological modes of analysis and critical vocabularies to create a holistic critical approach. It falls naturally into three parts; the opening establishes the relevance of the focus on folk song with discussion of Carter's life in the 1960s and the archival material; the middle section performs close literary and musicological analysis of Carter's texts against the songs she knew and, in some cases, sang; the final section reveals, through interview with a contemporary singer, the power of Carter's onward musical influence. While current musico-literary analysis attracts a vital and growing critical community, it has so far been mostly focused on influences from music to literature and has been less focused on ways in which musically influenced literary pieces might provoke musical responses in return. Significant critical interventions have also tended to focus more on either 'classical' and 'jazz' forms[118] or 'popular' musics;[119] the folk song tradition's tentacular influences on the literary imagination have received very little attention by comparison.[120] Both in its focus and its methods, therefore, this book presents an original critical workflow: for while it presents a close examination of how folk song performance profoundly influenced Carter, in so doing it also offers a holistic methodological model for increasing our understanding of how forms of music and literature interact more generally.

In the book as a whole, I analyze how Carter imbues her prose with some of the figures, shapes and structures familiar from folk songs to reveal moments where musicality interferes with lexical content to create a new experience, and I examine how Carter borrows folk song's rhythmic patternings and melodic shapes to subvert and contradict her own thematic and narrative content, creating subliminal messages we can receive if we are attuned. I consider how folk song's lyrical elements have enriched Carter's thematic palette, and how a deeper pan-cultural awareness of symbology specific to folk song might illuminate and even shift the terms of previous debates. I explore Carter's utilization of 'voice' in her texts, both in terms of characterization and structure, and suggest that an awareness of the resonance of Carter's own potential singing voice, present in her writing, might alter our perceptions of her syntactical choices. Finally I investigate concepts of performance as they relate to Carter and to us, her living readers, and how Carter's manipulation of 'songfulness' demands that we perform her prose musically by proxy.

In Chapter 2, I gather and present the evidence of Carter's folk singing praxis from Paul and Angela Carter's Folk Music Archive,[121] Carter's published essays and articles, her authored album sleeve notes, her unpublished diaries and letters, and her unpublished undergraduate dissertation. Together, these materials reveal unequivocally the extent of Carter's involvement with the 1960s folk song revival.

In Chapters 3, 4, 5 and 6 I move from archival analysis to a form of musico-literary criticism, reading a selection of Carter's fiction texts through lenses of folk songs she knew and/or sang, to reveal their influences upon her imaginative output. In Chapter 3, I discuss how folk song's startlingly modern notions of gender fluidity, whereby men routinely sing women's songs and vice versa, colour Carter's presentations of gender in her debut, *Shadow Dance*. I reveal how folk song's melodic shapes such as chiasmus infuse her syntactical constructions, and how folk song figures such as the vulpine anti-hero Reynardine appear in the character of Honeybuzzard. In Chapter 4, I argue that Carter uses her experience of folk singing to create imaginary spaces in her fiction, focusing in particular on the folk song locus of the greenwood, to suggest that Carter conjures the greenwood in her short story 'The Erl-King' (and elsewhere) by utilizing and repurposing prosodic features from songs. I scan dactylic rhythmic figures in her syntax, tying them to dactylic rhythms in songs set in the greenwood, and suggest that Carter transcodes the disquieting affect of modal scale shifts from music into grammar through nauseating pronominal and temporal shifts, to become a sonic geographer.

In Chapter 5, I examine Carter's rendering of the picaresque in her short story 'Reflections' and her novel *The Infernal Desire Machines of Doctor Hoffman*, to propose that her understanding of the topos of the journey was deeply influenced by her folk singing practice. I argue that Carter attunes us in these two texts to the pleasurable oscillation, implicit in the folk song tradition, between wanderlust, a desire for movement and comprehension and stasis, lacunae and bewilderment. In Chapter 6, I analyze the hybrids and chimeras of the bird-girls in 'The Erl-King' and the bird-woman Fevvers in *Nights at the Circus*, tracing through their strange bodies the very chimera that is song, and discovering within them the embodiment of Carter's singing voice. I give this song-prose a name: 'canorography', from 'canorous', meaning melodious or resonant.

In each chapter I use a subtly fluctuating semantic field to convey these ever-shifting relationships between Carter's folk song experience and her prose; in particular the verbs I use to describe the intermingling of folk song and prose throughout the musico-literary chapters are carefully selected. In Chapter 3, I write mainly of infusion and seepage; in Chapter 4, I describe attunement; in Chapter 5 I refer to weaving, burial and retrieval of musical treasure; in Chapter 6 I talk of hybridic splicing and chimeric conjoining. I augment this descriptive language, with which I can perhaps only ever hope to convey these relationships partially, with references to actual recordings of performances of the songs themselves. Throughout, I refer to a process of transcoding, expressing the idea that Carter is continually using her muscle memory of singing to convert meanings from one form of coded representation into another.

In Chapter 7, I reveal Carter's onward musical trajectory, and the influence her prose continues to have on music makers, through a series of interviews with the contemporary folk musician Emily Portman. With musicological analysis of Portman's repertoire and compositional practices, I show how musical features concealed within Carter's prose are extracted and repurposed by musically minded artists in an onward cycle of influences. My final chapter, Chapter 8, envisages future research which could result from the re-imagining of prose as audial event.

Maurice Merleau-Ponty writes of the corporeal occupation of the reader: 'I create Stendhal; I am Stendhal while reading him. But that is because first he knew how to bring me to dwell within him.' This concept of becoming-another is familiar to the folk singer, who becomes the subject of the folk song as s/he sings. Merleau-Ponty goes on,

> As long as language is functioning authentically, it is not a simple invitation to the listener or reader to discover in himself significations that were already there. It is rather the trick whereby the writer or orator, touching on these significations already present in us, makes them yield strange sounds. At first these sounds seem false or dissonant. However, because the writer is so successful in converting us to his system of harmony, we adopt it henceforth as our own. From then on, between the writer and ourselves there remain only the pure relations of spirit to spirit. Yet all this began through the complicity of speech and its echo, or to use Husserl's lively phrase referring to the perception of others, through the 'coupling' of language.[122]

Carter, through her manipulation of prose-songfulness, brings herself to dwell in us bodily and creates with us these 'pure relations of spirit to spirit'. Carter uses her understanding of the mechanics of singing, of the performing body as it breathes and the song's resonance within a listener's body, to situate 'songfulness' at the heart of her writing, to create 'invisible music', a 'canorographic' or song-infused prose. I maintain that Carter is singing to us and through us through her writing, and she can do this because she knew – very well – how to sing.

2

'a singer's swagger': Angela Carter, the folk singer

I have vivid recall of Angela singing solos because we sang fortnightly together at her Bristol club 'Folksong and Ballad'. She'd adopt a traditional singer's swagger with hands thrust into her pockets, eyes shut, maybe a grin.

Christine Molan, 'Authentic Magic'[1]

As the first of the two recordings begins, one can feel a palpable sense of excitement and anticipation in the room. Clothing brushes briefly against the microphone, a chair scrapes, a concertina note whines out to provide the starting note, and a singer takes to the floor. She begins, opening on the sixth note of the scale and spiralling upwards with the melody to the tonic before swooping down in an accomplished octave dive:

'If I – were King of Erin's Isle, and had all things at my will . . .'[2]

We are in the Cheltenham Folk Club, it is 15 January 1967, and Angela Carter is singing 'The Flower of Sweet Strabane' [1]. She and her husband Paul are caught on tape by chance as support singers to the club's guest booking for that night, the Newcastle singer Tommy Handle.

This is one of only two known extant recordings of Angela Carter performing folk music live in the 1960s. She sings unaccompanied, and one is immediately arrested by the serpentine melody, which rises from her like a coil of smoke, and by her sweet voice, laden with sympathy for the song's persona whose love for Martha, the most beautiful girl in Ireland, goes unrequited. Unaccompanied folk voice is an acquired taste; it is rarely polished, but always emotive: Carter's voice swells on the high notes and feels its way intuitively around the lyrical dactyls as the rejected first-person protagonist sets sail for America. Unlike many folk songs, its provenance is relatively clear: in 1915 it appeared in the popular *Derry Journal* newspaper column 'Come-All-Ye'[3] and in 1928 featured in Sam Henry's American newspaper column 'Songs of the People'; at Henry's estimation a likely composition date is 1846.[4] A tantalizing recent post in an online chatroom for folk song enthusiasts suggests there may remain present-day links to the eponymous 'flower', Martha.[5] Carter's version on this recording follows the singing of Paddy Tunney from his 1965 Topic album *A Wild Bees' Nest*;[6] the Carters were friends of Tunney and this was one of his favourite songs.[7] A second recording from the same night captures Carter playing an instrumental piece on English concertina, a medley of two polka tunes, 'Saint Mary's' and 'Church Street' [2] which, it has been suggested, she may have learned orally from the version on the 1963 debut LP from The Chieftains.[8]

These evocative recordings from 1967 form part of a privately held archive to which I have been granted generous access, which also contains Carter's folk song research notes from the 1960s, her jottings from folk song texts and her musical notations of folk song tunes, along with the books and records she shared with her first husband Paul Carter. Her musical notebooks were carefully preserved amongst Paul Carter's own papers, and only recently surfaced when, upon Paul's death in 2012, they were passed to Christine Molan, a Bristol-based artist and friend of the Carters who sang with them in Bristol during the 1960s, both at The Bear in Hotwells and later at their own club, 'Folksong and Ballad Bristol' which met fortnightly at The Lansdown in Clifton.[9]

A bio-chemistry lecturer by day, Paul Carter was one of the lesser-known folk record producers and field recordists of the late 1950s and 1960s, collecting and recording tracks which appeared on the Collector and Topic labels, alongside the works of more well-known collector producers such as Bill Leader, Peter Kennedy, Ken Stubbs and Seamus Ennis. He recorded studio performances of widely acclaimed revival singers such as Anne Briggs, Ewan MacColl, Bert Lloyd and Peggy Seeger, as well as field recordings of traditional singers such as Tom Willett, Sarah Makem and Phoebe Smith. One therefore might assume that Paul introduced Angela to folk song; in 1962 she claimed that Paul 'taught me all I know about the trad fad',[10] from which her biographer Edmund Gordon concludes, it 'was perhaps his most important gift to her'.[11] However, this could be a misreading on two counts: firstly, the phrase 'trad fad' at this time usually referred not to trad folk music but to trad jazz (and Paul was also a fervent jazz enthusiast);[12] secondly, Carter had an earlier folk song teacher, her maternal grandmother, with whom she lived for a portion of her childhood:

> My granny taught me songs that celebrated the wily fox, the poacher's comrade, and his depredations of bourgeois farmyards:
>
>> Old Mother Flipperty-flop jumped out of bed,
>> Out of the window she stuck out 'er 'ead –
>> 'John, John, the grey goose is gone
>> And the fox is off to his den, oh!'[13]

This lyric fragment comes from a set of songs known as 'The Fox' (Roud 131), sometimes 'The Hungry Fox', 'Daddy Fox' or 'A Fox Jumped Up', part of a group of anthropo-/zoomorphic songs which include 'Reynardine' and 'The Cottage in the Woods'. These songs were to become important touchstones in Carter's imaginative and creative relationship with folk song and its tropes. Elsewhere Carter emphasizes the importance of the physicality of her grandmother's performance of the 'Red Riding Hood' story:

> She liked, especially, to pounce on me, roaring, in personation of the wolf's pounce on Red Riding Hood at the end of the story, although she could not have known

that [Charles] Perrault himself suggests this acting-out of the story to the narrator in a note in the margin of the manuscript.[14]

The somatic element of her grandmother's transmission of these oral cultural artefacts to her granddaughter was to have dramatic repercussions on Carter's subsequent literary creations.

Notwithstanding her grandmother's early interventions, Carter's marriage to Paul Carter, and their shared experience of folk songs and folk singers, surely deepened her understanding of and reverence for the folk song form. Amongst the books in their shared archive, scrawled inside the cover of *The Everlasting Circle* by James Reeves (a collection of folk songs published in 1960 on which Carter was to draw heavily in her folk song scholarship), there is a touching dedication from Angela to Paul (signed with her maiden initials 'AOS', which suggests the gift predates their marriage in September 1960) which encapsulates this association most neatly:

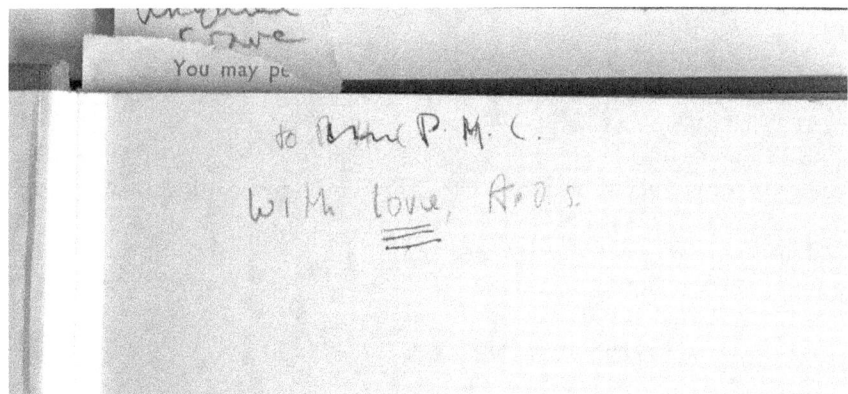

Figure 1 Photo detail of hand-written inscription on inside cover of James Reeves, *The Everlasting Circle* (1960), from Paul and Angela Carter's Folk Music Archive. Copyright © Christine Molan. Reproduced with kind permission of Christine Molan.

The form's connections with Paul may also go some way to explaining why, when their marriage ended in 1969, she cut off all links with the folk revival scene, and rarely mentioned its impact upon her life and work again. But folk song's influences on her prose announce themselves through musically nuanced prosody, imagery, tropes and motifs, musical shapes and rhythmic undercurrents, which together present a prose style steeped in folk song.[15]

Even without the discovery of the archive and the recordings of her singing and playing, it would be possible from extant sources to stitch together an understanding of the importance of Carter's interest and investment in folk song, which was not only pleasurable and intellectually stimulating for her creative imagination as she found her writer's 'voice', but also profoundly influential on the ways in which we continue to 'read' her. Folk song 'sings back' to us through her prose, the influence of its somatic memory on her singing body presenting itself in its various symbiotic components, all essential expressions of the one form – text, melody, and voice – which I shall now examine in turn.

Carter's textual engagement with folk song

Carter's fascination with traditional folk song can be seen, in part, to be a preoccupation with the form's complex systems of textual significations and unorthodox, internally calibrated historicities. Carter was intrigued and inspired by the potentially ancient poetry of folk song, the resonant imagery locked up in its lexicon, and the recurring motifs and latent structural shapes which had, she insisted, accumulated potent literary value and significance. Whether balladic or lyrical in mood,[16] Carter believed folk song poetry to be of 'great beauty';[17] she spontaneously expressed her admiration for it in various parts of her unpublished journals. She transcribed lines from the folk song 'The Twa Corbies' (Child 26) onto the inside cover of her 1961 journal:

> O'er his white bones, when they are bare,
> The wind sall blow for evermair.[18]

and on 10 November of that year, she cited 'The Unquiet Grave' (Child 78) [3]:

> I suppose, by true poetry, I mean, for example,
>   'Cold is the wind tonight, my love,
>   And a few drops of rain
>   I never had but one true love,
>   In cold earth he was lain.'[19]

In February 1964, she wrote out in her marginalia an extract from 'One Moonlight Night', sometimes also known as 'The Cottage In The Wood' (Roud 608):

> One moonlight night as I sat high,
>   Waiting for one, but two came by,
> The boughs did bend, my heart did quake
>   To see the hole the fox did make.[20]

This aesthetic revelling in folk song's rich store of images soon spilled over into a scholarly interest, for which Carter found several outlets.

Firstly, Carter wrote sleeve notes for commercial album releases, in which she discusses folk song poetry as literary artefact. These hermeneutic exegeses allowed her to use and share her growing knowledge of folk song, and her developing intertextual understanding of its position in wider culture. In her sleeve notes to Peggy Seeger's 1962 EP *Troubled Love*, for example, she uses a more canonical 'literary' source to elucidate (and perhaps validate) the record's thematic content:

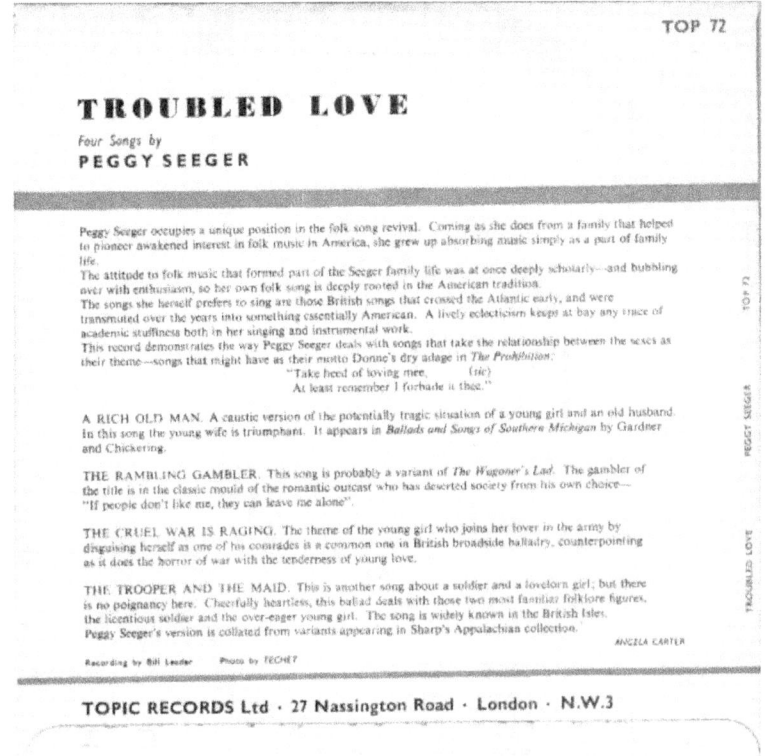

Figure 2 Peggy Seeger, *Troubled Love* EP, back cover (Topic Records TOP72, 1962). Copyright © Topic Records. Reproduced with kind permission of Topic Records.

This record demonstrates the way Peggy Seeger deals with songs that take the relationship between the sexes as their theme – songs that might have as their motto John Donne's dry adage in *The Prohibition*:

'Take heed of loving mee, (sic)
At least remember I forbade it thee.'[21]

On Seeger's 1962 EP *Early In The Spring* (see overleaf), Carter attempts to decipher the

considerable symbolism in the imagery of the text, but this version is perhaps easier of interpretation than many, and could mean that a woman, no longer young, is regretting a youthful misadventure with a sexual opportunist. The gardener perhaps represents a fertility element.[22]

Carter contextualizes 'The Cock' in her sleeve notes to Louis Killen's 1965 album *Ballads and Broadsides*, comparing this version's narrative elements with other permutations:

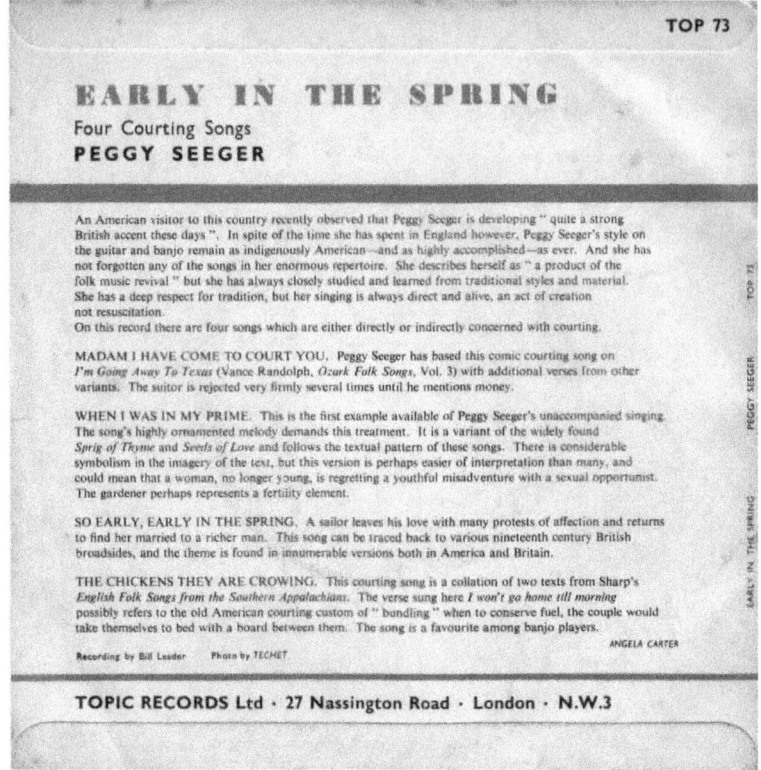

Figure 3 Peggy Seeger, *Early in the Spring* EP, back cover (Topic Records TOP73, 1962). Copyright © Topic Records. Reproduced with kind permission of Topic Records.

In some of this song's relations, notably the ballad 'The Grey Cock', cock-crow has a supernatural significance; it summons a dead lover back to his grave after a last night with a living true love. But here, it breaks the embraces of earthly lovers and the young man trudges off over the cold fields, thinking ruefully of his girl in her snug bed.[23]

Despite the vernacular medium, Carter is careful to apply the same scholarly rigour to her analyses as she does to her university essays. She is concerned with the narrative elements of folk songs, but her attention soon begins to turn to resonant imagery, recurring motifs and the interchangeable language of symbols.

The title of Carter's 1964 essay 'Now is the Time for Singing' is a nod to the 1961 LP *Now Is The Time For Fishing* by Norfolk singer Sam Larner, whom she greatly admired. In the essay, she explores what she perceives to be the profound contemporaneous cultural significances of folk song and its revival. Carter declares that the 'study of the traditional song of these islands is something of a liberal education in itself' and that 'it is possible to find great beauty – by any standards – in the texts alone, even apart from their beauty, as a skeleton has beauty of its own'. She uncovers resonances and relevances in the evocative imagery of traditional folk songs and their 'pictorial images of great clarity' for a modern readership; one image in particular, from 'The Dowie Dens of Yarrow' [4], she finds especially arresting:

> The extraordinary image [...] – the girl letting down her long, yellow hair and wrapping her dead lover up in it, to protect him or to keep him warm – we know to be one created by the working over of a text. [...] It is also quite clearly not a naturalistic image. It is meant to work on an allusive and symbolic level; as is the sympathetic magic of the oak that bends and breaks.[24]

Carter sometimes strains in her attempts to forge links between folk song lyrics and more canonical poetry. She suggests, for example, that 'The Threshing Machine' might remind us of 'the pylon poetry between the great wars', or the 'keen, unpassion'd' beauty of Rupert Brooke's great machine';[25] these attempts run the risk of undermining her goal to attain more institutional validation for the folk song form, although the institution in which she was participating at the time, the English Department of the *über*-Leavisite LC Knights, was unlikely to admit this kind of literature into the academy. But this is the sort of affective text that Carter was instinctively attracted to; she wrote later,

> I was drawn to that section of our native literature which is actually mostly about monsters. Old English and medieval literature [is] the part of our literature, our inheritance, in which literal truth isn't important at all. In *Beowulf*, for example, it's not a question of do monsters exist or can a monster have a mother? It's: how does a monster's mother feel?[26]

She was actively seeking that part of the canon where, as with folk song poetry, preconceived rules of normalcy do not apply; in the medieval department, under the supervision of Basil Cottle, she found it.

Carter was given an opportunity with Cottle to develop these lines of argument in more depth when she wrote her undergraduate dissertation, 'Some Speculations on Possible Relationships between the Medieval Period and 20th Century Folk Song Poetry', in which she attempts to formalize links between the folk songs she was discovering in contemporary collections, hearing on records and singing in folk clubs, and the medieval poetry she was reading in books. She suggests striking resemblances between songs and medieval poems can be discerned, not in their narrative detail, but in the palette of circulating images, symbols, motifs and loci, what David Atkinson calls the peculiar 'vocabulary and "grammar" of balladry',[27] which appear to have percolated through the poems and into popular song and which may have proved more resistant to processes of variation.

For example, Carter compares the folk song 'The Streams of Lovely Nancy' [5] to 'The Castle of Love and Grace', a Marian hymn-parable contained within the *Cursor Mundi*,[28] a fourteenth-century Northumbrian poem, expanding on an argument initially proposed in 1913 by Lucy Broadwood and Anne Gilchrist that the origins of the former can be found in the latter. Gilchrist suggests that 'Nancy' may have survived the Reformation because of mutations over time which buried its overt Marian references, but which maintained a network of recognizable images. The image of the magnificent castle in the poem, for example, resurfaces with mysterious signification in the song:

> At the top all of this mountain where my love's castle stands,
>   'Tis all overbuilt with ivory to the bottom of the stand,
> Fine arches and fine porches and a diamond stone so bright,
>   It's a pilot for a sailor on a darn'd stormy night.[29]

Whilst the poem may have been stripped of overt religious references in its song version, its resonant imagery hints, argues Carter, towards a possible Marian past.

Carter argues folk song texts reveal their ancient literary origins not just in images and motifs; she also suggests form and structure hold latent memory. She notices medieval roots entangled in successful formulae such as the rubric 'As I Roved Out', mapping it across more than 70 songs, and noting how it has survived because it functions on a structural level:

> This is not so much the wholesale survival of a patch of medieval culture as the retention by the creators of folk-song of certain forms of expression that suited them particularly well. The 'As I Roved Out' formula can be varied to fit almost any situation, just as the folktale introductory formula, 'once upon a time', can be; the essence of this formula is the idea of the chance happening as the narrator is walking by himself.[30]

Carter also alerts us here to structural processes of 'bricolage' at work deep in folk song's haphazard construction:

> Under examination, traditional song in the English language begins to take on the appearance of collage; a collection of bits and pieces, odds and ends, haphazardly assembled upon a background that is the property of nobody but the people themselves.[31]

Perhaps influenced by the figure of the 'bricoleur' in Claude Lévi-Strauss's *The Savage Mind* (1962) but remarkably ahead of both Jacques Derrida's *Writing and Difference* (1967) and Roland Barthes' *Image Music Text* (1968), Carter's prescient sensitivities to processes of 'collage', intrinsic to the performed folk song form, illuminate ways in which her growing understanding of folk song was to influence her creative processes.[32] Elsewhere she describes this process in similar terms: 'I used bits and pieces from various mythologies quite casually, because they were to hand.'[33] Ahead of her time, Carter was finding methodologies in the folk song tradition which would resonate with and inform her own postmodern creative experience.

Medieval poetry also shares structural currency with the folk song form through its authorial anonymity. In 'Now' Carter celebrates the many authors and imaginations who have worked over folk song, whom A. L. Lloyd refers to as the 'ghosts of so many pasts [...] looking back out of the mirror whose emotions and experiences have been imprinted into the songs themselves'.[34] Carter agrees, observing that 'many of the most pleasing verbal effects in a song are not the result of one person's creative talent, but the cumulative talents of years, even centuries, working over a song'.[35] Vladimir Propp asks us to liken folklore 'not to literature but to language, which is invented by no one and which has neither an author nor authors'.[36] Folk song is the product of many talents, many lives, many experiences; the past is built up into the textual expression of songs like a patina of past lives, past ghosts, past voices. Carter found herself drawn to it.

She was equally drawn to folk song's unkempt, unruly, sense of its own history, its myriad relationships to fluid pasts and presents flowing from a joyfully disordered and rambunctious oral tradition, allowing for the development of simultaneous trajectories, versions and variants. Just like folk tales and fairy tales, other oral traditions which had in the nineteenth century begun a migration to more bibliocentric forms, folk song's sprawling genealogy smacks of a gloriously promiscuous creativity. Multiple song versions coexist in many locations; there is no claim to authorship, no progenitor, no original. This non-authoritative, non-linear, anti-patriarchal mode appealed to Carter's leftist magpie imagination and rang true with the 1960s post-structuralist zeitgeist she embraced, in which she loved to 'loot and rummage'[37] in the treasure-chests of European culture, because the locks were off. Imaginatively promiscuous in her own artistic life, I suggest she admired and learned this tendency towards irreverence from her folk song praxis, and revelled in the prospect of building new creations from 'raw material in the lumber room of the Western imagination'[38] because, among other influences, her folk singing and scholarship – and perhaps even the great folk song collector and singer Bert Lloyd himself[39] – had shown her how to do it.

But before Carter was to find a public platform for her own artistic identity, at the heart of her 1965 undergraduate dissertation there exists an awareness of a problematic relationship between tradition and modernity, an uncomfortable contradiction between the need for tradition and its simultaneous repulsion, an oscillation that would persist throughout her fictions. For, on the one hand, Carter can be seen to be seeking validation from the 'academy' for folk song by finding evidence of the roots of 'respectable' medieval poetry within its family tree. Starting with carols, she progresses to seemingly 'historical' songs such as those that commemorate specific battles:

> Those ballads concerned with the wars between England and Scotland can be regarded fairly confidently as medieval in origin.
> The battle of Otterburn took place in 1388 and the earliest ballads composed about it date from 1400. The best known are 'The Battle of Otterburn' (Child 161) and 'The Hunting of the Cheviot' (Child 162), usually known as Chevy Chase.[40]

But on the other hand, she proceeds to dismantle any historical certainty there may be surrounding these songs, suggesting instead that the folk song mode has a different understanding of time, of what the past might mean in relation to us, and what folk song's purpose might be:

> The traditional ballad is largely unhistorical, changing the size of the armies engaged, omitting actual leaders such as the Earl of Mar, reporting the killing of Macdonald and the actual duration of the conflict incorrectly. Folksong has its own historicity, which is not necessarily that of the history text books, having been composed for other purposes.[41]

Walter Ong describes this seeming movement of details in orally transmitted folk materials as nevertheless consistent with the idea of 'homeostasis' for, as he puts it, the 'integrity of the past [is] subordinate to the integrity of the present'.[42] In other words, the details may change in oral narratives, but the singer is consistent in his or her singing, and in using the vehicle of the song to explain an ever-changing present to an audience. Singers will change the texts of songs to suit themselves, demonstrating 'the almost magical ability of a great traditional singer to create a whole new out of elements of text and tune'[43] – singers like Jeannie Robertson who while singing 'My Son David' [6], a variant of the Child ballad 'Edward', would remember her own dead son and so imbue the song with new tender resonances, weaving her own personal history into the fabric of the song and adding another layer to its complex historical patina.[44] As Carter explains,

> Traditional song is always in a state of flux. Since the singer is, to some extent, a creator, he can reformulate the text and tune he is singing to please himself; there is, finally, no standardised form to which he must adhere.[45]

Carter observes this oscillation between the personal and the historical in folk song praxis when she observes how Peggy Seeger 'has a deep respect for tradition, but her singing is always direct and alive, an act of creation and not resuscitation'.[46] Similarly she notes how Louis Killen refuses to make concessions to commercialism yet 'stamps each performance with his own musical individuality and dynamism through keeping to the disciplines of traditional singing, a paradox which is the basis of the serious folk song revival'.[47] This utilitarian recycling of the old to forge the new was to become a resonant theme throughout Carter's analysis of her own work: the favoured metaphor of 'old wine in new bottles' (ironically itself already 'upcycled' from Matthew 9:17) to illustrate a point about reading in her now-famous essay 'Notes from the Front Line' first appears, for example, in her unpublished 1965 dissertation, where she concludes:

> These songs survived the centuries, being continually re-moulded to suit each new generation of country singers, but often retaining ancient features; and newly written or adapted songs were often, new wine in old bottles, cast in ancient forms.[48]

In 'Now' Carter ruminates on the idea of historical foregrounding to songs, but concludes that what matters is not the unhinged, possibly erroneous historicity of textbook-fact-gone-wrong, but the veracity of the performer's *own* lyrical historicity brought to bear on the song through performance. When discussing the background to the folk song 'The Bonny Bunch of Roses' [7] for example, Carter explains its context:

> From the song, which is a conversation between young Napoleon and his mother detailing Bonaparte's ambitions and their defeat, and his son's tragically early death before he could avenge his father, one learns all one needs to know about the historical context of the song ...

but then, through the compelling use of the conjunction phrase so recognizably hers, subordinates its historical features to the more relevant, more appropriate intentions of the singer:

> for it is not really about Napoleon and the Napoleonic Wars at all, not when Heaney sings it, say, in a folk-song club in 1964; his song is about how all brave men must finally meet their Moscows, and how all worldly ambition is finally brought to nothing.[49]

Similarly in her dissertation she describes the way singers obliterate 'official pasts' and bring them into the service of their own specificities, their own times and spaces:

> Ballads quite genuinely have no time and place because those who sing them tend to assimilate them into their own experiences and details like the time and place and setting of the original version is not particularly important and may be changed or ignored in the singing.[50]

She further explains how the singer

> is not primarily concerned with the historical or geographical provenance of a song he has learned from his father, or from a ballad sheet, or from a stranger he had met in a pub or market place. He is concerned, rather, with the core of emotional truth, or human drama, which a song contains and which is applicable to the life he himself leads.[51]

The singer's personal and emotional history forms their core response to the song, and it is this which proves consistent.

And yet, in almost direct contradiction to this positing of the personal into the historical, there is a counter-tendency in folk song towards an obliteration of the individual in the face of the song itself. In her folk song notebook preserved in the archive, Carter notes Cecil Sharp's observation of the folk singer: 'When he sings his aim is to forget himself and everything that reminds him of his everyday life.'[52] In 'Now' she contemplates the repressive, pressurized nature of the relationship between the singer and her/his material: she praises Harry Cox's

> musical personality – and it is his musical personality only which he imposes on a song, he never allows his own emotional responses to a song to come through but lets it speak for itself...[53]

The singer's experience is perhaps one of sublimation, of transformation, a 'folding-in' to the song of personal experience which is then transformed, through a 'folding-out' process of the act of singing, into something entirely new, entirely other. As Carter describes it, the 'performer is something more than the interpreter of his material: he is helping to formulate it'.[54] The folk song is shaped by the performer, as much as the performance is shaped by the song.

Across her private journals, her dissertation, her essays and notes, Carter reveals this dynamic textual engagement with folk song as alternative history, alternative historicity. While Carter may have wanted initially to use 'official pasts' to validate folk song, it becomes apparent that as she tries to do so, folk song challenges that very notion, creating instead an unofficial but compelling accumulation of human experiences which becomes semantically more akin to music than to text, loaded with a different kind of meaning in which human experience, while unspecific, is recognizable. This is the element of 'story', rather than 'history', lying latent in folk song narratives, which Carter seized upon. In her unpublished papers there exists a creative writing teaching plan, possibly dating from her visiting professorship at Brown University (1980–81), in which she makes narrative connections between the Child ballad 'Lady Isabel & The Elf-Knight' and the Bluebeard complex of folk tales. She boils each down to essences, observing how in the ballad 'the elf-knight is erl-king & demon lover' and how 'the claustrophobia of "Bluebeard" and "Mr Fox" turn out to not have been important [...] we are left, oddly enough, with fine clothing – with a demon lover – & with a triumphant, nay, a vengeful virgin'.[55] Folk song narratives, alongside other traditional forms, occupied an important place in her storytelling arsenal.

Carter was also adamant that the textual fabric of folk song was only one part of its materiality, and is therefore only one part of the story of the influence folk song was to have on her as a writer.

Carter's prosodic engagement with folk song

In her journals dating from a similar period, Carter is thinking about the prosodic quality of words to convey an internal musical meaning, a 'melody of letters'.[56] In 'Now', Carter shows awareness of the musical understanding of language needed to write singable lyrics:

> ...not only did [the songs] have a certain sort of verbal creativity, but it was closely linked with a musical creativity, and a working technical knowledge of how some phrases are poetry but unsingable and others become poetry when sung.[57]

Around the same time, she was reading Northrop Frye's *Anatomy of Criticism*[58] and in her diary she notes with interest his observations about 'melos': on 8 January 1963 she describes 'melos' as:

> a musical quality; & by musical he means rhythmic, language following an elaborate internal scheme of balances, chords and discords, with metre and relations of harsh consonants very pronounced, also speeds.

She abbreviates Frye's categorizations of different writers:

> Browning, Skelton, Dunbar, Smart – musical
> Keats, Tennyson, Shelley – unmusical

and then quotes directly Frye's observations about musical phrasing innate in the English language:

> the *melos* of physical absorption in sound and rhythm, the pounding movement and clashing noise which the heavy accentuation of English makes possible ... tendency to ragtime in English poetry that can be traced back through Poe's *Bells* and Dryden's *Alexander's Feast* to Skelton and to Dunbar's *Ane Ballat of Our Lady* ...[59]

Here we can witness her ruminating on critical thinking surrounding prosody, musicality and embedded rhythms in poetry, and forging in the crucible of her imagination links between these observations and the melodic elements of her own prose.

There is more evidence to suggest that Carter was thinking sounds and words together as she composed texts designed to be voiced, such as her radio plays. As she begins to write 'Vampirella', she describes the scene:

> I ran the pencil idly along the top of the radiator. It made a metallic, almost musical rattle. [...] I alliterated her. A lovely lady vampire. And she must be plucking those twanging, almost musical notes out of her birdcage because, like me, she was bored ...[60]

When Carter states, 'I alliterated her,' she suggests a deep and nuanced relationship between word, sound and imaginative creation. She sings her 'lovely lady vampire' into being; Carter carries her songful relationship between word and sound, honed through her folk singing praxis, deep into her texts for radio, and even further into her prose.

Carter's understanding of the power of prosody to convey meaning is fictionalized in the language of the River People in her 1972 novel *The Infernal Desire Machines of Doctor Hoffman*, who 'speak in a kind of singing [...] The only way to transcribe their language would be in a music notation.'[61] Desiderio's new name amongst them is 'Kiku. The two syllables were separated by the distance of a minor third. The name meant "foundling bird"; it seemed to me most wistfully appropriate.'[62] As the patriarch, Nao-Kurai, tells a story, he 'rambled on in a drowsy voice, inadvertently flattening notes here and there, which subtly altered various meanings, but I continued to listen because these picturesque ancient survivals were, were they not, the orally transmitted history of my people.'[63] Music, history, identity, language, song: Carter was learning how to write the intricate inter-relationships of these states into her prose by doing the same as her character: singing the 'ancient survivals' of her own culture into her writing.

Carter's melodic engagement with folk song

The melodic component of a folk song, its tune, is just as vital a carrier of semantic signification as its words, as Carter and others have highlighted. Surprisingly, not all folk song scholars agree on this point: F. J. Child omitted any reference to melodies in his definitive collection of folk songs,[64] which focused entirely on the etymology and diaspora of the songs' textual, lyrical components.[65] But other collectors, such as Cecil Sharp, George Gardiner, the Hammond Brothers (Henry and Robert) and Sabine Baring-Gould were more careful to notate the tunes alongside the lyrics they found, and their collectors' notebooks are filled with musical notations alongside lyrical jottings.

In her own private folk song notebook, Carter noted the tunes of folk songs she was interested in as carefully as the words, perhaps so that she could perform them herself. Here, for example, is her notation of the tune of 'Lucy Wan,' which Molan remembers her performing, written out from the 'Penguin Book' as stated in the marginalia:

Figure 4 Photo detail of 'Lucy Wan' notated by Angela Carter, from Paul and Angela Carter's Folk Music Archive. Copyright © Christine Molan. Reproduced with kind permission of Christine Molan.

Here is another folk song Carter transcribed musically in her notebook, this time learned from a recording, of Phoebe Smith's 'Higher Germany', and therefore presumably written down by ear:

Figure 5 Photo detail of 'Higher Germany' from Paul and Angela Carter's Folk Music Archive. Copyright © Christine Molan. Reproduced with kind permission of Christine Molan.

In her 1963–64 journal, Carter wrote out a list of 80 folk song titles, which includes a sub-list of songs intriguingly entitled 'to learn':

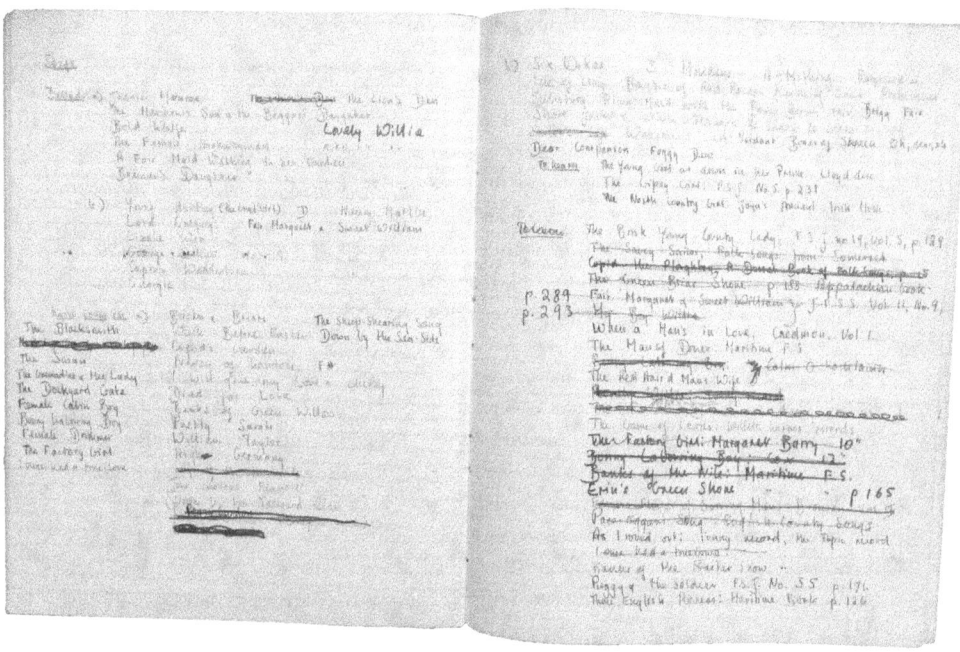

Figure 6 Photograph of a page in Angela Carter's *1963-64 Journal*. Copyright © The Estate of Angela Carter. Reproduced with kind permission of the Estate c/o Rogers, Coleridge & White Ltd., 20 Powis Mews, London W11 1JN.

Christine Molan has clarified that this list does not constitute a personal repertoire; Carter herself only sang eight of the songs listed here in their folk group, and other songs were sung by other members. However, the presence of this list (and its notable bias towards songs of female agency) suggests Carter was engaging with this material for some other purpose. It might even be read as an early example of her curatorial and editorial skills which would find full expression in *The Virago Book of Fairy Tales* and *The Second Virago Book of Fairy Tales*, anthologies she compiled and edited in 1990 and 1991, and in her collation of contemporary women writers' short stories, *Wayward Girls and Wicked Women* (1986). Learning the musical components of these songs, it seems from her folk notes, was as important to Carter as the textual elements, because she understood the semantic impact of melodies upon words, evident in her vivid description in 'Now' of the 'enormously virile tune' of the folk song 'Blow the Candle Out'.[66]

The notoriously complex, ambiguous relationship between words, music and meaning has occupied the theoretical musings of philosophers from Plato to Adorno.[67] The phenomenological approach of American musicologist Samuel P. Bayard perceives a political relationship between melodic shapes and the lived experiences of regional communities:

> the English style is characterized by a certain solidity of melodic build – an emphasis throughout the tune on the strong notes of the mode, like the tonic or

dominant tones – and by a preference for the sort of melodic movement which 'gets somewhere', which is not held up by hesitating progression or undue overlay of ornamental features. In general, the style is firm and forward-moving, with vigorous rhythm, bold, long-ranging sweeps, and simple melodism.[68]

By contrast, he notes the difference in the Irish style, which displays

> a striking tendency to emphasize and dwell on scale-tones that are inconclusive or indecisive – the weak or passing tones, the ones that do not contribute to resolution or finality in the entire phrase or musical utterance, but rather to easy flow and facile continuity. These qualities taken together give the purest Irish airs a peculiarly melodious, graceful softness of flow and outline; a sweetness and smooth ease that seem often on the point of slipping into diffuse weakness.[69]

Recognizing Bayard's (arguably prejudiced) distinctions between English and Irish melodic styles, A. L. Lloyd constructs a Marxist reading of England's changing melodies; he senses a shift in English folk melody style during the eighteenth century, from Bayard's recognizably English style to a more Irish flavour. Rather than being caused entirely by the influences of increased Irish migration, Lloyd wonders whether these melodic fluctuations could be a more subtle expression of economic insecurity amongst the village poor as enclosures robbed them of their livelihoods and common lands disappeared. Carter herself readily recognizes hegemonic relations at play in melodies and claims her 'big man striding up and down in boots' is 'the anti-middle-class figure of Jack', whom she frames with glee as the antithesis of 'tongue-tied' 'John', the 'cold unemotional Englishman' who is far too busy out 'empire-building' to be sneaking in through any girl's window.[70]

Carter is also sensitive to the central role of the singer and the singing voice as purveyor of meaning in the folk tradition, and the ways in which singers find depths of expression in timbre and phrasing. As Georgina Boyes explains, meaning in folk song is supra-linguistic, for

> meaning is at the core of performance. And what a song means to its singer doesn't necessarily or only reside in its words. Through a song an individual can express something they feel is most significant about themselves or evoke a specific person or event.[71]

Moreover, meaning is generated not just by the singer in performance, but by the rapport of that singer with the audience, in a process of semantic exchange. Niall MacKinnon describes 'the direct and inter-communicative form of the audience-performer relationship' in folk performance, and how meaning 'does not flow from a performer to an audience but is created within performance'.[72] Carter describes in detail the beauty of Harry Cox's singing as 'he modulates the tune of a song from verse to verse' and how he sings 'from the heart'.[73] She admires Sam Larner's 'spectacular timing and control',[74] Joe Heaney's 'almost magical ability [...] to create a new whole out of elements of text and tune'[75] and Louis Killen's talent to sing 'with power and authority [which] wakes the same echoes'.[76] These singers all use the power and dexterity of their singing voices to bind the past and the present together, to make these songs of the past relevant to a present audience. Emily Portman, the contemporary folk singer, speaks of 'the actual magic' between herself and the audience when she performs (see Chapter 7).

The folk singer's central, crucial, defining role as singer means that printed or notated folk songs, divorced from any voiced performative element, are only ever partial, fragmentary shadows of the whole form. Singing is the only way a folk song can exist; as Carter reiterates,

> One learns more about the importance of style from hearing Cox [...] than one ever will learn from looking at books.[77]

The folk song only comes into existence when sung by a singer;[78] for the artefact to exist it must be embodied, performed, breathed into life, and in this regard, the folk song form with its predication on voice bears some resemblance to ancient literature. Homer's *Iliad* opens with the commandment 'Sing, goddess, of the anger of Achilleus, son of Peleus',[79] while in the *Odyssey*, song moves the body of the singer spatially:

> When a singer selects a particular theme, he is said to be stirred within his heart or mind (his *thumos* or *noos*) to go in a particular direction: 'The Muse has given *aiodê* [song] to the singer / to give pleasure, in whatever direction (*hoppêi*) his heart moves' (Od. 8.44–45); [...] The moving of the poet's mind is like a ranging over space...[80]

In Hesiod's *Theogony*, song-in-language has transformative effects of divination on the body of the poet-performer. Hesiod 'learned the art of singing [...] from the Muses (*Theog.* 22, cf. Od. 8. 481, 488) who breathed into him a "voice filled with the words of a god" (*Theog.* 31–32).'[81] In the voice we find the origin of all language; for Aristotle its innate musicality is the beginning of meaning: 'for words are imitations, and the voice, the most mimetic of all our parts, was there to start with'.[82] So singing is always already present in literature, and because of her folk singing praxis, Carter is connected with her singing voice and aware of its positive imbrication in her writing; that its physical, sounded elements are *sine qua non* is what sets folk song apart from the other oral traditions from which Carter was influenced.

Carter is not alone in noticing the truncated nature of the unsung, unvoiced ballad. For Frost, as mentioned before, the unsung ballad 'stays half-lacking'.[83] Frank Sidgwick goes so far as to define the sung ballad as anti-text, as 'so far from being a literary form that it is, in its essentials, not literary', and stresses its formal antiquity: 'It is of a *genre* not only older than the Epic, older than Tragedy, but older than literature, older than the alphabet. It is *lore*, and belongs to the illiterate.'[84] Ethnomusicologist Constantin Brăiloiu explains how

> folk melody has no tangible reality by itself. It only exists at the moment when it is sung or played and [only] lives by the will of its interpreter and in the manner he

chooses. Creation and interpretation merge together here – it must be repeated constantly – in a way that musical practice, based on writing or printing, ignores completely.[85]

The figure of the singer and the performer's role is central to Ginette Dunn's anthropological observations of Suffolk pub folk singing in the late 1970s. In that specific rural community, where late modernity has not quite erased certain aspects of village life,

> the individual singer assumes a special role in performance since he becomes spokesman for a group and gives voice not only to personal but to social concerns, dynamics and emotions [...] Song is an expression of self, but since self has no meaning outside society, song expresses man's understanding of his humanity, his contact with others, his view of the world, and his realisation that the world has a view of him. Therefore it is the sung song and not the textual song that is crucial here.[86]

Carter felt particularly free to play with the folk song form because she understood it from the inside out, because she knew what it felt like to sing. With singing comes physical understanding: words are seen to work on the body, creating physical responses. The voice is in constant dialogue with its environs, folding in and folding out, 'reading back' in a cycle of influences. It engenders its own corporeal intelligence, its own way of understanding the world.

With this somatic knowledge and experience of singing in mind, Carter's descriptions of the idiosyncrasies of the folk singers she admires and her empathetic knowledge of the corporeality of singing take on a new authority:

> Sam Larner, the octogenarian Norfolk singer, speaks like a song, it is his idiom of speech [...] he is a splendid conscious performer [...] To hear the present Harry Cox is to be immediately aware that one is listening to an artist [...] His style is a compound of subtle and beautiful rhythms; there is a marvellous pulse to his singing and he modulates the tune of a song from verse to verse and decorates, with great taste and economy, the basic melodic line so that it grows with organic logic, with the rightness and inevitability of a natural growth. [...] Heaney sings totally without sentiment. His tune is sharply angular, almost spiky; he stylises it through superb control and this very free, very beautiful decoration...[87]

Folk song's sonic features – its rhythmic, temporal and melodic structures, its phrasal patterns, inversions, decorations, and the repeating refrains and burdens – provide powerful frameworks for Carter the writer to appropriate and manipulate. Through performance she somatically absorbs audial features in the way Barthes describes when he suggests that performed music 'goes much farther than the ear; it goes into the body, into the muscles by the beats of its rhythm, and somehow into the viscera by the voluptuous pleasure of its *melos*'.[88] Combining her structural knowledge of the musical form from a practitioner's perspective with her understanding of the narrative elements of melody and her muscle memory of singing, I propose Carter embedded, through processes of accretion, layers of musical intelligence into her prose, in a process entirely consistent with Sharp's famous dictum on folk processes of 'continuity, variation and selection',[89] one which illustrates her active participation in an evolution of folk song mediation.

She could do this because she was a folk singer. The singer of a folk song becomes temporarily occupied, and transformed, by the performance of the song itself; the life and character of the persona of the song enter the singer somatically. As Dunn explains: 'The singer is always singer, that is socially accepted, but he actualises the role only in performance [...] once he has crossed the threshold from audience to performer, he changes. Perhaps he expresses his fantasy life as he sings.'[90] This is 'the occupied "I" position' in folk song praxis. For a singer approaching the singing of a folk song, narrative perspective is an important consideration – 'Who is it that I am becoming?' – and loaded within this question 'Who?' are further questions of gender, time, place, morality, identity, and being – questions that Carter would revel in asking again and again.

Carter's engagement with folk song performance

Carter had a physical understanding of folk song's real-time performance by the living human voice. Embodied performance, the somatic manifestation of the song in the voice, in the breath, in the body, exists in the Hegelian sense as 'a time-object in the sense proper'[91] and gives, alongside text and tune, vitality to the form:

> And so she's going to have a baby, and she's so unhappy she wants to die. And even with the moving sparseness of the language of this text, one must realize that it is the tune which is an elegiac, lamenting one, and the gentle unsentimental singing of the English gypsy, Tom Willett, that gives it is true poetic life.[92]

Carter in the 1960s does not seem to have discriminated between recorded and live voices.[93] The Carters owned many LPs,[94] and Paul Carter was an active field recordist of source singers so tapes cluttered up their house.[95] In 'Now', she asserts that the recorded folk voice plays a valuable role in the revival: 'You can hear Joe Heaney on record, which is a great thing.'[96] But she also loved the live form, and expressed fervent opinions about 'correct' and 'incorrect' methods of performance. An early example of Carter's music journalism is a review of a folk club night, in which she critiques the various talents on display at The Swan & Sugar Loaf: Garry James, who 'eschewed accompaniment (very properly) to sing a selection of fairly esoteric and markedly attractive English and Irish folk-songs' is praised, while 'Two young men, who shall be nameless as they have hitherto shown themselves to be fair performers' are savaged for playing 'non-ethnic guitars'.[97] She really cared about the mode of live performance and its appropriateness to the material.

Carter lived her convictions, declared emphatically in 'Now', that the 'whole – the song – does not exist except in performance'. Angela and Paul Carter were both regularly attending the 'Ballads and Broadsides' folk club at The Bear in the Bristol district of Hotwells, a club they had founded when they moved to Bristol in 1961. This was a place where fellow enthusiasts might get together to sing traditional material. Molan reminisces, 'Friday night at The Bear. We all squeezed into the back-room.'[98] In 1965, the Carters founded a new club at a different location, 'Folk Song and Ballad, Bristol'. Ian Anderson, a folk artist living in Bristol during the 1960s and the former editor of *fRoots* Magazine, recalls a reputation of strictness surrounding the Carters' club: 'We were told that you weren't allowed in with guitars and stuff like that, so we never went there.'[99] He remembers a time Paul and Angela saw him playing at the 'Ballads and Blues' club and invited him to play at their club, though he never dared.[100] He told me,

> they and their club at the Lansdown had a bit of a fearsome reputation among local folkies – for being 'purists' and for not suffering fools gladly! Looking back, I'm sure it was only partly deserved, and were I to meet them knowing what I know now I'm sure we'd get on like a house on fire. But I was young and probably foolish, only 19, and they were older and certain of their views and scared me to death![101]

So, with Paul, Angela Carter can be seen to have held some local authority, and her strong opinions about performance style and live interpretation held some sway among the folk enthusiasts around her.

Paul and Angela's joint club manifesto in the archive (see Appendix 1) states explicitly its intentions: to promote 'a wider appreciation and deeper understanding of the great heritage of traditional folk song, ballad and music of the British Isles, and especially that of England', and 'to further the natural evolution of contemporary work within the framework described by tradition'.[102] From the outset, the Carters were expressing a desire to favour the songs of England over songs from other parts of the British Isles. They also wanted to facilitate the form's onward evolution, an ambition this intervention suggests Carter achieved, not necessarily so much through the activities of the folk club, but through the migration and sublimation of folk song forms into her own prose writing, a migration which has gone on to have profound influences on subsequent writers and musicians.

Carter also expressed an awareness of music's affect on her own writing. In her 1960 journal she wrote, 'Probably because of coming increasingly aware of myself as a writer, I'm finding it more difficult to <u>bother</u> about other art-forms – unless I can immediately synthesise them with literature [...] Music is different. It's heaven's order.'[103] She stated in a letter in 1966 that it was her express desire to repurpose her folk song experience into prose: '... I believe in not wasting anything and all these years' work on folk-song and traditional verse will be a waste of time unless I can assimilate it, somehow, into my writing.'[104] As ever, Carter was acutely aware of her processes and intentions.

But it is the acoustic materiality of the recordings of her performance in that folk club in 1967 which demonstrates best the expansive depth and breath of her somatic engagement with, and investment in, the folk song form, and presents best the multimodal reach of its influence upon her creative imagination: for they prove beyond doubt that she knew what these songs felt like to sing. The shift and growth of her interest, from intellectual curiosity to somatic praxis and muscle memory, and then into fiction, is most poignantly embodied by her arresting singing voice on tape. In the bold octave jumps and the haunting, unresolved final notes of each verse, one can hear a young Carter undergoing an act of transformation, slipping out of herself, and slipping into the skin of an imagined other.

3

'me and not-me': folk songs, narrative perspectives and the gender imaginary in *Shadow Dance*

'I like,' he said obscurely, 'I like – you know – to slip in and out of me. I like to be somebody different each morning. Me and not-me. I would like to have a cupboard bulging with all different bodies and faces and choose a fresh one every morning.'
Angela Carter, *Shadow Dance*[1]

In 1964, when Angela Carter was busy writing her debut novel *Shadow Dance*,[2] her lucid essay in defence of the folk song form 'Now is the Time for Singing' appeared in the Bristol University magazine *Nonesuch*; around this time she co-founded a folk club, and she listed 80 folk song titles and fragments of other folk songs in her journal; she was to submit her 95-page undergraduate dissertation on links between twentieth-century folk songs and medieval poetry the following year.[3]

I suggest that, alongside the plethora of other rich intertextual influences already well-documented by critics such as Sarah Gamble[4] and Anna Watz,[5] the folk songs with which Carter was preoccupied at the very moment she was writing *Shadow Dance* have seeped into the fiction text she was writing structurally and thematically, and that new readings of Carter's prose emanate from deeper understandings of the accretive effects of song performance upon (perhaps unconscious) meanings accumulating in her work. I will examine specifically Carter's presentation of the performance of gender in this her first novel, to suggest that her experience of folk singing and her familiarity with the gender blindness inherent in the folk singing tradition gave her first novel a sense of gender fluidity critics have until now failed fully to appreciate.

Carter understood from the performance of folk songs that she could 'sing' a man's point of view and that, as a result, she could explore ideas – of self, sexuality and gender – through occupying the 'I' position of all her created characters, not just her female ones. Her later apologies for being a 'male impersonator'[6] may suggest that this exploration of performances of gender identity through the occupation of a male perspective was the result of what she sensed later as 'colonialisation of the mind', or a byproduct of growing up in the linguistic matrix of patriarchy. But I propose rather that her lived practice of the gender-ambivalent 'I' position in folk songs (considered necessarily alongside her simultaneous absorption of contemporaneous developments in theories of narratology being pioneered by Tzvetan Todorov and others, in which she was also well versed)[7] led her to a corporeal understanding of 'being' inside other gendered experiences; because of singing folk songs, she felt free to explore versions of selfhood not just through the lives of her female protagonists (such as Melanie in *The Magic Toyshop*, or Marianne in *Heroes and Villains*)[8] but through her male characters such as Honeybuzzard and Morris in *Shadow Dance*. While it could be argued that folk song does not have a monopoly on gender ambiguity, and that other forms of performed music may lay claim to such instances of degenderization, there is no evidence that Carter herself was as invested in them. In the recording of 15 January 1967 Carter stands up and performs a folk song – and the folk song she sings is a (heteronormatively assumed) male persona's lament for unrequited love.

Marc O'Day suggests that Honeybuzzard and Morris in *Shadow Dance* represent two sides of the same personality;[9] I take this proposition one step further to suggest they represent an early example of Carter experimenting with versions of herself. Edmund Gordon notes Carter's irritation than no-one spotted she was Lee, the male protagonist of her fifth novel, *Love*:

> 'LOVE is autobiographical,' she wrote to Carole [Roffe] after the book was published. 'I might well be Lee; I even put in clues like knocking out his front tooth, dammit, and nobody guessed!' In another letter she wrote, 'if some biographer of the far-distant future got hold of the reference to Paul ... in which I compared him to Annabel in LOVE – oh, there'd be meat there!'[10]

Gordon goes on to notice Carter's double-investment in Lee's troubled brother Buzz, whom one might suggest was borne from the same character-nursery as Honeybuzzard:

> If Lee and Annabel are dream-versions of Angela and Paul, then Buzz comes from an altogether more shadowy part of Angela's psyche. When she reread the novel almost twenty years later, she wrote: 'he's come out of the pages to haunt me, whoever he was, the creation of my discontent ... he is something to do with my libido, I think, the perpetually renewed fountain of desire who is the female myth or fantasy or dream of the male, the woman's imaginary idea of male sexuality.'[11]

If Carter was prepared to inveigle versions of herself into the skins of her male characters for this later novel, it doesn't seem far-fetched to suggest she was applying the same modus operandi in her earlier work, even if subconsciously.

Honeybuzzard, the vulpine antihero of *Shadow Dance*, can be seen through the prism of Carter's folk song practice as a vehicle for exploring multiple potentialities of selfhood: the potential for innate cruelty, selfishness, libido; the apologetic, conciliatory Morris might be read as a more dutiful version of herself, who tolerates begrudgingly the obligations of marriage; in Morris's kind but long-suffering wife Edna, one might read a version of Paul who, according to Carter's own diaries and corroborated by Gordon, suffered from bouts of depression.

This reading contradicts previous arguments proposed by critics such as Paulina Palmer, who argues that Carter's (mis)use of sexual violence in her early novels inadvertently reinforces the very 'self-perpetuating and closed nature of patriarchal structures and institutions' that Carter was purportedly trying to challenge,[12] or Christina Britzolakis, who suggests that, through Carter's ornate and fetishised language her fiction comes dangerously close to 'complicity with the structures of domination against which these texts are often ranged'.[13] Sarah Gamble doesn't entertain the possibility that Carter could be 'experimenting with female points of view' by slipping inside male characters.[14] But what if Carter is assuming the male position to pluralize gender identities, including her own, subverting all expectations of the nature of domination?

Honeybuzzard has been framed rather clumsily until now either as a pantomime stock villain or as a chilling representative of a devastating patriarchal force. Linden Peach describes him as 'a comic stereotype of the Gothic villain'[15] and a patriarchal abuser who sets out to commodify, defile and destroy female victims remorselessly; Peach focuses on Honeybuzzard's indifference to his murderous cruelty, and reads Marxist messages in Honeybuzzard's choice of location (graveyard) and props (crucifix) in his ritualistic violations of Ghislaine:

> These details compound the horror arising from the way in which women are seen as 'flesh' and 'meat', especially as Honeybuzzard also thinks of selling pornographic photographs of Ghislaine on the crucifix. The interrelated but contrasting tropes of flesh signifying pleasure and of meat as signifying economic objectification occur throughout Carter's fiction, which seeks to explore the boundaries between them.[16]

Rebecca Munford agrees with Peach, labelling Honeybuzzard 'the sadistic anti-hero' and Ghislaine the archetypal Gothic heroine, an 'orphaned, passive and masochistic adolescent' entwined in a sadomasochistic model designed to expose 'the mystification and mythologisation of female virtue and victimhood'.[17] She suggests that Ghislaine's suffering should be seen through the lens of 'a narcissistic, *male* imaginary'[18] and that through it her 'complicity with the structures and narratives of male desire' can be 'interrogated'.[19] But Maggie Tonkin argues that Carter's 'use of irony is inextricable from [her] deployment of dialectical images of femininity', and that it has been missed in some of these readings.[20]

Other observations fail to see Carter's exploration of multiple expressions of selfhood in the twinning of Honeybuzzard and Morris, implying that Carter's portrayal of her male characters is merely superficial, just a case of 'dressing up'. Carter is repeatedly accused of intellectual drag: Britzolakis suggests that her relation to literary history 'frequently involves a cross-dressed or masculine narrative perspective',[21] noting her sometime implication in a 'double drag, [...] an imaginary identification with or impersonation of femininity'.[22] Robert Clark has accused Carter's writing of being 'a feminism in male chauvinist drag, a transvestite style', and that 'her fascination with violent eroticism and her failure to find any alternative basis on which to construct a feminine identity prevent her work from being other than an elaborate trace of women's self-alienation'.[23] One might argue this 'self-alienation' for Carter includes her own, and becomes in her hands a positive, multifarious exercise in the proliferation of subjectivities.

Lorna Sage gets closest when she suggests that 'sex-roles come out reversed. Beautiful boys, called things like Jewel and Precious [...] are described caressingly and coolly as sexual objects'[24] – and when she observes that Honeybuzzard 'alone belongs to two worlds, in gender terms and, in terms just as vital to Carter the writer, the real (life) and the shadow (art)'.[25] But she doesn't go as far as to suggest Carter is doing the same with versions of herself. In this regard I propose that, through her intimate portrayal of male characters, Carter is revelling in the possibilities of variations of her own selfhood, interrogating the darker, crueller sides of fluid gender experience to conceive of fiction as a series of spaces where she can perform many selves into existence. Carter's regular folk-singing praxis would have encouraged this subliminal naturalizing of the occupied 'I' position in genders other than her own, this proliferation of positions, because 'so many ghosts of so many pasts are looking back out of the mirror' at the very moment the singer takes to the stage.[26]

Folk singing and the gender-fluid 'I' position

In the folk song tradition, while many songs normalize misogyny, sexual violence, domestic abuse and rape, there is no essentialist conception of gender when it comes to the performing singer. To stand and sing is a social performance: singers who identify as female can sing what might be termed 'men's' songs (or, songs positioned from a heteronormatively assumed 'male' perspective), and singers who identify as male can sing 'women's' songs (or, songs positioned from a heteronormatively assumed 'female' perspective). Folk song is by no means unique as a popular musical form to embrace this singer-persona gender inversion; in indie rock, for example, see Patti Smith's 'Gloria' [8], or Jack White's heart-breaking rendering of Dolly Parton's 'Jolene' [9]. But in these cases, gender inversion can be seen as a decisive act, a self-conscious violation of expectations intended to promote a counter-cultural subversion of heteronormative social hegemonies. In contrast, traditional folk song's quotidian disregard for singer-persona gender parity feels unselfconscious, unaware, almost innocent, and is all the more disarming given the form's otherwise stifling atmospheres of heteronormativity and misogyny. More importantly, within the contexts of this study, it is the only form we know for sure that Carter performed, and performed repeatedly. The folk songs Carter chose to list in her 1964 journal reflect this disregard for gender parity between singer and song, and vary wildly in terms of their narrative perspective. Some songs, such as 'Died for Love' [17] or 'The Banks of Red Roses' [10], position themselves in the first person from a female perspective:

> 'Oh, when I was a young girl I heard my mother say
>   That I was a foolish lass and easy led astray.
> And before I would work, I would rather sport and play
>   With my Johnny on the banks of red roses.'[27]

while 'The Week Before Easter' (also known as 'The False Bride') [11] is sung from the first-person perspective of a man watching his beloved marrying another:

> Now the first time I saw my love she was dressed all in white,
>   Made my eyes run and water quite dazzled my sight,
> When I thought to myself that I might have been that man
>   But she's left me and gone with another.[28]

Some songs, such as 'Reynardine' [12], are first-person testimonies rendered via the frame-narrative technique of an accidental, anonymous, gender-neutral, eavesdropping 'I'-observer:

> One evening as I rambled among the springing thyme,
>   I overhead a young woman, conversing with Reynardine.[29]

Others are presented from a third-person omniscient narrator's storytelling perspective in which the gender-ambiguous storyteller-observer's attention closely follows certain identified protagonists to either sticky or happy endings:

> George Collins walked out one May morning,
>   When May was all in bloom . . .[30]

or

> Down into this country, there lived a wealthy squire,
>   Who had a only daughter, was charming, young and fair. . .[31]

or

> Fair Lucy she sits at her father's door,
>   A-weeping and making moan,
> And by there came her brother dear:
>   'What ails thee, Lucy Wan?'[32]

The third-person narrator of 'George Collins' [13] presents the demise and ghosting of jack-the-lad George at the hand of a girl because he has broken too many hearts. In 'Jackie Munro' [14], the narrator's attention closely follows the eponymous Jackie as she dresses up as a man and enlists to follow her love into the war, rescuing him and receiving a promotion to boot. In 'Lucy Wan' [15] the omniscient narrator's unflinching gaze relays how pregnant Lucy is brutally dismembered by her brother-lover. Although the narrators' stances are third person, their chosen protagonists dominate and occupy privileged positions within the narratives. Narrative positions might even fluctuate within the same song. 'Bold Wolfe' [16], for example, opens with an exclamatory implied-second-person imperative rallying cry: 'Come all ye young men all!', moves to a first-person male perspective ('I went to see my love, / Thinking to woo her') and then shifts to a third-person narrator ('Bold Wolfe, he took his leave') who relays the facts of the battle and then finally reports Wolfe's direct speech: 'I will die in pleasure.'[33] All of these songs appear on Carter's journal list.

From the list of 80 songs (in which there are four duplications and two unknown titles), 26 are presented from a male first-person perspective, 18 from a third-person narrative position, and 13 from a female first-person perspective.[34] Carter could have sung any of these songs[35] – she and Paul owned the books and LPs from which they learned them. In the only known recording of Carter singing, she performs the Irish ballad 'The Flower of Sweet Strabane' [1] in which the 'I' of the song is a lovelorn young man who, spurned by his love, is setting sail for America.[36] 'The False Bride' [11] is presented from the point of view of a male jilted lover 'I' who sees his girl marrying another, which was collected by Cecil Sharp from a female singer, Lucy White, in Hambridge, Somerset in 1904; Carter would have known contemporaneous recorded versions of this song by Bert Lloyd (1960), George 'Pop' Maynard (1960) and Shirley Collins (1963). Tom Willett sings a beautiful version of 'Died for Love' [17], recorded by Paul Carter, from a (heteronormatively assumed) female perspective: ('Now my love he is tall and handsome too ...'). In unpublished teaching notes, Carter writes that in the 'folk trad., both sexes may be virtuosi performers & the audience is unisex'[37] – she was immersed in and aware of a startlingly 'modern' gender neutrality the folk singing art form expresses within performance, in spite of its simultaneous reinforcements of patriarchal hegemonies in constrictive narrative and character representations.

One way of framing this gender ambiguity in performance might be to see the folk singer as a kind of everyman Tiresias, a transparent window or mirror, through which certain histories, experiences and stories may be gleaned. There is nothing strange about a singer not conforming to the gender of the 'I' of the song, for it is understood that there is an occupation taking place, a possession, a process in which 'so many ghosts of so many pasts are looking back out of the mirror'.[38] The individual folk singer disappears, to be replaced by a collective occupancy whose gender is necessarily multivalent.

But while singers erase themselves in performance, at the same time they also bring their personal experiences to the song as it passes through them. Suzanne Gilbert summarizes the findings of the ethnomusicologist James Porter on his singer-subject, Jeannie Robertson, whose ballad-singing 'became a "transformative" act, "a way of distilling the life-world and its experiences into a ritualising gesture that compresses feeling, cognition and volition."'[39] Edward Cone also notices this process of assimilation, distinguishing in his study of singing performance between the *person* (the implicit composer) and the *persona* (who 'sings'):

> the two aspects of person and persona fuse. The physical presence and the vitality of the singer turn the persona of the poetic-musical text into an actual, immediate, living being: the *person* of the singer invests the *persona* of the song with *personality*. If the impersonation is successful, if the illusion is complete, we hear this embodied persona as 'composing' his part – as living through the experience of the song.[40]

Through this process of fusion, songs accrue a patina, they become composites of all the singers who have sung them, all the 'ghosts' in the mirror, all the emotions that the song has channelled through the years. Lloyd notices how

> ... after [the folk song] has come into being a multitude of other singers are likely to get to work on it, altering it about, de-composing and re-composing it, producing sometimes richer sometimes poorer versions of the original; now deepening the emotional and ideological content, now making it more shallow; now bringing the tune into sad decay, now re-creating and renewing it happily.[41]

This collective 'remembering, repeating and working-through'[42] via performance might be seen as a response to the trauma of modernity, a macrocosmic, societal compulsion to remember across generations and communities; for, as Nigel Thrift and John-David Dewsbury have suggested, performance is 'itself a form of knowledge, an intelligence in-action'.[43] Carter recognized these processes of communal intelligence at work in folk-song imagery, such as the yellow hair motif in 'The Dowie Dens of Yarrow' [4] (see also p. 25):

> The song it comes from, the classic Scots ballad 'The Dowie Dens of Yarrow', is of some considerable antiquity; and these verses seem to have been transposed into it at an early date from another song from the times when young men themselves had long, yellow hair, for the song concerned a girl who pulled her drowned lover out of the river by his long, yellow hair. It was obviously something that cried out to be worked over.[44]

In this example, the image of the hair has been transferred from the male to the female; there is little or no gender distinction. Carter has osmosed from folk singing that gender is infinitely fluid and transferable.

Pauline Greenhill finds ambiguity of sexual orientation lying latent in the internal narratives of the cross-dressing female warrior ballads, such as 'The Handsome Cabin Boy', 'Polly Oliver' and 'Blue Jacket and White Trousers', in the 'possibility of same-sex attraction and nonheterosexual activity' and the ways in which certain singers have teased out this interpretation in performance.[45] Diane Dugaw elaborates on this destabilizing latency, seeing sexuality as one aspect of a wider question about gender ambiguity in these ballad worlds:

> the preoccupation with homosexual attraction – both for women and for men – that stories of female transvestites almost always feature, brings with it the larger implication that gender-based attraction is a fragile construction – indeed, that gender itself may be a fragile construct.[46]

Because it is necessary to maintain tight focus on the specificities of gender identity and performance, there is no opportunity here to explore in more depth the implications of expressions of diverse sexualities secreted within the seemingly heteronormative fabric of the folk song tradition, nor the possible implications of these concealments on Carter's writerly imagination, and on cultural production more widely. Future research might follow this rich vein of enquiry.

Despite its overarching traditionalist assumptions, the folk song form is continually blurring boundaries between performances of male and female identities, fulfilling Judith Butler's ideas of performances of gender as 'the repeated stylization of the body, a set of repeated acts within a highly rigid regulatory frame that congeal over time to produce the appearance of substance, of a natural sort of being'.[47] From her folk singing praxis, Carter was able to magpie-pick (as she did from so many other areas of culture) from the folk song tradition's ambivalent and sometimes difficult historical treatments of gender: whilst rejecting those aspects that perpetuate misogyny, she embraced the tradition's gender fluidity, and percolated it through the fiction she was concurrently constructing. I suggest she actively migrated those very ideas of gender fluidity, learned from her occupation of the gender-ambiguous 'I' position in the songs' performance, into her own writing.

Through close analysis of several folk songs Carter was considering during the time of writing *Shadow Dance* – 'Reynardine',[48] [12] 'Blow the Candle Out'[49] [18] and a brief look at 'The Game of Cards'[50] [19] – and their various impacts upon accretive layers of meaning in Carter's writing, it becomes possible to read Honeybuzzard, the dangerously attractive, murderous central villain of *Shadow Dance*, as a performance of one aspect of Carter's perceived selfhood, and his violent sexual aberrations as an exploration (explosion?) of female sexuality and energy, rather than an assumed representation of an oppressive and sadistic patriarchal hegemony, over whom so much feminist ink has already been spilt.

The songs – overview

'Reynardine' [12] shot to folk-revival fame thanks to one of the second wave's main proponents, A. L. Lloyd (fondly known as 'Bert'), who recorded the song in 1956[51] and again in 1966,[52] and included it in his live repertoire at folk club performances. Christine Molan remembers how Lloyd 'took the club by storm' one night performing 'Reynardine' at the Carter's club, where he elided the song into a reading of the folk tale 'Mr Fox' from Joseph Jacobs' *English Fairy Tales* to create a terrifying Gothic set piece.[53] As Molan recalls,

> he held folk club audiences spellbound, and his theatrical timing was masterly. Angela was there. He was staying with them. Perhaps she'd asked him to do the act. She and Paul knew (as Rod [Stradling] says) that 'Bert always took over the evening'. Maybe she'd heard of him doing the act elsewhere and asked for a repeat performance that night (?) Anyone but anyone who heard Bert tell this tale around the clubs in 1963 will remember the spine-chilling effect of hearing that modal tune, sung in his light high voice, run on ghost-like from the bloody finale of the tale. The verses were surely tweaked for effect each time by the artist according to his 'fancy'.[54]

Carter also refers to this performance in her journal in the spring of 1964: she writes firstly, 'See: Joseph Jacobs "English Fairy Tales" for Mr. Fox. (Bert's Mr. Fox?)' and then, in a different pen, later, she's added – '(Yes, it's Bert's Mr. Fox all right)'.[55] In the song 'Reynardine', an anonymous first-person narrator witnesses the seduction and abduction of a young girl by an irresistibly attractive, mysterious man:

> One evening as I rambled among the springing thyme,
>   I overheard a young woman, conversing with Reynardine.
> Her hair was black, her eyes were blue, her mouth as red as wine,
>   And he smiled to look upon her, did the sly bold Reynardine.[56]

In the sleeve notes to his 1956 version, Lloyd alludes to the dangerous attraction and zoomorphic ambiguities of the song's eponymous villain: 'Who was Reynardine, with his irresistible charm, his glittering eye, his foxy smile? An ordinary man, or an outlaw maybe, or some supernatural lover?' In his second recording, Lloyd makes a very specific lyric alteration, changed shining 'eyes' to shining 'teeth', emphasizing Reynardine's carnivorous nature as he leads the girl 'over the mountain' to his 'castle' and her fate.[57]

Another song of seduction on which Carter was ruminating during this period was 'Blow The Candle Out' [18], which she analyzes musicologically in 'Now'. Peter Kennedy's recording of Jimmy Gilhaney, an Irish traveller, singing it in the Orkney Isles featured on the LP *Songs of Seduction*, which was in the Carters' record collection.[58] Here is the tune as sung by Gilhaney, represented by my own (imperfect) musical notation:

Carter describes the shape of this 'enormously virile' melody using the aforementioned simile of boots going up and down the stairs, and venerates the song as

> one of the great love songs in the English language and it expresses no yearning, no phony idealisation, no sentimentality, but a great warmth, a kind and easy loving that accepts men and women as they are with no fogging notions of sin or shame. [...] On the printed page, this looks like a piece of doggerel; sung, it becomes a celebration of sexual enjoyment, a piece of complete emotional honesty. For the texts are nothing without the tunes, which give them a further dimension of meaning.[59]

Carter notices a relationship between the song's melodic shape and its subject matter, the tune which mimics the illicit climbing of the stairs, and its matter-of-fact acceptance of the quotidian reality of extra-marital sexual encounters, its depiction of a real truth concerning sexual relations: that women and men do have extramarital sex, that unplanned pregnancies do occur, that men may not necessarily return to accept their responsibilities as fathers, and that women may not necessarily want them to. She developed this understanding of the complex interrelations between melody, rhythm, lyrics and voice, gleaned and then lived out in her folk song praxis, as she constructed her own prose compositions.

The songs – rhythmic influences

The rhythmic landscape of 'Reynardine' is comprised of quatrains of iambic tetrameter, iambs which drive us compulsively along with the young maiden 'over the mountain' and create a surreal, dream-like atmosphere, a milky liquidity in which many possibilities present themselves:

```
    ˘     ′  | ˘     ′  | ˘    ′    | ˘    ′  |
One eve- |ning  as  | I  ramb- |-led  (x) |

       ˘    ′  | ˘    ′    | ˘    ′    | ˘     ′ |
     a- mong | the spring- |-ing thyme | (x)  (x)|

    ˘   ′  | ˘   ′    | ˘    ˘    ′  | ˘    ′  |
   I  o- |ver- heard| a  young  wo |-man  (x) |

         ˘      ′  | ˘      ˘   ′  | ˘    ′     | ˘    ′  |
     con-vers- | ing  with Rey- | nar - dine. | (x) (x) |
```

'Blow the Candle Out' may be another song of seduction using the framework of iambic tetrameter, but there are differences: this time the female is doing the persuading, and the iambs create an atmosphere of quotidian familiarity, a compulsive earthy drive and libidinous desire of two young lovers who could be anyone:

```
  ˘    ′   | ˘     ′  | ˘    ′   | ˘    ′   |
My fa- | ther and | my mo- |(x) -ther, |

          ˘     ′  | ˘     ′    | ˘    ′   | ˘    ′  |
      next bed- |-room they | do  lie,| (x)  (x). |

   ˘  ′   | ˘    ′   | ˘    ′    | ˘    ′  |
  (x) Kiss |- ing and | em-brac- | (x)  - ing,|

     ˘     ′  | ˘    ′  | ˘    ′  | ˘     ′ |
   Then why | not you | and  I? | (x)  (x) |

   ˘   ′   | ˘    ′   | ˘    ′    | ˘    ′  |
  (x) Kiss |- ing and | em-brac- | (x)  - ing,|

       ˘    ′  | ˘    ′  | ˘    ′   | ˘     ′  |
   with-out | a  fear | or doubt, | (x)   So |

         ˘   ′  | ˘    ′  | ˘    ′    | ˘    ′ |
     come roll | me  in | your arms,| (x) love, |

            ˘     ′ | ˘    ′   | ˘    ′    | ˘    ′ |
       and we'll blow | the can- | dle out. | (x)  (x) |
```

Both songs use four-line stanzas to create discrete rhythmically spaced units of action, and both deploy various kinds of syntactic repetition as part of their structure: in 'Reynardine' it is the villain's mysterious name, connoting carnivorous mischief, which repeats itself in epistrophe to conclude stanzas 1, 2, 7 and 8. The recurring burden of 'Blow the Candle Out', 'Come roll me in your arms, love / And we'll blow the candle out', repeats at the end of every four-line verse to complete a discrete idea; the pathos of the final lines, 'he never said when he'd come back to blow the candle out' is increased by the expectation of the repeating burden.

The euphemistic 'blowing out of the candle' is of course another way to describe sexual activity, and alongside this kind of *double entendre*, polyptotonic repetitions, where words derived from the same root are repeated, are also used in folk songs to create humourous ensnaring nets of recognition and shared meaning. In 'The Game of Cards' (which also appears in Carter's long journal list of songs), playing a game of cards becomes another extended metaphor for sexual activity, and repeated ideas of 'play', 'game', 'playing' and 'gaming' and anaphoric repetitions of 'I'm not given' bind us into the light-hearted sensuality of the song.

> Now as we were a-walking and talking together
>   Those sweet pleasant banks, I set myself down
> Then I says pretty fair maid, would you sit yourself beside of me
>   And then I will show you a sweet pleasant *game*.
>
> I'm not given to *gaming*, I'm not given to *gaming*
>   I'm not given to *gaming*, kind sir, she did say
> But if I do *play* you, then it must be *All Fowers*
>   And then I will gave you two chalks to my one.[60] [my emphasis]

Similarly polysyndetic repetitions, strings of conjunctions, are used to build tension in folk songs; the repetition of 'and' in every stanza of 'Reynardine' suggests through syntax the relentlessness of the villain's assault, the girl's loss of consciousness and her eventual collapse of resistance:

> Her cherry cheek *and* ruby lip, they lost their former dye,
>   *And* she fell into his arms there, all on the mountain high. [my emphasis]

So rhythmic quatrains of iambic tetrameter, and repetitive rhetorical devices such as epistrophe, anaphora, polyptoton and polysyndeton play an important role in creating the rhythmic landscapes so recognizable in folk song.

Carter's *Shadow Dance* – rhythmic figures

When one begins to read *Shadow Dance* as musical prose, one starts to hear the rhythms and figures of these songs transfused into Carter's writing. Iambs underpin Carter's milky, surreal descriptions, such as this description of Ghislaine's facial scar:

```
       ˘     ´     |  ˘    ´   |  ˘        ´    |    ´      ´    | ˘    ˘       ´     |
    The scar  | was like  |  a     big,  |  red   crack  | a-   cross    ice |

       ˘     ˘     |   ´    ˘    | ˘        ´     |  ˘     ´   |
    and might  | sudden-  | -ly    o-   | -pen   up  |

       ˘    ´     |  ˘   ˘   |  ´    ˘    | ˘   ´   |
    and swa -  | -llow her |  in-to   | herself, |

       ´    ˘     |  ˘    ´   |  ˘  ´    |   ˘   ´   |
    scra-ming, | herself  | in-to  | herself. ⁶¹
```

When Morris floats in and out of reality, Carter borrows iambs from folk song:

```
       ˘    ´   |  ˘    ´     |  ˘        ´      |  ˘      ´   |  ˘    ´     | ˘
    'This is - | - n't real," | thought Mor- | -ris.   'I  |  am dream- | ing⁶²
```

to sound out his seduction by Honeybuzzard and to obfuscate his ability to 'see' the destructive nature of their friendship.

Four-line stanzas from folk song structure persistently cut across Carter's prose syntax in repetitious, folded descriptions which fall into canorous quatrains. Ghislaine is described in four parts as 'a beautiful girl, a white and golden girl, like moonlight on daisies, a month ago'⁶³ and when she surrenders herself to Honeybuzzard she does so in a prose that sings like a four-line stanza: 'I've learned my lesson, I can't live without you, you are my master, do what you like with me.'⁶⁴ Carter also uses rhetorical devices of epistrophe and anaphora to echo the folk song technique of a recurring burden. An early description of Ghislaine, for example, uses a kind of weakened epistrophe to stitch us rhythmically into the scene:

> She was a very *young girl*. She used to look like a *young girl* in a picture book, a soft and dewy *young girl*. She used to look like the sort of *young girl* one cannot imagine sitting on the lavatory or shaving her armpits or picking her nose.⁶⁵ [my emphasis]

Using a similar strategy with anaphora, Carter repeatedly sounds out the name of Honeybuzzard, Ghislaine's murderous former lover:

> They belonged to *Honeybuzzard*.
>   Who came in pat, like the catastrophe in an old comedy. *Honeybuzzard*, lithe and slick as a stick of liquorice in his black leather jacket and corduroy trousers. *Honeybuzzard*, who seemed to be affecting a Groucho Marx stunt walk, his black legs scuttling in the wake of his thrust-forward torso. *Honeybuzzard*, crowned with an extremely large peaked cap, checked in screaming orange and shouting purple...⁶⁶ [my emphasis]

Carter also uses polyptotonic repetitions to tumble descriptions over one another in syntactical rivers within clauses and sentences. Morris '*ran* down the road, faster and faster till he thought he might leave the ground and start flying, so fast was he *running*,

running to get away from the flat and all the rank memories it contained'.[67] [my emphasis] She also deploys polysyndeton, creating songlike strings of dream-prose, such as when Ghislaine is 'pulling both flowers *and* grass *and* nettles *and* piss-the-beds'[68] or the longer description of her childlike appearance:

> *And* she had long, yellow, milkmaid hair *and* her eyes were so big and brown they seemed to gobble up her face [...] *And* her darkened lashes swept down over half her cheeks.
> *And* she was so light and fragile *and* her bones so birdy fine *and* little *and* her skin was almost translucent.[69] [my emphasis]

Carter is tugging at the sounds and images of folk songs in her writing, borrowing rhythmic features with which she would have been familiar, such as the iambic feel, the four-line quatrain shape and internal repetitions such as epistrophe, anaphora, polyptoton and polysyndeton so intrinsic to folk song, in her own syntactical constructions.

The songs – melodic influences

The songs' melodies also have structural impacts on ways in which Carter builds her prose. Carter took a great interest in the tunes of folk songs, as shown by her careful musical notations in her folk notebook. One can see, for example, in her notebook in the archive the child-like notation of the folk song 'Three Pretty Maids', sometimes known as 'The Blackbird' or 'The Bird in the Bush':

Figure 7 Photo detail of 'Three Pretty Maids' notated by Angela Carter, from Paul and Angela Carter's Folk Music Archive. Copyright © Christine Molan. Reproduced with kind permission of Christine Molan.

Carter transcribed 32 other songs in this fashion, revealing a sensitivity to, and an awareness of, individual melody shapes, the repetitions in pitch and rhythm undulations, the semantic messages encoded within folk song tunes, and the different ways in which melodic movement and repetition could contribute to a song's overall meaning.[70] I propose she understood the melodies of all the songs with which she engaged in similar terms. In particular, she noticed in 'Reynardine' and 'Blow the Candle Out' melodic shapes of parabola and chiasmus, which she then imported into her own prose constructions.

The melody of 'Reynardine' creates the shape of a parabolic arc which complements the song's disturbing narrative. The eponymous Reynardine is a devilishly vulpine antihero, an enigmatic man-beast, a villain with what we infer are only ill intentions for the vulnerable girl caught in his sway. 'Her hair was black, her eyes were blue, her mouth as red as wine': her physical description, reminiscent of 'Snow White' from fairy tale tradition, alerts us instinctively to danger through ancient chains of association, and labels this girl a victim in the Sadeian sense; she will never escape this narrative, and must succumb to the rake's 'sly, bold' advances every time the song is sung, to be led over the mountain by him to his mysterious 'castle' – and her fate.

The Mixolydian ABCD melodic structure of the tune intensifies the meaning, suggesting a dragging, a pulling, a resistance, a darker and more menacing compulsion. The tune opens with an optimistic spiral-climb phrase up the scale only as far as the VI (so its Mixolydian nature remains hidden without the revealing flattened VII expression), before lowering its eyelids flirtatiously to the IV to rest; a second hopeful spiral up, an attempt to escape, in line 3 touches the VI once more before descending back to the tonic through a flattened VII – revealing its dark Mixolydian truth – and then rotating back between the III of the scale and the flattened VII below, to come to rest on the tonic. There's an unsettling queasiness to the shape, from the two moments of attempted escape represented in the recurring VI's, to the nauseating final circumnavigation of the tonic and the undertow of the Mixolydian flattened VII.

The chiastic melodic shape of 'Blow The Candle Out', in contrast, reveals what an honest, everyday seduction might sound like from a musical point of view. The tune consists of four phrases which together form a chiastic ABBA figure; the first phrase makes a brave, bold opening octave jump up and marches back down the Ionian scale to the tonic with a kind of rumpus authority which smacks of male confidence. The second line plaintively lingers between the V of the scale and the top octave, teasingly questioning as it jitters back and forth to the V – it tickles, flirts, and cajoles, and the focus on the V sounds like a kind of pleading; this tentative, flirtatious tune repeats itself on line three, whereupon on line four we return to the bolder octave jump, reinforcing the persona's persuasive line of argument. The neediness of seduction takes on a chiastic form, according to the melody of this song.

Carter's *Shadow Dance* – melodic influences

Because of her folk singing praxis, Carter absorbed these melodic figures of the parabolic arc and the chiasmus and translated them into both the narrative structure and the imagery of *Shadow Dance*. In structural choices suggestive of Schenkerian analysis,[71] Carter builds the novel's entire shape like that of a tune: it climbs from the 'tonic note' of Morris's initial mundane life and his drab marriage in which the 'voluptuous shadows of the city trees moved with black shadows'[72] to the parabolic and feverishly life-affirming homoerotic dance with Honeybuzzard, which lies at the very heart of the novel as Chapter 6 closes.

In this scene, Honeybuzzard dismisses their friends – 'They are all shadows. How can you be sorry for shadows?'[73] – before he and Morris perform the eponymous 'shadow dance':

> Morris came into his arms and they circled the room. Because of his greater height, Morris found himself taking the man's part and Honey bending himself to the girl's movements. Who was he being now? A great lady, a grand-dame collecting hearts like butterflies, stabbing them through with her hairpins and keeping them in a glass case? Morris was gradually drawn into the game, too.[74]

Carter warps conventional ideas of gender here, suggesting how gender becomes irrelevant, almost superfluous, in the annihilation of their embrace. This ludic performance of gender roles reflects the fluidity of gender to which Carter was accustomed in folk song praxis, where men sang women and women sang men as a matter of course. Morris and Honeybuzzard forge new identities from their 'stylized repetition of acts'.[75] And so the men's dance (another sexually charged extended metaphor) reaches fever pitch –

> Laughing, breathless, they whirled to the invisible rhetoric of a hundred violins. The patches of candlelight illuminated only their feet for odd moments, and then they were back, dancing in darkness again. They neared the extravagant climax of the dance.[76]

Their movements become violent, and the dance (reminiscent of the dance of the clowns in *Nights at the Circus*) threatens to annihilate the world:

> But when the time came for parting and bowing and curtseying to one another, Honeybuzzard instead convulsively crushed his partner in a fierce embrace, pressing his sweating face deeply into the other's shoulder, straining bruised fingers into neck and back, wet mouth fastened on his throat, clinging as if he would never let go until the round world toppled into the sun and the last bell-tower rang midnight and everything was extinguished.[77]

Honeybuzzard, sexually aroused by this homoerotic encounter, translates his feelings into heterosexual rage: '"I'm going to stuff my Emily rigid," he said, thrusting the keyring into Morris's hand.'[78] Homoerotic arousal incites in him a desire to dominate and punish his female partner.

Viewing this encounter through the lens of Carter's gender-fluid folk song praxis and her native ability to sing the voice of men in folk song, it becomes increasingly apparent that Honeybuzzard embodies some kind of fantasized projection of a cruel version of Carter. Through Honeybuzzard, Carter allows a ludic, cruel, destructive version of the self to emerge, the selfish dandy who experiences without censure what it feels like to make the world dance to one's whims and desires. The dance of Honeybuzzard and Morris represents the apex of the parabolic arc which declines after this point; Honeybuzzard's spiral into murderous madness and Morris's inability to extricate himself from Honeybuzzard's destructive thrall together bring about the fall back into the influence of the 'shadows' into which Morris ambiguously vanishes; the parabola completes its final descent.

Chiasmus appears microcosmically in imagery Carter uses during moments of remembered or projected near-perfection. In the fantasies of both Morris's escape and the seduction of Ghislaine, Carter recreates the similar melodic figure of the confident A-sequence, the two more tentative B-sequences and the return to the A-sequence of 'Blow The Candle Out'. Morris dreams of escape from the shadows and Honeybuzzard: 'He would go away, really go away, (A) and forget about them all, (B) really forget about them all, (B) and find an honest job, glass-blowing or gas-fitting or building roads, somewhere far, far away (A)'.[79] A repetitive, choric quality similarly surrounds those descriptions of Ghislaine mentioned before: 'A month ago, (A) she was a beautiful girl; (B) how could such a girl not be beautiful? [...] She was a beautiful girl, a white and golden girl, (B) like moonlight on daisies, a month ago. (A)' The chiastic structure of this description opens and closes with the comforting deictic referent of 'a month ago', a safe time; the internal oscillation and repetitive questioning of 'how could such a girl not be beautiful?' and the repetition of the diminutive 'girl' rock back and forth beseechingly, before returning to the closing 'a month ago'. This structure highlights the innocent and honest nature of Ghislaine's sexual energy, her practical promiscuity, and yet Carter finds something unsettling in it too: the shape carries within it the shape of a specific kind of self-reflexion; Honeybuzzard's sadistic abuse of Ghislaine ('The scar was all red and raw') and her irrepressible masochistic desire to be annihilated in turn by him ('you are my master, do what you like with me') create a Sadeian mirroring of death and desire which will come to obliterate them both. Chiasmus encapsulates at once the innocence and the corruption of their trajectory.

Songs and *Shadow Dance* – thematic influences

Carter's influence from these songs doesn't stop with structural features; she also absorbed their thematic influences, the rich allusive layers of imagery and the dense semantic associations embedded within them. The text of *Shadow Dance* is infused with the figures of 'Reynardine': both the mysterious bestial villain whose 'teeth so bright did shine', and the song's anonymous victim-girl-lover who is compelled to follow him to her doom. Honeybuzzard shares many of the characteristics of the mysterious Reynardine; their bestial charactonyms are just the start. Honeybuzzard is described, like Reynardine, as disturbingly vulpine:

> He had a pair of perfectly pointed ears, such as fauns have and, curiously, these were also covered with down; his pointed ears poked whimsically through his golden love-locks, under the shadow of the extraordinary cap. And then, disquieting, strange, at odds with the cherub-face, there was the mouth.
>
> It was impossible to look at the full, rich lines of his dark red mouth without thinking: 'This man eats meat.' It was an inexpressibly carnivorous mouth; a mouth that suggested snapping, tearing, biting, a mouth that was always half-smiling in a pretty, feline curve; and showing in the smile, hints of feline, tearing teeth, small, brilliantly white, sharp, like wounding little chips of milk glass. How beautiful he was, and how indefinably sinister.[80]

His teeth, like Reynardine's, shine brightly; Lloyd might have written this description of Honeybuzzard for his show. Carter also imports from the song the self-sacrificing, sadomasochistic victim-girl in Ghislaine, whose desire for the dangerous lover overwhelms her. Carter describes Ghislaine in passive terms: 'doll', 'automaton', 'Jumping Jack'; Carter suggests she is nothing more than Honeybuzzard's puppet: 'Why not? She always did jump when I pulled her string, poor little girl.'[81] Ghislaine's subjugation to Honeybuzzard's will represents an annihilation of the self, an obliteration: 'I've learned my lesson, I can't live without you, you are my master, do what you like with me.'[82] This feels like a fantasy of stylized victimhood, not one which can be sustained in any kind of reality; it is the *Justine* of feminine behaviour: humility to the point of annihilation. Honeybuzzard and Ghislaine's relationship is choreographed, one could argue, to resemble two extreme aspects of *feminine* sexuality, examining through exaggeration the sexualized aggrandizement or capitulation of the self as sexual being, rather than making any comment on an exterior 'battle of the sexes'.

When one witnesses Carter's folk song praxis up close and understands its narrative positioning as wholesale occupation, it allows for a reading of Honeybuzzard as occupation: Carter can be read as the singer within the character she has created, a version within a version, and her authorial voice 'sings' to us through the text:

> 'I like,' he said obscurely, 'I like – you know – to slip in and out of me. I would like to be somebody different each morning. Me and not-me. I would like to have a cupboard bulging with all different bodies and faces and choose a fresh one every morning.'[83]

Honeybuzzard's plurality adds to his macabre attraction; like 'Reynardine' he is ultimately unknowable, he is nothing but surface and performance, and as such Carter can use him to perform multiple versions of self. Carter was regularly standing up and singing from different perspectives at folk clubs, singing herself into other personae: in addition to the gender-fluid identity of the singer, some of the songs (such as 'Jackie Munro' and 'Polly Oliver') sang narratives of cross-dressing women. As Dugaw explains, the formulaic structure of the ballads regularizes to predictability a world which is criss-crossed, inside-out, upside-down. Although the outline of the story is strenuously upright – the separation and reunion of separated heterosexual lovers – almost anything in fact is possible, for inversion and reversal rule this world. Daughters overturn the wishes of lovers and fathers; the pressgang which enslaves her sweetheart becomes an avenue of liberation for the heroine; women matter-of-factly decide to pass themselves as men and play the rescuing role; sailor sweethearts and merchant fathers weep and repent while female heroines smile, set things right, and earn and bestow rewards.[84]

Reading versions of Carter within versions of Honeybuzzard through the lens of her folk song praxis reveals Carter, very early in her career, eschewing any essential sense of a unified self for a fragmentary, illusory performance – an understanding gleaned directly from her experience of folk singing.

The narrative of the stoical and practical Emily, who without fuss decides to raise Honeybuzzard's baby without him, echoes the narrative of the song 'Blow the Candle Out', and its 'kind and easy loving that accepts men and women as they are with no fogging notions of sin or shame.'[85] Emily encapsulates the song's spirit of independence, its fearlessness of autonomy: 'If it hadn't been him, it would have been somebody else, sooner or later. So it can be sooner and I'll have my baby.'[86] Morris describes her attitude as 'peasant fatalism' but Emily's simple acceptance of her situation also illustrates the kind of folk pragmatism Carter so admired in 'Blow The Candle Out', that 'there's no room for regret when the young man goes away [...] And that's that, and there's no point in grieving.'[87] Honeybuzzard's cruel indifference is rendered powerless here; he is erased from the history of this baby and its mother, and Emily becomes an expression of a new independence, a new self-sufficiency to replace the old 'shame', a new social construct of the elective single mother, a new voice in the panoply of Carter's polyvocal explorations of the many different ways one can imagine the self.

Conclusion

This new understanding of Carter's folk song praxis provided by the archive reveals that, even in a work as early in her career as *Shadow Dance*, Carter shows herself to be in a process of exploration of versions of selfhood through imagination and occupation, learned from her folk singing praxis. Carter becomes everyone and anyone; regardless of gender, she is free to 'slip in and out of' bodies to make both male and female versions of herself because she is at once male and/and-not female, female and/and-not male. Her semi-credible apology in 'Notes from the Front Line' about being a young 'male impersonator' flies in the face of her far more authentic confessions in letters about Lee, Buzz (and by extrapolation Honeybuzzard) being 'something to do with [her] libido'. This is not 'impersonation' but occupation, which can be seen as a direct result of her folk singing experience, and which embodies a freedom of gender performance and gender identity that would become one of the main creative tenets of her oeuvre.[88]

Carter creates these fictive spaces in which we can 'slip in and out' of performances of 'dreams' of the male and female, spaces which are culturally specific and therefore always expressive of power relations, in order to choose how to perform gender identity. The problematic nature of folk song material may ultimately have contributed to Carter's discontinuation of active participation in the folk community, but I propose that the act of folk singing in these early years naturalized gender fluidity for her, a naturalization that manifests itself in the intricate matrices not just of Honeybuzzard/Morris/Ghislaine in *Shadow Dance*, but in so many of her other works that followed (Joseph/Charlotte/Annie in *Several Perceptions*, Lee/Buzz/Annabelle in *Love*, Anna/the narrator in 'Reflections', Desiderio/Albertina in *The Infernal Desire Machines of Doctor Hoffman*, Evelyn/Eve in *The Passion of New Eve*, Fevvers/Walser in *Nights at the Circus* and Dora/Nora/Peregrine/Melchior in *Wise Children* to name but a few. Through them all, Carter harnesses and appropriates the capacity, learned first from her own folk singing, for a radically traditional, traditionally radical gender imaginary, and through embedding such musicality within her fiction, demands that the reader re-perform her performances of self, so that the reciprocity between writer and reader grows to resemble that between singer and listener: a system of sympathetic resonances.

4

'an invented distance': folk songs, sonic geographies and the Erl-King's greenwood

The woods enclose and then enclose again, like a system of Chinese boxes opening one into another; the intimate perspectives of the wood changed endlessly around the interloper, the imaginary traveller walking towards an invented distance that perpetually receded before me. It is easy to lose yourself in these woods.

Angela Carter, 'The Erl-King'[1]

Angela Carter expressed a keen understanding of a correlative relationship between space and imagination, and repeatedly associated her sense of space with her imaginative life. From the microcosm of the room in which she worked or the house in which she grew up, to the macrocosm of the nation in which she lived, her various expressions of space suggest ceaselessly oscillating sensitivities towards states of belonging and/or estrangement which were to pervade her oeuvre: as Marina Warner has observed, hers was a spatial imagination.[2] This chapter will explore how Carter, the writer, used her folk singing experience to conjure imaginary spaces and how, through aspects of her prose writing such as dactylic rhythmic figures, and shifts in pronoun and tense, she was able to deploy her somatic understanding of oscillating spatial relationships in songs to become a sonic geographer, a cartographer within her own texts, conjuring imaginary landscapes through musical affect.

In the house of her childhood where 'a curious kind of dream-time operated',[3] Carter's journalist father would, at midnight, bring her the next day's papers in bed – 'all the fresh print would smudge the sheets in a delicious way and get on to my fingers'[4] – and in this very specific space she remembers reading John Wyndham's *The Day of the Triffids* in instalments: 'It was the idea of a blind world that obsessed and indeed terrified me.'[5] As her imaginative life developed, rooms themselves began to influence her creative output:

> I started to write short pieces when I was living in a room too small to write a novel in. So the size of my room modified what I did inside it and it was the same with the pieces themselves.[6]

Her observations on the interrelations between spatial occupancy and imaginative output expand from the domestic to the regional and national. In her early journalism on folk song, she reproduces received views on folk song's intimate relationships with the land from which it is purported to emanate:

> A nation can be known by the traditions of its people. Not the publicised but the far deeper traditions, those, for example, that express themselves in its folk songs – spontaneous creations springing from a level of the mind that reaches below consciousness for its symbols and images.[7]

Here she boldly tethers regional musical traditions to the collective unconscious creativity of its local people, in line with Cecil Sharp and others, expounding at the same time a confidence in her own sense of ethnicity and nationality. In the folk club manifesto she co-authored with Paul Carter (see Appendix 1), she states that the club will be 'concerned exclusively with the promotion of a wider appreciation and deeper understanding of the great heritage of traditional folksong, ballad and music of the British Isles, and especially that of England'.[8] This young folk singer appears exceptionally sure about what and where England is, and how she relates to it.

But this confidence was to be short-lived, both in terms of her domestic comfort and her surety of national identity. To suggest Carter was making 'home' with her new husband would be disingenuous: aged only twenty when she married him, their relationship was not to be as straightforward as she had hoped; a distressing diary entry in 1961 reveals feelings of regret and alienation: 'I'm unhappy enough to die. I want to go home. I want to go home. I want to go home.'[9] Wherever 'home' was, she wasn't in it. Edmund Gordon concludes from her diaries and letters from this period that she never really settled into their marriage; friends such as Edward Horesh have implied that, from the outside at least, the marriage appeared doomed.[10] But accounts from other friends, such as Christine Molan, suggest happier times and highlight Paul's positive influences on Carter's creative development, not least through their shared love of folk song. Molan reminisces,

> without [Paul] she would definitely not have had access to unique experiences – she was so incredibly fortunate to arrive on the scene at a pivotal moment in folk-song history with Paul as quiet unassuming guide [...] Paul respected her as a working partner [...] Through accompanying Paul on field-trips for Topic after 1960, Angela was able to actually witness Sarah Makem and many others – not only at the peak period of their singing life – but to meet them in their own home environment... an experience to die for. [...] Paul was a bio-chemist as well as an experienced musicologist – an interesting combination. He encouraged her to work on the subject in an analytical, academic way throughout her degree.[11]

Human relationships are infinitely complex; both interpretations (and many more besides) may paint a truer portrait of their living marriage: but after the personally tumultuous 'Year One'[12] of 1968, Carter was to disentangle herself from Paul, from her home with him, from Bristol and England, in a quest to redefine herself and her spatial relationship with the world.

Carter underwent a series of seismic shifts in attitudes towards seemingly 'familiar' concepts during her travels in Japan between 1969 and 1972; the first was a shift in self-awareness. She describes herself, viewed by her lover, as a foreigner in Japan, a 'mysterious other' who

> had become a kind of phoenix, a fabulous beast; I was an outlandish jewel. He found me, I think, inexpressibly exotic. But I often felt like a female impersonator. [...] I wore men's sandals because they were the only kind that fitted me...[13]

She drew on her musical understanding to describe her cultural isolation as dissonance, in this space where the 'notes' of her body played a different 'tune' to those around her:

> My pink cheeks, blue eyes and blatant yellow hair made of me, in the visual orchestration of this city in which all heads were dark, eyes brown and skin monotone, an instrument which played upon an alien scale. In a sober harmony of subtle plucked instruments and wistful flutes, I blared. I proclaimed myself like a perpetual fanfare.[14]

She described the 'painful and enlightening experience to be regarded as a coloured person, for example; to be defined as Caucasian before I was defined as a woman, and learning the hard way that most people on this planet are *not* Caucasian and have no reason to either love or respect Caucasians'.[15] Sozo Araki, the most significant of her lovers in Japan, proposes that she relished and exaggerated this feeling of incongruity: 'I think it was probably important to her that her culture be odd or exceptional, no matter good or bad. Presumably, she couldn't bear the thought that she and her world were commonplace.'[16] Araki's account implies that Carter needed to feel alienation in her surroundings, that she actively sought out a sense of cultural agitation.

Whether she experienced or invented this discomfort, Carter underwent a personal and political sea-change in Japan, metamorphosing from the young revivalist folk-singer-wife who seemed possessed of a clear sense of place, to a person newly awakened to her own strangeness, her own incongruity. She later noted that her 'female consciousness *was* being forged out of the contradictions of my experience as a traveller',[17] travels which kindled in her a problematic new relationship with the nation she called 'home':

> I always felt foreign in England, and I realized the reason I'd always felt foreign was that I was. My father's [...] Scottish, you understand. [...] He never perceived himself as Scottish, as being different, but it is different, I think.[18]

Her sense of England fascinated her throughout her life. Lorna Sage claims that she was

> interested in the question of what it meant to be English, but earlier on she found herself looking to outsiders of all sorts for inspiration. She would have said that this was entirely appropriate: she was a great believer in the kind of reverse-anthropology which involves studying your own culture as if from elsewhere, cultivating the viewpoint of an alien in order to defamiliarize the landscape of habit.[19]

The death of her English mother at the end of 1969, and her father's subsequent sale of their London home and removal back to Scotland, disarmed her.[20] At the start of her 1970 journal, just before returning for a second sojourn in Japan, she wrote: 'I feel so strange. No home. Nothing familiar, any more. I feel quite empty, like a husk with the kernel gone, quite lacking in energy & prey to vague fears.'[21] In Carter's 'imaginative topography houses stood in for mothers',[22] and, with the simultaneous loss of her mother and family house, she felt cut adrift. These processes of estrangement, which began during her time in Japan, were to continue upon her return: 'I came back to England in 1972. I found myself in a new country. It was like waking up, it was a rude awakening. We live in Gothic times.'[23] By now for Carter all sorts of concepts of 'space' and 'home' – ontological, domestic, national – had become imaginary.

Carter's problematic expressions of her various experiences of space – at once sure and/and-not unsure, native and/and-not foreign, remembered and/and-not unknown – were attuned by her folk singing practice. The tradition's cultural collective expression of location and memory oscillates in the same way between the familiar and the strange. As Carter wrote, folk songs claim to be accessing that 'far deeper' national collective memory associated with locality, representing 'spontaneous creations springing from a level of the mind that reaches below consciousness for its symbols and images', as if these songs have bubbled up from the land itself. Sharp frames folk song in this way:

> Now, as a matter of fact, in every land we do find music of a distinctive and often of a very beautiful quality, prevalent among the unlettered classes; bound, it is true, by certain limitations, but of a beauty and character of its own [...] This spontaneous utterance is called folk-song.[24]

Folk songs are therefore seen on the one hand as textured, local, and specific, expressing a particular politics of the local, and carrying encoded within them particular histories of communal singing traditions and associations with particular landscapes.

But on the other hand, folk songs are also felt to exist *outside space*. Carter noted in her dissertation the instability of spatial conjurings within songs; even songs which pretend to record localized historical events, such as battles, are strangely unconcerned with accuracy.[25] She notes rather the dependence for spatial specificity upon the figure of the singer.[26] Elsewhere in unpublished notes, she describes oral cultural artefacts as the 'invisible luggage' of migrating people, 'intended to be portable, [which] can be tailored to fit the locality in which they find themselves.'[27] Through myriad variations, folk songs know of no geographical boundaries and their lack of spatial specificity is exactly what makes them so transferable, forming an intrinsic aspect of their protean strength.

The dichotomy of this situated placelessness, oscillating at the heart of the folk song tradition, is expressed personally in the body of the singer. For while the song exists outside space and time, the singer standing up to sing takes occupancy of the song in a moment, in a location; in the song's performance it not only comes into being ('only in so far as it is sung does the folk song really exist')[28] but it takes on the associative significances which relate to that event, that time, that place, that person. Folk song is therefore *at once* specific and/and-not equivocal, historical and/and-not ahistorical, particular and/and-not general. Songs carry innate abilities to recreate their own sonic geographies and auditory landscapes through the voice, the body and the locus of the singer. They also possess a wondrous power to retrieve, remember, forget, reconstruct, lose, disperse, move, shrink, expand and conjure myriad imagined spaces: in this very dexterity lies their power.

Owain Jones and Joanne Garde-Hansen describe as 'slippery' the relationship between space, memory, imagination and identity when discussing intersecting relationships of geography and memory:

> memories of who we are now, who we were, who we wanted to become, are wrapped up in memories of where we are, where we were, and where we will be (would like to be).[29]

They discuss ways in which memory breaks up space, and describe how we are undergoing constant processes of reconstructing ourselves in these present moments from fragments of past spatial relations and memories:

> We are thus becoming creatures of spatial remains. Our spatial relationships of the moment are shaped by previous (spatial) experiences. Memory (of one kind or another) is then a fundamental (geographic) aspect of becoming, intimately entwined with space, affect, emotion, imagination and identity.[30]

Places, they suggest, present a powerful intersection of memory and geography, and our own senses of place, belonging and dwelling are built on the accumulation of memories within a location. Carter's variously expressed relationships with the spaces of her room, her parents' house, Bristol, London, England or Japan are all constructed from her own memories of feelings, perceptions, impressions, reflections, in which she uses spatial contours to construct an image of herself situated within that space. But at the same time Carter uses these places to disturb and ruffle, as part of a self-prescribed regimen of discomfort, heightening her (our) awareness that she does not (we do not) belong *anywhere*. She is engaged, as Araki observes, in ongoing processes of deliberate auto-estrangement, exclusions and retreats from any kind of belonging which might induce intellectual stupor, led by her driving 'singular moral function: that of creating unease', because, to her, 'contradictions are the only things that make any sense'.[31] Her folk singing praxis, with its own sense of situated placelessness, attuned her to these productive oscillations between the familiar and the strange, and she could draw on her singer's muscle memory when she came to imagine new spaces within the fictive landscapes of her writing.

The topography of folk songs

Folk songs generate and occupy their own powerful imaginary spaces, ideas and memories of homes abandoned and regained, of battlefields yielded and conquered, of magical forests and dangerous shorelines negotiated and navigated, which they carry within them.

Folk songs quickly become part of the spaces in which they resonate. William Motherwell observed their flexibility of locale: 'a ballad, when it has become a favourite of the people in any particular district, is soon fitted with localities, drawn from the immediate neighbourhood'.[32] In his analysis of folk song poetry, Roger Renwick seeks evidence of spatial origins: according to David Atkinson, Renwick 'employs a structuralist methodology to identify a set of codes inherent in the language of folk songs and other kinds of vernacular poetry, and to seek to relate those codes to the environment in which the songs were sung or the poetry produced'.[33] More recent geographical scholarship suggests that auditory landscapes, sonic geographies, are created by local sounds which are perceived to be appropriate to and associated with certain spaces, and folk song becomes included in the topography of these specific places. In his study of church bells, Alain Corbin observes the 'intense power of the bell to evoke, to impart a feeling of time passing, foster reminiscence, recover things forgotten, and to consolidate an individual's identification with a primordial auditory site',[34] while David Matless raises questions specifically about folk music and its relationship to place: 'Are certain musics in the regional cultural grain? Which styles of voice belong in the landscape? Does nature make music, noise, both or neither?'[35] Matless equates human folk song with bird song as a 'natural' sound which 'feels' part of a landscape: 'Local humans could also appear as unselfconscious sounding fauna expressing the region, whether children singing "John Barleycorn" or adult folk song presented as local cultural essence'.[36] He notes the disappointment observed when folk song is no longer heard in a region where it has become expected: 'Private leisure diaries also record song, and mourn decline: "For the first time on record there was no 'John Barleycorn' at Stokesby this year, either time we passed it."'[37] It is not just that the environment is shaped by song; in this symbiotic spatial relationship, song is reciprocally shaped by its environment, in particular by the human geography of the environs in which it is produced:

> The performance environment is created by each village community, its blood and marital ties, its common employment sources, and its shared activities. Within this context, the singer and his audience reside.[38]

Idyllic projections of the 'English village' and the 'village community' themselves seem to have undergone transformations as the twentieth century progressed, receding more and more into the realms of the imaginary, as critics such as Georgina Boyes, Dave Harker, Benedict Anderson and Trish Winter and Simon Keegan-Phipps (among many others) have debated.[39] These imagined spaces, they suggest, have been mediated and appropriated by socially powerful individuals and movements for political, sometimes nationalistic, ends.

Boyes argues that the 'rescue' and 'revival' of folk song in the nineteenth and twentieth centuries was in part motivated by a collective invention of an 'imagined village', that perfect English hamlet somewhere, a place where Sharp's 'folk', seemingly uncorrupted by the encroachment of technology, capitalism, literacy and all the other symptoms of modernity, could continue to sing their folk songs in a form uninterrupted since antiquity. Winter and Keegan-Phipps share Boyes' scepticism, suggesting that Sharp's 'folk' were nothing but 'a whimsical ideal that was both symptomatic and a perpetuating construct of the essentialising nationalism to which he and his numerous followers subscribed'.[40] They suggest that to 'perform Englishness through doing English folk music and dance is, then, to produce and circulate particular images and concepts of nation and national identity'.[41] Dave Harker is unforgiving in his assessment of these agenda-driven political motivations for folk revival: these concepts 'are conceptual lumber, and they have to go'.[42]

The folk singer Peggy Seeger conversely finds that, to imagine lost villages of the American Appalachian mountains, the origin-places of the songs she sings, is positively productive; these places may no longer exist materially but they perpetuate as powerful imaginary spaces within songs, within culture, capable of empowering the vulnerable, or exposing abuses, spaces to where we can travel through the medium of the songs themselves. Perhaps this is one of folk song's most powerful attributes, its ability to transport the listener to its imagined spaces.[43] In a similar way, the artist Iain Biggs uses the physical Bronze-Age site of Tamshiel Rig in the Scottish Borders to reimagine the fictive forest of Carterhaugh from the folk song 'Tam Lin'. He explains how 'Carterhaugh as an extant, if wholly fictional, place [is] summoned back into existence through each performance'.[44] Biggs argues that song reifies this imaginative space through memory and performance, and that:

> the space of innumerable identity narratives-so-far that make up the undisciplined landscape – one that escapes reduction to dualistic categories – becomes that 'sought-after place' where the two great classes of narrative (history and fiction) may be productively interwoven as distinct but mutually informing strands of deep mapping as a factually informed poetic imagining of our place in the world that is both other than the human subject – as land, place, nature – and a space for projection: a 'sublimated self-portrait'.[45]

Ethnomusicologist Martin Stokes describes '"places" constructed through music', and how 'music is socially meaningful not entirely but largely because it provides means by which people recognize identities and places, and the boundaries which separate them'.[46] Music can, for example, summon 'home' wherever we are.

Through her folk song praxis, Carter was to become profoundly attuned to these multi-directional notions of sonic geography: how folk songs can belong to specific places and yet be of no place at all, how they are at once the products of spaces and yet free of them, and most importantly how songs evoke and conjure space, lost spaces, and how the singing voice has the power to create, harness and modify its own imaginative space. She learned an awareness of the creative power of the performing voice to conjure and manipulate imagined places, sonic geographies, and she carried this spatial awareness into her prose.

The folk song greenwood

From the many examples of imaginary topographies folk songs generate, occupy and nourish across the tradition which could have become the focus for this chapter (shorelines, water-sides, roadsides or mountains, to name but a few), the topography of the greenwood is one of the most terrifying and exciting. Carter knew the folk song greenwood from such songs which depict this strange, productive, magical space as 'The Unquiet Grave' [3], 'The Cruel Mother [26], 'King Orfeo' [25], 'The Outlandish Knight' [21] (also known as 'Lady Isabel and the Elf-Knight' [20]), 'Babes in the Wood' [22], 'Tam Lin' [23] and 'Hind Etin' [24].

Carter writes about 'The Unquiet Grave', 'The Cruel Mother' and 'King Orfeo' in her dissertation;[47] she discusses 'Lady Isabel and the Elf-Knight' at length in unpublished teaching notes in relation to the 'Bluebeard' cycle of tales and songs.[48] She loved 'The Unquiet Grave' so much that in her 1961 journal she used its opening lines as an example of what she called 'true poetry',[49] and, in an article, she notes the origins of 'The Outlandish Knight', which

> began life as a folktale in the beginnings of human history. It is related to the story of Bluebeard and is still widely sung in the countryside. Fred learnt his version from the gypsies.[50]

Christine Molan remembers Paul singing 'Babes in the Wood' at their folk club.[51] Paul was imbricated in Carter's deep appreciation and performance of these folk songs; there is a sense from the anecdotes from Molan and others who knew them in the 1960s that 'the Folk Singing Carters'[52] absorbed folk song tropes like the greenwood into the vernacular of their everyday lives, and that, alongside the picture Gordon paints of a failing marriage, the flat they shared at 38 Royal York Crescent was also filled with interesting people, laughter, and music.

Carter knew the greenwood, from singing such songs with Paul and their friends, as an ancient locus of 'grave, hideous and elemental beings',[53] a dangerous space situated on the perimeter of civilized society, culture and legislature, a place just out of the corner of one's eye, where transformations, corruptions, mutations and violations may be quietly ignored. The greenwood is a place for 'things that can live only on the margin of the mind',[54] where the hegemonic rules of society, law, propriety, reality, even time, are diluted because of their distance from 'the centre'.[55] The greenwood exists at once outside civilization and yet is constructed by it, a sort of controlled liminal explosion, or what David Atkinson describes as a 'cultural safety-valve',[56] where culture attempts to control its own deviations and desires. I suggest that the greenwood, far from being an archaic social construct from an imagined 'olde England', is always with us: the Allies' post-9/11 political practice of 'extraordinary rendition',[57] the reported rapes in New Orleans following Hurricane Katrina in 2005,[58] or the 'Jungle' refugee camp in Calais,[59] are all contemporary cultural expressions of the greenwood. Every small English town has a greenwood: Michael Symmons Roberts and Paul Farley call its liminal boundary 'edgelands': 'If you know those places where overspill housing estates break into scrubland, wasteland; if you know these underdeveloped, unwatched territories, you know that they have "edge"'.[60] The greenwood is para-historical, para-linguistic, para-juridical and blind to class and gender; anyone's daughter or son is in danger; it is a place of unprejudiced peril, where rapes and murders are routinely perpetrated, where unwanted babies are dumped and lovers slain, a Castle Silling against which society discreetly and conveniently blocks its ears and averts its gaze. Carter was well aware of its potency; no wonder she loved it.

The folk song greenwood is recognizable because it exhibits five shared characteristics wherever it appears. Firstly, it is synonymous with adventure, flight and danger: seduced by the mysterious Elf-Knight's musical notes, the rebellious Lady Isabel in 'Lady Isabel and the Elf-Knight' [20] elopes with him to the greenwood:

> He leapt on a horse, and she on another,
>   Aye, as the gowans grow gay,
> And they rode on to the greenwood together,
>   The first morning in May.[61]

But when they arrive there, he tries to kill her as he has done seven/ten/twelve girls before her. In other greenwood songs such as 'Tam Lin' [23], young girls receive ample and explicit warnings not to go into the greenwood unless they are looking for 'trouble':

> O I forbid you maidens a',
>   That wear gowd on your hair,
> To come or gae by Carterhaugh,
>   For young Tam Lin is there.[62]

Secondly, lengthy incarceration in the greenwood is common: in 'Hind Etin' [24] Lady Margaret follows 'a note' into the greenwood and is trapped there for 'six long years and one' by Hind Etin/Young Akin, with whom she has seven sons. Tam Lin has been seven years the prisoner of the Queen of the Fairies when Janet/Margaret rescues him. King Orfeo must sit in the wood until his hair is grown over, and play his instrument for the fairies in order to win back his captured wife [25]. Thirdly, the folk song greenwood is inhabited by supernatural beings. Tam Lin, once a nobleman, is now a woodland sprite; the Elf-Knight seduces Lady Isabel with his supernatural, magical music; the Cruel Mother [26] is haunted by the talking ghosts of her dead babies, while the protagonist of 'The Unquiet Grave' [3] wakes the ghost of his/her lover murdered in the greenwood through excessive grieving.

Fourthly, the folk song greenwood is the site of transformations, perhaps supernatural in nature (from human to animal or sprite), or perhaps relating to perceived status (from virginal to violated). In 'Tam Lin' (as in other songs such as 'Down in the Meadows' and 'Died for Love' [17]) the plucking of the rose is a common metaphor for the compromise of a woman's virginity. Janet/Margaret is 'deflowered' by the plucking of the 'double rose' in her encounter with Tam Lin, the magical elf of the woods –

> She had na pu'd a double rose,
>   A rose but only twa,
> Till up then started young Tam Lin,
>   Says, 'Lady, thou's pu nae mae'.[63]

When she returns to her father's house she discovers she has conceived Tam Lin's baby in the woods of Carterhaugh, and will have to fight formidable supernatural forces to save him from hell and return him to human form. Tam Lin has been changed in the greenwood too, seven years before, from nobleman to sprite –

> When we were frae the hunting come,
>   That frae my horse I fell;
> The Queen o Fairies she caught me,
>   In yon green hill to dwell.[64]

Lastly, death, the most profound and permanent transformation of all, is often undergone by unfortunate greenwood wanderers. Murder is commonplace in the greenwood: the eponymous Cruel Mother gives birth to, and then kills, her illegitimate babies from shame in the greenwood:

> She took out her wee pen-knife
>   Sing hey alone and alonie O
> She twind them both of their sweet life
>   Down by yon greenwood sidie O.[65]

She assumes she can kill her babies and return from the greenwood a maid once more; she is proved wrong by their ghosts. The dead lover in 'The Unquiet Grave' has been murdered in the greenwood; Isabel might be murdered like the other girls before her, unless she can extricate herself from the Elf-Knight's embraces. The two lost children of 'Babes in the Wood', like the twin babies of 'The Cruel Mother', are destined to perish –

> They sobbed and they sighed, they sat there and cried,
>   Those two little babies, they laid down and died.[66]

while Isabel is the latest in a long line of girls enticed into the greenwood to die.

Carter knew all these songs and she borrowed recognizable elements from them which manifest the greenwood in folk song – elements connoting danger, adventure and flight, incarceration, supernatural transformation, and murderous death – and transposed them into the structures of her own writing, creating her own form of spatial imaginary.

The greenwood's rhythmic influences

Folk songs which depict adventure, danger and flight associated with the greenwood are often presented within a dactylic rhythmical framework.[67] The lines of these folk songs may be acephalous in nature which can make them harder to spot (and can lead to them being erroneously identified as anapaestic), but the drive and excitement incited by the dactylic canter transports one phonically during a close analysis.[68] In greenwood folk songs such as 'The Outlandish Knight'/'Lady Isabel and the Elf-Knight' and 'Babes in the

Wood', dactylic tetrameter is a compelling ingredient in the overall composition, emphasizing the extremes of danger and excitement the greenwood locus evokes.

Werner Wolf identifies in 'musicalized fiction' the 'common acoustic nature of both music and literature' which 'provides the basis for a whole set of more detailed similarities between the two arts'.[69] Here I focus on just one of the similarities that Wolf highlights: rhythm. One can 'hear' the dactylic gallop at work in the song 'Lady Isabel and the Elf-Knight', using specifically the musical scansion methodologies developed by Geoffrey Leech, which acknowledge 'silent beats', and which require us to 'hear' the text musically with its associated rests.[70]

'Lady Isabel and the Elf-Knight' [20] depicts a young lady's seduction by a dangerous magical music-man, their elopement into the greenwood, and her cunning escape from his murderous clutches (essentially the same story as Carter's 'Erl King'). Read the following stanza aloud, following the schema of stressed (´), unstressed (ˇ) and silent (x) syllables as indicated. Strike your finger on a table wherever you see a silent beat (x) to get the feel of it:

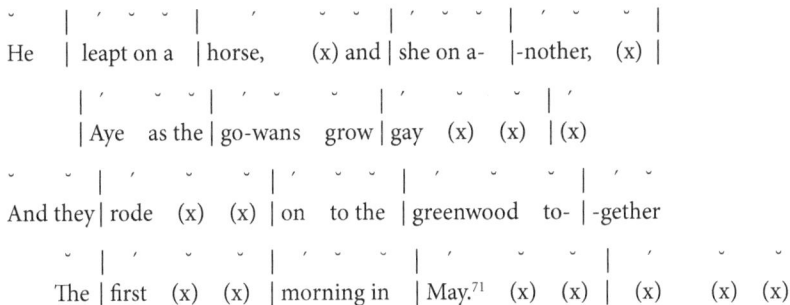

'Babes in the Wood' similarly employs a hypnotic, driving dactylic rhythm to draw us into the horror of the greenwood and the children's plight:

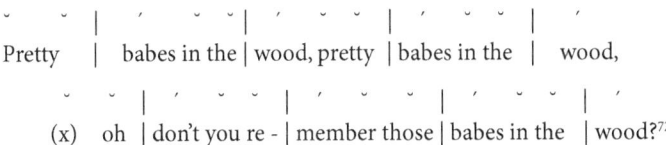

This dactylic drive is the sound of the heartbeat pounding away in the ears, the sound of galloping hooves drumming on the earth: it is the sound of primal fear. The relentless dactylic feel embodies in rhythmic terms the irresistible draw of the greenwood, and expresses a paradox oscillating at the heart of the Edenic greenwood between attraction and repulsion, wonder and horror, excitement and danger: this is the rhythm of concupiscence.

By taking this rhythmic figure, learned from feeling its effects corporeally in her singing, and weaving it into her prose passages, Carter is able to evoke an auditory greenwood landscape, drawing on its sounds and associations 'remembered, repeated, and worked through' to provoke subliminally, through affective reader response, that 'unease' she saw as her writing's 'singular moral function'.⁷³ Carter transcodes into her prose the claustrophobic dactylic rhythms she remembers from these folk songs to construct the sonic topography of the Erl-King's greenwood forest:

```
 ´   ˘     ˘  |  ´   ˘   ˘  |  ´    ˘    ˘  | ´  -e-  ˘   | ˘
per-fect trans- |-par- ency | must be im- |-pen-e- tra - | ble,
```

```
 ˘   |  ´   ˘    ˘  |  ´    ˘     ˘  |  ˘    |  ´      ˘    |  ´    ˘
these | vert- i- cal | bars of    a  | brass-coloured | distill –
```

```
 ´   ˘    ˘  |  ´    ˘   ˘   |  ´    ˘
a- tion of | light coming | down from ...
```

'Listening' to the following canorous paragraph from the Erl-King forest's description, one might find its rhythmic patterns and assonant, alliterative threads interweaving to stitch it into a kind of song. Dactylic canters erupt, highlighted here in bracketed prose 'feet':

> [*There was a*] little tangled [*mist in the*] thickets, [*mi-mick-ing*] the tufts of old man's beard that [*flossed the lo-*]wer [*bran-ches of*] the trees and bushes; heavy [*bun-ches of*] red [*be-rries as*] [*ripe and de-*] [*-licious as*] [*go-blin or*] enchanted fruit [*hung on the*] [*haw-thorns but*] the old grass withers, retreats. One by one, the [*ferns have curled*] [*up x their*] [*hun- x - dred*] [*eyes x and*] [*curled x back*] [*in-to the*] earth.⁷⁴

In particular, one can hear the dactyls at play in the following phrases:

```
    ´    ˘   ˘.  |   ´   ˘    ˘  |   ´    ˘   ˘  |   ´    ˘     ˘
...berries as | ripe and de- |-licious as | gob- lin or ...
```

```
     ´    ˘   ˘   |  ´     ˘    ˘
...hung on the | haw-thorns but ...
```

```
 ˘  |  ´    ˘    ˘     |    ´    ˘   ˘  |  ´   ˘    ˘  |  ´   ˘  |  ´   ˘
the | ferns havecurled |  up (x) their | hun-(x) -dred | eyes (x)
```

```
 ˘  |  ´    ˘    ˘  |  ´    ˘   ˘  |  ´   ˘    ˘
and | curled (x) back | in-to the | earth (x) (x)
```

Once attuned, we can start to feel the rhythm of the greenwood wherever Carter is conjuring it as auditory landscape. In Carter's 1969 novel *Heroes and Villains*, Marianne wanders into a primeval forest where

```
 ˘  |  ´    ˘   ˘  |  ´    ˘   ˘ |  ´     ˘     ˘  |  ´    ˘    ˘  |  ´   ˘    ˘  |  ´   ˘
the | curd-ed white | blo-ssom of | haw-thorn closed | ev-ery surr- | ound-ing per- | spect-ive⁷⁵
```

In the short story 'Penetrating to the Heart of the Forest' (1974), twins Emile and Madeline wander into the transformative 'enchanted forest' and walk beneath the

```
  ´    ˘   ˘  |  ´    ˘    ˘   |  ´    ˘   ˘  |  ´   ˘    ˘  |  ´    ˘    ˘   |  ´   ˘
pines in a | hushed (x) in- | ter-ior like | that of a | sent-ient cath- | e- dral
```

where

>   ´ ˘ ˘ | ´ ˘ ˘ | ´
> Ferns (x) un - | curled as they | watched,

and there are

>   ´ ˘ ˘ | ´ ˘ ˘ | ´ ˘ ˘ | ´
> trees that bore [...] brown, speckled | plu-mage of | birds.⁷⁶

The relentless dactylic rhythm of the syntax manifests a 'remainder', a murmur of the irresistible allure of the greenwood pulling beneath the narrative.

One can map in the assonant word-play and dactylic rhythm the rising and falling of the seasons and the potential for corruption in the height of ripeness, with the oscillation of the heroine's enthralment and repulsion. Carter simultaneously disturbs and attracts with the passage's prosodic beauty, just as the Erl-King's 'lass |-o of in- | -human (x) | music' both seduces and admonishes the heroine. Assonance also plays its part in the canorous composition of syntax: the asphyxiating short /ɪ/ sounds – 'little', 'mist', 'thickets', 'mimicking' – wind tightly round us, strangle us; the /e/ sounds of 'heavy', 'red' and 'berries' suggest an opening, a wideness, a fecundity. Immediately this ripeness is negated by 'old grass' which 'withers, retreats'; the ferns have 'curled up their hundred eyes' – they don't want to bear witness – 'and curled back into the earth': the repetitive /ɜː/ sound of 'curled', 'earth' and 'turn' suggests collapse, a return, a cyclic closure – 'the year, in turning, turns in on itself.' This phonetic cycle of /ɜː/ and /ɪ/ echoes itself in the /ɜː/ and /ɪ/ of the Erl-King's very name. This innate musicality, drawing on folk song's rich store of resonances through prosody and rhythm, intensifies the power of the Erl-King's melodious two-note seduction, and draws a line through our collective memory back to folk song's dangerous, wonderful, terrifying greenwood, and its capacity for inciting transformation. The greenwood is/is-not at once deliciously enticing and repulsively terrifying. Read this way, the rhythmic turn of Carter's prose is working to forewarn us, long before the words reveal it, attuning us to the rhythm of the danger to come, and our desires for it, transposing it within the assonant interplay of her prosody.

It would be myopic to assume Carter's greenwood always needs to be a forest. Through rhythmic chains of association, Carter is able to conjure the unease of the greenwood anywhere she chooses: in urban spaces such as hotels, which assume the greenwood's sonic topographies in *Wise Children*:

> ˘ | ´ ˘ ˘ | ´ ˘ ˘ | ´ ˘ ˘ | ˘ | ´ ˘ ˘ | ´ ˘ ˘ | ´
> The | leg-end-ary | For-est of | Ard-en, the | re-si- | den-tial mo- |-tel of the | stars

or alongside the overblown 'woods near Athens' film set,

>   ´ ˘ ˘ | ´ ˘ ˘ | ´ ˘
> Bindweed in | stream-ers and | con-kers

where

        ′ ˘ ˘ | ′ ˘ ˘ | ′ ˘
What I missed | most was il- | -lusion.⁷⁷

or the Weinsteinian power-spaces of the Hollywood producer Genghis Khan which become just another greenwood through dactylic transformation, and where the 'big Grünewald crucifixion'⁷⁸ oversees the action in the

    ′ ˘ ˘ | ′ ˘ ˘ | ′ ˘ | ′ ˘
ho-ly of | ho-lies, the | orchid | arbour

All are transformative greenwood spaces which, Dora confesses, 'changed me for good and all'.⁷⁹ Even Morris's bric-a-brac shop in *Shadow Dance* becomes a greenwood through sound:

˘ | ′ ˘ ˘ | ′ ˘ ˘ | ′ ′ | ′ ˘ ˘ | ′ ˘ ˘
a | sort of sub | aqu-e-ous | deep-sea | at-mos-phere | (x) in which

′ ˘ ˘ | ′ ˘ ˘ | ˘ ′ ˘ | ′ ′
piles (x) of | furn-i-ture. | and rags and | tea-chests

′ ˘ ˘ | ′ ˘ ′ | ′ ˘ ˘ | ′ ′
seemed the en- | crust-ed, drowned | car-goes of | long-dead ships.

˘ | ′ ˘ ˘ | ′ ˘ ˘ | ′ ˘
There | should have been | limp-ets and | seaweed⁸⁰

Carter forewarns us of dreadful events to come there. Ghislaine, raped by Honey in another urban greenwood, the 'padlocked and deserted' city cemetery, irradiates her dactylic acquiescence with greenwood rhythms:

˘ | ′ ˘ ˘ | ′ ˘ ˘
'I | can't live with- | -out you, (x)

′ ˘ ˘ | ′ ˘ ˘
you are my | ma-ster, (x)

′ ˘ ˘ | ′ ˘ ˘
do what you | like with me.'⁸¹

Ghislaine is sickeningly complicit in her own suffering; but by the time the narrator-heroine-victim of 'The Erl-King' wanders into her greenwood, the protagonist's complicity with her executioner is more complex, more nuanced; what both share is the rhythmic context of the greenwood; its menacing, enticing, exciting rhythmic force is a constant. Through rhythmic patterns in her syntax, Carter transcodes the pulse of the greenwood from folk song into prose, and it is this driving force which sends us there ourselves, where through the prosodic 'deep mapping' of the dynamic paradox of attraction and repulsion at the heart of the greenwood, all the contradictory implications of wonder and horror are working to estrange us from ourselves.

'Wooziness': the greenwood's melodic influences

Carter also drew on her rudimentary knowledge and understanding of the musical modes, the different types of scales with their concomitant characteristic behaviours and affects, to create auditory landscapes in her writing. Her basic understanding of modal scales and their interrelations, an understanding most likely gleaned from Paul as documents from the archive suggest, would have provided her with structural frameworks for understanding how folk song melodies provoke unease in a listener, affective models she could borrow and translate into grammar.

The nature of modality and its relation to folk song melodies has been the cause of near-vituperative dissent amongst ethnomusicologists and collectors such as Cecil Sharp, Percy Grainger, Annie Gilchrist, B. H. Bronson, Harold Powers, James Porter, Richard Sykes and Julia Bishop.[82] Sharp argues that modality is one of folk song's key features that proves its antiquity; the polarization in the eighteenth and nineteenth centuries of this spectrum of scales into the two scales of 'major' and 'minor' was a process which had, claims Sharp, passed the rural singer by, and which thereby offers hard evidence of the 'long, unbroken chain' stretching back into 'the mists of the past', which he is convinced folk song represents.[83] However, Sharp is not convinced about internal modulations within a song. Percy Grainger notices, from early experiments with phonograph recordings, some folk song melodies which were marked by a series of modal shifts in feel:

> Of seventy-three tunes phonographed in Lincolnshire, forty-five are major, and twenty-eight modal. None of the latter are definitely Aeolian, though some mainly Dorian tunes occasionally have quickly passing minor sixths. Most are in a mongrel blend of Mixolydian and Dorian. I can recall no song starting *purely* Mixolydian or Dorian that becomes during its progress purely Dorian or Mixolydian, though I have instances of songs starting *mainly* in the one mode and ending *mainly* in the other.[84]

Sharp disagrees, declaring that 'folk-airs modulate with extreme rarity', although he does note the phenomenon occasionally. He admits, begrudgingly, that

> there are a few folk-tunes which, judging by their finals, are Mixolydian, but which are, nevertheless, major rather than Mixolydian in character ...

but he denies that any flickering is intentional, but rather erroneous:

> I have always suspected the cadences to these tunes to be corrupt and due to the imperfect recollection of the singers, and the other day a case occurred which confirmed my suspicions.

Collecting a version of 'The Unquiet Grave', Sharp observes an internal modulation from the 'major' (Ionian) to the Mixolydian mode, but refuses to admit it is 'correct':

Although, strictly speaking, it was Mixolydian, yet I felt sure the tune was really a major one. I accordingly prevailed upon the singer to repeat the ballad several times. When she had sung the air *ten or twenty times*, she suddenly repeated the last line of one of the verses to the following phrase: [he then notates the altered melody] I have no doubt but that this was the correct form of the tune, and that in her previous repetitions the singer had forgotten to 'double' the last line. The tune was, after all, a major one in the key of G; not a Mixolydian in D, as it at first appeared to be.[85] [my emphasis]

Rather than use the blunt instrument of repetition, I would rather examine the various extant melodies of songs where internal modal modulations appear to be present. Julia Bishop cites Fleetwood Sheppard's important, sometimes overlooked, analysis of modal shifts[86] which he notes are sometimes perceived of as 'mistakes' but which he believes 'are often marks of antiquity, and are found in the folk-songs of all nations.'[87]

Whatever their provenance, these internal modal modulations, where a song's melody moves through more than one modal scale, evoke a very specific affective response, a sense of somatic disturbance in the listener, a discombobulating nausea. The contemporary folk artist Emily Portman[88] tells me how she feels the affect of these perceived modal shifts in tunes she knows and sings:

EP: I got really into a lot of traveller singers from the south, south east... [...] Queen Caroline Hughes, Mary Ann Haynes... and Phoebe Smith... [...] Caroline Hughes, she would sing in this amazing style, bending notes, suggesting microtones in a way that seemed to be intentional, not just a happy accident..... the way that she played with modes really interested me... I think it was her that did...

> Oh for that dear girl she roamed those meadows
> She was picking these flowers by one, two or three,
> She picked, she plucked until she gained,
> Until she gathered her apron full ...

That kind of thing.... bits of Lydian, the sharpened fourth ...

PP: But then pulling out of it again, modulated ...

EP: Yes, all of that ... when I hear a tune like that that plays between modes, I've always just gone *oooo! amazing!*

PP: Because it's kind of creepy isn't it, it creates this very unsettling, slightly nauseating atmosphere ...

EP: ... the wooziness ...[89]

Modal scale modulations convey in melodic terms the eerie threat of dangerous spaces such as the greenwood in the way that dactyls use rhythm.

I suggest that Carter capitalizes on her melodic awareness of folk song's affective 'wooziness' engendered by modal scale modulations, by seeking to translate that sensation in readers through grammar, fulfilling her mission to provoke 'unease'.[90] In 'The Erl-King' she translates modal scale modulations into pronominal and temporal shifts, rendering through grammatical ripples the same disorientating confusion that modals provoke by undermining or defying anticipation. In this way, the affective response of 'wooziness' is provoked in the reader, catapulting us into the ancient greenwood through ancient chains of association and memory.

Modal scales occupy a hinterland between what the modern Western musical ear understands as 'major' and 'minor', and, in this regard, they emit a liminal, non-committal, creatively unfinished feel to the modern ear. The interconnecting relationships between the Ionian, Dorian, Phrygian, Lydian, Mixolydian, Aeolian, and Locrian is well represented by B. H. Bronson's figure of the 'modestar'; below see Bronson's diagram, and next to it a version contained in the archive, drawn by Paul.

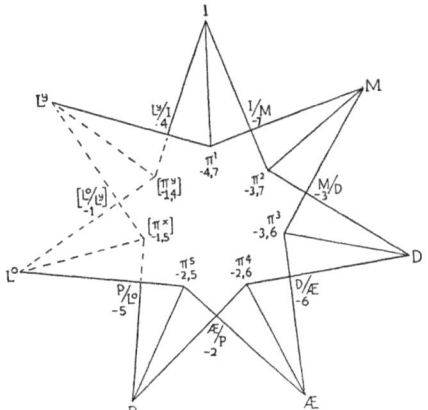 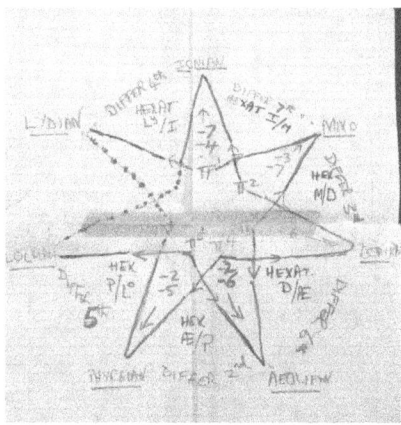

Figure 8 Photo detail of B. H. Bronson's 'modestar' diagram. Republished with permission of Princeton University Press from B. H. Bronson, *The Traditional Tunes of the Child Ballads* (Princeton, NJ: Princeton University Press, 1959), p. xlii; permission conveyed through Copyright Clearance Center, Inc.

Figure 9 Photo detail of Paul Carter's 'modestar', from Paul and Angela Carter's Folk Music Archive. Copyright © Christine Molan. Reproduced with kind permission of Christine Molan.

While, in Bronson's collation of Child ballad melodies, some of the tune variants of 'The Unquiet Grave' stick to one mode, several variants use fluctuating modal scales, such as 'Cold Blows the Wind', published by the collector Charlotte Sophia Burne in 1886, and which is represented by Bronson once more as Aeolian with an inflected VII (see overleaf).

This melody, which spends much of the time in G minor, represents an unsettling modulation between Aeolian and Ionian modes, with the third phrase taking on the Ionian feel of the B♭ major in an otherwise Aeolian melody.

Another supernatural greenwood song to reveal internal modal modulation in some of its versions is 'Tam Lin', a song which Bert Lloyd cherishes: 'We haven't all that many fairy ballads, and this is by far the finest.'[91] Child observes a reference to 'The Tayl of the ȝong Tamlene' made in 1549,[92] and, according to Lloyd, the first broadside

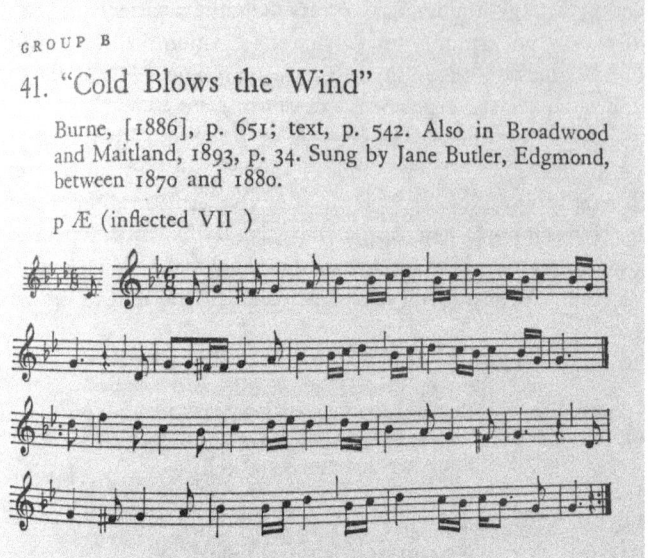

Figure 10 Photo detail of Charlotte Sophia Burne's tune for 'Cold Blows the Wind' (a variant of 'The Unquiet Grave'). Republished with permission of Princeton University Press from B. H. Bronson, *The Singing Tradition of Child's Popular Ballads* (Princeton, NJ: Princeton University Press, 1976), pp. 203–5 (p. 205); permission conveyed through Copyright Clearance Center, Inc.

printed the lyrics in 1558; however, the first recorded melody for 'Tam Lin' of which I am aware appears in Johnson's *Scots Musical Museum* of 1803. While the song is sung partly in the Aeolian mode (Æ) there is a decidedly un-Aeolian inflected VII which creeps into the melody with the C# at bar 3, which suggests there is some kind of internal modulation at work.

The modes of this tune, to my ear, are in a state of flux; the over-riding sense of this melody is Aeolian (suggested here in D); however, the opening two bars of the song strongly suggest the more major Ionian mode (here in F); at bar 3 we move into Ionian D, which makes the C# in bar 4 not an inverted VII as Bronson suggests in his later reproduction of this tune, but the expected VII in that scale; the long jump from the top F to the A in bar 4 is full of pathos, pulling us down into the order of the over-riding Aeolian D scale, which has the mournful feel of what our modern musical ear associates with what we know as the more minor key. There is a deliciously tragic pull of danger about this melodic arrangement; the optimism of the more Ionian-flavoured opening translates into the dark pull of the Aeolian mode, as we realize Janet/Margaret will have to undergo great trials if she is to rescue Tam Lin from the clutches of the powerful Fairy Queen. Nicholas Cook suggests of these shifts that 'the way you experience the sound depends on the harmonic context,'[93] and, within the cyclic structure of folk song melody, we contextualize and experience an oscillating cycle of emotions from pleasure to danger and back again, over and over again, verse after

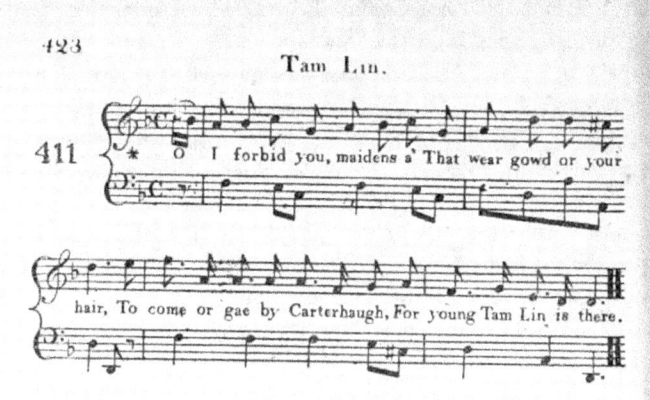

Figure 11 Detail from 'Tam Lin' in James Johnson's *Scots Musical Museum* (1803). Image taken from the National Library of Scotland website <https://digital.nls.uk/special-collections-of-printed-music/archive/87802922> [accessed 18 February 2022]. Image reproduced with the permission of the National Library of Scotland.

repeating verse.[94] This oscillation is a recognizable feature of the imagined sound of the dream of the greenwood.

Carter was familiar with these modes and their idiosyncrasies, perhaps because of, or at the very least aided by, Paul's interest in them. Paul made copious notes about the relationships between physics and music in his notebooks, making notes such as: 'Pleasure in music not explainable but displeasure – dissonance is to some extent.'[95] Tracing the history of the understanding of consonance and modes back to Pythagoras via Jean le Rond d'Alembert and Heinrich Glarean, Paul describes the 'chord of nature' and observes how the 'Greeks of course knew of these modes long before'.[96] Angela may have absorbed from Paul an interest in modal relationships and their effects; in her

Figure 12 Photo detail of 'George Collins' notated by Angela Carter, from Paul and Angela Carter's Folk Music Archive. Copyright © Christine Molan. Reproduced with kind permission of Christine Molan.

own musical notation of 'George Collins' she can be seen to include the abbreviation 'mix' for Mixolydian as part of her record of the tune:

Occasionally in her fiction Carter uses this knowledge of modes thematically: in 'The Smile of Winter' she describes how 'the storms themselves are a raucous music and turn my house into an Aeolian xylophone'.[97] But more often, she expresses her grasp of the disorientating, vertiginous affective power of these shifting folk song modes on the imagination in more structural terms.

The relentless pronominal and temporal shifts in 'The Erl-King' are nauseatingly unsettling in their circular recurrences, and relentless not just in their gyroscopic inversions of perspective but in the repetitive waves of assonant vowel sounds. The moves of person and tense are constantly rippling under us; just when we think we have our balance, Carter disorientates us again.[98] In this ever-shifting greenwood story, the boundaries between person (I/you/she/he) and tense (past/present/future) are transgressed in ways which migrate the unnerving mode modulations from folk song and reconfigure them into prose.

In the opening paragraphs of 'The Erl-King', we are introduced to a generic 'you': 'there is not much in the autumn wood to make you smile', which we, as readers, are invited to imagine is ourselves: 'You step between the first trees and then you are no longer in the open air.' Within a few paragraphs, however, 'you' has modulated momentarily into the magical Erl-King: 'though the cold wind that always heralds your presence', who then quickly shifts into 'he': 'He smiles. He lays down his pipe.' At this point 'you' is reclaimed by the 'you'-reader-*qua*-character: 'Erl-King will do you grievous harm.'[99] This cycle, this oscillation, between he/you continues throughout the story, repeating like the verses of a song. The person of the Erl-King oscillates rhythmically, relentlessly, between 'he' – 'he can make soft cheese', 'He knows all about the wood', 'he laughs at me', 'he lays me down', 'he combs his hair' – and 'you' – 'I feel your sharp teeth', 'you sink your teeth', 'If I strung that old fiddle with your hair', 'I could lodge inside your body', 'What big eyes you have'.[100] This oscillation occurs so frequently across the story it begins to take on the feel of a repeated burden, a cyclic pattern of 'him' merging into 'you' and back into 'him', as if in the music of the modulation there is an emergent conflagration of the two states, that, like in the greenwood itself where wonder and horror both 'are' and 'are-not', so the Erl-King is at once alien and part of us.

Similarly, our narrator-persona modulates her person, but in her case it only occurs at the beginning and end of the story. She walks into the story in the third person: 'A young girl would go into the woods [...] she will be trapped [...] the interloper, the imaginary traveller', but within a few lines 'she' has modulated into 'I'/'me', who realizes 'my girlish and delicious loneliness had been made into a sound'. She remains in the first person for the majority of this story, a position which intensifies our personal experience of the narrator's adventure in the greenwood, inserting us within the action, only to be pulled back out into the third person in the closing paragraphs: 'Then she will open all the cages [...] She will carve off his great mane [...] she will string the old fiddle...' This change in person is a change of mode, a shift from the emotional confusion and solipsism of the first person singular position to the objectivity and cold clarity of the third person, with its dispassionate glare into possible futures.

Tense shifts also take place throughout this story; sometimes within one paragraph we find ourselves catapulted from simple present ('The woods enclose') to simple past ('changed endlessly') and back again ('It is easy') in the space of a few lines. Carter also deploys deft usage of modal auxiliaries in her construction of the future tense, which share with modal scales that sense of unfinished, non-committal possibility. Modal verb constructions such as 'I shall take', 'I will strangle', 'you could swallow', and 'it will play' all resonate with the sense of possibility and potential latent in the unfixed, loose, endlessly deferred musicality of the modal scales.

In an astute and detailed essay, Monika Fludernik names these pronominal and temporal shifts in Carter's writing 'strategic' and their result 'defamiliarisation, and with a subsequent need to step out of the grooves of one's reading experience', but she can ultimately attribute no 'true textual "meaning" or function' to these changes of pronoun or tense.[101] I answer her with a musicology-led explanation of their function, at least: that these pronominal and temporal shifts are consistent with the effects of modal scale modulations within folk songs, and that they work to invoke a 'wooziness' in the reader which summons up the greenwood space through disorientation. Carter wants to nudge us into the greenwood before we even realize we are there, and, through these undulating shifts, she manages it.

Lorna Sage writes that '[v]ertigo, the loss of stability, is meat and drink to Carter';[102] pronoun and tense shifts provided Carter with a way, using methodologies of undermined anticipation she learned from singing folk songs through modal scale shifts, to compose vertiginous imaginary landscapes, and spatial imaginaries.

The greenwood's thematic influences

Rhythmic and melodic influences from greenwood-situated folk songs that pervade 'The Erl-King' are reinforced by strong thematic influences, seeping into Carter's motivic arsenal from singing and listening, upon which she drew so heavily to create the unsettling greenwood landscape of the Erl-King's forest.

Debates abound regarding the source materials for Carter's story. She revelled in what Martine Hennard Dutheil de la Rochère has dubbed 'translational poetics' – 'translation was for Carter the laboratory of creation in which she conducted her literary experiments'[103] – and Carter was as familiar with the works of European writers such as Charles Perrault and Johann Wolfgang von Goethe as she was with English language authors. From unpublished papers[104] we learn she was consciously borrowing elements from Goethe to construct her 'Erl-King'[105] – elements such as the name of the strange genius loci, the forest setting, the cry *'Erlkönig hat mir ein Leids getan!'*[106] and the gutteral sound 'Ach!'.[107] As she drafts and redrafts, she highlights more intertextual influences from Christina Rossetti, William Blake, Frances Hodgson Burnett and Charles Baudelaire. But once more, her conscious list is incomplete: whether by accident or design, she has omitted another important yet obvious influence: the 'constellation' of English folk songs surrounding Child ballad 4, 'Lady Isabel and the Elf-Knight' [20] that she knew so well, all set in the greenwood.[108]

In these folk songs, the danger of the greenwood is personified by the figure of the magical music-man, who seduces his victims with supernatural melodies. His musical language is all the more potent in the greenwood, where words, along with rationality and law, are less effective.[109] In 'Lady Isabel and the Elf-Knight', 'The Elfin Knight' and 'The Banks of Red Roses' [10], dangerous music-men use irresistible tunes to lure their victims to harm. Lady Isabel hears 'an elf-knight blawing his horn', whom she longs 'to sleep in my bosom'; instantly he appears at her window.[110] The eponymous magical being of 'The Elfin Knight' 'blaws his horn both lowd and shril' to begin the riddling conversation with the clever lass who is drawn to him.[111] In 'The Banks of Red Roses' the murderous Johnny 'pulled out his charm flute and played his lass a tune' before luring her to a cave.[112] The music of these men is distilled into the ethereal, ensnaring 'magic lasso' of the Erl-King's music, which 'went directly to my heart. [...] He smiles. He lays down his pipe, his elder bird-call'. We know from these folk songs that to succumb to such music will do us 'grievous harm', and yet we follow. The Erl-King's bestial attributes (his 'white pointed teeth with the spittle gleaming on them') are drawn from folk song antiheroes such as 'Reynardine' [12] (see Chapter 3), and his integral relationship with the forest ('as though he were a tree') and its animals ('little brown bunnies [...] crouching at his feet') are reminiscent of 'King Orfeo' [25] whose harping, after ten years in the forest, inspires 'all the beasts and birds [to] flock to him'.[113] These resonances work to heighten our sense of the danger our wandering heroine is in.[114]

The excitement and flight synonymous with the greenwood is embodied in the figure of Carter's 'dauntless heroine', another trope Carter lifts from the folk song greenwood to populate her Erl-King forest.[115] Folk song is full of such spirited, independent women, for whom, as Dianne Dugaw suggests, 'assertiveness seems a predisposition, indeed an ideal.'[116] In the ballad, Isabel appears at first to be at the Elf-Knight's mercy, having willingly abandoned the safety of her father's house, and now finding herself in the greenwood and beyond the jurisdiction of the known world. But rather than yielding, she formulates a plan:

> 'O sit down a while, lay your head on my knee,
> That we may hae some rest before that I die.'

she sings to him, lulling him to sleep on her lap to disarm him:

> She stroakd him sae fast, the nearer he did creep,
> Wi a sma charm she lulld him fast asleep.

and then she stabs him with his own dagger:

> Wi his ain sword-belt sae fast as she ban him,
> Wi his ain dag-durk sae sair as she dang him.[117]

Isabel saves herself with her quick thinking and her singing voice, one dauntless heroine amongst a plethora of brave, 'clever lasses' in the folk songs Carter so admired.

Carter's narrator-protagonist in 'The Erl-King' is Isabel translated into prose: she has wandered into the wood freely, and is drawn to the Erl-King 'on his magic lasso of inhuman music',[118] his 'diatonic spool of sound, one rising note, one falling note', the sound of the nightingale migrated into prose and imbued with centuries of association with female violence.[119] Like Isabel, her life is threatened in the greenwood and she is faced with a stark choice: whether to avenge her assailant's victims and escape, or become like them. Like Isabel, she plans to lull her assailant to sleep with her singing voice, and then she will kill him; unlike Isabel however, her plan hangs ambiguously in the future tense:

Sometimes he lays his head on my lap and lets me comb his lovely hair for him [...] I shall take two handfuls of his rustling hair as he lies half dreaming, half waking, and wind them into ropes, very softly, so he will not wake up, and softly, with hands as gentle as rain, I will strangle him with them.[120]

Like Isabel, Carter's heroine oscillates between attraction and repulsion for her abductor. She is one minute overjoyed ('how pleasing, how lovely') and enthralled ('He knows all about the wood and the creatures in it') by the Erl-King, and the next repulsed ('his flesh is of the same substance as those leaves that are slowly turning into earth') and panic-stricken ('I was shaken with a terrible fear'). Her abductor is a sexualized being for whom she feels unmitigated desire – 'he has stiff, russet nipples ripe as berries' – and yet he is 'gaunt'. She recognizes this oxymoron: 'His touch both consoles and devastates me.' This is the true nature of their destructive love: 'His embraces were his enticements and yet, oh yet! they were the branches of which the trap itself was woven.'[121] Carter translates the greenwood paradox of attraction/repulsion into the oscillating emotions of her narrator-heroine, who concludes that Erl-King really does mean her 'grievous harm', just in time to aspire to extricate herself from his devastating embraces. But escape is only a potentiality for Carter's narrator-heroine, suspended as her escape is in the future tense.

Zoomorphic imprisonment in the greenwood is another common trope in folk song: in Child ballad 20, 'The Cruel Mother' [26], the woman, having murdered her babies, will endure incarceration in zoomorphic form as punishment: in Thomas Moran's sung version she'll be 'seven long years a wolf in the woods';[122] in Child's J version she will become 'seven years bird on the tree' and 'seven years fish i the sea'.[123] In Child ballad 41 'Hind Etin' [24], Lady Margaret is incarcerated in the greenwood by her assailant the Etin who, Child notes in his C-variant, 'pull[s] up the biggest tree in the forest [...] to scoop out a cave many fathoms deep, in which he confines Margaret till she comes to terms, and consents to *go home* with him, wherever that may be'.[124] Tam Lin [23] is trapped in the greenwood for seven years by the Queen of the Fairies; King Orfeo [25] must sit in the wood until his hair is grown over, and play his harp for the fairies in order to win back his captured wife. In Carter's greenwood incarceration is evoked in the songs of the Erl-King's prisoners, his 'wall of trapped birds', who are confined because of their talents: 'the sweetest singers he will keep in cages'. She describes this greenwood as 'bird-haunted', and hears the uncanny phenomenon of how the 'birds, at random, all singing, strike a chord' – but at other times they

> don't sing, they only cry because they can't find their way out of the wood, have lost their flesh when they are dipped in the corrosive pools of his regard and now must live in cages.[125]

As with the Elf-Knight's previous victims, these girls are numerous and transformed; but unlike them, they are still alive and salvageable: 'she will open all the cages and let the birds free; they will change back into young girls, every one, each with the crimson imprint of his love-bite on their throats.'[126] In Carter's story, there is hope of liberation and escape from the 'bird-haunted solitude' of the forest and the 'reducing chamber' of the Erl-King's gaze.

Carter evokes the arbitrary brutality of the greenwood space through her evocation of the 'singing bone' folk song trope as 'The Erl-King' closes. The accusation 'Mother, mother, you have murdered me!', which will be sung out by the fiddle strung with human hair, is strongly reminiscent of Child ballad 10 'The Twa Sisters' [27],[127] which Molan specifically remembers Carter singing.[128] The 'singing bone' trope, of which this ballad is perhaps the finest example, connotes betrayal and injustice: a sinister, self-playing instrument, fashioned from body parts, summons ancient collective memories of danger and transformation via a rich system of shared symbology, which Carter can here be seen harnessing as she reconstructs the irrational, capricious horror of the greenwood space.

Conclusion

Carter combines the raw musical elements of the folk song greenwood – its cantering rhythmic dactyls, its unsettling modal scale modulations, its recognizable thematic tropes and figures – with myriad other intertextual influences to fabricate the spatial construction of the Erl-King's labyrinthine forest home, harnessing the power of ancient chains of semantic association in the service of her prose. In particular she uses components of music-in-language to construct what she calls '"landscapes of the heart" [...] the Romantic correlation between inside and outside that converts physical geography into parts of the apparatus of the sensibility'.[129] Simon Frith explains the processes a singer experiences in terms of the singability of words:

> The singer finds herself driven by the physical logic of the sound of the words rather than by the semantic meaning of the verse, and so creates a sense of spontaneity: the singing feels real rather than rehearsed; the singer is responding (like the listener) to the musical event of which they are part, being possessed by the music rather than possessing it.[130]

I suggest here that, at times, Carter is doing the same in reverse through lexical and syntactical choices: she is momentarily driven by the 'physical logic of the sound of the words rather than by the semantic meaning', and this is a direct consequence of her singing experience. Here, in the oscillation between the excess of her musical prose and the loss of specificity engendered by it, the 'curious abyss' opens up, the gap at the spinning heart of this prehistoric musical language of concupiscence. The Erl-King and his greenwood home are built on the movement of Carter's many musical iterations.

Aware of the oscillating 'and/and-not', 'is/is-not' nature of folk song, Carter applies its ambivalent nature to her Erl-King, who is at once the figure of her narrator's fear: 'Erl-King will do you grievous harm', and her desire, 'the tender butcher who showed me how the price of flesh is love'. The narrator feels the riptide of these dynamic feelings towards him emerging and merging, 'becoming', at once; he is simultaneously hospitable, kind, and loving, and yet devastating, threatening, and devouring.

The Erl-King can be seen as a personification of the greenwood space itself. He is historical and/and-not ahistorical; temporal and/and-not timeless; moral and/and-not amoral. We enter the woods on a specific day of the year, a 'cold day of late October' but, once inside, time is fluid: its occupants have 'all the time in the world' while the Erl-King's eyes are a time-negating 'green liquid amber' in which the narrator will be trapped 'forever'. The Erl-King provides sustenance: 'we shall eat the oatcakes he has baked on the hearthstone' and shelter: 'Rattle of the rain on the roof', but he also threatens annihilation: 'in his innocence he never knew he might be the death of me'. The Erl-King bestows the same kinds of mindless, unintentional gifts and threats as the forest itself.

The Erl-King *is* the greenwood, and vice versa. Like Tam Lin or King Orfeo, he is supernaturally interchangeable with the forest, 'like bubbles of earth, sustained by nature, existing in a void [...] he came alive from the desire of the woods'; and yet, she is the one in danger of being swallowed by him, not the other way around: 'I will be [...] consumed by you'. The Erl-King and his greenwood are conjured by Carter partly through these ancient associations, and partly through Carter's engagement with the sounded spatial structures learned from folk song, enabling her to build her spatial imaginary through sonic geographies and auditory landscapes.

Oscillating emotions are evoked within this greenwood space. Terror is inspired by this greenwood, yes, but there is also an overwhelming sense of sadness and regret: in 'the melancholy of the failing year' and the 'haunting sense of the imminent cessation of being' there is a deep sense of melancholy; the tune of the Erl-King, like that of the nightingale Philomela, is 'as desolate as if it came from the throat of the last bird left alive'.[131] Yet, paradoxically, Carter's greenwood is also a place of enrichment, intense production, transformation and negotiation, and creativity lies in its 'intimate perspectives [that] changed endlessly', because in estrangement there is the possibility of revelation: 'I have seen the cage you are weaving for me'. In the greenwood, we undergo 'the negotiations we have to make to discover any kind of reality. I tend to think it's the world that we're looking for in the forest'.[132]

In her syntactical recreation of the imaginary greenwood space, Carter reveals an engagement with folk song's rhythms, melodic shapes, themes and tropes which transcends influence. Like the 'singing bone', Carter is repurposing elements of folk song, borrowing audial parts which worked on her imagination when she was performing, or listening to performance, so that her reader might not only 'hear', but actually 'perform', those affective responses to the songs, the 'invisible music' spilling from Carter's songful prose. Carter creates a 'creature of spatial remains' in her Erl-King heroine lost-and-found, a narrator tiptoeing through fragmented spatial networks of greenwoods from past texts, using the susurrating sounds and flickering images of old songs to navigate collective rememberings, recreating her own '(spatial) experiences [...] intimately entwined with space, affect, emotion, imagination and identity' through musical, spatial, and somatic recall. She breaks the greenwood's 'magic silence'[133] by the final victorious stringing of the fiddle, using the sonic matter of old songs within her prose to forge new auditory landscapes where meaningful transformation might, at last, be possible.

5

'moving through time': folk songs, journeys and the picaresque in 'Reflections' and *The Infernal Desire Machines of Doctor Hoffman*

> *I returned slowly through the mists of winter. Time lay more thickly about me than the mists. I was so unused to moving through time that I felt like a man walking under water. Time exerted great pressure on my blood vessels and my eardrums, so that I suffered from terrible headaches, weakness and nausea. Time clogged the hooves of my mare until she lay down beneath me and died.*
> Angela Carter, *The Infernal Desire Machines of Doctor Hoffman*[1]

Angela Carter revelled in the creative freedoms afforded her by the literary genre of the picaresque and the topos of the journey. As she explained to Lorna Sage,

> I suppose the picaresque is a mode I fall into, because you can get so much in, you can talk one minute about a castle, the next about a railway station, and move through space and time, with just the structure of the journey.[2]

What she does not reveal to Sage, however, is how much she owed her understanding of the picaresque mode to her immersion in the folk song tradition, nor how much her singing of these songs steeped her imagination in the mode's images, figures and narrative shapes.

Although the picaroon, the clever rogue, has been a stock character in Western literature for centuries (see, for example, Encolpius from the Roman *Satyrica*,[3] or the Reynard fox-figure in the medieval *Ysengrimus*),[4] and the figure of the wandering adventurer features in the songs of twelfth-century *trouvères*[5] and fourteenth-century *chansons d'aventure*,[6] the novelistic picaresque form is generally understood to have crystallized as a genre in sixteenth-century Spain, and has been imitated, appropriated and repurposed ever since.[7] The picaresque form itself, by its very definition, is at once within a historical tradition and at the same time achronological. As Ulrich Wicks illustrates, there is

> a kind of paradox in our usage of the term that is not unlike the picaro's situation in his fictional world: just as he is plunged into the very thick of it and yet remains an outsider, so criticism has left us with a term that must do double – and

confusingly contradictory – duty. On the one hand, we have a historical approach that sees the picaresque as a 'closed' episode in the fiction of sixteenth- and seventeenth-century Spain, and, on the other, we have an ahistorical approach that sees it as an 'open' fictional tradition, until in contemporary usage the term 'picaresque' seems to be applied whenever something 'episodic' tied together by an 'antihero' needs a name.[8]

Just as the picaresque narrative itself is beset by digressions, flashbacks, jump-cuts and other structural interruptions, so the very ways in which we perceive it are inconsistent and out of time. This appropriateness of form would have appealed to Carter.

Some of the most celebrated elements of the picaresque – the wandering rogue, the deflowering of maidens, the random episodic occurrences, the plain language – permeate through the folk songs Carter was singing and listening to in the 1960s, songs such as 'Died for Love' [17], 'The Banks of Sweet Primroses' [28], 'The Young Girl Cut Down in Her Prime' [29], 'Reynardine' [12] and 'As I Roved Out' [30], which all sport a charming, dangerous, semi-criminal, opportunistic, irredeemable 'rascal of low degree'[9] for a protagonist who 'roves out' into the countryside, seducing young girls as he goes without regret. Folk songs which chart the deviating paths of these travelling rascals and their variously doomed, spurned, or lost lovers have repeatedly been (and continue to be) performed by contemporary artists working within the tradition[10] and share many recognizable characteristics with their more 'literary' cousins.

For example, an internal structural tension between motion and stasis develops in both picaresque literary narratives and picaresque songs. In picaresque narratives, a discrepancy emerges between the incessant movement of the peripatetic journeying hero and the peculiar stasis of the text's narrative development, its inability to get anywhere: the narratives often display a characteristic lack of either plot or character progression; digressive and deviational paths lead us to dead ends; picaroons neither learn or grow; they remain incorrigible reprobates. The peripatetic antiheroes of folk songs, cut from the same cloth, will be forever wandering out on May mornings: their state of being perpetually bound on a restless journey and propelled forward in endless motion is itself unchanging and unceasing. The tension even expresses itself within the songs' grammar. Intransitive verbs of picaresque adventure, so common in folk song – to 'journey', to 'ramble', to 'rove', 'to walk out' – lack any specific direction or drive, they suggest both semantically and grammatically a digressive, perverse path, in search of unspecified opportunities, which is by very definition 'structureless'; they present 'little more than a series of thrilling incidents impossible to conceive as happening in one life'.[11] Their trajectories meander, suggesting that the rovers are eternal wanderers; their wandering is ever so; their status quo is forever the same. Their lack of development creates a form of stasis, because they are destined never to change.[12] This innate tension between motion and stasis is then perpetuated by the form itself, for the songs have wandered across continents enduring processes of 'continuity, variation, and selection',[13] are both transformed and yet preserved by their repetition. Folk songs require performance as a living form, and yet at the same time they need preservation and remembrance; they occupy antithetical states of motion and stasis at once: for whilst every performance creates a fresh instance of a song's reification and memorial, it also presents new opportunities for mutation and change.

Carter's expression of the picaresque form and its innate ability to achieve a kind of stasis in its perpetual motion, takes musical shape in her prose, I suggest, because of her immersion in the folk singing tradition. This chapter will ask, firstly, how Carter's refiguring of the picaresque and her expression of the 'journey through space and time' was inflected by her understanding and performance of folk songs, focusing on two of her prose works, *The Infernal Desire Machines of Doctor Hoffman* (hereafter *Hoffman*) and 'Reflections', and, secondly, to what result.

Particular focus on *Hoffman* (written in 1971) and 'Reflections' (written sometime in 1972), is precipitated by two counts of biographical interest. Firstly, when Carter wrote them, she was on a journey of her own: physically from England to Japan, and emotionally from her first marriage into the unknown. Secondly, both works were written shortly after she had left behind the folk singing community in Bristol: proof of influence from folk singing in these particular texts would suggest that folk song continued to shape her creative output after her practical involvement in the revival had come to an end.

Carter wrote *Hoffman* in Japan during the winter of 1970–71, whilst living in idyllic, if temporary, seclusion with her lover, Sozo Araki, in a seaside cottage in Chiba Province.[14] In letters home Carter reveals a fatalistic gloom about their future: as Gordon puts it, *Hoffman* was 'in a sense an elegy to her relationship with Sozo'.[15] While Cornel Bonca reads *Hoffman* as concerned only with the male perspective, concluding that there is 'only the dead end of sexual domination',[16] others such as Maggie Tonkin have read in *Hoffman* a more sexually nuanced universe.[17] I read Desiderio, *Hoffman*'s picaresque hero, as another gender-ambivalent embodiment of a version of Carter herself,[18] the disaffected, bored, nonchalant traveller, fuelled only by unquenchable desire, whose charactonym expresses a dual sense of both longing and, crucially, loss.[19] One can almost hear Carter from Sage's interview speaking through Desiderio in *Hoffman*'s opening pages: 'And so I made a journey through space and time, up a river, across a mountain, over the sea, through a forest. Until I came to a certain castle. And ... But I must not run ahead of myself.'[20] I suggest Desiderio stands in for Carter, and her own deviating journey of insatiable desire for freedom from what she saw as the 'mind-forg'd manacles' of her former life. And if Desiderio stands in for Carter, so Albertina stands in for Sozo: Natsumi Ikoma has noticed how 'Albertina [...] is modelled after Sozo';[21] Carter expressed such intentions as she was planning the novel:

> It's interesting for me because it will be in the first person – male; the heroine will look exactly like S. on one of his good days, i.e. when I love him. It is to be called 'Doctor Hoffman's Desire Machine'.[22]

Sozo's youthful beauty, mystery and complete lack of ambition can be seen embodied in Carter's configuration of 'Albertina as narrative enigma',[23] in which sexual fulfilment is constantly deferred.

Carter wrote 'Reflections' (published in the 1974 short story collection *Fireworks*) later, sometime between April and December 1972, after the end of her relationship with Sozo and her return to England.[24] It shares some striking similarities with *Hoffman*: its wandering male picaresque hero;[25] its meditations on music-as-language;[26] its hallucinogenic hyper-reality, the other-world through the mirror reminiscent of the Doctor's strange manipulations; its central androgyne who, like Albertina, exhibits both the male and female principle; knitting as metaphor for the narrative act;[27] graphic and violent depictions of male rape from the first person perspective. These texts also share a conscious rejection of realism, examples of 'a fiction that takes full cognisance of its status as non-being, that is, a fiction that remains aware it is of its own nature, which is of course a different nature than human, tactile immediacy'.[28] Carter was embracing a new 'strange, hallucinatory'[29] style.

I suggest that, in Carter's handling of journeying and the picaresque in these texts, there is a remembrance of the implicit tension at work in folk songs between motion and stasis that Carter knew how to express in musical terms from performing it: the tension between needs for, on the one hand, wanderlust, movement and understanding, and on the other, stasis, lacunae and bewilderment.

The picaresque in the folk song tradition

Folk songs, often perpetuated by itinerant communities, have a natural affinity with the picaresque mode and the topos of the journey.[30] The folk singer-narrator habitually invites the listener to rove, to ramble, to leave the comfort of now and come along on an adventure:

> As I was a-walking one morning in May,
>   I saw a young couple a-making of hay,
> O one was a pretty maid, and her beauty shone clear,
>   And the other was a soldier, a bold grenadier.[31] [31]

or

> And as I roved out on a May morning, on a May morning quite early,
>   I met me love upon the way, oh lord but she was early.
> Her hair was dark, her teeth were white, her buckles shone like silver,
>   She had a dark and a roving eye, and her hair hung o'er her shoulder.[32] [30]

or

> As I walked out one May morning when flowers were all in bloom,
>   I went into a flowery field and smelled a sweet perfume,
> I turned myself all round and round and listened for a while,
>   And there I saw Cupid the ploughboy and he my heart beguiled.[33] [32]

Roger Renwick notes the rubric's affinity to the liminal nature of journeying, of existing on the 'interstitial' boundary between one state or place and another, and the significance of the time of year:

> May, in the pragmatic world, is the interstitial period between spring and summer, two temporal categories that are firmly delineated ones in the seasonal calendar, while 'roving out' indicates the interstitial space between the known and fixed home environs and the similarly unambiguous locus of a journey's destination.[34]

This motion between states of time and place creates myriad opportunities in folk song for singer-narrators to find adventure on the road, and Carter knew it well both from singing and from study. She celebrates the rubric's remarkable utility in her dissertation, comparing it to 'once upon a time'.[35] Carter unpacks the rubric *in situ*, noting how it is used in folk songs to create seemingly endless opportunities for (mis)adventure:

> A song which one collector has called 'far and away the most common and most popular folk song found in the British Isles today' is often simply called 'As I Roved Out', though Harry Cox of Norfolk calls it 'Seventeen Come Sunday'. It is a straightforward, rather cynical account of a rural seduction perhaps connected with the longer and more explicit narrative ballad, 'The Trooper and the Maid' (Child 299); the narrator cheerfully leaves the poor young girl behind, 'undone forever'. This song begins:
>
> As I roved out one bright May morning,
>   one May morning early,
> I met a maid upon the way,
>   she was her mama's darling.
>
> Songs of this type – simply accounts of rural seduction in the greenwood in springtime – surely, however remotely, echo the *chanson d'aventure*, that development from the *pastourelle* of the *provençale* troubadour poets which recounts the poet's amorous adventures on a trip to the country.[36]

Carter draws a compelling line between the singer-narrators of folk songs in the living tradition in which she is performing, and the roaming young man seeking adventure in the medieval *chansons d'aventure*:

> Like so many English love songs, the opening magically recalls the breathless evocation of spring in medieval poetry, when leaves grow green, flowers bud out, small birds sing and the young man says, 'Now springes the spray. All for love I am so sick That slepen I ne may.'[37]

As Nicolette Zeeman explains, the homodiegetic narrator of the medieval *chanson d'aventure* is usually 'errant', travelling with no specific intention, no object of desire, a singer who is irresistibly drawn to another singing figure in the landscape. Zeeman notes Anne Middleton's assessment of the audience's 'decentred and decentring experience'[38] from this lack of direction, but suggests nevertheless that

> 'intent', feeling, and desire are at stake. Even if the singer is not initially able to articulate his desire, he usually finds it in the landscape – sometimes his own desire, and sometimes that of another person.[39]

Carter's short story 'Reflections' opens with one such errant narrator: 'I was walking in a wood one late spring day of skimming cloud and shower-tarnished sunshine.'[40] This wanderer sounds as if he has walked into the story from a folk song; indeed Carter reveals in an unpublished essay that 'Reflections' was inspired by the cover of a folk album by Anne Briggs:

> Actually, this story started off with a record cover – cover of a record made by a wonderful girl I used to know who was a folk-singer, I hadn't seen her for years and picked up this record cover with a photograph of Anne with a dog and a gun, striding through a grove. (Most English folk-songs begin, 'As I walked out one May morning.')[41]

Figure 13 Anne Briggs, *Anne Briggs* LP, front cover (Topic Records 12T207, 1971). Copyright © Topic Records. Reproduced with kind permission of Topic Records.

Carter deleted this paragraph from the final version of this essay when it was published in 1975 as 'Notes on the Gothic Mode', but this early draft reveals how much folk song was still influencing her imaginative output. In 'Reflections', Carter articulates this desire in the landscape through the depiction of the wandering young man, drawn (following medieval convention) to an acousmatic singing voice in the landscape ('Then I heard a young girl singing'[42]), and 'the possibility that the landscape and what the narrator finds in it are a manifestation of something in him'.[43] While Carter's young male narrator appears to be wandering aimlessly into this wood, perhaps without realizing it, he is searching for something.[44]

Journeys in folk songs may not be random wanderings; they can sometimes be undertaken deliberately to forget the beloved, or to escape a crime. Carter knew 'The Flower of Sweet Strabane' from the singing of it, but she forgot some of the verses in the recording that survives, perhaps due to nerves;[45] in the longer version sung by Paddy Tunney, whom Carter greatly admired, Martha's spurned lover sets sail for America:

> But since I cannot win her love,
>   no joy there is for me
> I'm going to seek forgetfulness
>   in a land across the sea.[46]

The incestuous brother in 'Lucy Wan', another favourite of Carter's to sing, similarly hurls himself upon an endless journey:

> I shall dress myself in a new suit of blue
>   And sail to some far country.[47]

But to leave on these journeys is not the kind of motion it may at first appear; it is not in search of discovery, but rather in search of 'forgetfulness', oblivion, an attempt to obliterate the painful memory of the beloved, which is a desire for nothingness, for stasis.

Carter was to infuse the picaresque narrative of *Hoffman* with this productive dichotomy between journeying and forgetting from folk songs: after murdering Albertina, Desiderio 'returned slowly through the mists of winter. Time lay more thickly about me than the mists'.[48] Behind Desiderio the storyteller stands Carter the storyteller, and his fractured experience of moving through time is steeped in Carter's own experience of writing:

> Narrative is written in language but it is composed, if you follow me, in time. All writers are inventing a kind of imitation time when they invent the time in which a story unfolds, and they are playing a complicated game with *our* time, the reader's time, the time it takes to read a story. A good writer can make you believe time stands still.[49]

When Desiderio 'writes' his own story, he simultaneously 'cannot remember exactly how it began', yet remembers 'everything'; both states can be true simultaneously, for in the motion of the picaresque journey lies the lacuna of forgetfulness and unknowing.

Lacunae in meaning and sense can also emerge as folk songs travel through time and space, sometimes to such an extent that the songs appear to lose their meaning altogether.[50] Carter observes how seemingly nonsensical tag-verses, such as the verse about the rose and briar growing together in the graveyard, recur across so many songs:

> These verses always seem to me to occur simply as a 'pretty fancy', inserted to draw a narrative to a fitting close. They are applied to such a great number of romantic ballads that they seem to exist only as a meaningless bit of prettiness...[51]

Their function appears to supersede content, and yet, empty of meaning as they are, the 'charm' of their imagery and their functionality arms them with resilience. Repetitive burdens may also contain a loose semantic content, such as 'all alone and alone ee',[52] 'Lay the bent to the bonny broom' or 'Jennifer gentle and rosemaree',[53] or they may be nonsense lines, such as 'Ba, ba, ba, lilly ba'.[54] More often than not, they are rhythmical devices, sung more for their satisfying sounds, and as *aides-memoire*, giving the singer time to recall the next lines of the song. They might also be corruptions of words from other languages, such as 'scowan orla grona', the seemingly nonsense-burden in 'King Orfeo' which Patrick Shuldham-Shaw asserts is likely a corruption of the Scandinavian 'skoven arle grön' or 'Early green's the wood'.[55] Walter Ong explains that these rhythmic repeated burden lines are intrinsic elements of orally communicated texts:

> Fixed, often rhythmically balanced, expressions of this sort and of other sorts can be found occasionally in print, indeed can be 'looked up' in books of sayings, but in oral cultures they are not occasional. They are incessant. They form the substance of thought itself. Thought in any extended form is impossible without them, for it consists in them.[56]

These mnemonic features become vessels with which folk songs (like other orally transmitted narratives) are capable of carrying impressions, ideas and affective associations through time.

Some changes to folk songs that occur through time are less accidental, more deliberate. Changes in social mores motivate conscientious tinkering, especially by interfering, well-meaning collectors: Carter reveals in her sleeve notes to Louis Killen's version of 'One May Morning' that the song had been 'deemed sufficiently indelicate to bring a blush to Edwardian cheeks and was duly doctored for publication'[57] – Killen chose to sing an undoctored (and therefore seemingly more 'authentic') version. In other cases, religious persecution may have driven imagery underground; folklorists have speculated, for example, on the 'true meaning' of the enigmatic song 'The Streams of Lovely Nancy':

> Oh, the streams of lovely Nancy are divided in three parts,
> Where the young men and maidens they do meet their sweethearts.
> It is drinking of good liquor caused my heart for to sing,
> And the noise in yonder village made the rocks for to ring.
>
> At the top of this mountain, there my love's castle stands,
> It's all overbuilt with ivory on yonder black sand,

Fine arches, fine porches, and diamonds so bright.
It's a pilot for a sailor on a dark winter's night.[58]

Lucy Broadwood and Anne Gilchrist speculate on the song's submerged meanings: Broadwood localizes the song to Cornwall (emphasizing the significance of words 'nance' and 'Marazion'), and identifies the castle as St Michael's Mount. Gilchrist proposes a more theological reading, discussing the song's resemblance to 'The Castle of Love and Grace' in the *Cursor Mundi*, and interpreting the poem as parable: 'The polished rock is Mary's heart; [...] the clear streams [...] are her mercy'.[59] Gilchrist recognizes the protective power of ambiguity from religious persecution:

> If this song be really in its first form a mystical hymn to the Virgin, the obscurity due to its allegorical character may well have enabled it to survive the Reformation and Puritan periods in popular use, whether or not the transformation to its present form has been deliberate or due to a natural and gradual process by which singers and printers have substituted new for forgotten verses and the familiar for the incomprehensible, making good the *lacunae* in the text and sense in their own way.[60]

Gilchrist proposes that the song's survival on its journey through violent times in British history has been facilitated by the emergence of 'lacunae' – areas of stasis, spaces in the text for ambiguity, which has given the song quasi-Darwinian advantage.

Carter read Broadwood's and Gilchrist's arguments when she wrote about this song in her dissertation. Like them, she lists the song's common picaresque elements – 'the mountain, the castle, the pilot light, the river or sea at the foot of the mountain'[61] – and observes that the 'extreme confusion, almost surrealist quality, of this text is constant':[62] after its corrosive journey through time, its arrival at nonsense is a stabilizing factor.[63] Through the stripping-out of meaning, the song has travelled safely through time to arrive finally in a position of stasis.

But from this stillness, movement begins anew, instigated by Carter, for she grabs the imagery of the castle in 'Nancy', and splices it with a recurring medieval concept of the Otherworld, situated

> on a mountain, perhaps, or on an island, or cut off from the every-day world by some sort of water barrier [...] a splendid castle, usually guarded by armed figures; and a garden, with a beautiful fountain or fair running streams, and trees and remarkable birds.[64]

This castle-composite is repurposed by Carter variously in, for example, the country house of 'Reflections', or the Doctor's castle in *Hoffman*, or the Marquis's amphibious castle in 'The Bloody Chamber'. In the otherworldly garden surrounding the house in 'Reflections', 'ragged robin and ground elder conspired to oust the perennials from the borders and a bright sadness of neglect touched everything as though with dust'.[65] Doctor Hoffman's Teutonic castle is 'a romantic memory in stone' and it shines: 'as the light faded, the castle began to open eyes of many beautiful colours for all the windows were of stained glass'.[66] The Marquis's 'luminous murmurous' castle in 'The Bloody Chamber' echoes the watery isolation of the castle in 'Nancy':

> And ah! his castle. The faery solitude of the place; with its turrets of misty blue, its courtyard, its spiked gate, his castle that lay on the very bosom of the sea with seabirds mewing about its attics, the casements opening on to the green and purple, evanescent departures of the ocean, cut off by the tide from land for half a day ... that castle, at home neither on the land or on the water, a mysterious, amphibious place, contravening the materiality of both earth and the waves, with the melancholy of a mermaiden who perches on her rock and waits, endlessly, for a lover who had drowned far away, long ago. That lovely, sad, sea-siren of a place![67]

Writing about 'Nancy', Carter reveals a deep understanding of the potent combination of loss of meaning coupled with potential for aesthetic beauty within these imagic fragments:

> this song contains a wealth of the commonplaces of medieval allegorical imagery, retained over the centuries with no notion of a further meaning than the sheer beauty of such imagery in itself, the magic of the pictures in the mind which it creates. Any meaning, any abstruse religious significance, earlier forms of this song may have had is now totally lost to us; it is a puzzle to which the clues have been forgotten.[68]

Folk song's ambiguous imagery, 'the magic of the pictures in the mind', becomes power in Carter's hands and she moves it on in a perpetual process of reconfiguration. She is stripping out the sung images from 'Nancy' and repurposing the sound of them, like a burden, weaving them back into her prose, so that they can enjoy a continued trajectory.

These songs, shapes and images are travelling through time, and become transformed by their journeys into objects of beauty and mystery; meaning is stripped from them; 'clues'[69] and 'keys'[70] are lost; origins are necessarily eclipsed, 'always already withdrawn',[71] and passed on only through a continuous process of 'displacement and 'non-understanding';[72] any attempt at hermeneutical comprehension in the ethnographic sense becomes speculative.[73] But singing these images gains the songs a space of sympathetic resonance with the incomprehensible, a physical understanding of the movement of words as just-words, muscle memory, a performative element of language akin to ritual and religion which imbues the act of enunciation with meaning. Just because we struggle to interpret the songs, does not mean they lack value or meaning. Nonsense, as Winfried Menninghaus argues in relation to fairy tales and folk tales, is '*ipso facto* proper to the [form] itself, a constituent of its "origin"', for 'displacement and incomprehension [are] positively indispensable'[74] aspects of mode of being; intrinsic, essential, *a priori*.

Carter used the songs she knew both as 'material',[75] infusing her own narrative with the substance of their characters and narratives, and at the same time used them as 'architecture',[76] emptying them of their meanings (as they have emptied themselves out through time) and absorbing their shapes, the 'magic of the pictures in the mind'. In *Hoffman* and 'Reflections', Carter spliced these various elements of 'Died for Love' and

'The Leaves of Life', together with a host of other cultural materials, developing simultaneously 'material' and 'architectural' modes of infusing her prose with their useful oscillations between movement and stillness.

'Died for Love' [17] and *Hoffman*

The folk song 'Died for Love' is one of the most pervasive in the folk singing tradition, and it seems to have preoccupied Carter's creative imagination because references to it pop up like weeds across her oeuvre. The song charts various overlapping journeys; the girls' initial journeys into the 'meadows' and their inevitable despoilment there, the girl-narrator's emotional journey towards a painful realization of her erstwhile lover's indifference, and her final intention to die, heading towards her grave 'both long and narrow'. In picaresque terms, the song relays the result of the picaroon's waywardness; he has impregnated the girl, abandoned her and moved on, and the song charts the resultant damage. But at the centre of all this movement, there rests the static, unchanging story of the abandoned woman's agony at being left holding the baby.

As well as the song's content, its journey through time, its various mutations and preservations, would have interested Carter. Many variants can be found in print, including 'In Woodstock Town',[77] 'My True Love Once He Courted Me',[78] and 'A Brisk Young Sailor'.[79] Recorded versions of the song also abound: in 1908 Joseph Taylor sang 'Died for Love' for the collector Percy Grainger, who recorded him onto wax cylinder.[80] Carter may have known Taylor's crackled version, and possibly Shirley Collins' banjo-accompanied 1959 rendition recorded by Alan Lomax,[81] but I proffer she knew Tom Willett's *a cappella* version best, because Paul Carter recorded Willett himself in 1962.[82] Given the date, it is entirely possible she was there in the room when it was recorded, as she accompanied Paul on some of his field trips.[83]

Figures 14 and 15 The Willett Family, *The Roving Journeymen: English Traditional Songs* LP, front cover, inner label (Topic Records 12T84, 1962). Copyright © Topic Records. Reproduced with kind permission of Topic Records.

Oh, it's down the green meadow where the poor girls they roam,
    A-gathering flowers just as they grow,
She gathered her flowers and way she came,
    But she left the sweetest rose behind.

Now there is a flower that I've heard say
    That never dies nor fades away,
But if that flower I could only find
    I'd ease my heart and tormented mind.

Now there is an alehouse where my love goes,
    Where my love goes and sits himself down,
He takes a strange girl on his knee,
    Now don't you think that's a grief to me?

Now a grief, and a grief, I'll tell you for why,
    Because she's got more gold than I,
But her gold will glitter, her silver will fly,
    And in a short time, she'll be as poor as I.

Now my love he is tall and handsome too,
    My love he is tall and slender too,
But carries two hearts in the room of one.
    Won't he be a rogue when I'm dead and gone.

Now dig my grave both long and deep,
    A marble stone, both head and feet,
And in the middle a turtle dove,
    To show the wide world I died for love.

Carter was referencing 'Died for Love' long before *Hoffman*. She was pondering its significance in a discussion on innocence in her journal on 22 May 1960 (see overleaf). Carter's careful description in *Several Perceptions* of a folk singing pub scene in which Anne Blossom is reduced to tears by a rendition of 'Died for Love' presumably comes from Carter's first-hand experience. She describes how the singer

> had a strident voice like honey on the blade of a knife. She was loving to show off and shone with exuberance. All the Irishmen joined in her song. She vamped out a thumping waltz time on the bass and sang with a brisk, pure lack of sentiment:
>
> He went upstairs to go to bed
>   And found her hanging from a beam,
> He took a knife and cut her down
>   And in her bodice a note he found.

> satisfy his natural & rightful desire for pleasure
> the greater part of his life must pass
> unhappily & without self-respect.
> But now I do see that Morris
> is soft where Trotsky is hard – a
> genuine love of mankind & an almost futile
> logical hatred of the machine are his most vital
> characteristics; but Morris is all right.
> Even Engels preferred the Tories
> to the Whigs.
>
> May 22 Why do they talk so much crap about
> innocence? As if lack of knowledge could
> ever be a good thing?
> I hate innocence.
>
> The Bloody Gardener
> Died for Love

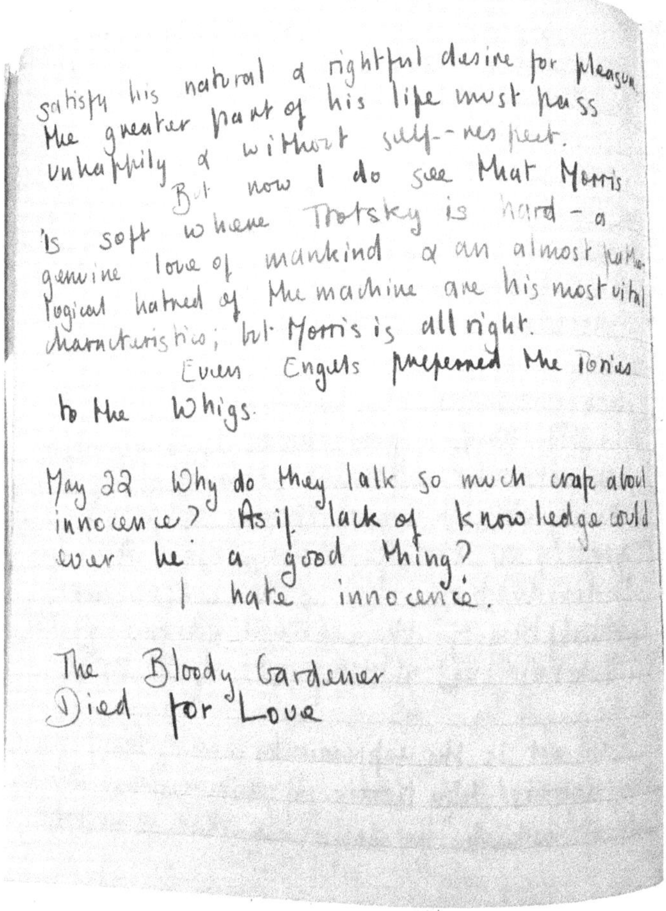

Figure 16 Photograph of a page in Angela Carter's *1960 Journal*, BL Add MS 88899/1/100. Copyright © The Estate of Angela Carter. Reproduced with kind permission of the Estate c/o Rogers, Coleridge & White Ltd., 20 Powis Mews, London W11 1JN.

> I wish I wish but it's all in vain,
>   I wish I was a maid again;
> But a maid again I'll never be
>   Till cherries grow on an apple tree.
>
> Dig me a grave both wide and deep,
>   A marble stone at my head and feet
> And in the middle a turtle dove
>   To tell the world I died of love.[84]

By evoking 'Died for Love' at this moment, Carter is deliberately infusing the story of Anne and her lost baby with 'the old, old story'[85] of the picaroon figure's destructive path through women's pre-contraceptive lives. The song surfaces again in Carter's 1983 essay 'Alison's Giggle', in which she borrows two stanzas from 'Died for Love' to posit an argument about sexual politics, education, and non-canonical women's cultural production:

> Since performance of traditional song is fairly evenly divided between women and men, and the anonymous material is kept alive and often considerably altered in performance, it is fair to assume that women not only shape the songs they sing but invented some of them, long ago, in the first place.
>
> When I wore my apron low
>   He followed me through frost and snow.
> Now I wear it to my chin
>   He passes by and says nothing.
>
> Although always found in the song called 'Died for Love', this is a 'floating verse', that may be used at appropriate moments in all manner of different versions of different songs. Sex; pregnancy; desertion. That is a woman's life.
>
> I wish my baby little were born
>   And smiling on its nurse's knee
> And I myself were dead and gone
>   For a maid again I'll never be.[86]

Carter can be seen repurposing the materiality of the song, its specific meaning of abandonment and its sexual-political-historical contexts, to elucidate her chosen narrative or argument.

In *Hoffman*, two overt references to this song surface at pivotal points in the novel's narrative arc, alerting us to the song's powerful material influence on the novel. Mary Anne the 'beautiful somnambulist', questions Desiderio dreamily, 'Don't you think it would be very beautiful to die for love?'[87] – and later, Albertina declares, as he plunges the knife into her chest, 'I always knew one only died of love'.[88] Carter summons this song at these two moments, asking it to work on us, perhaps using its associations to cast Desiderio in the role of the picaroon of folk song tradition, whose objects of sexual desire lie dead or dying in his arms, or casting him rather as the victim who will soon be abandoned by his lover forever – or perhaps playing on the ambivalence between the two to suggest he can play both roles at once.

But there are more obfuscate ways in which Carter borrows the song and puts it to work when we come to examine its influence on *Hoffman*. Carter can be seen experimenting with a method of borrowing the 'architectural' features of the song, its structural constituents, its shape, while discarding the less relevant details of its semantic or historical content. In *Hoffman*, Carter appropriates the 'architecture' of the song, not for the sake of the content, but for the sake of the form, and her handling of the raw components develops, from thematic references in narrative or polemical arcs, into architectural evocations of rhythm, narrative positioning, and symbology. She 'resolves' the song 'to its constituents',[89] taking useful elements onwards and jettisoning the rest – a technique she will later describe, when discussing *The Bloody Chamber*, as her intention 'to extract the latent content from the traditional stories and to use it as the beginnings of new stories'.[90] One can reverse-engineer this intentionality to see its origins in *Hoffman*, in the ways she extracts the 'latent content' from the folk song 'Died for Love' and uses it as the 'beginnings' of a new interrogation through her writing into the journeys of desire.

Carter's intimacy with the rhythmic shapes of 'Died for Love', through hearing it in oral contexts such as live performances and records, results in a prosodic engagement with the song, one which seeps into her imagination on a semiotic level and resurfaces in her writing through syntactical choices. The poetic act of dying-for-love in the song becomes sublimated within the rhythm of the iamb, the lilting, tripping rhythm of the heartbeat. The iambic rhythm of the final stanza in particular drips with sorrow and regret, leading us towards the grave of the mournful lover-singer:

```
  ˘    ´   |   ˘    ´   |   ˘     ´   |   ˘    ´
Now   dig  |  my  grave |  both  long |  and  deep
  ˘    ´   |   ˘    ´   |   ˘    ´    |   ˘    ´
A    mar-  | -ble  stone, | both  head | and  feet
```

'Died for Love' is not the only song to harness the iamb in such a way. The iambic journey towards death provides the prospect of reunion for separated lovers in 'Barbara Allen' (Child 84) when Barbara asks her mother to

```
  ˘    ´   |   ˘     ´   |   ˘     ´   |   ˘    ´
Make  my   |  bed   long |  and   nar- |  -row[91]
```

while Fair Margaret dies for love in violent iambs when she sees her sweet William marrying another in Child 74:

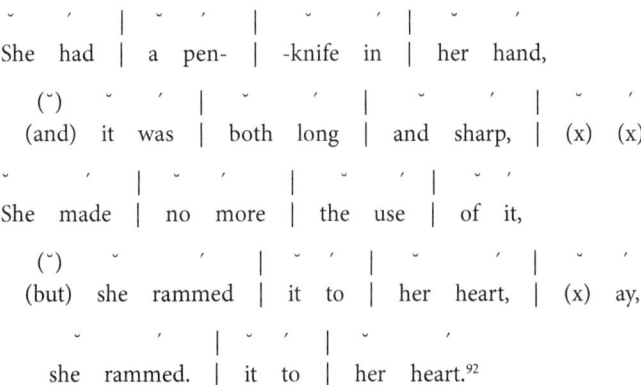

```
  ˘     ´   |   ˘    ´   |   ˘     ´   |   ˘    ´
She   had   |  a   pen-  | -knife in   |  her  hand,
  (˘)    ˘    ´   |   ˘    ´   |   ˘     ´   |   ˘    ´
 (and)  it  was   | both  long |  and  sharp, | (x)  (x)
  ˘    ´   |   ˘    ´   |   ˘    ´    |   ˘    ´
She  made  |  no   more |  the  use   |  of   it,
  (˘)    ˘    ´   |   ˘    ´   |   ˘    ´   |   ˘    ´
 (but)  she rammed | it   to   |  her  heart, | (x)  ay,
          ˘    ´   |   ˘    ´   |   ˘    ´
        she  rammed. | it   to   |  her  heart.[92]
```

In *Hoffman*, Carter repurposes the iambic shape of doomed lovers separated in life, united in death, from 'Died for Love' and these other songs. The iambs pump themselves out like heartbeats in pained, off-kilter beats, and remind the listener of other fundamental corporeal two-beat rhythms, rhythms such as sex, breathing, and walking:

```
 ˘   ´  |  ˘    ´
As  I  | roved out
```

Carter uses these iambic patternings in *Hoffman* to draw audial rings of delayed agony around the various manifestations of Albertina, who, we have been forewarned, will die at his hands:

```
 ˘    ´   |  ˘     ´    |  ˘    ´   |  ˘    ´
She  did  | not  speak; | she  did  | not  smile.⁹³

 ˘    ´   |  ˘     ´    |   ˘    ´    |  ˘    ´
mi-ra-   | cu-lous    | bou-quet   | of  bone⁹⁴

 ˘   ´   |  ˘     ´    |  ˘   ´   |  ˘    ´   |  ˘    ´
As  it  | drew  near | I  saw  | it  was  | a  swan.⁹⁵

  ˘    ´    |  ˘   ´   |  ˘    ´    |  ˘   ´   |  ˘   ´    |  ˘
Because   | I  know | I  looked | like Al- | -berti-   | -na⁹⁶

 ˘    ´    |  ˘   ´   |  ˘    ´    |  ˘    ´    |  ˘    ´   |
she  spoke | to  me | be-fore  | she  died. | She  said:

 ˘    ´   |  ˘     ´    |  ˘    ´    |  ˘    ´   |  ˘   ´
'I  al-  | -ways  knew | one  on-  | -ly  died | of  love.'⁹⁷
```

Even her name,

```
   ´   |  ˘    ´   |   ˘
Al-  | -ber  ti- | -na
```

can be read as a catalectic iambic construction, unfinished, endlessly deferred. Carter is infusing her prose with the rhythmic architecture of this journey towards the lover's grave, learned from the singing of it.

Dying for love in Carter's works is voiced, incanted even, by various characters across her oeuvre and, in each case, iambic connections can be threaded back to this folk song's rhythmic patterning. Suicidal jilted Joseph in *Several Perceptions* notes how

```
   ´   |  ˘     ´    |  ˘    ´    |  ˘    ´    |  ˘    ´   |  ˘    ´
Gas  | and dark- | -ness slow- | -ly gath- | ered  in | the room
```

how the clock

```
   ´   |  ˘    ´   |  ˘    ´   |   ´   ˘   |   ˘    ´
ticked | a- way | the last | beats of | his heart
```

and how the

re-morse | of grief | will make | a stone | throb like | a heart.⁹⁸

Even the 'love-| -ly la- |-dy vam- | -pire' in *Vampirella* insists

I al- | -ways knew | that love, | true love | would kill | me.⁹⁹

The rhythmic evocations, wherever they appear, trace the shape of the folk song 'Died for Love'.

Other architectural features borrowed from this song's infusion within Carter's depiction of the lover's journey towards the grave can be discerned in *Hoffman*'s narrative structure. Desiderio the protagonist is a careless traveller and lover, a self-declared picaroon, while Desiderio the narrator is an old man looking back on his life:

> Expect a tale of picaresque adventure or even of heroic adventure, for I was a great hero in my time though now I am an old man and no longer the 'I' of my own story and my time is past, even if you can read about me in the history books – a strange thing to happen to a man in his own lifetime. It turns one into posterity's prostitute.¹⁰⁰

He describes his young travelling self as 'bored', 'sardonic' and 'disaffected',¹⁰¹ a young man who sets off on 'the road that led north' without any clear destination: 'There was once a young man named Desiderio who set out upon a journey and very soon lost himself completely.'¹⁰² Albertina becomes the only object he can identify and, by killing her, he finally becomes 'a traveller who had denied his proper destination'.¹⁰³ He describes his journey in alliterative phrases reminiscent of folk song: 'So I left the highway and took a green path between hedgerows drenched with dew where soon the sweet birds sang.'¹⁰⁴ His journey, like that of music itself, is a continual series of expectations and frustrations, 'an enclosed system of tensions and releases, of resolutions (or non-resolutions) of discords and harmonies'¹⁰⁵ – a quest in which anticipation is created and forever inhibited.

Desiderio's love for Albertina will never be consummated, only frustrated and delayed, perverted – but like any good picaroon, along the way he will be randomly promiscuous. He despoils Mary Anne who sleeps through his attentions 'as if she were feeling my caresses through a veil',¹⁰⁶ and copulates with the grandmother of his betrothed among the River People 'while a pan of shrimp danced and spluttered on the charcoal stove'.¹⁰⁷ Carter imbues her protagonist's actions with the dalliances and depravities of the folk song rover, and her narrative begins to take on the recognizable shape, the architecture, of the picaresque song.

Positioning of the narrator also plays a part in seeping the song's shapes into the text: both the song narrator of 'Died for Love' and the prose narrator Desiderio, having lost their lovers, sit on the hinge between life and death. While the song narrator of 'Died for Love' asks us to memorialize her experience, to mark her grave 'to show the wide world I died for love', old Desiderio writes the 'thick book' of his 'memoirs' and dedicates 'all my memories to Albertina Hoffman with my insatiable tears'. As the song narrator's memorial will be a 'marble stone', so his shall be 'a fat book to coffin young Desiderio'. We are asked to 'read' them both.

The architecture of the song bleeds into the structure of the novel through borrowed symbols, too. The rose is an ancient symbol of female virginity (appearing in many other songs, such as 'Tam Lin' and 'Cupid's Garden'), and the girl who 'left the sweetest rose behind' is understood to have given sexual favour to her sweetheart.[108] Carter seeps this symbolic architecture into *Hoffman*; Mary Anne sleepwalks into Desiderio's bedroom, holding

> a rose in her outstretched fingers [...] A thorn under the leaves pierced my thumb and I felt the red rose throb like a heart and saw it emit a single drop of blood as if like a sin-eater it had taken on the pain of the wound for me. [...] When I woke in the common-place morning, nothing was left of her in the bed but some dead leaves and there was no sign she had been in the room except for a withered rose in the middle of the floor.[109]

Mary Anne will leave 'the sweetest rose behind' with him, but it is the presence of the rose which symbolizes Desiderio's unquenchable desire for Albertina: 'the rose [...] shook off its petals as if shuddering in ecstasy to hear her voice'[110] and with her death: 'I had unconsciously tucked that handkerchief stained with Albertina's blood into my breast pocket, where it looked just like a red rose.'[111] Desiderio's only penetration of Albertina is with the knife, which slips into her body in a parody of the ever-deferred sex act, and so the rose is not real, but a representation of a rose, the shape of a rose, formed from clot and cloth, because Desiderio's consummation of his love for Albertina is never a real consummation, only a representation of a consummation, achieved at one remove.

Carter can be seen in these ways to be handling 'Died for Love' both as a material object and as an architectural shape. Its materiality is useful, but not useful enough, for, while the lyric speaks of some kind of generic 'female' experience, it also proves that no such thing exists, reverberating to us across a chasm of time, from a lost world of archaic sex interrelations which can no longer be deemed 'universal' – in fact, which can barely be described as recognizable in Western modernity. Carter is a liberated woman – writing in the 1970s, sexually free, having left her first husband, living with her new lover in Japan, promiscuous, brave – the song's cautionary morality is redundant. Carter sees herself as 'a new kind of being [...] the pure product of an advanced, industrialised, post-imperialist country in decline [...] unburdened with a past. The voluntarily sterile yet sexually active being [...] a being without precedent'.[112] The dying-because-pregnant-and-ashamed semantics of the story have become nonsensical in the brave new Western world of women's rights, contraception, the morning-after pill and legalized abortion.

But this non-sense, this non-communication of past stories, the 'losing of the key' and the 'forgetting of the clue', is both an intrinsic part of the ways in which folk songs work on modern audiences, and an intrinsic part of how *Hoffman* works on its readers. As Susan Rubin Suleiman argues, the hallucinogenic insanity of *Hoffman* and its surrealist inscrutability become part of its power.[113] Carter's *Hoffman*, and within it her treatment of 'Died for Love', is an attempt at an interpretation of signs. Doctor Hoffman himself cryptically exclaims,

> All things co-exist in pairs but mine is not an either/or world.
> Mine is an and + and world.
> I alone have discovered the key to the inexhaustible plus.[114]

This oscillating relationship between comprehension and confusion expresses a dynamic paradox spinning at the heart of the material and architectural usage of these ancient songs in Carter's prose works, a paradox between the importance of interpretation, the extraction and application of some kind of material resonant meaning, and the endless deferral of meaning, the production of an excessive non-sense, the perpetuation of that 'curious abyss'[115] Carter found so deliciously productive.

'The Leaves of Life' [33] and 'Reflections'

As *Hoffman* is infused with 'Died for Love', so 'The Leaves of Life' (sometimes known as 'Seven Virgins') percolates through Carter's short story 'Reflections', via the song sung by Anna in the woods – 'Under the leaves,' she sang, 'and the leaves of life'.[116] In the song, the narrator Thomas is walking alone 'under the leaves' when he comes across Mary and her six female friends; they tell him to go down into the town to see Jesus in the last throes of his execution. Despite the movement of the followers along their trajectory to see Jesus, there is at the song's heart the stillness of the Christ figure, nailed to a peculiarly anglicized yew tree.

Although it was an Anne Briggs record cover that inspired Carter to write 'Reflections', Briggs never actually sang 'The Leaves of Life'.[117] Carter heard others singing it, either live or on record: she may have known Ewan MacColl's rendition[118] but, more likely, Norma Waterson's version on The Watersons' 1965 LP, *Frost and Fire*:[119]

> All under the leaves and the leaves of life
>   I met with virgins seven.
> And one of them was Mary mild,
>   Our Lord's best mother in Heaven.
>
> 'Oh what are you seeking you seven pretty maids
>   All under the leaves of life?'
> 'We are seeking for no leaves, Thomas,
>   But for a friend of thine.'

'Go down, go down into yonder town
    And sit in the gallery,
And there you'll see sweet Jesus Christ,
    Nailed to a big yew tree.'

So down they went into yonder town
    As fast as foot could fall.
And many a bitter and a grievous tear
    From them virgins' eyes did fall.

'Oh peace, mother, oh peace, mother,
    Your weeping does me grieve.
But I will suffer this,' he said,
    For Adam and for Eve.'

'Oh how can I my weeping leave
    My sorrows undergo?
While I do see my own son die
    And sons I have no more.'

He's laid his head on his right shoulder
    And death has struck him nigh.
'The Holy Ghost be with your soul,
    Sweet mother, now I die.'

Oh the rose, the gentle rose,
    The fennel it grows so strong.
Amen, good Lord, your charity,
    Is the ending of my song.

A song overlooked by Child, the earliest known version is in a small Manx manuscript carol-book dating from the 1820s; the song then appeared in broadsides through the nineteenth century and in a Staffordshire chapbook, *A Good Christmas Box*, in 1847. Mary McCabe suggests its provenance is far older, and that it was 'certainly composed before the Reformation, since it contains ideas and even phrases drawn from English religious lyrics dating from the thirteenth to the early sixteenth centuries.'[120] McCabe charts its journey through time, including some changes, like 'The Streams of Lovely Nancy', 'which must have been made after the Reformation'; she credits the song's survival on the successful ways in which it combines 'the devotion and pathos of the religious lyric with the narrative and dramatic strength of the traditional ballad'.[121] While 'The Leaves of Life' / 'Seven Virgins' is repeatedly classified as a Christmas carol by collectors, its themes seem more related to Easter-tide: Lloyd squares the circle by labelling it a 'spring-time ballad-carol', and discusses how the song's imagery recalls the 'handsome illuminations' of the 1075 Arundel Psalter, the 'sombre tree of death with its dismal birds, and the dazzling tree of life with iridescent leaves'.[122]

Figure 17 Image of *The Arundel Psalter* (1075). Copyright © British Library Board (Arundel MS 60, f.52v). British Library Online Gallery <http://www.bl.uk/onlinegallery/onlineex/illmanus/arunmancoll/c/011aru000000060u00052v00.html> [accessed 2 March 2022].

Here are the holy 'leaves of life' to which the song refers, although through the ballad-carol's evocation of the greenwood one might also glean suggestions in the foliage of mortal corruption and transformation.[123]

Carter's short story 'Reflections' takes the tensions between interpretability and inscrutability Carter developed in *Hoffman* and intensifies them, so that the oscillations between interpretation and obfuscation not only become a concern for the internal narratorial voice but also start to leak into Carter's anxieties surrounding her own authorial control. Carter is once more using folk song's material substance and architectural shape in her prose, emptying out the song and seeping its excessive inscrutability into her text. 'Reflections' is steeped in the folk song 'The Leaves of Life' from its very opening, and indeed the song momentarily offers (and then retracts) a glimmer of hope that it might provide a 'key' to unlocking some of the story's arcane mysteries. The wandering narrator-protagonist of the story is 'roving out' into the wood like any good errant *trouvère* when he hears a young girl singing:

> Her voice performed a trajectory of sound far more ornate than that of the blackbird, who ceased at once to sing when he heard it for he could not compete with the richly crimson sinuosity of a voice that pierced the senses of the listener like an arrow in a dream. She sang; and her words thrilled through me, for they seemed filled with a meaning that had no relation to meaning as I understood it.
>
> 'Under the leaves,' she sang, 'and the leaves of life' – Then, in mid-flight, the song ceased and left me dazzled.[124]

The acousmatic voice is, of course, singing the opening lines of 'The Leaves of Life'. At first the narrator hears only the disembodied voice before he sees 'Anna' (nearly 'Anne'), the girl singing. Steven Connor has observed the level of disquiet induced by the acousmatic voice: 'Sound, and especially the sound of the human voice, is experienced as enigmatic or anxiously incomplete until its source can be identified';[125] Carter infuses her prose with this ancient anxiety through the voice of the unseen singing girl.

The incomprehensible voice which 'thrills' through the narrator of 'Reflections' recalls the effect Albertina's 'hieratic chant'[126] as black swan has on Desiderio in *Hoffman*:

> there issued from her throat a thrilling, erotic contralto. Her song was a savage, wordless lament with the dramatic cadences of flamenco in a scale the notes of which were unfamiliar to me yet seemed those of an ultimate Platonic mode, an elemental music.[127]

But the incomprehensible voice in 'Reflections' is not always thrilling or inviting; as Anna prepares to rape the narrator, it seems as if her song has become performative, an intrinsic element of the violent act:

> Then, once again, she began to sing; I saw the mute, dark, fire burning like Valhalla in *Götterdämmerung*. She sang a funeral pyre, the swan's song, death itself, and, with a brusque motion of her gun, she forced me forward on my knees while the dog stood over me as she tore open my clothes.[128]

As 'Reflections' closes and the world through the mirror is shut off, the aged androgyne echoes Anna's song of the leaves:

> 'Did you not realize who I was? That I was the synthesis in person? For I could go any way the world goes and so I was knitting the thesis and the antithesis

together, this world and that world. Over the leaves and under the leaves. Cohesion gone. Ah!'[129]

Jesus' passion is evoked in the story via the song's reference at the moment the androgyne disintegrates and the mirror-world collapses around the emboldened narrator. Symbols from the song, such as the 'the rose, the gentle rose', which Gertrud Schiller explains is also a symbol of Christ's passion,[130] and fennel for flattery, reinforce the sense that the story is encouraging us in our desire for it to all *mean something*, a desire to furnish us with some kind of insight into the nature and purpose of the mystery of messianic sacrifice, or the true nature of the gender principle. The story seems weighed down with a burgeoning need for signification which exceeds its own explanation, laden with a mystery as profound as divinity, as if it were itself 'filled with a meaning that had no relation to meaning as [we] understood it.'

This inscrutability, this inexplicability, is perhaps the most important result of these songs' various journeys seeping through Carter's imagination. Both *Hoffman* and 'Reflections' repeatedly invite and then defy interpretation, asking us to move towards some kind of understanding before bringing us to a deliciously bewildering standstill. Robert Coover, in admiration of 'Reflections', describes it as 'a most mysterious tale: violent, magical, comic, menacing, seemingly transparent, but, like the mirror through it displays itself, bewilderingly deceptive'; Susan Sellers finds accounts within it 'vague' and 'confusing'.[131] Anna Kérchy describes *Hoffman* as a 'violent surrealist collage'[132] while Susan Rubin Suleiman calls it an intertextual 'web' and suggests there is pleasure if we simply admire it, 'even bask in it, without trying to untangle it' (although she cannot resist trying).[133] These critics repeatedly oscillate between double-desires of elucidating/comprehending these obfuscate texts and at the same time acquiescing into bewilderment.

Carter expresses the same oscillation through the figures of both Desiderio and the androgyne. Desiderio seeks to impose writerly control on the chaos of his life so that we might better understand him:

> So I must gather together all that confusion of experience and arrange it in order [...] I must unravel my life as if it were so much knitting and pick out from that tangle the single, original thread of my self, the self who was a young man who happened to become a hero and then grew old.[134]

The androgyne in 'Reflections' attempts through writing/knitting to stitch up the universe, 'knitting the thesis and the antithesis together'.[135] Through her very writing Carter is 'gathering together' her thoughts and 'arranging' them 'in order' to expose what she sees as society's lies: she is, after all, 'in the demythologising business';[136] even in her musicological writing – her sleeve notes for folk records, or 'Now is the Time for Singing' – she expresses a deep, underlying demonstrative tendency: 'And so she's going to have a baby';[137] she glosses old songs for us, makes them relevant for modern audiences, identifies new semantic resonances, justifies their presence through understanding. She declares that 'to understand and to interpret is the main thing'[138] – her hermeneutic efforts can be seen as an attempt to travel towards understanding.

But in the same sentence she confesses, 'but my method of investigating is changing'.[139] All this 'gathering together' and 'arranging' serves only to further confound and conceal interpretation. Robert Coover reveals from his private correspondence with Carter that sometimes, much to her own discomfort, she was unable to arrive at an interpretation of her own work. She wrote to him that 'Reflections' was

> one of the very few pieces that I made up as I went along. I usually work to a very tight schema, and I *still don't know what it means*. The imagery was in charge of me instead of vice versa.[140]

Carter appears not only to be surprised that she can neither understand nor interpret her own work, but also that she can attribute value to her own bewilderment.

Carter's repurposing of these folk songs and their infusion within her enigmatic texts resulted in a change in her writing methods. She now did not always want attempts at elucidation to be successful: there was a new creative intentionality to her enthralled bewilderment. Carter's folk singing praxis, and in particular her handling of picaresque songs, and mysterious songs whose lyrical content has, from journeys through time, become unintelligible, enabled her to infuse her writing with their inherent creative dichotomy between motion and stasis: the logical empiricism of the Minister versus the surrealist imaginative power of the Doctor, the quotidian reality of the forest versus the upside-down world through the mirror; the rational systems of bald explanation versus 'the lacunae of the text'.

Understanding Carter's changing attitudes towards unintelligibility in her fiction, a development I suggest she owed to her understanding of folk singing, reveals a double desire emerging in her work for stasis from movement, and elucidation from bewilderment.

Conclusion

Carter realized from her intimate engagement with the folk song form that semantic transformation of songs (both intentional and unintentional) was the pragmatic result of their journeys through time, space, generations and communities:

> Surely the 'mystery' of much folk-song springs from as unromantic an origin as the widespread diffusion of an original song-pattern, filtered through a multitude of sensibilities all privileged to alter a text as they please. Naturally, there is effected a gradual stripping away of the original circumstances of the song, such as the town in which the event described took place and the real names of the participants, or these names are altered, to fit the song to another community.[141]

But while these songs have been moving towards us, and while their vagabond heroes have been roving across the eternal springtime of the English countryside, they have paradoxically and simultaneously been creating 'lacunae in the text', spaces of still ambiguity to which the 'keys'[142] and 'clues'[143] of understanding have gradually been lost.

Carter saw the potentiality of these 'lacunae', these diffused pools of imagery, to provoke deep recognitions and resonances and, putting her intuitive understanding of them to work, she infused her writing in *Hoffman* and 'Reflections' with their mysteries. This process of 'assimilation',[144] and its product, 'shimmer',[145] Carter achieves in *Hoffman* and 'Reflections' through the music of the language itself and through the provocation of meditations on the ability of musical meaning to exceed verbal communication. In 'Reflections', the rambling narrator describes the voice singing in the woods as having 'no relation to meaning as I understood it':[146] the acousmatic singing voice, exceeding verbal communication, creates a 'shimmer' of non-verbal signification for the listener-narrator, in which we are immediately immersed and bewildered. In *Hoffman*, Carter creates an entirely musical system of communication in the language of the River People: Desiderio, like the picaroon of 'Reflections', is arrested by a disembodied female voice: 'the sound of a woman's voice speaking a liquid and melodious language which took me back to my earliest childhood'.[147] He hears, then acquires, the language of the River People through sounded learning, and formulates a mental grid of its functions:

> the meaning of their words depended not so much on pronunciation as intonation. They speak in a kind of singing; when, in the mornings, a flock of womenfolk twitter about the barge emptying the slops over the side and getting the breakfast, it is like a dawn chorus. The only way to transcribe their language would be in a music notation.[148]

This outsider's observation of the phonic, musical quality of non-comprehended language is reminiscent of Carter's own immersion in the Japanese language she could not understand, although Desiderio's willingness to learn it differs from hers. In her essay 'Tokyo Pastoral' Carter described the 'clickety-clackety of chattering housewives, a sound like briskly plied knitting needles, for Japanese is a language full of Ts and Ks'.[149] Sozo Araki recalls that Carter resisted learning the Japanese language when she lived there: 'I was truly surprised, not only by the fact that she was not keen to learn Japanese, but that she had zero interest in the language itself.'[150] Carter contradicts him when she writes, 'I kept on trying to learn Japanese, and kept on failing to do so', but she seems to have enjoyed the workaround she developed: 'I started trying to understand things by simply looking at them very, very carefully, an involuntary apprenticeship in the interpretation of signs.'[151] It was as if she were deliberately keeping herself estranged from it, to develop what Barthes describes as 'a delicious protection, [...] an auditory film which halts at [the] ears all the alienations of the mother tongue'.[152] She was thinking of language as music, enjoying the 'lacunae' in her understanding not because of her failure to understand it, but conversely because of her ability to create from it a sounded semantic imaginary.

Language and music share an essential quality: they necessarily must be experienced in time, unfolding along a temporal plane;[153] but paradoxically, Carter described her writing experience as atemporal – 'Doing *Dr H.* just isolated me completely from the passage of time'.[154] These oscillating states, at once historical and/and-not ahistorical, dynamic and/and-not static, oscillating and hallucinogenic, and/and-not nonchalant and disaffected, infuse her writing.

I propose Carter created the spectacular temporalities in 'Reflections' and *Hoffman* – queasy, mutable, immeasurable – drawn from her understanding of 'folk time'[155] and her singing and study of folk songs, cultural artefacts which sit both inside and outside time, with 'their own historicity' which they systematically defy, with an elastic relationship between the 'now of the time of singing' and the myriad pasts which folk songs at once summon, occupy, utilize, politicize, own and deny. Carter can be seen in 'Reflections' and *Hoffman* actively interpolating her musical understanding of the journey, and all the temporal tensions at work between song and singer, between timeless artefact and grounded nowness of the singer's embodied performance, surrounded by all the body's cyclic repetitive rhythmic micro-time-markers – heartbeats, breaths – enmeshed within the structure of the song's journey of verses, burdens, and choruses. Carter's understanding of the 'time for singing' overspills into the rhythms, symbols and structures of her prose in these texts and others, informing ways in which she represents the imagined audial relationship between text and reader, with its necessary temporal movements and simultaneous 'lacunae' of semantic collapse.

She knew these productive spaces, these lacunae within folk songs, because she sang them, and the developmental leap she reveals in *Hoffman* and 'Reflections' suggests a mediation made possible because of her own journey, and a determination to repurpose these gaps in memory and meaning, these gaps in time and space, to create not dry hermeneutics or even rational explanations, but new lacunae, new mysteries. By dissolving folk songs into these abstruse texts, she creates new kinds of productive semantic imaginaries, weaving 'invisible music' within, between and beneath her words, to create an architecture for the productive onward journeys of folk song elements. And this is how I believe Carter fulfils the commitment she made in her folk club manifesto, 'to further the natural evolution of contemporary work within the framework described by tradition'.[156] She was furthering folk song's 'evolution' by infusing her prose with its audial artefacts, and this book proposes that these songs were carried along within her prose on another journey, a journey into the future where musicians might 'hear' her prose, and become inspired by the 'songfulness' infused within it.[157]

6

'only a bird in a gilded cage': folk songs, avianthropes and the canorographic voice in 'The Erl-King' and *Nights at the Circus*

> 'Singing is to speech what is dancing is to walking.' [...] To speak is one thing. To sing is quite another.
>
> Angela Carter, *Nights at the Circus*[1]

In previous chapters, I have presented some of the evidence emerging from the newly discovered archive[2] that supports the supposition that Angela Carter's practice- and performance-based musical understanding, her muscle memory of performance, her singing and breathing of traditional folk songs into rich and renewed oral life, came to influence profoundly both her creative textual output and her imaginative life. I have been demonstrating how Carter incorporated her experiences of folk singing into her work, how she allowed 'the richness and allusiveness of imagery in folk poetry, which reaches one through singing almost on a subliminal level' to infuse her imaginative life, enabling a development of her 'appreciation', her 'imagination', her 'ability to think in images', her 'sensibility' and her 'perceptions', as she proposed, just as she was becoming a writer, in 1964.[3] I have so far presented ample evidence that, through writing, Carter was effecting the intention she professed to Father Brocard Sewell in 1966.[4] I have shown how, thanks to her deep immersion and lived praxis of the folk song form, Carter's writing is infused with its fluid gender identities, its fragmented spatial networks and its endlessly mutable temporalities.

Now I identify one of the resultant products of these influences: 'canorographic' writing, or, the embodiment of a quality of 'songfulness' Lawrence Kramer observes in sung poetry, applied here atypically to prose.[5] This identification of 'canorographic' writing (derived from the adjective 'canorous' meaning 'songful' or 'melodious') is itself a discursive continuation of Anna Kérchy's scholarly identification of 'corporeographic' writing in Carter's 'body-texts',[6] and it endeavours to isolate the hybrid/chimera of the singing 'voice' as it presents within Carter's prose style, embodied in structural features such as rhythm, syntax, and motif.

In the crucible of her fiction, Carter forges hybrids and chimeras, imaginary beings whose mixed bodies blur the conventional, expected boundaries between human, animal, vegetable, mineral, and 'other'. As she zoomorphizes, botanizes and crystallizes her humans, and anthropomorphizes her animals and plants, she creates uncategorizable beings, taxonomic mash-ups which provoke in the reader ruminations on the most profound ontological questions. Carter said she wanted to use her fiction to 'ask questions that can't be asked in any other way [...] to adequately describe ourselves to ourselves' and understood that 'literal truth might not be the whole truth'.[7] Her chimeric creations in particular, especially those which chart the 'becoming' of one thing into another, frame ontological anxieties for critics such as Elaine Jordan, Margaret Atwood and Anna Kérchy:[8] what exactly *is it* to be human, what (if anything) differentiates us from the rest of the natural world, what 'social fictions' require exposing and dismantling through this method of estrangement? What assumptions/delusions is Carter challenging in 'The Tiger's Bride' when her heroine's skin becomes 'beautiful fur',[9] or in *Nights at the Circus* (hereafter, *Nights*) when Fevvers spreads her 'notorious and much-debated wings',[10] or in 'Penetrating to the Heart of the Forest' when Emile and Madeline suck 'a sweet, refreshing milk' from the nipples of a tree,[11] or in *Love* when the doomed, suicidal Annabel morphs into a 'marvellous crystallization' of metal and jewels?[12] I propose that these figures come to represent Carter's hybridized canorographic style, and that they embody ways in which she hybridizes prose, voice, melody, lyric and performance. Carter's canorography is therefore operating at any one time on two levels, the hybridized and chimeric bodies of her fictive creations enacting the stylized hybridity and chimeric quality of her song-infused language.

The songs Carter was studying and performing address these ontological questions head-on. In their subject-matter, songs of transformation with which Carter was familiar such as 'The Twa Magicians' (Child 44)[13] and 'The Cruel Mother' (Child 20)[14] persistently worry and traverse perceived lines between states of being and, within their ancient repeated story structures, they normalize hybridic and chimeric interchange. In particular, the talking-bird complex in songs such as 'Lady Isabel and the Elf-Knight'[15] and 'Young Hunting'[16] revels in the ambiguity between bird and human, song and speech. David Atkinson explains, 'The talking bird episodes in anglophone ballads are capable of [...] disclosing at one and the same time the existence of, and the urgent desire to suppress, important secrets; and embodying the idea that all is not what it may seem with ballad characters.'[17] Barre Toelken emphasizes the multivalent significances of birds in folk song: 'The bird as messenger, as possible carrier of the soul, and as dramatic parallel to the male character clearly does at least triple duty.'[18] Stephen Benson describes birds and birdsong in folk narratives as 'straightforwardly a mark of otherness in being, precisely, otherworldly'.[19] Ruminations on birds, women, song, incarceration, and silence reverberate through Carter's oeuvre, and I propose Carter used the trope of the 'becoming-bird', the avianthrope – in particular the bird-girls of 'The Erl-King' and the bird-woman Fevvers of *Nights* – as the perfect vehicle for exploring the interface between narrative voice and singing voice in her prose. The 'dizzy uncertainty about what was human and what was not'[20] repeatedly evoked by these avian creations springs, in part, from Carter's repetitive hearing and singing of these strange folk song universes which, while they share with their folk-tale cousins migrations across taxonomic boundaries in a fluid world of wonders and terrors, crucially deliver that anxiety, and were handled by Carter, within primarily oral contexts.

We might look at Carter's chimeric creations through the lens of Gilles Deleuze and Félix Guattari's 'becoming-animal', the object 'not only of science but also of dreams, symbolism, art and poetry', and their observation that 'the relationships between animals are bound up with the relations between man and animal, man and woman, man and child, man and the elements, man and the physical and microphysical universe.' Transformations between these states can be seen as 'alliance', for the 'becoming-animal of the human being is real, even if the animal the human being becomes is not; and the becoming-other of the animal is real, even if that something other it becomes is not.'[21] Carter's chimeras and hybrids, viewed in this way, can be understood as being in a perpetual process of revealing 'ourselves to ourselves'; incongruous imaginary 'alliances' designed to expose our supposedly 'real' material states.

The terms 'hybrid' and 'chimera' may seem interchangeable; Donna Haraway, for example, could be using them as synonyms when she describes our dislocated contemporary experience: 'we are all chimeras, theorized and fabricated hybrids of machine and organism'.[22] Both terms have been used to describe the imaginary creatures that slithered out of Carter's imagination; Mary S. Pollock calls the Erl-King an 'animal/plant/human hybrid',[23] while Rosemary Hill, writing of Carter's 'mutable, unhuman creatures', describes Fevvers as 'a chimera, human only up to a never quite clarified point'.[24] But the terms do have subtly discrete meanings worth pausing to unpack.

Primary Oxford English Dictionary definitions of 'chimera' suggest a mythological being fabricated from disparate parts, a 'fabled fire-breathing monster of Greek mythology, with a lion's head, a goat's body, and a serpent's tail'. Secondary definitions include a 'grotesque monster, formed of the parts of various animals' or 'an unreal creature of the imagination, a mere wild fancy; an unfounded conception'. Carter forged creatures across her oeuvre who could comfortably be described by any of these definitions – caged prostitutes who are 'part clockwork, part vegetable and part brute',[25] or 'trees that bore, instead of foliage, brown, speckled plumage of birds'.[26] The word 'hybrid', by contrast, describes a being which is the result of more 'natural' reproductive processes between different sources, 'produced by the inter-breeding of two different species or varieties of animals or plants; mongrel, cross-bred, half-bred', or more loosely, an object which is 'derived from heterogeneous or incongruous sources; having a mixed character; composed of two diverse elements; mongrel.' A chimera might therefore be understood as a being in which there coexists discrete elements, whereas a hybrid is in a state in which elements are mixed to such an extent that discretion disappears. While both chimeras and hybrids share the same sense of incongruity, between these two terms there emerges a tension between 'discrete' and 'mixed', 'real' and 'unreal', 'born' and 'fabricated', 'natural' and 'simulated'.

I want in this chapter to develop conversations surrounding the hybrids and chimeras across Carter's oeuvre to expose a different, yet parallel, set of questions which relate to the presence of the singing voice in Carter's writing.[27] Carter knew intimately from her folk singing praxis another kind of hybrid or chimera: the song – a sounded form created by the voice from the 'alliance' of discrete yet symbiotic elements of lyrics, melody and voice. A relationship emerges between Carter's 'becoming-animals', especially her 'becoming-birds', and qualities of 'songfulness'. Carter knew that to sing words and music together is to forge a chimera: for in song 'words and music remain forever in dialogue with each other: born together, always separating and yet also always recombining and imitating each other.'[28] Simon Frith observes that 'to sing words is to elevate them in some way, to make them special, to give them a new form of intensity. [...] Singing seems to be self-revealing in a way that speaking is not.'[29] To sing is to 'become' immersed, merged, blended, hybridized, with one's environment, and with others. Victor Zuckerkandl describes this singer's 'becoming' experience as 'a living bridge':

> A person using words only is never with things in this sense: he remains at a distance from them; they remain for him 'the other', that which he is not, 'outside' him. By contrast, if his words are not merely spoken but sung, they build a living bridge that links him with the things referred to by the words, that transmutes distinction and separation into togetherness. By means of the tones, the speaker goes out to the things, brings the things from outside within himself, so that they are no longer 'the other', something alien that he is not, but the other and his own in one. [...] Only then can the tones fulfil their purpose: remove the barrier between person and thing, and clear the way for what might be called the singer's inner partition in that of which he sings – for an active sharing, an experience of a special kind, a spiritual experience. This experience is not a dreaming-oneself-out-of-oneself, not a dreaming-oneself-into-something-other, as though one were different from what one is. The singer remains what he is, but his self is enlarged, his vital range is extended: being what he is he can now, without losing his identity, be with what he is not; and the other, being what it is, can, without losing its identity, be with him.[30]

This somatic experience of 'becoming', of being linked to the world through the singing voice, blooms within Carter's prose in a voiced songfulness, a hybridized, chimeric, song-infused, resonant writing style: 'canorography'.

Paradoxically, while the state of the hybrid or chimera is incongruous and disparate, it is also unified, for it is a new entity. And while disparate elements in the form of the song – lyrics, melody, voice – are identifiable as separate parts, at the same time they are integrated to make a new object which cannot exist without the amalgam of its components, and which in its execution always exceeds the sum of its parts.[31] Folk songs are both the product of deliberate chimeric splicings[32] of discrete and often interchangeable elements of lyric, melody and narrative,[33] and yet, through osmotic oral transference, they are also accidental or 'natural' hybrids, ancient versions muddling together through unpremeditated folk processes in the melting-pot of intergenerational and transnational dissemination.[34]

Folk songs have of course, for centuries, also appeared in text form, in chapbooks and broadsides, in published collections such as Thomas Percy's *Reliques* (1765) or William Motherwell's *Minstrelsy* (1827), in text-only collations such as Child's five-volume *English and Scottish Popular Ballads* (1882–1898), or text-and-tune volumes such as Sabine Baring-Gould's *Songs of the West* (1905). As Steve Roud explains, 'There has not been a pure oral tradition for at least 500 years, and most folk songs owe their continued existence to their regular appearance in print.'[35] The boundaries between textuality and orality in folk song tradition prove to be porous at best.

But an argument persists amongst folklorists that a folk song written down is only a partial artefact, and that a folk song can only wholly be rendered in sung performance. As I discussed in Chapter 2, Zuckerkandl declares that 'only in so far as it is sung does the folk song really exist';[36] Robert Frost complains that the unsung ballad 'stays half-lacking'.[37] Ethnomusicologist Constantin Brăiloiu claims that the folk melody 'only exists at the moment when it is sung or played and [only] lives by the will of its interpreter and in the manner he chooses. Creation and interpretation merge together here – it must be repeated constantly – in a way that musical practice, based on writing or printing, ignores completely'.[38] Carter herself writes of folk song that 'the texts are nothing without the tunes [...] The whole – the song – does not exist except in performance'.[39] Although textual modes of transmission have played and continue to play an important role in the tradition's survival, only in its oral manifestations is it seen to thrive as 'living music'.[40]

I propose that Carter's conjuring of hybridic, chimeric beings in her fictions springs from that part of her imagination she describes as being influenced by the singing of ballads, and that it is therefore associatively sonorous, phonic, and canorous, stemming from her own personal and repeated oral engagement with folk song. Her writing begs us to listen to its 'word-notes'[41] as music, a demand traced through the figure of the bird-woman, who 'becomes' the embodiment of Carter's transformed and transcoded singing voice within the text.

Some critics have interpreted Carter's bestial hybrids and chimeras as metaphors for our complex human social interactions. Jordan reads Carter's engagement with animals in *The Bloody Chamber* anthology as self-reflexive, that which 'reminds us that we are animals'.[42] Atwood similarly interprets Carter's chimeras in *The Bloody Chamber* as extended metaphors for differences in human nature between 'lambhood' and 'tigerishness'.[43] Pollock and Anja Müller-Wood advocate more nuanced readings; Pollock proposes a Kristevan interpretation, situating them 'in a borderland between human consciousness and the consciousness of other species, the realm of the almost/not quite human'[44] while Müller-Wood notes Carter's 'repeated reminders that humans are animals'[45] and her wider naturalism.

These readings appear to miss intrinsic 'corporeagraphic' relationships between form and content in Carter's prose, a term I borrow from Kérchy who, while exploring Carter's predilection for 'disturbing corporealities' argues that Carter's persistent 'violations of human anatomy's frontiers'[46] are the result of a structural fusion in Carter texts between 'corporeal and textual performances'.[47] In *Nights*, Kérchy affiliates the textual performance of Fevvers' 'freakish' body and the corporeal performance of her laughter:

> The laughing bodies produce a laughing text via *somatized* complex sentences in which we find encoded a laughing person's rhythmic deep breathing. An overwritten, periodic style invites readers to enjoy the oral quality of Carter's text, to read it out loud, to model physiologically the functioning of the laughing body by embodying its very vibration. [...] It is especially on reading out loud *NC*'s carnivalesque, corporeally vibrated, complex sentences when we can fully enjoy the oral, vocal, tonal quality of the text. [...] the reader's breaths taken between the

too long clauses within one single sentence enact the rhythmic respiration one experiences during laughter.[48]

Kérchy's acoustic engagement with Carter's language evokes the presence of a physical musicality in Carter's prose which calls to mind her specifically somatic singing praxis. Developing Kérchy's theory of 'corporeagraphic' writing, my 'canorographic' approach exposes a fusion between prose and song located at the interface between narrative voice and singing voice in Carter's writing. To better understand this 'canorographic' writing style, which I suggest emerged from Carter's engagement with folk song, we need to examine the songs.

Avianthropes in folk songs

Folk songs in the British tradition, like their tale cousins, are steeped in metamorphic transformations, and Carter drew deeply on her intimate knowledge of them when she created her own unsettling fictional hybrids and chimeras. Songs Carter knew, such as 'The Cruel Mother' [26] and 'Tam Lin' [23], present human/animal transformations with quotidian comfort, and while she was to deploy across her oeuvre many different kinds (wolf, jaguar, tiger, and lion, to name but a few), I want to focus here on her female avianthropes, the bird-girls whose hybridic/chimeric bodies and singing voices come to signify not just the latent violence of female experience, but the hybridized canorographic voice in the text.

'The Cruel Mother' is a ballad of multi-elemental transformation which Carter analyzes in detail in her undergraduate dissertation.[49] A woman who murders her illegitimate twin babies in the greenwood to protect her reputation is haunted by their ghosts and set a penance of 'transmigration, and shape-shifting'.[50] Carter knew 'Tam Lin'[51] both from her textual knowledge of Child, and from her familiarity with Anne Briggs, who sang the variant 'Young Tambling' on her eponymous 1971 LP.[52] In Margaret's arms, Tambling changes first into 'a lion that runs so wild', then 'a loathsome snake', then 'a red hot bar of iron', and finally 'a naked man'; in other variants, he becomes an eel, a dove and a swan. This may appear at first to be a story about a transforming man, but, as Child explains in his hermeneutic notes, the Scandinavian ballad 'Natergalen'[53] is buried palimpsestically within the song's etymology. The 'natergalen' or nightingale is a bird/woman figure, who

> relates to a knight how she had once had a lover, but a step-mother soon upset all that, and turned her into a bird and her brother into a wolf. The curse was not to be taken off the brother till he drank of his step-dame's blood, and after seven years he caught her, when she was taking a walk in a wood, tore out her heart, and regained his human shape. The knight proposed to the bird that she shall come and pass the winter in his bower, and go back to the wood in the summer: this, the nightingale says, the step-mother had forbidden, as long as she wore feathers. The knight seizes the bird by the foot, takes her home to his bower, and fastens the windows and doors. She turns to all the marvellous beasts one ever heard of, – to a lion, a bear, a

variety of small snakes, and at last to a loathsome lind-worm. The knight makes a sufficient incision for blood to come, and a maid stands on the floor as fair as a flower.[54]

One can feel lurking behind 'Tam Lin', and behind 'Natergalen', an ancient shared story which might also have been the source for Ovid's Philomel, the princess raped, mutilated and silenced by her brother-in-law Tereus, who murders her nephew and is transformed into a nightingale. Spirited, disobedient women, incarceration, avian transformations, infanticide and sexual violence are topoi shackled together for millennia in the collective Western consciousness of shared stories.

The song 'Polly Vaughan' [34] tells of a girl accidentally shot by her lover when he mistakes her for a swan. Carter must have known intimately Briggs' recording of 'Polly Vaughan'[55] on *The Hazards of Love*: Paul Carter was its recording supervisor. Christine Molan also regularly performed 'Polly Vaughan' after the singing of Briggs at their club. Bert Lloyd was adamant that the tragedy of mistaken identity at the heart of 'Polly Vaughan' was an echo, a memory, of a more ancient song of shape-shifting:

> Modern scholars have little doubt that in fact 'Polly Vaughan' is a fine relic of a very ancient ballad concerning one of those magic maidens, familiar in folklore, who are girls by daylight but swans (or white does) after sunset, and are tragically hunted and killed by brother or lover.[56]

Carter was aware of other variants of this song, and notated in her folk notebook a different version (with a different story, but still associating a female subject with a swan), collected by Helen Creighton:[57]

Figure 18 Photo detail of 'The Swan' notated by Angela Carter, from Paul and Angela Carter's Folk Music Archive. Copyright © Christine Molan. Reproduced with kind permission of Christine Molan.

The figure of the swan, and its relation to violence, was to haunt Carter's creative imagination. It surfaces not only in *The Magic Toyshop* and *Nights at the Circus* via the Leda-myth, with its intimations of male sexual violence perpetrated upon a female victim, but conversely as the embodiment of female violence perpetrated upon a male victim.

In *Hoffman*, Albertina's song as black swan in Desiderio's dream communicates danger to him in metalinguistic terms (see chapter 5).[58] In 'Reflections', Anna's song is compared to 'the swan's song' as she prepares to rape the male protagonist in the through-the-mirror wood.[59] The opening description of her acousmatic singing voice is more reminiscent of Briggs' actual voice on the 'Polly Vaughan' recording: Carter describes it as like the song of a blackbird, 'the richly crimson sinuosity of a voice that pierced the senses of the listener like an arrow in a dream.'[60] Anna's acousmatic voice in Carter's wood evokes anxiety, its uncanny sourcelessness reigniting 'ancient and long-lived fantasies of the powers of the autonomous, dissociated, or quasi-objectified voice',[61] and providing the perfect example of the 'acousmatic situation'.[62] In its disembodiment it resembles the eerie voice in 'The Twa Sisters' [27] of the murdered girl's voice, the drowned girl mistaken for a swan, whose voice sings out from a musical instrument to announce the guilt of her sister: 'And then bespake the strings all three, / "O yonder is my sister that drowned mee."'[63] Through its macabre speaking and its swan-body imagery it too, must have seeped into Carter's imagination and waited. Carter was to draw on the power of the disembodied voice, and the singing-bone motif, when she came to write 'The Erl-King'.

These complex and ancient interconnecting elements of female voice, birdsong, violence and metalinguistic meaning are structurally regurgitated in the cante-fable 'The Story of Orange', which Carter discusses in her 1963–64 journal. The cante-fable form, in which a repeated song, embedded within a tale, takes on vital narrative functionality, is perhaps the most striking example there is of a working chimera between folk tale and folk song, in which both prose and song elements remain discrete and yet are entirely symbiotic. Carter transcribed 'The Story of Orange' in her journal, and included the dead girl's eerie song that, in this version, rings out from the cellar:

> My mamma did kill me & put me in pies,
> My dadda did eat me and say I was nice;
> My two little sisters came picking my bones,
> And buried me under cold marble stones,
> > *Cold marble stones,*
> > *Cold marble stones,*
> And buried me under cold marble stones.[64]

Although Carter was also reading Joseph Jacobs' *English Fairy Tales* at the time,[65] the primary source for her transcription of the 'Orange' story is not Jacobs' version but an essay in *The Journal of the Folk-Song Society* from 1906, co-authored by folk song collectors Frank Kidson and Anne Gilchrist.[66] Kidson transcribes 'The Story of Orange', introducing it as a cante-fable 'only dimly (and perhaps imperfectly) remembered by my niece, Miss Ethel Kidson', and includes a musical notation of the tune for the sung refrain portion. Gilchrist then elaborates, discussing various collected versions of the cante-fable before turning to Jacobs' version in *English Fairy Tales* called 'The Rose-Tree': 'The dead girl, transformed into a bird, *sang* this verse in the branches of the rose-tree under which the "little brother" had reverently buried her bones'. The cante-fable's alternating of song and prose, as both W. F. H. Nicolaisen and Gilchrist stress, emphasizes the importance of oral performance in its rendering.[67] As Stephen Benson explains, the potency of the repeating song motif within the tale creates a new chimera:

> The birdsong in 'The Juniper Tree' is extraordinary, a moment of excess in what is an infamously excessive story [...] The eightfold repetition of the refrain is bludgeon and lyrical incantation, while acting also as one of those delightfully cunning fairy-tale devices, a recounting of events that becomes an event in itself: a lesson in how to do things with song. The song is artful contrivance and a thing of nature; it is human and it is animal.[68]

Courageous women, bird-transformations, infanticide, and sexual violence are topoi bound together by story, elements Carter would appropriate and hybridize, blending them with her own 'canorographic' writing/performing 'voice' to create the hybrid/chimera of the 'songful' or 'canorographic' text which, through its acoustic texture, is itself in the process of 'becoming' every time it is read.

Birds and voice in 'The Erl-King'

Carter wrote 'The Erl-King' sometime between October 1976 and July 1977, as she was penning other stories which would comprise the collection *The Bloody Chamber*.[69] 'The Erl-King' differs from its siblings: it does not, to my knowledge, have roots in Charles Perrault's fairy tales (a feature it shares with 'The Snow Child'), but springs more from a blend of Carter's deep knowledge of European texts such as Goethe's 'Erlkönig' and Grimm's 'Fitchers Vogel' with English and Scottish folk songs she knew such as 'Lady Isabel and the Elf-Knight' and 'Hind Etin' (see Chapter 4).[70] If, as I propose, Carter had these folk songs ringing in her ears as she wrote 'The Erl-King', then the new archive proves the extent to which she was drawing on a specifically oral sets of materials, from her own listening and singing of these forest-men and bird-girls from the tradition. Such knowledge points to the possibility Carter was hybridizing her own orally framed understanding and experience of singing into textual language, merging sounded understanding with textual influences (texts themselves arguably springing from orally situated *ur*-texts), to arrive at her own chimeric, 'canorographic' style.

Carter described her Erl-King as 'a non-human genius loci'[71] whose physical attributes were inspired, in part, by her partner Mark Pearce, whom she describes in her journal as

> a tree, with birds in it; a gaunt, tall, woodland being, with the shyness natural to those who live elsewhere, not here, not among us [...] Grace & unsureness of a wild animal, a young horse, perhaps, or a deer, that comes to take bread from your hand & starts back when you speak to it.[72]

Her Erl-King's innate sexuality in particular emanates from her intimate knowledge of the magical sexually charged forest-men of folk songs: Young Tambling,[73] King Orfeo,[74] the Elfin Knight,[75] and the Elf Knight[76] are all forest-men Carter knew well, and they reverberate throughout her own greenwood story.

Evocations of bird-song, bird-women, and the search for 'meaning' in music permeate the story thematically, from which a series of vocal chimeras emerges: the voice of the bird and/and-not the human; the voice as speaking and/and-not singing; the voice as present and/and-not acousmatic; the voice as phonic and/and-not silent. Carter's narrator-protagonist, wandering into the wood, at first mistakes the Erl-King's pipe-song for bird-song: 'That call, with all the melancholy of the failing year in it, went directly to my heart.'[77] She associates it with the song of Philomel:[78] the 'two notes of the song of a bird rose on the still air [...] one rising note, one falling note'.[79] The nightingale's song has been repeatedly appropriated by poets 'from Homer to T. S. Eliot'[80] to express in sound the most complex of human emotional states: Micha Lazarus observes Petrarch puzzling 'over the meaning of the nightingale's song and its relation to his own [...] The poet knows the nightingale is singing his song [...] but he can't tell what, in fact, that song is about'.[81] Carter's narrator-protagonist attempts to interpret the Erl-King's faux-bird-song in the same way: she feels 'as if my girlish and delicious loneliness had been made into a sound'.[82] But this bird-song is fake: it has been made by a magical man with a musical pipe. The Erl-King is capable of verbal language ('skin the rabbit, he says!', 'He told me about the grass snakes')[83] but he is far more eloquent, far more dangerous, in the musical language of his pipe, raising questions of whether music as language is more human or more animal, and whether music might be a hybridic site of intersection between the two.[84]

The incarcerated bird-girls the narrator-protagonist finds in the woods are chimeras which give Carter's 'canorography' particular imagic shape. Differentiated from the wild birds in the woods, these are 'singing birds'[85] the Erl-King has trapped with 'his magic lasso of inhuman music'[86] because they are 'the sweetest singers'.[87] These bird-girls are 'natural' in the sense that they have been caught from the wild, but fabricated in another because, as we discover, they have not always been birds. A conflation begins to emerge between ideas of trapped birds and trapped girls; the narrator-protagonist senses she is being ensnared by the Erl-King's music like the birds in the cages: 'He winds me into the circle of his eye on a reel of birdsong,'[88] and she recognizes via Blake's caged bird[89] the imprisoning process underway in their relationship with which she is complicit: 'I shall become so small you can keep me in one of your osier cages and mock my loss of liberty. I have seen the cage you are weaving for me; it is a very pretty one.'[90] Her hoped-for defiance will reverse the incarcerated bird-girls' metamorphosis: 'Then she will open all the cages and let the birds free; they will change back into young girls, every one.'[91] The bird-girls and their bird-cages are symbiotic; free, the girls will regain human form; their dependence upon cages can be read not only as a critique of what Carter saw as illogical female dependences upon incarcerating patriarchal structures, but also as a comment on the need to engage the very words of the oppressor to think/write/speak/sing oneself out of captivity.

The narrator-protagonist translates the bird-girls' song into polyphonic human music: 'Sometimes the birds, at random, all singing, strike a chord,'[92] and finally their songs carry emotion: 'now I know the birds don't sing, they only cry because they can't find their way out of the wood'.[93] Despair, disorientation, anxiety: the bird-girls' songs 'only a bird in a gilded cage'   123

take on human intention. There persists an ambiguity between the voice of the narrator-protagonist and the song of the bird-women, a slipperiness of intention and location intensified grammatically by Carter's nauseating pronoun and tense shifts.

Carter also creates musical tensions between voices and silences. The narrator-protagonist decides at first to withhold her song from the Erl-King: 'I shall sit, hereafter, in my cage among the other singing birds but I – I shall be dumb, from spite.'[94] Bird-vocalization here is equated with female acquiescence to power; the incarcerated bird-girls' songs are a sign of collusion with their captor, and she therefore initially chooses silence as resistance.[95] For Carter, the relationship between music, meaning and silence is symbiotic; Carter's poem 'Leide'/'Liede',[96] appearing here in her 1972 journal, attests to this:

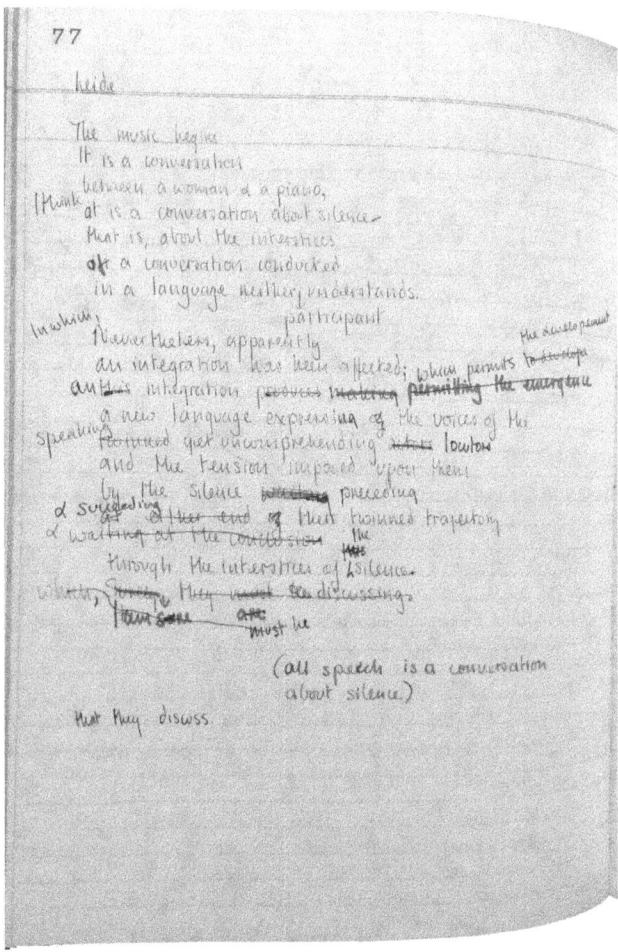

Figure 19 Photograph of a page in Angela Carter's *1972 Journal*, BL Add MS 88899/1/94. Copyright © The Estate of Angela Carter. Reproduced with kind permission of the Estate c/o Rogers, Coleridge & White Ltd., 20 Powis Mews, London W11 1JN.

At the bottom Carter has written: '(all speech is a conversation about silence)'. But, as Carol Gilligan proposes, for women to alter, or to silence, their voices in the face of patriarchal power, for whatever reason, is problematic in itself:

> Women's choices not to speak or rather to dissociate themselves from what they themselves are saying can be deliberate or unwitting, consciously chosen or enacted through the body by narrowing the passages connecting the voice with breath and sound, by keeping the voice high in the head so that it does not carry the depths of human feelings or a mix of feelings and thoughts, or by changing voice, shifting to a more guarded or impersonal register or key. Choices not to speak are often well-intentioned and psychologically protective, motivated by concerns for people's feelings and by an awareness of the realities of one's own and other's lives. And yet by restricting their voices, many women are wittingly or unwittingly perpetuating a male-voiced civilization and an order of living that is founded on disconnection from women.[97]

Carter's narrator-protagonist in 'The Erl-King' appears finally to concur with Gilligan, because she changes her mind and decides she won't be silent, or trapped: 'I had no wish to join the whistling congregation he kept in his cages'.[98] She ultimately refuses to comply with the Erl-King's desires; she refuses to become a trapped bird, she will neither be transformed, nor mute; she will neither sing, nor be objectified; for as Carter has stated elsewhere, to 'be the object of desire is to be defined in the passive case' and to 'exist in the passive case is to die in the passive case – that is, to be killed'.[99] She chooses rather to act; she will kill, and liberate, as she narrates. She aligns her self-reflexive, self-aware persona with the Petrarch-poet, the listener, who interprets the voice of the bird she hears, the voice of the Erl-King's desire, and bends its meaning to suit her desires, not his.

The mysterious disembodied voice, 'Mother, mother, you have murdered me!'[100] at the story's close forges a final, acousmatic chimera. The acousmatic voice here, a voice 'whose source one cannot see, a voice whose origin cannot be identified, a voice one cannot place',[101] serves as another manifestation of Carter's discarnate singing 'voice' within the text. At the same time it forges another chimera, one from folk song trope and classical allusion: the acousmatic 'voice' of the drowned sister in 'The Twa Sisters' singing from the bone-instrument strung with hair, a favourite ballad of Carter's to sing,[102] is fused with the cry of Ovid's Itys – 'Mother! Mother!' – as he is butchered by Philomel and Procne.[103] The acousmatic 'voice' that emanates from the Erl-King's fiddle evokes all the oral *ur*-stories that predate and nourish these texts, and with them Carter's own singing 'voice', dislocated from its body, yet embedded and resonating within us as we read.

Birds and voice in Carter's *Nights at the Circus*

Carter developed the bird-girls of 'The Erl-King' into Fevvers, the magnificent bird-woman of *Nights at the Circus*. The biographical details of Fevvers' upbringing and career echo the real-life story of Edith Piaf, 'The Little Sparrow'.[104] Fevvers' fictive etymologies and genealogies, I suggest, owe much to this songful and avianthropic significance.[105] If Fevvers hatched 'out of a bloody great egg'[106] and takes 'after her putative father, the swan, around the shoulder parts',[107] she is more hybrid than chimera, as she is the biological product of the union of unknown parents.[108] Yet, other descriptions suggest more deliberate, chimeric stitchings: 'not a woman at all but a cunningly constructed automaton made up of whalebone, india-rubber and springs.'[109] She is continually in a state of 'becoming', inventing herself as 'wonder' rather than 'freak' every time she steps onto the stage, experiencing 'the freedom to juggle with being'.[110] Fevvers is the consummate talking, singing bird, separating herself from humanity through the mechanics of the stage paradoxically in order to be more accepted by those who gaze upon her. In these terms, Fevvers is at once both hybrid and/and-not chimera; both 'natural' and/and-not 'constructed'; both 'hatched' and/and-not 'made'. Fevvers' wings are not just the wings of Apollinaire[111] and Cixous,[112] but of Philomel, the nightingale song-bird yoked through literary history to song, women, loss, and elusive musical meaning. She is one of Haraway's cyborgs; she has 'made thoroughly ambiguous the difference between natural and artificial, mind and body, self-developing and externally designed',[113] and a strange being, part animal and part human in a long chain emanating from folk song tradition, at once unnatural and yet a part of the magical, un/knowable, natural universe.

Fevvers may not live in the greenwood, but the overarching structure of *Nights at the Circus*, its three 'beats' of London, Petersburg and Siberia, sound out in Schenkerian terms the dactylic sound of the greenwood, and mortal danger, for anyone listening.[114] Like the trapped bird-girls, Fevvers is both a part of nature and yet excluded from it: 'hatched'[115] and yet carrying 'the great burden of my unnaturalness'.[116] While the bird-girls of 'The Erl-King' can 'change back into young girls',[117] Fevvers cannot – although perceptions of precisely what she is are just as mutable: Walser wonders if she is 'really a man?'[118] or perhaps and/and-not 'a real bird';[119] her 'quivering wings'[120] might be 'real' in the universe of the text, or they might be manufactured; Walser wonders, 'who had made of her a marvellous machine and equipped her with her story?'[121] She actively encourages the world's endless speculation: 'For, in order to earn a living, might not a genuine bird-woman – in the implausible event that such a thing existed – have to pretend that she was an artificial one?'[122] She is by speculation both trapped and/and-not independent, symbolized by her stage bird-cage prop: unlike the osier bird-cages of the Erl-King's bird-women, Fevvers' faux-cage is comprised of flimsy 'tinsel bars',[123] and with them she plays onstage with images of incarceration; yet, always fiscally insecure, always vulnerable to 'those unpredictable catastrophes that precipitate poor folks such as we into the abyss of poverty',[124] she never truly feels free. Lizzie asks, 'Does it seem strange to you? That the caged bird should want to see the end of cages, sir?'[125] The Grand Duke's magic-surrealist miniature golden bird-cage, in which he threatens finally to capture her, joins the Erl-King's cages and the gilded cage of marriage in Fevvers' signature song as symbols of the 'constraints the world imposes'[126] that Fevvers endlessly evades through performance.

Atkinson points out the figurative resonance of birds and cages ringing through the folk song tradition: 'For a social system that places a high value on female chastity, a bird in a gilded cage is a highly pertinent emblem.'[127] Caged birds, Atkinson argues, represent women safely under societal control; uncaged birds represent unrestrained female sexuality which threatens the patriarchal social order. Carter interrogates the nature of freedom by negotiating Fevvers around these variously perceived bird-cages, these restrictions on her magical, nearly-female body – does it matter whether the cages are/are-not? whether her wings are/are-not? whether her freedom is/is-not? For surely what matters is her/our perception of them – these figurative bird-cages are Blake's 'mind-forg'd manacles'[128] that Carter was so desperate for her fictions to expose and break open.

But more than her fantastical body, it is Fevvers' voice, the mesmeric acoustic performance of herself, which is, I argue, the real locus of Carter's most daring chimeric and canorographic construction of all, an identity emerging from disparate, incongruous parts, not just in terms of semantic content, but of musicality and sonic texture.[129] Fevvers' voice envelops and elides all the vocal chimeras Carter first conjures in 'The Erl-King': the voice as speaking and/and-not singing; the voice of the human and/and-not the non-human; the voice as present and/and-not acousmatic; the voice as resonant and/and-not silent.

Fevvers' voice is a chimera of speech-song-noise. Carter gives it fleshly, musical presence, a sonic texture, whether in her reported speech (just listen to 'a subtext of fertility underwrote the glittering sterility of the pleasure of the flesh available within the academy')[130] or her narratorial voice ('there slides past that unimaginable and deserted vastness where night is coming on, the sun declining in ghastly blood-streaked splendour ...'),[131] what Barthes calls 'the "grain" of the voice [...] the body in the voice as it sings',[132] what Benson describes as 'the imagination of sound, of the *sound* of a voice';[133] what Ihde portrays as: 'a "singing" of voice in writing.'[134] We 'hear' Fevvers' voice 'dipping, swooping';[135] Carter demands we imagine Fevvers in phonic terms, perform her, sing her into existence with our own 'inner voice',[136] creating another aural chimera – that between author and reader.

Carter fills our heads with the sounds of Fevvers' voice from the very first sentence – '"Lor' love you, sir!" Fevvers sang out in a voice that clanged like dustbin lids.'[137] Her textured voice speaks, sings and bangs, blurring the distinctions between words, speech, song and noise. Her discourse is musicalized with sounded rhetorical devices: alliteration ('I love the sight and stink and bustle of humanity'),[138] onomatopoeia ('Squeak, twang, bang and splash; squeak, twang, bang and splash'),[139] and linguistic fillers ('Oooo-er').[140] Her voice is sometimes bestial: it 'rasped like the tongue of a tiger'[141] – and sometimes 'raucous', raised 'in not unmelodious if brassy song. "Only a bird... in a gilded cage ...".'[142] Fevvers' voice performs on the margins of songfulness, for as Lazarus explains, 'the nightingale topos is *about* oscillation between semantics and sound [...] the acoustic dissolution of words into sound, words at the very edge of song.'[143] Fevvers' voice, like the Erl-King's elder-pipe, is mesmeric: it winds Walser (and the reader) to her on a magical spool of sound:

> Her voice. It was as if Walser had become a prisoner of her voice, her cavernous, sombre voice, a voice made for shouting about the tempest, her voice of a celestial fishwife. Musical as it strangely was, yet not a voice for singing with; it comprised discords, her scale contained twelve tones. Her voice, with its warped, homely,

Cockney vowels and random aspirates. Her dark, rusty, dipping, swooping voice, imperious as a siren's.[144]

Even Fevvers' silences are musical. Carter notates her discourse with rests, like musical staves, marked out in Empsonian terms[145] by bodily rhythms: 'She paused for precisely three heartbeats'[146] 'Pause of a single heartbeat';[147] 'Pause of three heartbeats.'[148] Her voice is materially present, and when Fevvers is silent, Walser feels physically abandoned:

> She said nothing else. Walser was intrigued by such silence after such loquacity. It was as though she had taken him as far as she could go on the brazen trajectory of her voice, yarned him in knots, and then – stopped short. Dropped him.[149]

Her voice might even be considered 'magical': Walser compares her and Lizzie to 'two Scheherezades, both intent on impacting a thousand stories into the single night'. But Fevvers' voice is also grounded in realia: 'Extraordinarily raucous and metallic voice; clanging of contralto or even baritone dustbins.'[150] Fevvers' voice, like her body, pivots on a perpetuated ambiguity between 'natural' and 'fabricated', 'hybrid' and 'chimeric', taking on seemingly acousmatic qualities:

> Yet such a voice could almost have had its source, not within her throat but in some ingenious mechanism or other behind the canvas screen, voice of a fake medium at a seance.[151]

Her voice is an endlessly shimmering chimera of natural musicality and intentional fabrication, her discourse a mash-up of classical and vernacular.[152] But while the incongruities of her chimera-body and her chimera-language make her appear strange, their compatibility, and their internal consistency-in-strangeness, create the impression of chimeric unity.

Fevvers' voice is quotidian, a 'dustbin lid' voice, the voice of popular culture, closer to the untrained voices in the folk clubs Carter sang in, or the music halls she would explore further in *Wise Children*, and therefore differentiated from the high-art voice of Mignon in *Nights*, whose recitations of 'Where the lemon-trees grow'[153] and 'Winter Journey'[154] Carter/Fevvers describes with such exquisite musicological detail:

> When we first heard her sing, in my room in the Hotel de l'Europe, it sounded as if the song sang itself, as if the song had nothing to do with Mignon and she was only a kind of fleshy phonograph, made to transmit music of which she had no consciousness. That was before she became a woman. Now she seized hold of the song in the supple lasso of her voice and mated it with her new-found soul, so the song was utterly transformed and yet its essence did not change, in the same way a familiar face changes yet stays the same when it is freshly visited by love.[155]

Mignon's voice is also the acousmatic voice in the wilderness that shakes Walser from his hallucinogenic torpor:

> Out of nowhere, or out of the pale blue sky, [...] there came a voice raised in song – a human voice, a woman's voice, a lovely voice. Such a voice you might believe would bring on spring-time prematurely. A voice to quicken all the little flowers...[156]

Carter does not suggest Fevvers' voice is any less potent for these associations – far from it – for it is the voice that will 'twist and shudder across the entire globe'.[157] Fevvers' voice in the text is Carter's voice, itself multifarious, not 'dead', for Carter 'went in for the proliferation, rather than the death, of the author'.[158] Fevvers' and Carter's voices blend and meld together until, like a hybrid, one can hardly discern a difference between them. This mixed voice protrudes through the text in the excessive 'self-irony'[159] of *Nights*, itself a chimera; for irony itself, says Haraway, is 'about the tension of holding incompatible things together because both or all are necessary and true'.[160] Carter through Fevvers is performing Haraway's 'cyborg', or Ihde's '"singing" of voice in writing', or Barthes' 'grain', using Fevvers to allow us to hallucinate[161] Carter's own voice. Fevvers can be read as the chimeric embodiment of Carter's 'songfulness', Carter's 'canorography', Carter's sounded folk-singing voice transcoded into her prose.

Conclusion

Fevvers' vocal and corporeal performance as bird/woman embodies Carter's canorographic prose, itself a chimera of body/voice/song/text. As bird-woman, Fevvers is the singer and the song: her voice sings, and her incongruous body performs hybridized, chimeric unions; in her discourses the vulgarities of the *illiterati* are hybridized with classical allusion, muddled in promiscuous folk-song melee. Our ontological anxiety around Fevvers stems not just from her 'freakish body'[162] but from her palimpsestic, chimeric vocal performances; as folk songs take old tunes and overlay new words, so Fevvers is a new tune to an old song, a phenomenon of lexical recycling, a translation in which 'something is being re-used, remembered, or re-sounded'[163] – Philomel, Winged Victory, Angel of Death, Azrael, Bird in a Gilded Cage – Fevvers is at once outside history ('You never existed before')[164] and yet, we know her, we've met her already; she bubbles up from our collective memory of ancient bird-women whose performances of suffering, incarceration, silence, and song is trapped forever in the resonance of recognition. Old bottles, new wine;[165] old images, new performances.

Fevvers' performance as bird/woman can be read as a direct expression of Carter's enmeshed and hybridized style, in which she embodies her vocal singing praxis to produce a canorous, oral, songful, acoustic text: song and/and-not prose. Through incongruous corporeal and linguistic combinations, embodied most completely in the chimeric voice and body of Fevvers, Carter is able to reify an 'alliance' between song and text, a song-infused writing, in which all the elements of song (music, lyric, voice) become embedded structurally within her prose, to create, not a 'New Age' or a 'New Woman', but a 'New Text' – a hybrid, a chimera – which is canorography: song-infused musico-literature. The becoming-bird-human-speaking-singing figure is the very enactment of this canorographic hybridity, and it flows directly from Carter's physical immersion in the folk song tradition.

Carter learned from the singing of ancient folk songs how to negotiate, repurpose and mediate old material, how to create hybrids and chimeras, how to sing old songs in new mouths, how to perform acts of 'creation, not resuscitation'.[166] Through the figure of the bird-woman, Carter sings herself into a new world, 'becoming-song', changing the world as she does so, her canorographic performances the inspirational springboards for new performances, new becomings, new songs.

7

'continued threads': Angela Carter and the folk singer Emily Portman

Those images that Carter was creating, both in the fairy tales and in her own writing, felt to me like continued threads from the folk songs that I'd been listening to. I think that was really exciting for me. [. . .] it did feel like she was a link between the songs and the stories for me.

Emily Portman[1]

The proposition I make – that Carter's folk song praxis had profound effects upon her prose production, and that she seeped her singing experience into her writing to create a song-infused 'canorography' – is fortified by the preponderance of contemporary folk, indie-folk, pop and rock musicians who cite her as a major musical influence.[2] Björk, PJ Harvey,[3] Bat for Lashes,[4] Aidan Baker,[5] Laura Marling,[6] Patrick Wolf[7] and Honeyblood[8] all either directly specify her influence on their creative outputs or have critics routinely forge such connections for them. The Blue Aeroplanes named a song after her on their 2001 album *Anti-Gravity*;[9] lead singer Gerard Langley was at Sheffield University when Carter was teaching there, and they collaborated on a literary project; he claims she made 'a lasting impression' on him.[10] Wolf Alice,[11] Wise Children[12] and The Tiger's Bride[13] invoke Carter by their very names.

Emily Portman

Emily Portman, the award-winning and critically acclaimed folk artist, openly discusses Carter's profound influence on her work.[14] To date, Portman has released three solo albums – *The Glamoury* (2010), *Hatchlings* (2012) and *Coracle* (2015) – and three further folk albums with The Furrow Collective. Having completed the Folk and Traditional Music BMus and MMus degree programmes at Newcastle University, she is now a published academic and has taught on these courses.[15] For the last decade she has been a key player in the 'current resurgence'[16] of traditional folk song, sometimes called the 'fourth wave', which is spearheaded by such artists as Eliza Carthy, Nancy Kerr, Jim Moray, Kate Rusby, Lady Maisery, Maz O'Connor, Sam Lee, and Stick in the Wheel. Portman has earned her prominent position in the movement through both musical and academic collaborations with grandees such as Martin Carthy, Norma Waterson, Lou Killen and Sandra Kerr.

Portman and I met at the Purbeck Folk Festival in August 2014, and discovered a shared love of Carter over wine at the bar. I promised to reconnect and continue our conversation; nearly five years on, in March 2019, I find myself in her house, surrounded by her welcoming family, her music, and her books. Portman explains to me that when she is songwriting, she repeatedly returns to Carter's writing for inspiration:

> EP: [...] it felt like a really easy connection to make as a musician into folk music, to move on to her [...] It felt very much part of the world of stories that I was already immersed in. And it seemed to be speaking to that, and adding something up in my head. It seemed to feed both sides. It made the ballads feel more relevant and it also fed into my writing, inspiring me. She almost felt like a guide, leading me to make creative connections, using folk tales as creative material. I felt more inspired to write, I think, just by returning to her books.
>
> PP: What kind of inspiration?
>
> EP: I think she inspired me to find new angles on the traditional stories, and gave me the courage to change things without feeling that I was treading on graves. So I think she gave me the permission to play with the material, for sure ... it was a big permission thing ... [...] I always end up returning to her writing. You know when you feel like you want to return to a text because you just feel like you're trying to get to the essence of why you're doing something? I felt like I returned to it in *Hatchling*, because I knew that it had somehow ignited something in *Glamoury*. I remember thinking, 'I need to go back to Angela Carter – I need to go and explore, open her fairy tale book – because I know I'll find something in there that will become song material.'[17]

In her song repertoire choices, Portman has actively sought out and promoted songs of female resistance. The traditional folk song genre has its vocal critics within feminist communities, and is sometimes accused of perpetuating universes which normalize misogyny and violence against women.[18] Individual singers respond differently to this quandary. Peggy Seeger told me in interview,

> many [traditional songs] are misogynistic, many of them have murdered women in them – I regard those as history, and I sing them with the names of people, of women, who were actually murdered by their husbands; people ask me, 'why do you sing them?', and I say, 'it's a roll of honour! You know, to remember these women'.[19]

In contrast, Portman recalls an anecdote from Martin Carthy, where he realized his own choice of repertoire had become unacceptable to a contemporary audience:

> EP: [...] I've talked to Martin Carthy about what he calls 'negative reaction songs', when you are in no doubt about the misogynistic perspective, or when it is endorsing oppressive behaviour ... So for example 'The Man of Burnham Town' was one that he sang, about domestic violence ... it was legitimizing wife-beating

... and he realized it, on stage, it got that far, before he realized that he wasn't going to be able to ever sing that again.[20]

Portman has actively searched for songs of female resistance, with woman and girl protagonists who challenge overarching patriarchal structures, answering misogyny with strength, defiance, and alternative modes of thinking. It is no surprise that Portman was drawn to Carter, whose agenda of excavating tales of female agency (demonstrated clearly in her curatorial and editorial choices for *The Virago Book of Fairy Tales* (1990),[21] *The Second Virago Book of Fairy Tales* (1992),[22] her anthology of short stories *Wayward Girls and Wicked Women* (1986),[23] translations of the tales of Charles Perrault,[24] and the list of folk songs in her 1964 journal discussed in Chapter 2) corresponds to Portman's own. Portman's songs use the folk song tradition to continue a conversation initiated by Carter both in her works of fiction and in her editorial decisions; Portman both intuitively and consciously stitches Carter and folk songs together within her own compositions, and did not realize until I interviewed her that Carter had herself been a singer of traditional songs, and that Carter was drinking from the same rich, nourishing lake of loci, topoi, symbols, motifs, and structural elements from which Portman draws.

As we talk, a series of seeming coincidences begins to reveal itself. I show Portman the song list from Carter's 1964 journal of songs,[25] and there is a startling (though, in hindsight, unsurprising) correlation between Carter's list and Portman's repertoire. Portman gasps and starts to laugh:

EP: .. Oh ... 'Bushes & Briars' ... wow! ..... [...] oh, 'Female Highwayman' ... I don't think I know 'Brewer's Daughter' ... 'Young Hunting', yeah,.... 'Lord Gregory', oh it's beautiful, 'Lord Gregory' ... 'Lizzie Wan', 'Captain Wedderburn ...' 'George Collins', oh I sing 'George Collins' ..., 'Georgie' ... these are so many songs that I've got in my repertoire ... maybe not surprisingly ... 'Bushes & Briars' ... 'Nancy of London ... 'Female Drummer' ... So she was totally into female empowerment ... it makes total sense but it's really amazing to see that written down ... 'Three maidens a-milking' which is risqué ... Oh yeah, 'Reynardine' ... [...] Oh look! 'Short Jacket and White Trousers' [...]

PP: Well this is interesting ... maybe you've been channeling her subliminally ...

EP: Yeah. ... I share a lot of this ... she had really similar interests in songs to me, that is amazing to find out ... wow! ... 'Gipsy Girl' ... that was one of the early ones that I learned, and again, you know, that involves a cheeky woman [laughs] ...

PP: It's a lot of feisty young girls, and wicked women and wayward girls ...

EP: Which is exactly what my repertoire was collecting as well, so I'm amazed by that ... [...] Oh yeah, 'Game of Cards' ... hmmm ....

[PP shows EP some musical notations from Carter's folk notebook]

EP: [looking at the staves] Well that's properly engaging with it, isn't it ... wow ... So neat! ... So she's got ... What songs is she looking for ...? 'Brown Girl', yeah, 'Lover's Ghost', 'Fair Annie' ... all of these ... such good songs she's choosing! ... oh, how exciting is that ... that's amazing ... my goodness![26]

Since my meeting with Portman, Christine Molan has confirmed to me that the list in Carter's 1964 journal does not represent Carter's personal singing repertoire;[27] the list might be more a list of the songs she wanted the group to sing as a collective: 'We all sang for each other at the small sing-around, and she wanted to hear these songs performed by someone, to hear them, to listen to what was 'happening' as text and tune [...] were put together.'[28] Nevertheless it is uncanny how Carter's list and Portman's repertoire focus on similar songs of female defiance and spirit (for example 'The Game of Cards', 'Polly Oliver' and 'Short Jacket and White Trousers'). Both Carter and Portman demonstrate an attraction to narratives with disobedient, spirited female characters at their hearts, a commonality which illustrates their shared mission to appropriate messages of female agency in the tradition to speak to contemporary concerns.

There also appears in several of Portman's songs a convergence with Carter in terms of drawing on influence, an assimilation I suggest reveals Portman's subliminal awareness of Carter's 'canorographic' affinity to the material. For example, until our conversation Portman has been unaware that Carter drew inspiration for 'The Erl-King' from the ballads which sit behind and beneath the story, sympathetically resonating through them – a resonance to which I suggest Portman is intuitively, unconsciously, musically attuned.

Both Carter and Portman have also been influenced by cante-fables, those half-song-half stories that use song as a vital element of the storytelling, such as 'The Story of Orange'. Carter transcribed the story in her 1963–1964 journal, and included the tale as 'The Juniper Tree' in the first *Virago Book of Fairy Tales*;[29] she suggested its grisly subject-matter would be suitable material for a 'horror movie'.[30] One can hear its influences in the transformed bird-girls of 'The Erl King', and in the eerie acousmatic voice that closes the story – 'Mother, mother you have murdered me!'. Portman, who refers to the same piece as 'Appley and Orangey', wrote the song 'Stick Stock' after being drawn to the Scots' traveller version:

> EP: I am really interested in metamorphosis and the different meanings it can have. And I think in 'Stick Stock' and 'The Juniper Tree', it's this feeling of a tale that must be told. [...] if a story is stifled and untold, it's burning to be told, and it will eventually come out, somehow. And, in the story of 'Stick Stock' / 'Juniper Tree', the story comes out in the transformation of the bird, singing the tale, and then the bird actually transforms back into the girl, in some versions ...[31]

As I gaze at the books on Portman's bookshelves, Portman tells me that many of the books were left to her in the will of Lou Killen, one of her most influential teachers. Portman asked Killen to sing 'Cockle Shell', part of a triptych of songs exploring the Selkie myth: although this track was not included on Portman's album, she shared the recording with me; Killen's performance is beautiful, tender, full of pathos. Portman did not know that Carter had written the detailed sleeve notes for Killen's 1965 album *Ballads & Broadsides*, nor that Carter greatly admired Killen as a singer.[32]

Portman has been, and continues to be, magnetically drawn to Carter for inspiration. I propose the reason for this is because Portman is responding instinctively to the 'invisible music'[33] Carter has successfully managed to thread, infuse, 'assimilate'[34] into her writing.

Listening to songs across Portman's three albums, one discerns at play a continuous reciprocity of influences between traditional folk songs and Angela Carter's works, which Portman claims she did not just read, but 'devoured'.[35] Portman's work is characterized by re-workings and re-imaginings of traditional folk songs, processes she describes as 'unravelling and reforming'[36] – another iteration of 'old wine in new bottles'. As Portman explains,

> My approach to traditional texts is to see them as a collection of malleable frameworks. To adopt the attitude of past folklore scholars in scorning so-called 'corrupted' fragments would be to ignore one of the elements that most excites me about the development of folk narratives: in their unruly transformations, brought about through their re-voicing and retelling, narratives are refocused and reformed anew, providing opportunities for contrasting meanings to emerge.[37]

Elsewhere she states what it is she does with them:

> My intention is to compose songs that draw upon traditional motifs that I find compelling and enduring and to re-contextualize them in the present. The result is a subjective re-interpretation of traditional material which does not attempt to subscribe to imagined authenticity, but recognizes the difference between the multifarious reformations of texts that occur in oral transmission and my own condensed editing process.[38]

Portman therefore frames herself as both an interpreter of traditional songs and a composer of new songs in the folk mode, taking thematic or narrative elements from traditional songs as starting-points or inspirations for new compositions.

As composer and interpreter, Portman employs four distinct methods to interact creatively with Carter. In the first method, Portman's song draws its subject-matter directly from Carter's fiction. Portman's song 'Hinge of the Year' [35] is a re-imagining of the scene from *Nights at the Circus* of Fevvers up on the trapeze, while 'Ash Girl' [36] is a direct response to Carter's short story 'Ashputtle'.[39]

In the second method, Portman's song originates from the same traditional folk song I have demonstrated in previous chapters that Carter knew well, and from which Portman departs to create her own composition. In this method, Portman is consciously employing Carter's methodology 'to extract the latent content from the traditional stories and to use it as the beginnings of new stories',[40] working to forge new, feminist reimaginings of old songs, prioritizing the voices of previously silent female characters – but using some of the same materials. I will examine in particular Portman's song 'Little Longing' [37], which Portman explains is a response to 'The Cruel Mother' [26], a folk song Carter analyzed in depth in her dissertation.

A third method demonstrates Portman drawing direct inspiration from a folk tale she has found in one of Carter's two edited *Virago* books of fairy tales. 'Tongue Tied' [40] and 'Mossy Coat' [39] are songs Portman composed after reading 'The Twelve Wild Ducks' and 'Mossycoat' in the *Virago* books, and, crucially, their accompanying editorial notes authored by Carter.[41]

Finally, there are songs Portman has written in which she draws both on Carter's fiction, and subliminally the traditional songs that influenced Carter. Portman's song 'Eye of Tree' [41] reveals Portman drawing a line of influence through Carter's story 'The Erl-King'[42] to the Child ballads 'Hind Etin' and 'Tam Lin' that lie behind it. Portman had instinctively 'heard' the ballads resonating in the story, not realizing Carter's prior experience as a folk singer and her familiarity with folk songs.

Close readings of Portman's songs against Carter's prose show the profound onward force of Carter's musical imagination, expressed by and impelled through her prose, to reveal how folk song features Carter wove so tightly into her writing perform the onward trajectory Carter so expressly hoped for.[43] Folk song's influences can be teased out of Carter's prose, and rethreaded into new musical creations, by a musician like Portman who is sensitive enough to hear them.

Method 1: direct influence from Carter's fiction

Some of Portman's songs are written in direct response to Carter's fiction. 'Hinge of the Year'[44] [35], for example, is a conscious reimagining of the fabulously winged Fevvers up on her trapeze in *Nights at the Circus*.[45] 'Hinge' is the song that initially alerted me to Portman's creative relationship with Carter, for Portman lifts directly from *Nights* both the song's title and its persona-protagonist. She hones in on a scene loaded with folk song allusion, where Mr. Rosencreutz[46] attempts to sacrifice Fevvers:

> '... do you not know what night it is, Flora?' [...] 'May eve, Flora, mia,' he assures me. 'In but a few moments, it will be *your* day, the green hinge of the year. The door of spring will open up to let summer through. It will be the merry morning of May!'[47]

As he prepares to kill her, Rosencreutz evokes objects and scenarios familiar to folklorists, the maypole and the village green:

> 'Maypole, phallus, lingam – ha! Up! heave ho and up he rises! up tomorrow on all the village greens of merrie England will spring the sacred phalloi of this blessed season and that is why, tonight of all nights, I chose to spirit you away.'[48]

Portman's song is not solely situated in this scene, but draws on images and sensations from a number of episodes, in keeping with the dizzying, swaying, drunken effects of the music. In the lyric 'I won't be anyone's bird in a cage', Portman conjures the Grand Duke's efforts to trap Fevvers in a tiny golden cage; with 'Here I sway', and 'might make these swirling lights clearer', Portman recreates Fevvers' dizzying stage act on the trapeze; when she imagines what it would be like 'to climb up on the roof, / See the lights of the city spread out like a galaxy', Portman recalls young Fevvers' first attempt at flight from the rooftops of Ma Nelson's brothel. There are references to the more decrepit aspects of night life, when 'nightclubs spill out onto the street' and there runs 'vodka and wine and blood in the gutters' – and allusions to Fevvers' monstrosity – 'no freak-show on a stage' and 'I knew I was different ever since I hatched out' – which reveal Portman's sensitivity to Fevvers' mission throughout the novel to tread a carefully maintained line of ontological uncertainty, to avoid the censure of humanity.

When I talk to Portman about 'Hinge', she tells me that she started to draft it while on holiday in Italy: 'I read *Nights at the Circus* during that holiday.' There is a sense in 'Hinge' that Portman's own experiences of being a performer seep into the song, and our discussion about Fevvers evolves into a meditation on the way we both feel as singers about the act of performance, and the transaction that takes place on stage between singer and audience, and that feeling of unique exchange:

> EP: [...] when I sing it, it feels a little bit like *playing a role* ... and I loved the descriptions of her performances under the lights as well, and...the magic of the performance, and that, *is she going to fly?* And I think that really did capture something about performance itself ... be it singing or whatever ... and that in-between space that you inhabit when you're performing ... [PP: tell me more about that] You know, when you're kind of ... [sighs] ... I don't know, you enter into ... maybe 'you' is the wrong word, maybe 'I' or maybe different performers feel this ... but there has to be a slight altered state (and I don't mean in terms of drinking wine!) but you have to not think about the words too closely, there has to be a certain trust that what you're going to do is just going to flow out of you and you can't think about it [PP: or you'll fall off your trapeze, right!] Yeah, and you just have to let it all flow ... [PP: it's that muscle memory thing ...] Exactly, muscle memory ... we were talking earlier about the lead-up to gigs, and I think that it's almost like you forget that that exists sometimes, that that muscle memory and the actual magic that can happen on stage when you and the audience are creating something that's alive and palpable, it just feels heightened and ... you don't feel wholly you ... I'm not saying that I'm channeling some kind of unknown force, at all, but there is, to a certain extent, a sense of just tapping into something ... There can be a kind of magic that occurs on stage between audience and performers, that requires both parties to hold the space. And for me, I perform best when I let go and relax, allow myself to get absorbed by the songs, to visualize the stories, almost to live them and pass them onto the audience, to invite them to live those stories too, for a moment ... It would be the biggest compliment to be called a story-teller, because I think the best folk singers draw me into the narrative and bring them to life.
>
> [...]
>
> EP: It is an exchange isn't it, with the audience, as well, which feels important.
>
> PP: I pick all that up from that song, that you've tapped in somehow to that description of Fevvers on stage but it's meeting you being on stage ...
>
> EP: Definitely in my mind were those wonderful descriptions of her up on the trapeze, and that moment where she flies, and she becomes this slightly supernatural ...
>
> PP: ... a 'pottering pigeon', I seem to remember her being ... [laughing] ... stuff that isn't so magical!

EP: Yeah, that's true, that's true! And that's also what I like about it, that it's always grounded in this *rude bolshiness* which is at odds with it all, before it gets too lofty and romantic.

PP: [...] I just get the feeling that Carter really did really know about performing, and I wonder if it's not just about her being a folk singer-y performer standing up in a folk club, but actually just the performance of *being her*, like *the projection of her*...

We talk further about the musical style of 'Hinge', which employs a dactylic 'um-pah-pah' swing which invokes the music-hall, the fairground, the carousel, and the circus. There is a solo performed on bowed saw, a wobbly, ethereal sound which encapsulates a turn-of-the-century giddiness, a playful innocence which would be snuffed out with the horror of the Great War:

PP: There's something very topsy-turvy about the music, and a bit fairground-y about the music...

EP: I do think I consciously went for a music-hall feel for that song, because it seemed to fit the era and story. I was just really taken with the character, and felt that that image of her on her night, when she was just about to try out her wings for the first time... just, it was brought to life to me, that idea of what if you had wings... and actually had to try them out for the first time... I think that's what the song is about, really. And it's also this idea of a drunken New Year's night out... [...] that kind of having to have a little bit of bravado behind you, before you take the leap...

Portman is melding and merging influences from Carter's novel with her own experiences of life, performance and giddiness to create a new musical artefact.

The song 'Ash Girl'[49] [36] is another direct response by Portman to Carter's fiction, written after reading the short story 'Ashputtle'.[50] Portman notes that part of her attraction to Carter's handling of the story was Carter's deviation from the more 'accepted' versions of the 'Cinderella' tale Portman had grown up with perpetuated by the Brothers Grimm and Disney. Portman liked the way Carter made the guiding force for good not a 'fairy godmother', but the benevolent ghost of the girl's actual mother:

EP: Having grown up with 'Cinderella', it felt like a really different tale when it was the mother giving her the instructions. And also, I just loved... when she says at the end, 'step into my grave'... that she needs to trust her mother to that extent, that she will fall into her mother's grave.

Portman is also drawn to the rich imagery embedded in Carter's prose:

EP: I just love the imagery of the bird pecking at its own breast, and the blood to make the tears... it's so different, and I think I was really captured by all of those images... the rubies, and the worms...

Portman's song recycles these lyrical elements from the story into her song: the black, red and white colour scheme from 'The Snow Child' and a host of folk tales resurfaces in the 'coal-black eyes', 'red calf', and 'white dove' who pecks 'at her breast / Til the ruby blood in torrents runs down'. The extinguished fire, the lost name, and the worms that turn to rubies are all symbols, 'keys' to 'latent material' which Portman deliberately turns in her song, expressing her desire to explore mother-daughter relationships and 'focusing on the gifts and burdens passed between them.'[51] While she was writing for her second album, she was expecting her first child, a girl:

> EP: [...] [...] That particular story 'Ashputtle', features a really positive mother, I feel she's just looking out for her daughter. Even beyond her death, she can't stop looking out for her daughter. There's this theme that comes up in a lot of folk songs about people saying, 'I can't rest [...] I can't rest because you're walking on my grave'... and she needs to rest. But she can't rest while her daughter's there walking around like a ghost herself ... I was pregnant as I was writing these songs for *Hatchling*, just about to enter motherhood, and so I was reflecting a lot on motherhood, and feeling the imminent sense of it ... so I think motherhood was on my mind throughout that whole album.[52]

Portman has chosen to focus her song on the second of Carter's three versions of the story, the version containing the helpful animals into which the mother's ghost has entered – the red calf and the white dove (Carter also includes a cat, which Portman omits). Portman's song is rendered in the imperative voice: it could be the voice of the mother, guiding the ash girl, culminating in stepping into the grave so that she can be transformed: 'Step into a grave, and cut all your losses.'

Portman can be seen here adopting an alphabet of symbols, made newly accessible by Carter's retelling, to fashion a new folk song about the gifts mothers bestow on their daughters. As part of her wider aim for this album 'to provide alternative conceptions of female voices, not necessarily rooted in a female body', she gives a voice to the benevolent mother ghost.[53]

Method 2: Same source material (song)

Some of Portman's songs spring from traditional folk songs that also influenced Carter: the two therefore share a common source. Child Ballad 20 'The Cruel Mother' [26] is a traditional ballad of which many versions have been collected,[54] most of which contain the following key plot points: a woman kills her illegitimate babies to conceal her extramarital sexual activity (often with a man of lower social standing), and is punished, often by their haunting, a crime for which she is usually required to perform some kind of penance in order to secure an uncertain redemption. In some versions, there appears the motif of a knife with blood that will not wash away.[55] Carter knew 'The Cruel Mother' well: she wrote about it at length in her dissertation where, rather than focusing on the woman's silenced voice, she concentrates on the strange metamorphic penances the mother must endure, and the image of the knife that cannot be washed of its blood.

The penances for the murderous mother fascinate the young Carter both in this ballad and 'The Maid and the Palmer', which 'consists not of exaggerated austerities but, partly at least, of transmigration, and shape changing; she is to be seven years a fish, seven a stone.'[56] She cites G. H. Gerould's analysis of the penances,[57] suggesting she has absorbed it as her own opinion:

> The actual forms of the girl's penance may be far older than the medieval period in origin. Gerrould [sic.] regards the frequent 'fish in the flood', 'bird in the wood' stanzas and their variants as a lingering survival of notions about metempsychosis.
>
> 'It is interesting,' says Gerrould [sic.], 'that the stages through which the wicked woman is doomed to pass vary somewhat in different versions, indicating that the idea has not been so alien to popular thought as to make changes impossible.'[58]

The motif of the blood-stained knife attracts Carter's attention: 'The indelible bloodstains, the river which turns to blood when the girl washes the bloodstained knife in it and the knife which refuses to be thrown away seem to be folklore elements.' She does not reveal her source for this assumption, but as Bert Lloyd reaches a similar conclusion, one might wonder if she is influenced here directly by him.[59] In her handling of these elements of the ballads, she can be seen to be putting down an imagic store, an alphabet of symbols, on which to draw later: in the 'The Bloody Chamber', for example, the knife image resurfaces in the form of the forbidden key: 'the key was still caked with wet blood and I ran to my bathroom and held it under the hot tap [...] I scrubbed the stain with my nail brush but still it would not budge.'[60] The heroine of 'The Bloody Chamber' disobeys and defies patriarchal order with a key, rather than a knife, but its blood proves equally stubborn.

Portman takes this harrowing song as the starting point to write two songs in sympathetic, compassionate response, 'Little Longing'[61] [37] and 'Borrowed and Blue',[62] which both retell the story of 'The Cruel Mother' but from the mother's point of view. Portman does not focus on the same metamorphic and motivic elements as Carter, but instead on aspects of the woman's dilemma. In Portman's detailed compositional notes for 'Little Longing', she explains that the song is a meditation on abortion,

> an 'anti-lullaby' for a child that is both wanted and unwanted; it is partly inspired by the seventeenth century ballad of 'The Cruel Mother', a tale of infanticide spurred by social misalliance. A glance at the shock-headlines in today's media displays how it is all too easy to demonize failed mothers and women who defy the 'natural' instinct towards motherhood. Songs like 'The Cruel Mother' display how women are quickly labelled monsters without an understanding of the social circumstances that influenced their choice. I call 'Little Longing' a lullaby as it is sung with tenderness from mother to unborn child, challenging the assumption that a rejection of motherhood through abortion only arises out of selfishness or desperation, not choice and even love. I am looking for a more pluralistic conception of femininity which does not place motherhood at its core, one which resists the construction of motherhood as singular and unchanging, a viewpoint

that upholds what Toni Bowers calls 'patriarchal privilege'. Like Bowers I believe that 'motherhood, far from a static 'natural' experience is a moving plurality of potential behaviours, always undergoing supervision, revision and contest, constructed in particularity.' In fairytales where 'good' mothers are so often absent, my attention to the mother and daughter relationship seeks to expand conceptions of motherhood within the genre.[63]

Portman has taken the story of 'The Cruel Mother' and, as Carter describes, has 're-moulded' the song 'to suit' the concerns of a 'new generation';[64] Portman also clearly states in this document the purpose of the overarching compositional project of which 'Little Longing' is a part – to give voice to the silent women of balladry:

Female voices and their persistence against silencing form a strand that runs throughout this vocal-centred album, particularly with regard to the problems that arise when encountering the silencing of female voices in traditional texts. In re-conceiving traditionally 'monstrous' characters such as sirens, witches, selkies or women who reject the maternal instinct, I attempt to unravel and unstitch the misogynistic undertones that underpin the monsters made out of women. I seek to expand conceptions of motherhood through investigating themes of abandonment and abortion.[65]

Portman's agenda uncannily resembles Carter's, which, as Harriet Kramer Linkin identifies, is 'to restore speech to the subordinated or silenced female voice'.[66] They are both about the business of re-voicing female silences.

Portman's 'Little Longing' is rendered in A, in the minor-feeling Dorian mode, with its characteristic raised VI and natural VII. It opens with a single cello note playing the tonic, behaving like a drone, a single note rooted beneath the fluctuating and gently ornamented vocal tune. The cello part develops in complexity as the song progresses, mimicking the complexity of conflicting emotions expressed: the heavy longing for the baby coupled with the relief that the baby is 'gone', both emotions coexisting, a duality reflected in emerging double-stops of the cello. The mother is envisioned as a tree: 'My boughs are heavy laden' and 'When the bough breaks', recalling the eerie nursery-rhyme 'Rock-a-bye baby', and also compared to empty fruit, a 'plum without a stone', evoking the fruits of Rossetti's illicit 'Goblin Market', and empty honeycomb, suggesting a barrenness, a lack of sweetness, a lack of tenderness.

The third and fourth stanzas are imbued with surreal imagery – the dream-like baby is formed from sawdust and sacking, and the woman addresses the baby as 'you'.[67] A paradox plays out that she can 'see [...] clearly' the baby's face in 'the murk of the night', but that in the 'bright morning' the baby's 'face, it fades': the logical clarity of sunshine is here pitted against the irrational opacity of the night, but paradoxically she can see in the gloom and cannot see in the light. In the morning, she can say, 'I'm happy that you're gone', because despite her longing she is not ready to receive this baby: 'For a seed sown out of season/ Will only do us harm.' Note the 'us' – the woman has taken a collective decision, although precisely who the 'us' is is not made explicit – perhaps the baby's father, perhaps the baby itself – perhaps all of them. She will endure her 'longing' for the collective good.

A mournful cello solo after the appearance of the second 'harm' here figures the complexity of emotions in musical phrasing. Leaping up from the lower V to the minor III, full of swelling pathos, the emotion spills over in the toppling movement of the tune. The demand of a rhetorical question, 'What woman am I?', accompanied by the delay of the raised VI, creates a sense of suspense and censure, encapsulating in musical terms the whispering disapproval of 'them'. And then Portman plays her master stroke, a harrowing lone sharpened VII on 'singing', shunting the song momentarily into a shocking harmonic minor scale, before returning to the soft mournfulness of the Dorian to conclude – 'Sleep my little longing, / Til I find you a home' – it is her responsibility to bide her time until conditions are right.

Tensions and paradoxes are held in place throughout this song: in the single cello drone-notes and the cello's increasing double-stops; between sleeping and waking in the voice; between the 'seeing' in the murk of the dark and the 'unseeing' in the light of the dawn; between the 'natural' imagery of a mother as tree, fruit and honeycomb, and the 'them' who denaturalize her with their question 'What woman am I?'; in the sinister whispering of the crowd contrasted with the clarity of the voice and cello. There is no room for clutter in the instrumentation here: it is frugal, spare, bare-boned, heart-breaking. Between the desperation of the longing to hold the absent baby, and the feeling expressed in the cold light of day – 'I'm happy that you're gone' – lies the attempt to process logically a lack which defies logic. But, as expressed in the elongated, aching cello lines, and the long-drawn-out eight-line tune arc of the vocal melody, this song is all about delay, deferment, not abandonment. The baby will come, just not now.

Portman and Carter have also both been influenced by the cante-fable 'The Juniper Tree', a 'singing bone' story.[68] Portman's haunting song 'Stick Stock' [38] was inspired by the same lesser-known variant of the story as Carter: 'The Story of Orange', or what Portman calls 'Appley and Orangey' – '"Appley and Orangey"... that's the one I based it on'.[69] Carter transcribed the entire story in her 1963–1964 journal, I suggest, from the 1906 Gilchrist and Kidson essay,[70] and she included the Brothers Grimm version of the story 'The Juniper Tree' in the first *Virago Book of Fairy Tales*. Critically, the sung portion of the cante-fable 'The Juniper Tree' / 'The Story of Orange' / 'Appley and Orangey', the eerie refrain, is a vital part of the narrative.[71]

Portman frames 'Stick Stock' in C with a grim child-like chanting refrain which throbs like an engine throughout the song, accompanied only by one single and rhythmic plucked note. She spots the melody with unsettling major III interventions at the end of the second line of each verse, so that the song heaves back and forth between major and minor feels. The rhythmic effects of the throbbing note and the stacked vocals create an atmosphere of derangement; unsettling thinning vocal effects on backing vocals, and the main vocal at 'Come in, come in, my sweetie pies', loads Portman's voice with the murderous menace of the stepmother.

Portman also refers to 'The Two Sisters' [27] several times during our conversation; she cites it as one of her more successful recordings, and she conjoins it with Carter in her head:

> EP: [...] I think that's partly what attracted me to [Carter] was the whole magic realism, and how for me that inhabited a very similar world to the ballads, because

that's what I was totally into about the ballads ... things like 'The Two Sisters', where there's the harp made out of her breast bone ... in ballad landscapes the magical and the mundane collide.

PP: ... and how it's totally normal! ....

EP: Yeah, and I love all that ... for me that's magical ... it's not that I'm necessarily attracted to the gore of it ... I feel like magazine interviewers often are like, 'oh, it so weird isn't it?' ... It's not that I'm just trying to be weird, I feel like there's something really powerful about the magic that's in there ... these things like the singing bone motif ... Those images that Carter was creating, both in the fairy tales and in her own writing, felt to me like continued threads from the folk songs that I'd been listening to. I think that was really exciting for me.

PP: I think it's really fascinating that you could see the link.

EP: I think I saw it, but I felt it as well – as an *ah! yes!* Someone who understands ... it did feel like she was a link between the songs and the stories for me.[72]

Portman revels in the thematic material encapsulated in the motif of the singing bone, 'the idea that if a story is stifled and untold, it's burning to be told, and it will eventually come out, somehow.'[73] Christine Molan remembers Carter singing 'The Two Sisters',[74] and she repurposed the image of instrument strung with human hair from this song for the dramatic ending of 'The Erl-King'. Carter's discordant pronoun and tense shifts in 'The Erl-King', as I suggest in chapter 4, are a rendering in prose of the kinds of key shifts Portman plays with in these eerie songs.

In all these examples, Portman can be seen to have been inadvertently drawing from the same sources as Carter for references, images and motifs, creating concentrations of complex musico-literary intertextuality.

Method 3: Songs inspired by Carter's tale collations

A group of Portman's songs have emerged from readings of folk tales collated by Carter in the *Virago Book of Fairy Tales* and the *Second Virago Book of Fairy Tales*, in particular 'Mossy Coat' and 'Tongue-Tied'. In the *Virago Book*, Carter includes a version of the folk tale 'Mossycoat',[75] the 'gypsy Cinderella',[76] collected by TW Thompson from Taimie Boswell at Oswaldwhistle, Northumberland in 1915, and reprinted in *Folktales of England*.[77] Carter's 'Mossycoat' text is already intensely audial, rendered in phonetic approximations of the oral teller's gypsy vernacular: 'A hawker came courting dis girl; came reg'lar he did, and kept on a-bringing of her dis thing and dat.' It tells of a young girl whose benevolent widow-witch-mother makes her a coat whose magical properties lead to her marriage to the young master of the house. Carter's notes highlight the social suspicions embedded in the tale – '"It is the technique of gypsies and tinkers to go to the front door, and try to see the mistress of the house," say the editors of *Folktales of England*. "They have a rooted distrust of servants and underlings. In many versions of the tale, it is the young master who ill-treats the heroine and not the servants."'[78]

This tale is presented by Carter as an exploration of social mobility, riddled with undercurrents of inverted snobbery.

Portman's song 'Mossy Coat'[79] [39], 'loosely based' on the tale 'Mossycoat' in Carter's edited collation, explores the gifts passed between mothers and daughters, and the freedoms afforded by transformation to traverse social boundaries. Portman focuses on the first half of the story, involving the mother and daughter, and emphasizes the useful gifts the mother passes on – not just the mossy coat, but the wisdom to recognize real value, not to be 'addled' by 'the glamourie', and the skill of 'needle and thread'.

> I started to wonder what would happen if, instead of going out to work or marrying a prince, Mossycoat got carried away with her new magical powers. The resulting moral tale is in part a reaction to the throwaway consumerist culture that makes skills like sewing and knitting redundant. 'Glamourie' is the magic that gypsies, fairy folk (and perhaps storytellers) cast over people's eyes to help them see another world, or to trick them into seeing beauty where there is none.[80]

Portman's song opens with playful single *pizzicato* notes which suggest opportunity, 'leaping' and 'lingering'[81] around the Mixolydian scale in A; they build in clockwork-like patterns, to be replaced with *arco* strokes on the long sung word 'sky'. Disorientating loops and repetitions in the fiddle, harp and cello parts spin us around as if in a dance, and the tunes repeat and interlink like a round, 'addling' us. Portman writes,

> I have [...] attempted to create sonic fragmentation and transformation in my arrangements by splicing and looping repeated patterns. This approach is particularly evident in 'Mossy Coat' and 'Tongue-Tied' which layer loops of fiddle, harp or cello to incrementally transform the sound, hopefully creating an effect of metamorphosis in the arrangement.[82]

The song concludes with a dizzying dance-like section in which accordion, strings and harp join together in a jig.

The Carter connection may be one of the reasons why Portman is compelled to use similar musical effects in both 'Mossy Coat' and 'Tongue-Tied'. 'Tongue-Tied' [40] is inspired by a tale Carter collated, 'The Twelve Wild Ducks', this time in her *Second Virago Book of Fairy Tales*. This story, which Carter reproduces from Sir George Webbe Dasent's translation from the Norwegian in *Popular Tales from the Norse*,[83] tells of a queen's rash bargaining of her twelve sons for a daughter, and that daughter's subsequent silent struggle to break the curse on her brothers to restore them to human form. The story uses a colour-palette which is instantly recognizable from more widely known tales such as 'Snow-White' from the Brothers Grimm:

> Once upon a time there was a queen who was out driving, when there had been a new fall of snow in the winter; but when she had gone a little way, she began to bleed at the nose, and had to get out of her sledge. And so, as she stood there, leaning against the fence, and saw the red blood on the white snow, she fell a-thinking how she had twelve sons and no daughter, and she said to herself –

> 'If I only had a daughter as white as snow and as red as blood, I shouldn't care what became of all my sons.'
>
> But the words were scarce out of her mouth before an old witch of the Trolls came up to her.[84]

Carter's reappropriation of this 'latent material' for her own short story, 'The Snow Child', although printed a decade before the *Virago* books appeared, suggests that Carter had come across 'The Twelve Wild Ducks' before she wrote her 'Snow Child', for imagic elements from this tale resurface:

> Midwinter – invincible, immaculate. The Count and his wife go riding, he on a grey mare and she on a black one, she wrapped in the glittering pelts of black foxes; and she wore high, black, shining boots with scarlet heels, and spurs. Fresh snow fell on snow already fallen; when it ceased, the whole world was white. 'I wish I had a girl as white as snow,' says the Count. They ride on. They come to a hole in the snow; this hole is filled with blood. He says, 'I wish I had a girl as red as blood'. So they ride on again; here is a raven, perched on a bare bough. 'I wish I had a girl as black as that bird's feathers.'
>
> As soon as he had completed her description, there she stood, beside the road, white skin, red mouth, black hair and stark naked; she was the child of his desire and the Countess hated her.[85]

Carter's editorial notes to 'The Twelve Wild Ducks' reveal her multimodal awareness of the many layers of symbolic meaning embedded in the visuals of the tale, their cinematic power:

> The film-maker Alfred Hitchcock thought nothing was more ominous than the look of blood on daisies. Blood on snow catches even more directly at the viscera. The raven, the blood, the snow – these are the elements of the unappeasable northern formulae of desire. [...] This carnivorous imagery expresses the depths of a woman's desire for a child in traditional stories. [...] 'The Twelve Wild Ducks', with its savage beginning and theme of sibling devotion, forms the basis of the Danish Hans Christian Andersen's lovely literary story, 'The Wild Swans'. Andersen upgraded the ducks to romantic swans although I feel that if wild ducks were good enough for Ibsen, they should have been good enough for him.[86]

Portman's song 'Tongue-Tied' [40] uses Carter's and Dasent's versions of the tale to springboard into investigations of the daughter's penance for the mother's 'rash words' – seven years of silence. Portman acknowledges the irony of singing about silence: surely to sing about silence is to break it:

> The idea of a song being sung by a voiceless narrator presents a paradox, which is still faced today knowingly or unknowingly by female storytellers. For as Warner observes:

> '[T]he very women who pass on the legacy are transgressing against the burden of its lessons as they do so; [...] woman narrators, extolling the magic silence of the heroic sister in 'The Twelve Brothers', are speaking themselves, breaking the silence, telling a story.'

This highlights the subversive potential in storytelling, for just as narrative meanings are moveable and multifaceted, songs that appear to enforce women's silence may have the opposite effect in performance, depending on the singer.[87]

Portman circumnavigates this paradox by creating from the outset a feeling of internal frustration in the song, alerting us to the interiority of the singer-protagonist's anguish. In Portman's version, the duck-brothers are 'raven kings': these black birds, the mother's red tongue, and the white thread work together to incorporate Carter's colour-palette of desire, the desire of the mother that spills over into the suffering of the daughter.

The song's awkward, lopsided 5/4 time signature, and D minor key (modulated at moments into the Mixolydian scale through tiny vocal ornamentations), plucked out in single string drone notes as the song opens, immediately create a sense of unease. The mournful bowed cello and harp parts that enter at 'seven years' suggest the length of time the daughter's silence must be maintained, and a menacing singing-round as the song concludes cascades in direct challenge to the enforced silence, suggesting the words are jumbling around in her head internally, unable to escape. A final haunting harp tune, misted with reverb, hangs in the air to reinstate and re-invite the silence.

Portman describes her engagement with this tale specifically through the prism of Carter's editorial notes:

> This is a song based on the first half a folktale which goes under various titles including 'The Twelve Wild Ducks'. Hans C. Anderson transformed the ducks into swans and although I like the connection between a mute bird and a silenced woman I am more drawn to the image of ravens, ambiguous birds with a motley symbolism which fits their roles in the tale. [...] Angela Carter, my source for this story, comments on the imagery that this combination creates [Here Portman quotes the Alfred Hitchcock passage mentioned earlier.] The colours red white and black are a recurring theme in the song, which bind mother and daughter: the red of blood upon snow and the flutter of raven wings become the colourful threads woven by the daughter once [...] she is sentenced to seven years' silence and given the job of sewing her brothers shirts of thistledown. As the daughter sews, she sheds blood on the white shirts from her work-worn fingers and the colours emerge once more.[88]

Portman refers to other influential myths in her notes, noticing parallels with the Philomel myth from Ovid's *Metamorphoses*, of a woman silenced by violence who must also sew, and which also contains avianthropic transformations.[89]

Carter's hand in the rendering of these stories, and in particular her illuminating accompanying notes, can be seen to be actively influencing Portman's interpretations, but not overtaking them. In each case, the tale provides a starting point, Carter an impetus, and Portman a new onward creative trajectory.

Method 4: Carter's fiction and traditional songs

Finally, in some of Portman's songs there seems to be an unexpected and unconscious convergence of influences from Carter and folk song appropriations, until now without Portman's awareness of Carter's folk song praxis. The best example of this confluence is Portman's song 'Eye of Tree'[90] [41]. Portman's initial explanation seems straightforward enough: 'when I was writing for *Coracle* I was writing inspired by "The Erl-King"'; but when she provides more detail she reveals that she and the cowriter of the song 'Eye of Tree' (the poet Eleanor Rees) were also using Child ballads 'Tam Lin' [23] and 'Hind Etin' [24] for inspiration:

> I got together with my poet friend Eleanor Rees and we were writing together inspired by ballads and we'd then do some writing . . . and we were looking at 'Hind Etin', we were writing inspired by the ballad and then it made me think of 'The Erl-King' . . . so I went and got down 'The Erl-King' . . . and we were like . . . *oh look!* we were having this conversation about the parallels . . .[91]

She had already spotted links between the two texts; she also mentions that 'Tam Lin' was an inspiration, and the source for the song's title and its repeating refrain:

> 'eye of tree, heart of clay' – that's a direct quote from 'Tam Lin' – 'I wish I'd plucked out your eyes and given you eyes of tree and heart of clay'. The fairy queen says it to him.[92]

As a footnote to the final draft of 'Eye of Tree' lyrics Portman sends me after our interview, there is the following very telling compositional note:

> *The words 'eye of tree' and 'heart of clay' feature in the ballad of 'Tam Lin'. This song is also inspired by Angela Carter's retelling of 'The Erl-King' and conversations with Eleanor Rees.

An earlier draft of Portman's song 'Eye of Tree' differs quite markedly from the lyrics of the finished recording, and contains more explicit references to Carter's 'Erl-King' story, revealing the song's bones. See both versions, side by side, in Appendix 5.

The rhythmic patterning of 'Eye of Tree' is a 3/4 dactylic patterning, a mesmeric gallop of 'DUH-duh-duh' phrases, consciously or unconsciously channelling the excitement and danger present in the dactylic constructions of Carter's prose, which themselves, as I argue in Chapter 4, were inspired by 'Lady Isabel and the Elf-Knight'. The song opens with an eerie, bone-rattling, arhythmic string-plucking section which lasts for 40 seconds, with a backwards-bell at 0.24 zooming us into an ethereal sonic universe. At 0.43 there enter strong, low piano octaves which drag us down amid the high plucks, and these continue, disorientating us and spinning us around as if entering the dangerous woods. It is not until 1.19 that, with another reversed bell, the pounding, exciting 3/4 gallop of the song begins, and the unison voices[93] that begin to sing 'So long I have strayed in the dark woods' create an eerie, echoing effect, drawing us into the interior universe of the song. The vocal melody plays on the harmonic minor scale of F, with Lydian flecks, while light bells sound like wind chimes. Bizarre, haunting, disturbing, crunching vocal harmonies are panned left and right in dizzying and disorientating spreads, including other voices such as the recognizably Scottish lilts of Rachel Newton. It is an effective musical rendering of the opening passage of 'The Erl-King', creating the 'vertical bars of a brass-coloured distillation of light' of this wood in which 'the foxes make their own runs in the subtle labyrinth'[94] in claustrophobic note-clashes and voice combinations, galloping dactylic rhythms, and hypnotic bell-chimes.

When one studies the details of the two Child ballads Portman and Rees were using as their primary sources – 'Hind Etin' [24] and 'Tam Lin' [23] – it becomes clear that Carter too must have been influenced by them as she wrote her 'Erl-King', alongside 'Lady Isabel and the Elf-Knight' [20], a 'constellation' of greenwood songs which I discuss in Chapter 4. In 'Hind Etin', Lady Margaret goes to Elmond's Wood and breaks a branch; Hind Etin appears, upbraids her, and then abducts her into the forest where he keeps her for seven years in a hidden den: 'He's built a bower, made it secure / With Carbuncle and stone / Though travellers were never so nigh / Appearance it had none.'[95] She bears him seven sons, but is sad they are never christened, nor she married. Her eldest son finally takes his mother and brothers out of the wood; in some variants, they are welcomed back to society; in all, the children are christened, and their mother wedded. The lengthy incarceration in the woods bears a strong resemblance to the threat of incarceration to the protagonist in 'The Erl-King', and the incarceration of all the bird-girls in his woodland den.

The opening sequence to 'Tam Lin' is similar: Janet/Margaret goes to the forest of Carterhaugh and plucks a rose; she is accosted by Tam Lin who promptly impregnates her, but in this story rather than incarcerating her he sends her home. When she returns to him, she discovers she can rescue him from the Queen of the Fairies by holding him through various metamorphoses, which she achieves, securing a noble father for her child. The sexually charged magical man of the woods and the bravery of the female protagonist are reminiscent of similar elements in 'The Erl-King'.

Portman's song, Carter's story, and the ballads that sit beneath them all share powerful common imagery and motifs: all are set in disorientating woods, all possess wilful, rebellious female protagonists and seductive, dangerous men with some overt or covert suggestion of magical powers. In some, music plays an important role: sometimes the female protagonist is drawn into the woods by magical music, and a stringless fiddle might feature. The excitement and danger of the greenwood and the man are conjured sonically by cantering dactylic rhythms.

Portman remembers the topics she and Rees were contemplating as they composed 'Eye of Tree':

> EP: I think that's what got us on to talking about it, was this whole idea of being captured in the centre of a forest, and this feeling of being held and then losing yourself in the forest ... [...] there was also a sense of it being about that search ... you know, the search for a fantasy ... ['Eye of Tree' describes] the trappings of losing yourself to somebody else and losing your own identity [...] There is a sense of getting lost in the woods [...] and actually finding that in the process you've become

a changed person ... are you fleeing the Erl King? Or are you searching? have you become something else, when you actually come across that person you've been searching for? Do you recognize them? Do you recognize yourself? [...] I feel like the character [in the song] becomes hard and strong in the process. And then, in finding your own strength, do you then need the fantasy any more? The fantasy of this Erl-King/lover or whatever ... [...] just the trappings that people make for each other, as well.... I say at the end, 'You have your cage waiting, And I have mine' ... this recognition of what we do to each other ... What people do to each other in their relationships, and actually choosing to run instead. I think I was talking to friends that were single and had this prolonged fantasy about finding the right person ... and it's a kind of fantasy that can be evasive and [...] ultimately the realities and the fantasy, they both have their lures don't they ... they both have their trappings and their cages ... [...] you suddenly realize that you actually want more ... you get one thing and you think, 'actually, that's not what I need.' [...] when you spend a lot of time yearning for somebody else, I think there can be the feeling of being unfulfilled, and then realizing that when you get into long-term relationships, that really, if you ever felt unfulfilled, you will continue to feel unfulfilled, because that person can't fulfil those empty parts of you ... nobody else can fix you.[96]

In her 1967 journal, Carter vents in similar terms her frustration and unhappiness within her marriage to Paul:

It seems to me with Paul that as I try & grow, as I submit myself to change to help him, as I make allowances & act tenderly & do all the things a good wife should, my fucking understanding, my kind heart, so I am building a better & stronger cage for myself every day & in every way [...] It seems to me I have only recently become a person and begun to apprehend the nature of the labyrinth & maybe see ways out.[97]

Recognizable imagery in Carter's journal entry of unwanted cages and labyrinths from which to escape were to emerge ten years later in the motifs and loci of 'The Erl-King'. But later, she would also describe her partner Mark Pearce as 'a gaunt, tall, woodland being'.[98] The complex figure of the Erl-King emerges from these contradictory experiences: the songs she knew of sexually attractive yet dangerous woodland men, and her positive and negative experiences of two of her most important relationships.

These ballads reminded Portman of Carter's story 'The Erl-King' precisely because they had already inspired Carter to write it. There is an active sympathetic resonance occurring here between old texts and new, and between traditional material, Carter, and Portman.

Conclusion

Emily Portman has, inadvertently, been responding to the folk song influences Carter threaded into her prose. Instinctively, Portman detected them resonating there, because she could read Carter from a musical perspective, and because of her practical and academic immersion in the folk song form. When I told her about Carter's folk singing history Portman said, 'I'm not surprised that she was influenced by folk music. And I'm not surprised that she was a musician.' For inspiration, Portman has delved into Carter as much as the tradition, reuniting Carter and folk songs in her own compositions to create sonic objects of rare beauty. But for all their delicacy, Portman's songs display a subcutaneous musculature, a discordant, unsettling, rippling undercurrent, which perfectly echoes and develops in musical terms the canorographic effects of Carter's prose. With the intense double-distillation of folk song via the prism of Carter, Portman's compositions create new micro-universes of dazzlingly uncomfortable beauty, transcoding the musical elements lying latent in Carter's prose back into song.

Further research is needed to understand better these intricate relationships between prose, song, voice, breath, 'influence', and 'inspiration'. 'Canorography' could be used as a new and valid literary-critical tool at a time when the academy is late to acknowledge the wider societal 'auditory turn'.[99] I register affective, somatic real-time responses to the excesses of 'songfulness' spilling from the canorographic prose text – my hairs stand on end when I 'read' or 're-perform' such 'canorographic' prose texts, as when I am moved by song. Identifying these cyclical relationships between experience, prose writing, song performance, 'songfulness', somatic resonance, empathy, 'influence' and 'affect' will open up rich new critical spaces for reimagining as porous the boundaries between song and prose.

8

Sympathetic resonances

> The music begins.
> It is a conversation
> between a woman and a piano,
> a conversation about silence –
> that is, about the interstices
> of a conversation conducted
> in a language neither participant understands
> in which, nevertheless, it would seem
> an integration has been affected,
> an integration which permits the development
> of a new language expressing the voices of the
> speaking yet uncomprehending locutors
> and the tension imposed upon them
> by the silence preceding
> and succeeding their twinned trajectory
> through the interstices of the silence
> they discuss.
>
> Angela Carter, 'Leide'/'Liede'[1]

This book is a celebration of the art of Angela Carter's canorography, her song-infused prose musicality, and an exposition of the profound impact of somatic performance of traditional folk song on her writing. I have argued that Carter the writer used her memory of listening, singing and performing to build sympathetic resonances between text and reader in much the same way that Carter the singer used vocal resonances, acoustic vibrations in air, to forge a 'living bridge'[2] between singer and audience in that folk club in 1967.

Carter loved all kinds of music. She enjoyed, voraciously consumed, reviewed, and allowed her writing to be influenced by many different genres and styles – classical, folk, rock, music-hall, jazz, opera – and a plethora of critics have observed those influences at work,[3] all in keeping with her famous 'magpie' eclecticism.[4] Sozo Araki, her most significant lover in Japan, remembers her diverse musical tastes and how music was capable of moving her:

Angela professed to like Bob Dylan. But, I think the singer she liked best was a German baritone, Dietrich Fischer-Dieskau. She repeatedly praised him with fervour, saying, 'When I hear him sing, I'm moved to tears.'[5]

Carter also enjoyed listening to spoken word recordings; at a seminal moment, a French teacher loaned her an LP of Baudelaire and Rimbaud's poetry. Martine Hennard, Edmund Gordon and I have deduced that this album, to which Carter referred more than once, was probably Jean-Louis Barrault's record, *Baudelaire et Rimbaud: Les Poètes Maudits (The Cursed Poets)*:

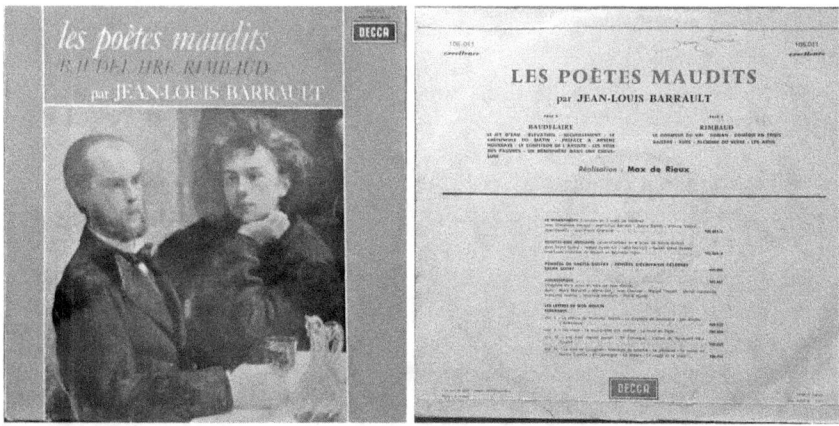

Figures 20 and 21 Jean-Louis Barrault, *Baudelaire et Rimbaud: Les Poètes Maudits* LP, front and back covers (Decca Records 105.011, 1953). Copyright © Decca Records. Reproduced with kind permission of Decca Records.

The result of Carter hearing this LP, according to Gordon, was 'critical':

> She 'wore that record out' before returning it, smitten by the 'dark, sinuous voice' of the actor, and by the renegade, dandyish flavour of the writing. It was after listening to it a few times that she decided she wanted to become a writer: 'That record was my trigger. It was like having my skull opened with a tin opener and all its contents transformed.'[6]

I have not to date been able to source an official list of Carter's record collection; but from the evidence of her fiction and non-fiction writing, her musical tastes were eclectic, and she imbibed music not just on record, but in live performance. Edward Horesh and Christopher Frayling remembered fondly their trips with her to see the opera;[7] she attended the first Cambridge Folk Festival in 1965 with Paul Carter.[8] In a 1966 concert review she expounded Bob Dylan's genius at a time when other critics were recoiling from his electrification, describing him as 'the first ever all-electronic, all existential rock and roll singer' and how he was 'singing for Kafka, Kierkegaard,

Dostoevsky, and all the boys down home on Desolation Row'. She recognized the literary value of Dylan's contribution, comparing him to 'Dean Swift and William Burroughs'.[9] There is even some evidence that she liked to sing pop tunes around the house; Araki records how they

> sang songs by Elvis or The Beatles. Angela's voice was quite deep when speaking, but when she sang, it rose in pitch. It was a crystal-clear voice, particular to Scandinavian white women. (I do not suppose many people except myself have heard Angela sing. Not many people in England sing in public, and Angela did not sing either at first whenever I sang. But gradually, she began singing as if she could not help but join me, because I seemed to have so much fun.)[10]

But, while acknowledging the contributory significances of all of these engagements with various musical genres, this book prioritizes the folk song form above all others, for one simple reason: this is the form that Carter performed in public before an audience: the 1967 recording proves that fact. It is my assertion that Carter's active public performance, singing before people as an act of communication and communion, the forging of a 'living bridge', the connecting of resonating bodies, and all just as her writing persona was taking flight, was uniquely to hard-wire folk song's rhythmic, melodic and thematic features into her fertile creative musico-literary imagination, because music performance is not just music – music performance is an act of physical communication.

When she wrote that the 'richness and allusiveness of imagery in folk poetry, which reaches one through singing almost on a subliminal level, means one's appreciation of the mode grows with one's knowledge',[11] Carter told us that to sing folk songs was to internalize them. Her corporeal folk song performance instilled in her a language; it enabled in her a capacity to communicate in a 'melody of letters',[12] a 'music of prose',[13] what I describe as canorography because of its innate 'songfulness',[14] which provokes in her readers all the paralinguistic physical affects that folk song arouses – pleasure, unease, recognition, horror, fear, relief – along with all the other non-verbal messages we receive from her works (such as the uneasiness of modal scales in tense and pronoun shifts, melodic patterns in narrative shapes, rhythmic patterns secreted in prosody) that I have outlined throughout this book. Carter's prose is ringing with the 'word-notes'[15] of her singing experience, and through her canorographic writing style she asks us to reimagine her prose as performance, to perform the 'invisible music'[16] of her prose as we read her, to bridge the dissonances of space and time between us to vibrate with her in acoustic, dynamic, trans-temporal, trans-spatial, sympathetic resonance.

The metaphor of the acoustic phenomenon of 'silvery' sympathetic resonance[17] is useful to describe observations in other fields.[18] For sympathetic resonance to occur between text and reader, one must presuppose in reading the presence of sound, and that to read prose is to partake in a sounded event. Whether read aloud or read silently, prose is sonorous: we 'listen' to prose when we read with our 'mental ears',[19] with our 'auditory imagination',[20] we pay attention to 'prose melos' with its 'musical characteristics',[21] we 'hear' alliterative and assonant repetitions, we perform syntactical constructions acoustically every time we read in 'that hall of the head' because '[e]verything a sentence is is made manifest by its music.'[22] Music and literature are 'the two temporal arts' that 'contrive their pattern of sounds in time; or, in other words, of sounds and pauses',[23] and as much as music, prose sentences need 'to gratify the sensual ear'[24] and create 'a satisfying equipoise of sound'.[25] Music and literature 'are arts presented through the sense of hearing, having their development in time',[26] and they share 'an intermedial presence' where there are 'signs of a "transposition" of music into narrative literature'.[27] It is not that literature merely 'imitates' music, nor that it shares 'similarities' with it; literature *is* a kind of music, and it always has been, for literature *is* language *is* music – sounded, musical, lexical meaning, representing the fully nuanced spectrum of our capacity for complex and varied sound expression. To listen and to read are acts of performance: '"listening" itself is a performance: to understand how musical pleasure, meaning, and evaluation work, we have to understand how, as listeners, we perform the music for ourselves'.[28] To sing, to write, to listen, to read, to receive, to resonate, to respond, to reciprocate: these are the mutually symbiotic acts of sympathetic resonance which coalesce in canorography: words-music-voice performed in time, manifest in prose.

We already think of, and know of, songs as audial experiences, and the production of a song as creating a reverberation between the singer and her/his world, forging a 'living bridge'. As we witness an 'audial turn' in literature more widely, with the rise in consumption of audio books[29] and performance poetry,[30] perhaps it is time to allow prose production to be viewed in similarly audial terms. For in both song and prose production, mediation and reception, sympathetic resonances can be perceived to be at work. In the live singing of a song, a singer can extend his/her acoustic self into the room towards the audience, and receive reactions and vibrations back from the audience, creating what Milla Tiainen describes as subtle 'foldings-out' and 'foldings-in' of influence.[31] Emily Portman describes her own experience of singing live as 'actual magic', as 'something that's alive and palpable', 'a sense of just tapping into something… there can be a kind of magic that occurs on stage between audience and performers, that requires both parties to hold the space.'[32] Simon Frith describes this 'holding of the space' as a continuous feedback loop, for 'the singer is responding (like the listener) to the musical event of which they are part, being possessed by the music rather than possessing it'.[33] These blurred somatic distinctions between 'originator' and 'recipient' in live music settings can feel profoundly moving for everyone involved.

In studio recordings, these precious moments of performance and reception are seemingly lost. The singer is in isolation; technology mediates between singer and audience; the sound travels to the recipient but the somatic feedback loop, the cycle of influences, is absent. Perhaps at first sight, prose production might resemble the disembodied recorded voice; written in isolation, connections between writer and reader appear lost. However, this would be to forget who performs the prose. In prose, the mediator *is* the recipient; the technology is the reading mind of the human, it is the reader who actively translates printed text back into (imagined or annunciated) sound, so, while the words of a novel are written, published, and printed in isolation, the performance of those words is not: it is acoustic, and fleshly, and noisy, and real-time.

We readers are singers; we perform the 'music of prose' on behalf of the dead, the 'dead', the 'proliferated', the absent, author. Prose is a form of song, an extended performance of the voice, in which we are asked to perform on behalf of the absent author. Writing, singing, reading, listening: there really is no gap between them; for to read is to perform, and to write is to sing. These forms come from the same source; boundaries between them are imagined. This is the 'living bridge' formed in the acoustic production of prose which creates an intimate somatic loop; it unites the reader with the author corporeally, for the reader is generating imagined sound on behalf of the author. The reader becomes the author in very intimate, phonological terms – 'I am Stendhal';[34] as such, there is no boundary between them; they are unified by the 'living bridge' of their shared production across space and time.

The corporeal imbrications of singer and audience necessary to realize song production are the same as those at work between author and reader. Canorographic prose forges 'living bridges' between cultures, genders, races, generations. Moreover, each and every performance is unique: my performance will differ from yours; today I will perform differently to the way I performed yesterday, or when I was fifteen; it will change from year to year, from moment to moment. A unique sympathetic resonance between author and reader emerges every time we read, a resonance that unites us in 'an active sharing, an experience of a special kind',[35] an audial vibration.

Both prose and song, therefore, use the combined production of words, sounds and voices – potential, imagined, actualized – to 'envelop',[36] infiltrate, resonate and conjoin sympathetically resonant receiving and emitting bodies. They both involve a sounded, physical interaction, and both provoke physical responses: what Norma Waterson purportedly called 'the goosies', or our 'second skin' – those impossible-to-feign goosebump reactions to pleasure, unease, recognition, horror, fear, relief. The skin, that reactive organ of truth, sets the hairs to rise when we are experiencing beauty: an immersive, corporeal experience.

Carter demands that we perform her prose as audial event, that we 'sing' her canorographic prose, every time we read her, and, if more evidence than the archive and her textual legacy were required, the swathes of songwriters and musicians who continue to cite her as inspiration prove beyond doubt her significant musical credentials.

This book opens entirely new, rich lines of enquiry within Carter scholarship with the discovery of the folk archive and the close analyses of its relations to Carter's oeuvre. I have shown that Carter was continually raiding the porous boundaries between her singing praxis and her prose production, and how she infused her prose with her experiences of live song performance to produce a prose style literally 'shot through with streams of song',[37] one that went on to influence subsequent musicians. This model, showing music's initial influence on a writer of literature, and its subsequent onward trajectory from literature back into music, can be seen to resemble a running stitch, with song diving in, through and out of prose again in a rich continuing seam of influence: this 'running stitch' move is a new, holistic methodological model which uniquely combines archival, literary, and musicological disciplines, and which might serve to examine further forms of writing, further forms of music, and uncover new resonances between them.

My hope for this book is that it suggests new avenues for further research. Carter is not, and will not be, the only canorographic writer; hers is by no means the only prose to have been influenced by an intimate physical knowledge and memory of song performance and she is not the only writer to imbricate that knowledge within syntax. Once attuned to ideas of canorography, and once resonating sympathetically with an understanding of literature as music, one might be in a position to identify different canorographic elements – the 'invisible music' – at work in the texts of authors such as Maya Angelou, Zadie Smith, or Kazuo Ishiguro, all of them singers as well as writers, or the prose works of Leonard Cohen, Tracy Thorne, Kerry Andrew, James Yorkston or Kathryn Williams, who have traversed perceived boundaries between novelist, poet, recording artist and live performer across their careers. One might analyze how experiences of songwriting and performance bleed into prose constructions, or manifestations of other intermedial forms of music performance, such as the influence of violin performance on Laurie Lee's syntax, or the influences of punk music on the work of William Gibson.[38]

Furthermore, I hope there may be important onward pedagogical implications for the teaching and reimagining of literature as audial event. It might, through further research, be deemed worthwhile to develop techniques which embrace the audial turn, liberating prose from the page, and this book may provide one building block in a new movement to create teaching methods which include performed prose and performance poetry, inviting new generations to engage (re-engage?) with literature as sound.

Carter foresaw a day when books no longer exist: 'I can contemplate with equanimity the science-fiction future world that every day approaches more closely, in which information and narrative pleasure are transmitted electronically and books are a quaint, antiquarian, minority taste.'[39] The entirely digitized literary future Carter predicted may be some way off, but I envisage a time soon in which we reimagine the act of prose reading as one of musical performance. In these divided times, we surely stand to benefit if we can become better attuned to the 'invisible music', the sympathetic resonances, that connect us.

Appendices

Appendix 1

The manifesto for Paul and Angela Carter's folk club in Bristol.

> FOLKSONG AND BALLAD, BRISTOL is a new organisation concerned exclusively with the promotion of a wider appreciation and deeper understanding of the great heritage of traditional folksong, ballad and music of the British Isles, and especially that of England. It also seeks to further the natural evolution of contemporary work within the framework described by tradition.
>
> All arts have form as well as content; we believe that performance styles grossly different to those used traditionally can abuse the songs, and hinder the appreciation of their musical and textual worth. Therefore the singers of fs and b,b. will, as far as possible, use styles assimilated from their knowledge of various traditional performers.
>
> The principal activity of the organisation is to present a series of informal meetings at which folksongs and music will be performed in broadly traditional style. Singers of national repute in this field of authentic folk music will be featured as often as opportunity and finances allow. Also, every opportunity of furthering the cause of folk music in the traditional style by means of lectures, discussions, press articles etc. will be pursued.
>
> Unlike some organisations involved in the current revival of interest in folk music, fs and b,b. maintains an impartiality to current politics and associated problems. This does not mean that we are non-political as individuals, rather that we do not consider political and 'protest' songs to be folksongs.
>
> fs and b,b. is a non profit making body. Funds that accumulate will be used to further our aims. Work performed by the resident singers and organisers is voluntary.
>
> FOLKSONG AND BALLAD, BRISTOL: FORTNIGHTLY: THE LANSDOWNE, CLIFTON ROAD, CLIFTON, BRISTOL. 8.

Figure 22 Paul and Angela Carter, 'Folksong and Ballad, Bristol Manifesto', from Paul and Angela Carter's Folk Music Archive. Copyright © Christine Molan. Reproduced with kind permission of Christine Molan.

158 *Appendices*

Appendix 2

Photographs of the books and magazines in Paul and Angela Carter's folk music archive.

Figures 23 and 24 Photos of archive books and journals, from Paul and Angela Carter's Folk Music Archive. Copyright © Christine Molan. Reproduced with kind permission of Christine Molan.

Appendices 159

Appendix 3

Photo of the LPs in Paul and Angela Carter's folk music archive.

Figure 25 Photo of archive LPs from Paul and Angela Carter's Folk Music Archive. Copyright © Christine Molan. Reproduced with kind permission of Christine Molan.

Appendix 4 – Cheltenham Folk Club sheets

Two club records sheets from the Cheltenham Folk Club, which show Paul and Angela Carter as guest singers, and their repertoires, on two occasions. The recordings in existence were made on 15 January 1967, but the couple also sang at the club in May 1966. That night's proceedings were not committed to tape, because, as Christine Molan explains, the Carters insisted on arranging the group into an egalitarian circle, which made recording more difficult. In January 1967 they were not afforded that opportunity, and so the recording was made. 'Christine Widgery', who appears singing with the Carters on the May 1966 sheet with 'Bill Molan' and other 'Bristol Singers', would later become Christine Molan, the custodian of the archive.

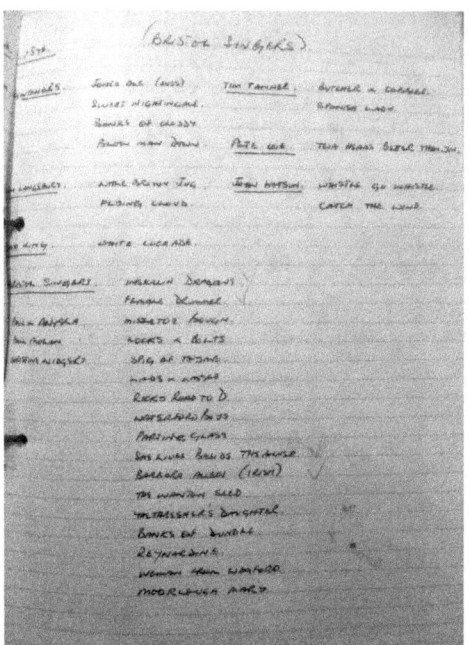

Figure 26 Photo of Cheltenham Folk Club log book page, 15 January 1967. Copyright © Christine Molan. Reproduced with kind permission from Christine Molan and Ken Langsbury of The Cheltenham Folk Club.

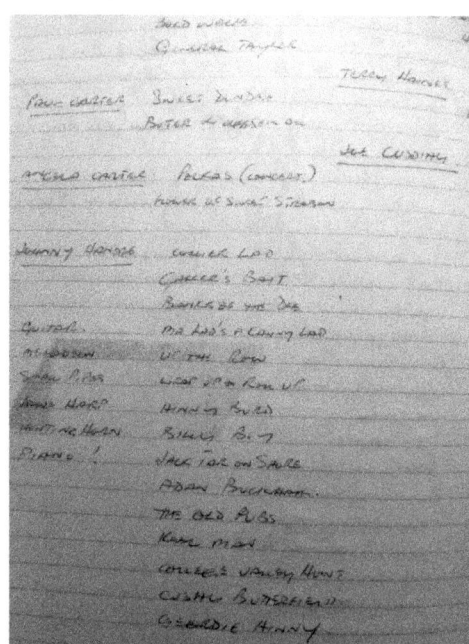

Figure 27 Photo of Cheltenham Folk Club log book page, 1 May 1966. Copyright © Christine Molan. Reproduced with kind permission from Christine Molan and Ken Langsbury of The Cheltenham Folk Club.

Appendix 5 – Emily Portman 'Eye of Tree' versions

EYE OF TREE Draft version	EYE OF TREE Finalized version
Harp Intro (free time into rhythm) *Bring in glitchy atmospheric sounds (flutters/ crackles) & fragments of 'eye of tree' in background.*	*[wind-like opening]*
So long I have strayed in the woods So long I have strayed in the heart of the woods That I am over-grown with lichen and velvet moss	So long I have strayed in the dark woods, So long I have strayed in the woods, jade heart, That I have forgotten to play my part
What did I seek in the woods What did I seek in the heart of the woods I have wondered so long that I have forgotten Was it the Erl king who promised me cathedrals?	Was I searching for you, or running away? I left a crumb trail of fine-pressed powder, Discarded my lace, whalebone and mirror, Gold-flecked eyes in black brook water,
I am overhung with shadows. My cloak is moss velvet The fallow hours of fern spiral tracing Tasting of sap and hard, bitter berries Sweet yellow raspberries and frosted bilberries Crystal cold brook water, young hawthorn in spring …	
I become a hunter and fashion arrows Make a bow string from sinew and gut	
And when at last I find you Your eyes are speckled with gold Time hangs in orbit I am changed No longer well-feathered, well powdered Under-ripe rosebud you plucked I leave no perfume trail My skin has a burnished chestnut sheen I have the woods on my side. I am wearing the forest's disguise	
Eyes of tree heart of clay	
First enticed by the wild bird's echo So long I have strayed in the woods	

continued overleaf

EYE OF TREE Draft version	EYE OF TREE Finalized version

So long I have strayed in the woods dark heart
That I have forgotten how to play the part
That I have forgotten what part to play
 	
I've overgrown with mosses and lichen
Hard as an unripe hawthorn berry
No longer well-feathered or fine-powdered
 	
Eyes of tree heart of clay
 	
So long I have strayed in the woods
So long I have searched in the woods dark heart
That I have forgotten the shape of your face
I have forgotten where my search started
I searched for you under leaf mould
 	
In cracking branches in echoing flutters
But the gold-flecked eyes in the dark pools
Were my own, grown bright in the woods,
The fluting tune was of my own making
My delight was in my own foot-fall's echo
Eye of tree heart of clay
 	
So long I have strayed in the woods
 	
So long I have searched in the woods dark heart
That when I finally see you I dart away
 	
I see my own double and run from the mirror
Wood crack upon twig crack, who can run faster?
You have your cage waiting and I HAVE MINE
Who will be the willing bird, after all this time?
Who will cage a wild bird
 	
Who will cage this wild wild bird?
Who will dare to shut me away with eyes of tree heart of clay?
	Eye of tree
	  Heart of clay
	
	What did I seek in the dark wood,
	Oh what did I seek in the woods, jade heart?
	First enticed by a wild bird's echo,
	Faint on your flute and gutless fiddle
	
	Now I search for your song in branch snap and wing flutter
	Was such neat entrapment all of my own making?
	Taking delight in a trick of my shadow?
	
	Eye of tree
	  Heart of clay
	
	So long I have craved in the dark wood,
	So long I have craved the woods, jade heart,
	When I finally find you, I dart away,
	I see my own double and flee from the mirror,
	Wood crack upon wood crack, who can run faster?
	You have your cage waiting and I have mine,
	Who will play the willing bird?
	After all this time ...
	
	Who will cage this pretty wild bird?
	
	Who will dare to steal you away?
	Who will cage this pretty wild bird?
	Who will dare to steal you away?
	Who will cage this pretty wild bird?
	Who will dare to steal you away?

Notes

Preface

1 Josienne Clarke & Ben Walker and Maz O'Connor performed memorable sets.
2 Melissa Gregg and Gregory J. Seigworth, 'An Inventory of Shimmers', in *The Affect Theory Reader,* ed. by Melissa Gregg and Gregory J. Seigworth (Durham, NC & London: Duke University Press, 2010), pp. 1–25 (p. 18).
3 Werner Wolf, *The Musicalization of Fiction: A Study in the Theory and History of Intermediality* (Amsterdam and Atlanta, GA: Rodopi, 1999), p. 1.
4 Emily Petermann, *The Musical Novel: Imitation of Musical Structure, Performance, and Reception in Contemporary Fiction* (Rochester, NY: Camden House, 2014), p. 5.
5 Wolf, *Musicalization*, p. 4.
6 Wolf, *Musicalization*, p. 229.
7 Wolf, *Musicalization,* p. 16.
8 Petermann, *Musical,* p. 3.
9 Roland Barthes, 'Musica Practica', in *Image Music Text,* trans. by Stephen Heath (London: Fontana Press, 1977), pp. 149–54 (p. 149).
10 Roland Barthes, 'The Grain of the Voice', in *Image Music Text*, trans. by Stephen Heath (London: Fontana Press, 1977), pp. 179–89 (p. 188).
11 Lawrence Kramer, *Musical Meaning: Toward a Critical History* (Berkeley, CA and London: University of California Press, 2002), p. 4.
12 Although Carter's prose shares some of the objectives of performative writing, such as a desire to 'discern possible intersections of speech and writing' and to 'make writing perform'. Della Pollock, 'Performing Writing', in *The Ends of Performance*, ed. by Peggy Phelan, Jill Lane (New York: New York University Press, 1998), pp. 73–103 (pp. 76, 79).
13 T. S. Eliot, *The Use of Poetry and the Use of Criticism*, first publ. 1933 (London: Faber & Faber, 1948), p. 118.
14 Walter J. Ong, *Orality and Literacy: The Technologizing of the Word* (London: Routledge, 2002), p. 171.
15 Ong, *Orality*, p. 168.

1 Songful influences

1 Angela Carter, 'Now is the Time for Singing', *Nonesuch*, 122 (1964), 11–15 (p. 15). I have taken the liberty of correcting what I believe to be a typo here. In the original essay, published in *Nonesuch Magazine*, 'one' was printed as 'on'. I have searched amongst Carter's papers, without success, for an original submission text of the essay with which to cross-check. However, I did receive this message of reassurance from Ian Coates, a member of the Special Collections Team at Bristol University's Arts & Social Sciences Library, where *Nonesuch* is archived: 'on reading the paragraph in

question, I think you are correct that it was a misprint'. Ian Coates, email to the author, 7 November 2017.
2. Carter wrote, 'About ⅔ of the way through "Shadow Dance"; another three or four chapters should see the first draft finished. It's coming along.' Angela Carter, *1963–64 Journal* (unpublished diary), BL Add MS 88899/1/89, 9 July 1964.
3. Marina Warner, 'Introduction', in *The Second Virago Book of Fairy Tales* (London: Virago, 1992), pp. ix–xvi (p. xiii).
4. The Child ballads are the 305 ballads collected by the philologist F. J. Child and published as *The English & Scottish Popular Ballads* across five volumes by Houghton, Mifflin and Co. between 1882–98. The Carters' copies of the Purslow and Reeves song books remain in the archive.
5. Charlotte Crofts, *'Anagrams of Desire': Angela Carter's writing for radio, film and television* (Manchester: Manchester University Press, 2003), p. 39.
6. Crofts, *Anagrams*, pp. 40–1.
7. Jack Zipes, 'Introduction', in *Angela Carter, The Fairy Tales of Charles Perrault* (London: Penguin, 2008), pp. vii–xxvii (p. viii).
8. Lorna Sage, *Women in the House of Fiction: Post-War Women Novelists* (Basingstoke: Macmillan, 1992), p. 173.
9. Paul Carter remembered fondly a trip he and Angela made from London in 1959 to hear some of the older Sussex singers at a pub reunion organized by young local collectors: 'Me 'n Angela were picked up by Reg Hall in South Croydon and we all went to one of those incredible Sussex do's. Angela and I had just discovered "Folkestone Murder" and the three of us thought "the dismal bell is tolling" very funny. I don't know why, in context it chills the heart.' Paul Carter, email to Christine Molan, cited in Christine Molan, 'Authentic Magic: Angela, Folksong and Bristol', in *Strange Worlds: The Vision of Angela Carter*, ed. by Marie Mulvey-Roberts and Fiona Robinson (Bristol: Sansom, 2016), pp. 29–32 (p. 31).
10. Angela Stalker, 'Come in, take a chair, lean on it and sing', *Croydon Advertiser*, 31 March 1961, p. 4. Angela Carter, 'Rich life behind the cool mask', *Western Daily Press*, 19 March 1962, p. 4. Angela Carter, 'The festival opens with folk music', *Western Daily Press*, 31 October 1962, p. 6.
11. Angela Carter, 'Some Speculations on Possible Relationships between the Medieval Period and 20th Century Folk Song Poetry' (unpublished BA thesis, submitted to Bristol University, 1965), BL Add MS 88899/1/116.
12. Carter's unpublished journals are peppered with folk song references. See for example BL Add MS: 1960 88899/1/100 (p. 5), 1961 88899/1/86 (p. 19), 1961–62 88899/1/87 (p. 21); 1962–63 88899/1/88 (p. 24); 1963–64 88899/1/89 (July 1964); 1965–66 88899/1/90 (pp. 8, 9, 11, 19), 1966–68 88899/1/91 (p. 16).
13. Paul and Angela Carter's Folk Music Archive is in private ownership in Bristol at the time of writing. The custodian, Christine Molan, was a folk singing friend of the Carters in the 1960s, and on Paul's death the box of folk song notes, books and LPs was passed to her.
14. Peggy Seeger, *Troubled Love* (Topic Records TOP72, 1962); Peggy Seeger, *Early in the Spring* (Topic Records TOP73, 1962); Louis Killen, *Ballads and Broadsides* (Topic Records 12T126, 1965).
15. Angela Carter, 'The Flower of Sweet Strabane' and 'Saint Mary's & Church Street Medley', recorded live at the Cheltenham Folk Club, 15 January 1967 © Denis Olding, 1967.
16. Cecil Sharp, *English Folk-Song: Some Conclusions* (London: Novello, 1907), p. 16.

17 Lorna Sage, *Angela Carter*, first publ. 1994 (Tavistock: Northcote House, 2007), p. 40.
18 Lorna Sage, 'The Savage Sideshow: a profile of Angela Carter', *New Review*, 4/39–40 (1977), 51–7 (p. 53).
19 Susannah Clapp, 'Introduction', in Angela Carter, *The Curious Room: Plays, film scripts and an opera* (London: Vintage, 1997), pp. vii–x (p. viii).
20 Carter's protagonists lead us to such conclusions: Dora in *Wise Children* exclaims, 'What a joy it is to dance and sing!' (*Wise Children* (London: Vintage, 1992), p. 232), while Fevvers in *Nights at the Circus* declares, 'To speak is one thing. To sing is quite another' (*Nights at the Circus* (London: Vintage, 2006), pp. 179–80).
21 Edmund Gordon, *The Invention of Angela Carter* (London: Chatto & Windus, 2016), p. 65.
22 Carter, 'Rich life', p. 4.
23 John Haffenden, 'Angela Carter', in *Novelists in Interview* (London: Methuen, 1985), pp. 76–96 (p. 84).
24 Although, as Stephen Benson observes, '*The Bloody Chamber* has not been swamped beneath the weight of critical comment it has generated.' Stephen Benson, 'Angela Carter and the Literary Märchen', first publ. in *Marvels & Tales*, 12/1 (1998), 23–51 (p. 43); repr. in *Angela Carter and the Fairy Tale*, ed. by Danielle M. Roemer and Cristina Bacchilega (Detroit, MI: Wayne State University Press, 2001), pp. 30–58.
25 Angela Carter, 'Introduction', in *The Virago Book of Fairy Tales* (London: Virago, 1990), pp. ix–xxii (pp. ix–x).
26 Danielle M. Roemer and Cristina Bacchilega, 'Introduction', in *Angela Carter and the Fairy Tale*, ed. by Danielle M. Roemer and Cristina Bacchilega (Detroit, MI: Wayne State University Press, 2001), pp. 7–25 (p. 11).
27 Benson, 'Märchen', pp. 41, 43, 25.
28 Anny Crunelle-Vanrigh, 'The Logic of the Same and *Différance*: "The Courtship of Mr Lyon"', in *Angela Carter and the Fairy Tale*, ed. by Danielle M. Roemer and Cristina Bacchilega (Detroit, MI: Wayne State University Press, 2001), pp. 128–44 (pp. 131, 133).
29 Marina Warner, *From the Beast to the Blonde: Fairy Tales and their Tellers* (London: Vintage, 1995), pp. 193–4.
30 Haffenden, *Interview*, p. 93.
31 Sarah Gamble, *Angela Carter: Writing from the Front Line* (Edinburgh: Edinburgh University Press, 1997), p. 29.
32 Gamble, *Front Line*, p. 24.
33 Angela Carter, 'Sugar Daddy', first publ. 1983, repr. in *Shaking a Leg: Collected Journalism and Writings*, ed. by Jenny Uglow (London: Vintage, 2013) (hereafter *SAL*), pp. 24–36 (p. 35).
34 Laura Mulvey, 'Cinema Magic and the Old Monsters', in *Flesh and the Mirror: Essays on the Art of Angela Carter*, ed. by Lorna Sage (London: Virago, 1994), pp. 230–42 (p. 241).
35 Marina Warner, 'The Uses of Enchantment: Lecture at the National Film Theatre, 7 February 1992', in *Cinema and the Realms of Enchantment: Lectures, Seminars and Essays by Marina Warner and others*, ed. by Duncan Petrie, BFI Working Papers series (London: British Film Institute, 1993), pp. 13–35 (p. 24).
36 Guido Almansi, 'In The Alchemist's Cave: radio plays', in *Flesh and the Mirror: Essays on the Art of Angela Carter*, ed. by Lorna Sage (London: Virago, 1994), pp. 216–29 (p. 221).

37 Angela Carter, 'Preface to *Come Unto These Yellow Sands*', in Angela Carter, *The Curious Room: Plays, Film Scripts and an Opera*, ed. by Mark Bell (London: Vintage, 1997), pp. 497–502 (p. 497).
38 Almansi, 'Cave', p. 229.
39 '... radio retains the atavistic lure, the atavistic power, of voices in the dark, and the writer who gives the words to those voices retains some of the authority of the most antique tellers of tales'. Angela Carter, 'Preface to *Come Unto These Yellow Sands*', in *The Curious Room: Plays, Film Scripts and an Opera*, ed. Mark Bell (London: Vintage, 1997), pp. 497–502 (p. 502).
40 Crofts, *Anagrams*, p. 40.
41 Crofts, *Anagrams*, p. 59.
42 Carter, 'Introduction', *Virago*, p. ix.
43 Stephen Benson, *Cycles of Influence: Fiction Folktale Theory* (Detroit, MI: Wayne State University Press, 2003), p. 216.
44 Julie Sauvage, 'Bloody chamber melodies: painting and music in *The Bloody Chamber*', in *The Arts of Angela Carter: A Cabinet of Curiosities*, ed. by Marie Mulvey-Roberts (Manchester: Manchester University Press, 2019), pp. 58–79 (p. 60).
45 Roemer and Bacchilega, 'Introduction', p. 8.
46 Jack Zipes, *The Irresistible Fairy Tale: The Cultural and Social History of a Genre* (Princeton, NJ: Princeton University Press, 2012), p. 22.
47 Carter, 'Introduction', *Virago*, p. ix.
48 Stith Thompson, *The Folktale* (New York: Dryden Press, 1946), pp. 8, 10.
49 Steven Swann Jones, *The Fairy Tale: Magic Mirror of the Imagination* (London: Routledge, 2002), pp. 5, 8.
50 Bruno Bettelheim, *The Uses of Enchantment: The Meaning and Importance of Fairy Tales* (London: Thames and Hudson, 1976), p. 7.
51 Jack Zipes, *Why Fairy Tales Stick: The Evolution and Relevance of a Genre* (Abingdon: Routledge, 2006), p. xi.
52 Jack Zipes, *Breaking the Magic Spell: Radical Theories of Folk and Fairy Tales* (London: Heinemann, 1979), p. 3.
53 Andrew Teverson, *Fairy Tale* (Abingdon: Routledge, 2013), p. 130.
54 Cay Dollerup, Iven Reventlow and Carsten Rosenberg Hansen, 'A Case Study for Editorial Filters in Folktales: A Discussion of the *Allerleirauh* Tales in Grimm', *Fabula* 27/1 (1986), 12–30 (p. 12).
55 Sharp, *Conclusions*, p. 3.
56 Maud Karpeles, 'Definition of Folk Music', *Journal of the International Folk Music Council*, 7 (1955), 6–7 (p. 6).
57 Raymond Williams, 'folk', in *Keywords: A Vocabulary of Society and Culture* (New York: Oxford University Press, 1985), pp. 136–7 (p. 137).
58 Steve Roud, 'General Introduction', in *The New Penguin Book of English Folk Songs*, ed. by Steve Roud and Julia Bishop (London: Penguin, 2012), pp. ix–xli (p. xii).
59 Frank Sidgwick, *The Ballad* (London: Martin Secker, 1915), p. 52.
60 'Such songs were, no doubt, intended to help proscribe extramarital sexual activity on the part of young village girls. Whether they had any effect on illegitimacy rates is now unguessable.' Angela Carter, 'Alison's Giggle', first publ. 1983, repr. in *SAL*, pp. 662–76 (p. 676).
61 EFDSS website Beginners' Guide <https://www.efdss.org/learning/resources/beginners-guides/52-english-folk-song/2456-efdss-themes-part1> [accessed 14 February 2022]. See Carter's 1969 novel of the same name.

62 Sharp, *Conclusions*, p. viii.
63 Reg Hall, interview with the author, 5 December 2014.
64 Sharp, *Conclusions*, p. 63.
65 Trish Winter and Simon Keegan-Phipps, *Performing Englishness: Identity and politics in a contemporary folk resurgence* (Manchester: Manchester University Press, 2013), p. 6.
66 Dave Harker, *Fakesong: The Manufacture of British 'Folk Song' 1700 to the Present Day* (Milton Keynes: Open University Press, 1985), p. 110.
67 Steve Roud, *Folk Song In England* (London: Faber, 2017), p. 10.
68 Roud, *England*, p. 10.
69 Victor Zuckerkandl, 'The Meaning of Song', in *Music, Words and Voice: A Reader*, ed. by Martin Clayton (Manchester: Manchester University Press, 2008), pp. 113–18 (p. 114).
70 Zuckerkandl, 'Meaning', p. 115.
71 Sharp, *Conclusions*, p. ix.
72 Roud, *England*, p. 11.
73 'Music points to true language in the sense that content is apparent in it, but it does so at the cost of unambiguous meaning, which has migrated to the languages of intentionality. And as though Music, that most eloquent of all languages, needed consoling for the curse of ambiguity – its mythic aspect, intentions are poured into it.' Theodor Adorno, *Quasi Una Fantasia*, first publ. 1963, trans. by Rodney Livingstone (London: Verso, 1992), p. 3.
74 Lawrence Kramer, *Musical Meaning: Towards a Critical History* (Berkeley, CA: University of California Press, 2002), p. 4.
75 Angela Carter, 'Now is the Time for Singing', *Nonesuch* 122 (1964), 11–15 (p. 12). This essay was reprinted in *SAL*, pp. 383–94.
76 Kramer, *Musical*, p. 4.
77 Carter, 'Now', p. 15.
78 Carter, 'Now', p. 12.
79 Zuckerkandl, 'Meaning', p. 115.
80 Robert Frost, 'The Hear-Say Ballad (1953)', in *The Collected Prose of Robert Frost*, ed. by Mark Richardson (Cambridge, MA: Harvard University Press, 2007), pp. 171–2 (p. 171).
81 George Herzog, 'song: folk song and the music of folk song' in *Funk & Wagnalls Standard Dictionary of Folklore, Mythology and Legend*, ed. by Maria Leach (San Francisco, CA: Harper Collins, 1996), pp. 1032–50 (p. 1033).
82 Roud, *England*, p. 16.
83 Stith Thompson, 'folktale', in *Funk & Wagnalls*, p. 408.
84 Francis Lee Utley, 'Folk Literature: An Operational Definition', *The Journal of American Folklore*, 74/293 (Jul-Sep 1961), 193–206 (p. 199).
85 Warner, *Blonde*, p. 24.
86 Hilda Ellis Davidson and Anna Chaudhri, *A Companion to the Fairy Tale* (Cambridge: DS Brewer, 2003), p. 2.
87 Roud, *England*, p. 13.
88 Roland Barthes, 'The Grain of the Voice', in *Image Music Text*, trans. by Stephen Heath (London: Fontana Press, 1977), pp. 179–89 (p. 188).
89 Kramer, *Musical*, p. 3.
90 A. L. Lloyd, *Folk Song In England*, first publ. 1967 (Frogmore: Paladin, 1975), p. 151.
91 Peggy Seeger, interview with the author, 4 January 2016.

92 F. J. Child, '"Ballad Poetry", *Johnson's Universal Cyclopædia* (1900)', *Journal of Folklore Research*, 31/1–3, Triple Issue: Ballad Redux (January–December 1994), 214–22 (p. 214).
93 Milla Tiainen, 'Corporeal Voices, Sexual Differentiations: New Materialist Perspectives on Music, Singing and Subjectivity', in *Sonic Interventions*, ed. by Sylvia Mieszkowski, Joy Smith and Marijke de Valck (New York: Rodopi, 2007), pp. 147–68 (p. 158).
94 Tiainen, 'Corporeal', p. 157.
95 Carter, 'Sugar', p. 35.
96 See Carter's description of Sunny the tramp playing an imaginary violin: Angela Carter, *Several Perceptions*, first publ. 1968 (London: Virago, 1995), p. 1. This description chimes with a non-fiction essay Carter wrote about a local character: see Angela Carter, 'A Busker (Retired)', *New Society*, 1967, 471.
97 Richard Schechner, *Performance Theory* (London: Routledge Classics, 2003), pp. 14, 24.
98 Kramer, *Musical*, p. 53.
99 Kramer, *Musical*, p. 59.
100 Kramer, *Musical*, p. 60.
101 Kramer, *Musical*, p. 64.
102 Carter, 'Preface', p. 499.
103 Marina Warner, 'Why Angela Carter's *The Bloody Chamber* Still Bites', *Scotsman*, 15 September 2012 <https://www.scotsman.com/arts-and-culture/books/marina-warner-why-angela-carters-bloody-chamber-still-bites-2461766> [accessed 17 February 2022]
104 T. S. Eliot, *The Use of Poetry and The Use of Criticism* (London: Faber & Faber, 1948), p. 118.
105 Jacques Derrida, *Of Grammatology*, first publ. 1967, trans. by Gayatri Chakravorty Spivak (Baltimore, MD: John Hopkins University Press, 1997), p. 17.
106 Jeremy Prynne, 'Mental Ears and Poetic Work', *Chicago Review*, 55/1 (Winter 2010), 126–57 (p. 126).
107 Lawrence Kramer, *Music & Poetry: The Nineteenth Century and After*, (Berkeley, CA: University of California Press, 1992), p. 8.
108 Angela Carter, *Shadow Dance*, first publ. 1966 (London: Virago, 2014), p. 4.
109 Angela Carter, *Nights at the Circus*, first publ. 1984 (London: Vintage, 2006), p. 47.
110 Dani Cavallaro, *The World of Angela Carter: A Critical Investigation* (Jefferson, NC: McFarland, 2011), p. 176.
111 Angela Carter, *The Magic Toyshop*, first publ. 1967 (London: Virago, 1992), p. 197.
112 Carter, 'Introduction', *Virago Book*, p. ix.
113 Crofts, *Anagrams*, p. 40.
114 Warner, 'Bites'.
115 Salman Rushdie, 'Introduction', in Angela Carter, *Burning Your Boats: Collected Stories* (London: Vintage, 1996) (hereafter *BYB*), pp. ix–xvi (p. x).
116 Kramer, *Musical*, p. 63.
117 Friedrich A. Kittler, *Gramophone, Film, Typewriter*, first publ. 1986, trans. Geoffrey Winthrop-Young and Michael Wutz (Stanford, CA: Stanford University Press, 1999), p. 10.
118 See Calvin S. Brown, *Music and Literature: A Comparison of the Arts*, first publ. 1948 (Hanover, NH: University Press of New England, 1987); Werner Wolf, *The Musicalization of Fiction: A Study in the Theory and History of Intermediality* (Amsterdam: Rodopi, 1999); Stephen Benson, *Literary Music: Writing Music in Contemporary Fiction* (London: Routledge, 2006); Emily Petermann, *The Musical*

Novel: Imitation of Musical Structure, Performance, and Reception in Contemporary Fiction (Rochester, NY: Camden House, 2014).
119 See John Street and Sara Cohen, *Popular Music,* 24/2 'Literature and Music Issue' (2005); *Litpop: Writing and Popular Music,* ed. by Rachel Carroll and Adam Hansen (Farnham: Ashgate, 2016).
120 See George Deacon, *John Clare and the Folk Tradition,* first publ. 1983 (London: Francis Boutle, 2002).
121 Paul and Angela Carter's Folk Music Archive is a newly discovered private archive of folk song notes, LPs and books made and owned by Paul Carter and Angela Carter, including two recordings, one of Angela singing, and the other of her playing the English concertina, in private hands in Bristol at the time of writing. See Appendices for images from the archive.
122 Maurice Merleau-Ponty, *The Prose of the World,* ed. by Claude Lefort, trans. by John O'Neill (Evanston, IL: Northwestern University Press, 1973), pp. 12–13.

2 'a singer's swagger': Angela Carter, the folk singer

1 Christine Molan, 'Authentic Magic: Angela, folk song and Bristol', in *Strange Worlds: The Vision of Angela Carter,* ed. by Marie Mulvey-Roberts and Fiona Robinson (Bristol: Sansom & Co, 2017), pp. 29–32 (p. 29).
2 Angela Carter, 'The Flower of Sweet Strabane' and 'Saint Mary's & Church Street Medley', recorded live at the Cheltenham Folk Club, 15 January 1967 © Denis Olding, 1967, contained in Paul and Angela Carter's Folk Music Archive.
3 *Derry Journal,* Friday Morning 14 May 1915, 'Come All Ye' column, p. 2 <http://www.britishnewspaperarchive.co.uk/viewer/bl/0001123/19150514/051/0002?_=1464951754261> [accessed 3 February 2022].
4 *Sam Henry's Songs of the People,* ed. by Gale Huntington and Lani Herrmann (Athens, GA: University of Georgia Press, 1990), pp. 390–1.
5 'Subject: RE: Lyr Req: The Flower of Sweet Strabane From: GUEST, Direct descendant Date: 06 Dec 15 – 07:30 PM @Frank Maher There are some words in your version that are wrong. I am a direct descendant of Martha Ramsey I still live in Strabane not to [sic.] far from where Martha was born actually. I shall post the proper version when I have time. The [sic.] are verses missed down through the years.' Mudcat Café website <http://www.mudcat.org/thread.cfm?ThreadID=8569#53604> [accessed 14 February 2022].
6 Paddy Tunney, 'The Flower of Sweet Strabane', on *A Wild Bees' Nest* (Topic Records 12T139, 1965). See also Paddy Tunney, *Where Songs Do Thunder: Travels in Traditional Song* (Belfast: Appletree, 1991), pp. 58–9.
7 'In Donegal, Paul and Angela met and befriended Paddy Tunney, an outstanding singer of great wit. [...] Angela was recorded by chance singing one of Paddy's favourites 'The Flower of Sweet Strabane'...' Molan, 'Authentic Magic', p. 32.
8 Rod Stradling, who played folk songs with the Carters and who now runs *Musical Traditions* <http://www.mustrad.org.uk>, suggested to Molan that Carter probably learned this medley from a similar version which appeared on the eponymous LP Chieftains, *Chieftains* (Claddagh Records CC02, 1963).
9 A manifesto for this club, co-authored by Paul and Angela Carter, also exists in the archive. See Appendix 1.
10 Angela Carter, 'Our Author of the Month', *Storyteller,* July 1962, p. 1.

11 Edmund Gordon, *The Invention of Angela Carter* (London: Chatto & Windus, 2016), p. 44.
12 Christine Molan points out, trad fad 'was what the late 50s fashion for trad jazz was always called'. Email to the author, 23 June 2020. See also George McKay, 'Trad jazz in 1950s Britain – protest, pleasure, politics – interviews with some of those involved', January 2010 <http://usir.salford.ac.uk/id/eprint/9306/1/trad_jazz_interviews_2001-02_PDF.pdf> [accessed 14 February 2022].
13 Angela Carter, 'The Mother Lode', first publ. 1976, repr. in *SAL*, pp. 3–19 (p. 6).
14 Angela Carter, 'Afterword', in *The Fairy Tales of Charles Perrault* (London: Penguin, 2008), pp. 71–8 (p. 74).
15 In Chapter 6, I shall describe song-infused prose as 'canorography', or 'canorographic' writing.
16 The balladic mood is seen to be more concerned with its compelling narrative, such as in 'Jackie Munro': 'Way out in the country there lived a wealthy squire'. A. L. Lloyd, 'Jackie Munro', *English Street Songs* (Riverside RLP12-614, 1956). 'Defined in simplest terms, the ballad is a folk-song that tells a story.' G. H. Gerould, *The Ballad of Tradition* (New York: Oxford University Press, 1957), p. 3. The lyric, by contrast, expresses, in the first person, the singer's emotions at that moment, such as in 'The Butcher Boy': 'I wish, I wish, but it's all in vain'. Sarah Makem, 'The Butcher Boy', *The Heart Is True (The Voice of the People Series) Vol. 24*, recorded by Paul Carter and Sean O'Boyle 1967 (Topic Records TSCD674, 2012). 'A distinctive feature of lyric seems to be this attempt to create the impression of something happening now, in the present time of discourse.' Jonathan Culler, *Theory of the Lyric* (Cambridge, MA: Harvard University Press, 2015), p. 37.
17 Angela Carter, 'Now is the Time for Singing', *Nonesuch*, 122 (1964), 11–15 (p. 15).
18 Angela Carter, *1961 Journal* (unpublished diary), BL Add MS 88899/1/86, p. 2.
19 Carter, *1961 Journal*, p. 19. Carter also uses 'The Unquiet Grave' as an example of a ballad of some antiquity in her dissertation: 'It seems to me that the "timelessness and placelessness" of ballads, their seeming isolation from any given place or time, the frequent atmosphere of mystery which CS Lewis notes in *The Discarded Image*, is not really a quality inherent in the narrative ballad itself, as a form. If these qualities are present in ballads of extremely venerable origin, such as "The Unquiet Grave" (Child 78) and "Thomas The Rhymer" (Child 37) (sic.), then they are also present, I think, in "As We Were A-Sailing" and, indeed, in many of the "shudder romances" of sexual murder.' Angela Carter, 'Some Speculations on Possible Relationships between the Medieval Period and 20th Century Folk Song Poetry' (unpublished BA thesis, University of Bristol, 1965), BL Add MS 88899/1/116, p. 12.
20 Angela Carter, *1963–64 Journal* (unpublished diary), BL Add MS 88899/1/89, February 1964. See also Carter's likely reference: A. G. Gilchrist, 'One Moonlight Night', *Journal of the Folk-Song Society*, 2/9 (1906), 297–9.
21 Angela Carter, sleeve notes for Peggy Seeger, *Troubled Love* (Topic Records TOP72, 1962).
22 Angela Carter, sleeve notes for Peggy Seeger, *Early in the Spring* (Topic Records TOP73, 1962).
23 Angela Carter, sleeve notes for Louis Killen, *Ballads and Broadsides* (Topic Records 12T126, 1965).
24 Carter, 'Now', p. 15.
25 Carter, 'Now', p. 11.
26 Angela Carter, 'Fools Are My Theme', first publ. 1982, repr. in *SAL*, pp. 39–45 (p. 40).

27 David Atkinson, *The English Traditional Ballad: Theory, Method, and Practice* (Aldershot: Ashgate, 2002), p. 13.
28 Ralph Vaughan Williams, Cecil J. Sharp, G. S. K. Butterworth, Frank Kidson, A. G. Gilchrist and Lucy E. Broadwood, 'Songs Collected from Sussex', *Journal of the Folk-Song Society*, 4/ 17 (January 1913), 279–324 (pp. 310–19).
29 *The Penguin Book of English Folk Songs*, ed. by Ralph Vaughan Williams and A. L. Lloyd (Harmondsworth: Penguin, 1959), p. 98.
30 Carter, 'Speculations', p. 47.
31 Carter, 'Speculations', p. 1.
32 See the epigraph for Chapter 1 for her pronouncement in 'Now' that singing folk songs was affecting her imagination.
33 Angela Carter, 'Notes from the Front Line', first publ. 1983, repr. in *SAL*, pp. 45–53 (p. 47).
34 A. L. Lloyd, *Folk Song in England*, first publ. 1967 (Frogmore: Paladin, 1975), p. 151.
35 Carter, 'Now', pp. 14–15.
36 Vladimir Propp, *Theory and History of Folklore*, trans. by Ariadna Y. Martin and Richard P. Martin, ed. by Anatoly Liberman (Minneapolis, MN: University of Minnesota Press, 1984), p. 7.
37 Carter, 'Notes', p. 51.
38 Carter, 'Notes', p. 49.
39 'Years ago, the late A. L. Lloyd, ethnomusicologist, folklorist and singer, taught me that I didn't need to know an artist's name to recognize that one had been at work. This book is dedicated to that proposition and, therefore, to his memory.' Angela Carter, 'Introduction', in *The Virago Book of Fairy Tales* (London: Virago, 1990), p. xxii.
40 Carter, 'Speculations', p. 29.
41 Carter, 'Speculations', p. 29.
42 Walter J. Ong, *Orality and Literary: The Technologizing of the Word* (London: Routledge, 2002), p. 47.
43 Carter, 'Now', p. 13.
44 See James Porter, 'Jeannie Robertson's "My Son David": A Conceptual Performance Model', *Journal of American Folklore*, 89/351 (January–March 1976), 7–26.
45 Carter, 'Speculations', p. 3.
46 Carter, on Seeger, *Spring*.
47 Carter, on Killen, *Broadsides*.
48 Carter, 'Speculations', p. 98.
49 Carter, 'Now', p. 14.
50 Carter, 'Speculations', pp. 14–15.
51 Carter, 'Speculations', p. 13.
52 Cecil Sharp and Olive Campbell, *English Folk Songs from the Southern Appalachians*, Vol. 1, first publ. 1917 (London: Oxford University Press, 1932), p. xxxvii.
53 Carter, 'Now', p. 13.
54 Carter, 'Now', p. 13.
55 Angela Carter, teaching notes on the 'Bluebeard' cycle, in 'Angela Carter Papers: Miscellaneous fairy tale material (1984, 1992, n.d.) (unpublished papers), BL Add MS 88899/1/82, pp. 123–4.
56 'Few writers, indeed, are probably conscious of the length to which they push this melody of letters.' Robert Louis Stevenson, 'On Some Technical Elements of Style in Literature', in *Essays in the Art of Writing* (London: Chatto & Windus, 1905), p. 40.
57 Carter, 'Now', p. 15.

58 Northrope Frye, *The Anatomy of Criticism: Four Essays*, first publ. 1957 (Princeton, NJ: Princeton University Press, 1971).
59 Angela Carter, *1962–63 Journal* (unpublished diary), BL Add MS 88899/1/88, pp. 9–10.
60 Angela Carter, 'Preface to *Come Unto These Yellow Sands*', in *The Curious Room: Collected Dramatic Works*, ed. by Mark Bell (London: Vintage, 1997), pp. 497–502 (p. 499).
61 Angela Carter, *The Infernal Desire Machines of Doctor Hoffman*, first publ. 1972 (London: Penguin, 2011), p. 79.
62 Carter, *Hoffman*, p. 88. For links between this described sound and the literary tradition of the nightingale, see Chapter 6.
63 Carter, *Hoffman*, p. 103.
64 F. J. Child, *The English and Scottish Popular Ballads, 10 Parts,* (Boston, MA: Houghton, Mifflin & Co, 1882–98). These 305 folk songs are now collectively and affectionately known as the Child ballads.
65 Carter criticizes Child for this omission of tunes in her dissertation: 'Child compiled a selection of largely para-ballads.' Carter, 'Speculations', p. 7.
66 See p. 10.
67 In Plato's *Cratylus*, Socrates identifies 'that things have natural names' and that 'only someone who looks to the natural name of each thing and is able to put its form into letters and syllables' is 'a craftsman of names'. He concludes that 'the best possible way to speak consists in using names all (or most) of which are like the things they name (that is, are appropriate to them), while the worst is to use the opposite kind of names.' In other words, there is a value judgement for the sound of words based on their proximity to likeness. *Plato: The Complete Works*, ed. by John M. Cooper (Indianapolis, IN: Hackett, 1997), pp. 109, 151. Adorno ruminates on the similarities between the language of music and the language of words. 'Music resembles language in the sense that it is a temporal sequence of articulated sounds which are more than just sounds. They say something, often something human. The better the music, the more forcefully they say it. The succession of sounds is like logic; it can be right or wrong. But what has been said cannot be detached from the music. Music creates no semiotic system. [...] Music points to true language in the sense that content is apparent in it, but it does so at the cost of unambiguous meaning, which has migrated to the languages of intentionality. And as though Music, that most eloquent of all languages, needed consoling for the curse of ambiguity – its mythic aspect, intentions are poured into it.' Theodor Adorno, *Quasi Una Fantasia*, first publ. 1963, trans. by Rodney Livingstone (London: Verso, 1992), pp. 1, 3.
68 Samuel P. Bayard, 'Prolegomena to a Study of the Principal Melodic Families of British-American Folk Song', *Journal of American Folklore*, 63/247 (January–March 1950), 1–44, (p. 34).
69 Bayard, 'Prolegomena', p. 35.
70 Carter, 'Now', p. 11.
71 Georgina Boyes, 'Introduction and Commentary (2004)', to A. L. Lloyd, *The Singing Englishman*, first publ. 1944, <http://www.mustrad.org.uk/articles/tse> [accessed 17 February 2022].
72 Niall MacKinnon, *The British Folk Scene: Musical Performance and Social Identity* (Buckingham: Open University Press, 1993), pp. 127, 15. See Emily Portman's discussion of performance in Chapter 7.
73 Carter, 'Now', p. 13.
74 Carter, 'Now', p. 12.

75 Carter, 'Now', p. 13.
76 Carter, 'Now', p. 14.
77 Carter, 'Now', p. 13.
78 'We can start with a simple statement: *A folk song is a song sung by a folk singer, and a folk singer is someone who sings folk songs.* Ridiculous as this may sound, it is actually useful to highlight the way we often use the term 'folk' in everyday situations. Many of us do slide between the singer and the song. . . .' Steve Roud, *Folk Song in England* (London: Faber, 2017), p. 16.
79 Homer, *The Iliad*, trans. by Martin Hammond (London: Penguin, 1987), p. 3.
80 Andrew Ford, *Homer: The Poetry of the Past* (Ithaca, NY: Cornell University Press, 1992), pp. 43-4.
81 Andrew Ford, 'Epic as Genre', in *A New Companion to Homer*, ed. by Ian Morris and Barry B. Powell (Boston, MA: Brill, 1997), pp. 396-414 (p. 407), unedited version <https://www.academia.edu/788503/Epic_as_Genre> [accessed 16 February 2022].
82 Aristotle, *On Rhetoric*, trans. by George A. Kennedy, 2nd edn (Oxford: Oxford University Press, 2007), p. 196.
83 Robert Frost, 'The Hear-Say Ballad', in *The Collected Prose of Robert Frost*, ed. by Mark Richardson (Cambridge, MA: Harvard University Press, 2007), pp. 171-2.
84 Frank Sidgwick, *The Ballad* (London: Martin Decker, 1914), pp. 7-8.
85 Constantin Brăiloiu, 'Outline of a Method of Musical Folklore', trans. Margaret Mooney, *Ethnomusicology*, 14/3 (September 1970), 389-417 (p. 394).
86 Ginette Dunn, *The Fellowship of Song: Popular Singing Traditions in East Suffolk* (London: Croom Helm, 1980), pp. 13-14.
87 Carter, 'Now', pp. 12-14.
88 Roland Barthes, 'Loving Schumann', in *The Responsibility of Forms: Critical Essays on Music, Art and Representation*, trans. by Richard Howard (Berkeley, CA: University of California Press, 1985), pp. 293-8 (p. 295).
89 Cecil Sharp, *English Folk-Song: Some Conclusions* (London: Novello, 1907), p. 16.
90 Dunn, *Fellowship*, pp. 47, 91.
91 Edmund Husserl, 'ein Zeitobjekt im eigentlichen Sinn', cited in HU Gumbrecht, *Our Broad Present: Time and Contemporary Culture* (New York: Columbia University Press, 2014), p. 4.
92 Carter, 'Now', p. 15.
93 The mediated nature of the folk singing voice by recordings, and the production of commercial albums, was to become a more contentious activity as the 1960s continued (see p. 8). Through similar processes of revised attitudes, Angela Carter may have come to align theoretically the practice of recording folk song with more patriarchal activities of oppression.
94 See Appendix 3 for photographs of the LPs in the archive.
95 Christine Molan remembers Paul and Angela making trips together to record singers: 'During academic breaks, Paul was often away on recording projects, and Angela went with him. Professional secrecy surrounded their work for Topic Records from 1961, one got used to not enquiring what was happening.' Christine Molan, 'Authentic Magic: Angela, Folksong and Bristol', in *Strange Worlds: The Vision of Angela Carter*, ed. by Marie Mulvey-Roberts and Fiona Robinson (Bristol: Sansom & Co, 2017), pp. 29-32 (p. 29). Elsewhere, Molan reminisces, 'Few of us knew that Angela was absorbing folk song on every level, in libraries, among singers, from Alan Lomax vinyl, and through listening to Paul's unique reel-to-reel tapes piled high in boxes at her Bristol home.' Christine Molan, 'Angela Carter', *fRoots*, 409 (July 2017), p. 21.

96   Carter, 'Now', p. 13.
97   Angela Stalker, 'Come in, take a chair, lean on it and sing', *Croydon Advertiser*, 31 March 1961, p. 4.
98   Molan, 'Authentic', p. 29.
99   JP Bean, *Singing from the Floor: A History of British Folk Clubs* (London: Faber & Faber, 2014), p. 146.
100 Mark Jones, *Bristol Folk: A Discographical History of Bristol Folk Music in the 1960s and 1970s* (Bristol: Bristol Folk Publications 2009), pp. 9–10, 142.
101 Ian Anderson, email to the author, 3 September 2018.
102 Paul Carter and Angela Carter, 'Folksong and Ballad, Bristol Manifesto', Paul and Angela Carter's Folk Music Archive. See Appendix 1.
103 Angela Carter, *1960 Journal* (unpublished diary), BL Add MS 88899/1/100, p. 9.
104 Angela Carter, 'Letter to Fr. Brocard Sewell', 11 January 1966, (unpublished letter), AYL MS.

3 'me and not-me': folk songs, narrative perspectives and the gender imaginary in *Shadow Dance*

1   Angela Carter, *Shadow Dance*, first publ. 1966 (London: Virago, 2014), p. 78.
2   'About ⅔ of the way through "Shadow Dance"; another three or four chapters should see the first draft finished. It's coming along.' Angela Carter, *1963-64 Journal* (unpublished diary), BL Add MS 88899/1/89, July 1964.
3   See Chapter 2 for a more thorough survey of these various materials.
4   Gamble forges links between Morris the dandy, Foucault and Baudelaire. Sarah Gamble, *Angela Carter: Writing from the Front Line* (Edinburgh: Edinburgh University Press, 1997), p. 50.
5   Watz suggests *Shadow Dance* reveals Carter engaging 'in a dialogue with surrealist ideas of transgression and subversion of accepted values'. Anna Watz Fruchard, 'Convulsive Beauty and Compulsive Desire: The Surrealist Pattern of *Shadow Dance*', in *Revisiting Angela Carter: Texts, Contexts, Intertexts*, ed. by R. Munford (Basingstoke: Palgrave Macmillan, 2006), pp. 21–41 (p. 22).
6   Angela Carter, 'Notes from the Front Line', first publ.1983, repr. in *SAL*, pp. 45–53 (p. 48).
7   See for example Tzvetan Todorov, *The Fantastic: A Structural Approach to a Literary Genre* (Cleveland, OH, 1973), which appears in the list of books read in her *1977 Journal* (unpublished diary), BL Add MS 88899/1/96.
8   Sarah Gamble suggests this was 'the period in which [Carter] began experimenting with female points of view, creating, in *The Magic Toyshop* and *Heroes and Villains*, heroines who are well able to withstand the seductive blandishments and murderous desires of the dandy.' Sarah Gamble, *Angela Carter: Writing from the Front Line* (Edinburgh: Edinburgh University Press, 1997), p. 63.
9   'They're perhaps the serious and frivolous sides of the same coin.' Marc O'Day, '"Mutability is Having a Field Day": The Sixties Aura of Angela Carter's Bristol Trilogy', in *Flesh and the Mirror: Essays on the Art of Angela Carter*, ed. by Lorna Sage (London: Virago, 1994), pp. 24–59 (p. 37).
10 Edmund Gordon, *The Invention of Angela Carter* (London: Chatto & Windus, 2016), p. 127.

11 Gordon, *Invention*, p. 127.
12 Paulina Palmer, 'From "Coded Mannequin" to Bird Woman: Angela Carter's Magic Flight', in *Women Reading Women's Writing*, ed. by Sue Roe (Brighton: Harvester, 1987), pp. 179–205 (p. 181).
13 Christina Britzolakis, 'Angela Carter's Fetishism', *Textual Practice* 9/3 (1995), 459–75 (p. 470).
14 Gamble, *Front Line*, p. 63.
15 Linden Peach, *Angela Carter*, first publ. 1998 (Basingstoke: Palgrave Macmillan, 2009), p. 23.
16 Peach, *Carter*, p. 26.
17 Rebecca Munford, '"The Desecration of the Temple"; or, "Sexuality as Terrorism"? Angela Carter's (Post-)feminist Gothic Heroines', *Gothic Studies*, 9/2 (2007), 58–70 (p. 64).
18 Nicole Ward Jouve, '"Mother is a Figure of Speech . . ."', in *Flesh and the Mirror: Essays on the Art of Angela Carter*, ed. by Lorna Sage (London: Virago, 1994), pp. 136–70 (p. 148).
19 Rebecca Munford, 'Angela Carter and the Politics of Intertextuality', in *Revisiting Angela Carter: Texts, Contexts, Intertexts,* ed. by R. Munford (Basingstoke: Palgrave Macmillan, 2006), pp. 1–20 (p. 11).
20 Maggie Tonkin, *Angela Carter and Decadence: Critical Fictions/Fictional Critiques* (Basingstoke: Palgrave Macmillan, 2012), p. 15.
21 Britzolakis, 'Fetishism', p. 466.
22 Britzolakis, 'Fetishism', p. 469.
23 Robert Clark, 'Angela Carter's Desire Machine', *Women's Studies*, 14/2 (1987), 147–61 (p. 158).
24 Lorna Sage, 'The Savage Sideshow: a profile of Angela Carter', *New Review*, 4/39–40 (1977), 51–7 (p. 52).
25 Lorna Sage, *Angela Carter*, first publ. 1994 (Tavistock: Northcote, 2007), p. 12.
26 A. L. Lloyd, *Folk Song in England*, first publ. 1967 (Frogmore: Paladin, 1975), p. 151.
27 Sarah Makem, 'The Banks of Red Roses', recorded by Paul Carter and Sean O'Boyle in Keady, Co. Armagh, 1967, on *Sarah Makem, Ulster Ballad Singer* (Topic Records 12T182, 1968).
28 Bob Copper, 'The False Bride', on LP *The Folk Songs of Britain Vol. I: Songs of Courtship* (Caedmon TC1142, 1961). See also first verse quoted in Carter, 'Now', p. 15.
29 A. L. Lloyd, 'Reynardine', on *First Person* (Topic Records 12T118, 1966).
30 Enos White, 'George Collins', on *The Folksongs of Britain, Vol. 4: The Child Ballads Vol. 1* (Caedmon TC 1145, 1961).
31 A. L. Lloyd, 'Jackie Munro', on *English Street Songs* (Riverside RLP 12-614, 1956).
32 'Lucy Wan', in *The Penguin Book of English Folk Songs*, ed. by R. Vaughan Williams and A. L. Lloyd (Harmondsworth: Penguin, 1959), p. 65.
33 'Bold Wolfe', in Elizabeth Bristol Greenleaf and Grace Yarrow Mansfield, *Ballads and Sea Songs of Newfoundland* (Cambridge, MA: Harvard University Press, 1933), pp. 96–8. The Watersons also sang a version, 'Brave Wolfe', on *The Watersons* (Topic Records 12T142, 1966).
34 Of the remaining songs, nine use the anonymous eavesdropper frame narrative device, three present a conversation between two lovers, two are a mixture of more than one method, and one is from the perspective of a horse.
35 Christine Molan explained to me, '. . .(unless there's something I didn't know about) only eight of these [songs] on this list did Angela sing herself. We all sang for each

other at the small sing-around, and she wanted to hear these songs performed by someone, to hear them, to listen to what was "happening" as text and tune (and twiddles and swoops, which I loved doing) were put together. Paul sung the songs "straight" in their approved manner. To sing someone else's song – even a variant – would have been very bad form. [...] I sang "The Factory Girl" (she wrote out Margaret Barry's words for me!). Also "Salisbury Plain", and later, Tunney's "When A Man's In Love". She wrote out "Fanny Blair" for Paul to learn and sing, which he did until he died in 2012. From 1963, he was singing "Lord Bateman", "The Demon Lover", "The Outlandish Knight", "The Brewer's Daughter", "Bold Wolfe", "Henry Martin", "Cupid's Garden", "Died for Love", "The Banks of Sweet Primroses", "Sweet Dundee" ... In fact, this is mostly Paul's repertoire! From this list, Angela sang only "The Lions Den", "Short Trousers", "Lucy Wan", "Female Highwayman", "William Taylor", "Jackie Monroe", "The Female Drummer", and "Bruton Town." Christine Molan, email to the author, 28 June 2020.

36 Angela Carter, 'The Flower of Sweet Strabane', recorded live at the Cheltenham Folk Club, 15 January 1967 © Denis Olding, 1967.
37 Angela Carter, teaching notes on the 'Bluebeard' cycle, in 'Angela Carter Papers: Miscellaneous fairy tale material (1984, 1992, n.d.) (unpublished papers), London, BL Add MS 88899/1/82, p. 57.
38 Lloyd, *England*, p. 151.
39 Suzanne Gilbert, 'Orality and the Ballad Tradition', in *The Edinburgh Companion to Scottish Women's Writing*, ed. by Glenda Norquay (Edinburgh: Edinburgh University Press, 2012), pp. 35–43 (p. 42).
40 Edward Cone, 'Song and Performance', first publ. 1974, repr. in *Music, Words and Voice: A Reader*, ed. Martin Clayton (Manchester: Manchester University Press, 2008), pp. 230–41 (p. 233).
41 Lloyd, *England*, p. 65.
42 Sigmund Freud, 'Remembering, Repeating and Working-Through (1914)', in *The Standard Edition of the Complete Psychological Works of Sigmund Freud*, ed. by Anna Freud, trans. by Joan Riviere (London: Hogarth Press, 1958), xii, 145–56.
43 Nigel Thrift and John-David Dewsbury, 'Dead Geographies – and How to Make Them Live', *Environment and Planning D: Society and Space*, 18 (2000), 411–32 (p. 425).
44 Carter, 'Now', p. 15.
45 Pauline Greenhill, '"Neither a Man nor a Maid": Sexualities and Gendered Meanings in Cross-Dressing Ballads', *Journal of American Folklore*, 108/428 (Spring 1995), 156–77 (p. 157).
46 Dianne Dugaw, *Warrior Women and Popular Balladry, 1650–1850* (Cambridge: Cambridge University Press, 1989), p. 145.
47 Judith Butler, *Gender Trouble* (London: Routledge, 1990), p. 33.
48 'Reynardine' appears on Carter's 1964 journal list.
49 Carter analyzes the melodic and lyrical content of 'Blow The Candle Out' in her 1964 essay 'Now is the Time for Singing'. She probably knew the song from Jimmy Gilhaney's version, 'Blow The Candle Out', on *The Folksongs of Britain, Vol 2: Songs of Seduction* (Caedmon Records TC1143, 1962).
50 'The Game of Cards' appears on Carter's 1964 journal list.
51 A. L. Lloyd, 'Reynardine', on *The Foggy Dew and Other Traditional English Love Songs* (Tradition Records TLP1016, 1956).
52 A. L. Lloyd, 'Reynardine', on *First Person* (Topic Records LP 12T118, 1966).
53 Christine Molan, *Angela Carter*, fROOTS Magazine, July 2017, p. 21.

54 Christine Molan, email to the author, 12 May 2020.
55 Carter, *1963–64 Journal*.
56 'Reynardine' as sung by Lloyd on *First Person* in 1966.
57 For more on this lyric alteration and a fascinating debate on how Lloyd may have created 'Reynardine' for his own purposes, see Stephen D. Winick, 'A. L. Lloyd and Reynardine: Authenticity and Authorship in the Afterlife of a British Broadside Ballad', *Folklore*, 115/3 (December 2004), 286–308.
58 Jimmy Gilhaney, 'Blow the Candle Out', on *The Folksongs of Britain, Vol. 2: Songs of Seduction* (Caedmon TC1143, 1961).
59 Carter, 'Now', p. 12.
60 Tom Willett, 'The Game of Cards', on The Willett Family, *The Roving Journeymen: English Traditional Songs* (Topic Records 12T84, 1962).
61 Carter, *Shadow*, p. 10.
62 Carter, *Shadow*, p. 138.
63 Carter, *Shadow*, p. 3.
64 Carter, *Shadow*, p. 166.
65 Carter, *Shadow*, p. 2.
66 Carter, *Shadow*, p. 55.
67 Carter, *Shadow*, p. 158.
68 Carter, *Shadow*, p. 3.
69 Carter, *Shadow*, p. 2.
70 A complete list of titles of the 33 folksongs notated by Angela Carter in this notebook is as follows: 'The Banks of Sweet Dundee', 'The Wagoner's Lad', 'Down in the Meadows'; 'Tom's Gone to Ilo'; 'The Gipsy Countess'; 'King Herod and the Cock'; 'The Undaunted Female'; 'The Dowie Dens of Yarrow'; 'George Collins'; 'Higher Germany'; 'Pretty Saro'; 'Earl Brand'; 'Come All Ye Fair and Tender Ladies'; 'Lucy Wan'; 'Three Pretty Maids'; 'The Bold Lieutenant'; 'Good Morning, My Pretty Little Miss'; 'Who is That that Raps at my Window?'; 'Geordie'; 'Peggy Gordon'; 'Down by the Seaside'; 'Bold Wolfe'; 'Polly Oliver'; 'The Banks of the Nile'; 'The Brown Girl'; 'The Swan'; 'The Duke of Argyle'; 'The Lover's Ghost'; 'The Courtship of Willy Reilly'; 'Girl from the North Country'; 'Fair Annie'; 'Tarry Wood'; 'The Small Black Rose'. Where she acknowledges a source they are mostly textual, although some are taken down from records, such as 'Higher Germany' for which she cites Phoebe Smith's recording as the origin.
71 In Schenkerian musical analysis, an underlying fundamental structure in its simplest form, known as the *Ursatz*, is shown to be that from which the whole work originates.
72 Carter, *Shadow*, p. 11.
73 Carter, *Shadow*, p. 86.
74 Carter, *Shadow*, pp. 92–3.
75 Judith Butler, 'Performative Acts and Gender Constitution: An Essay in Phenomenology and Feminist Theory', *Theatre Journal*, 40/4 (December, 1988), 519–31 (p. 519).
76 Carter, *Shadow*, p. 93.
77 Carter, *Shadow*, p. 93.
78 Carter, *Shadow*, p. 94.
79 Carter, *Shadow*, p. 159.
80 Carter, *Shadow*, p. 56.
81 Carter, *Shadow*, p. 125.
82 Carter, *Shadow*, p. 166.
83 Carter, *Shadow*, p. 78.

84 Dugaw, *Warrior,* p. 91.
85 Carter, 'Now', p. 12.
86 Carter, *Shadow,* p. 168.
87 Carter, 'Now', p. 12.
88 See Rachel Carroll, '"She had never been a woman": Second Wave Feminism, Femininity and Transgender in Angela Carter's *The Passion of New Eve* (1977)', in *Transgender and the Literary Imagination: Changing Gender in Twentieth-Century Writing* (Edinburgh: Edinburgh University Press, 2017), pp. 64–86.

4 'an invented distance': folk songs, sonic geographies and the Erl-King's greenwood

1 Angela Carter, 'The Erl-King', first publ. in *The Bloody Chamber and other stories* (1979), repr. in *BYB*, pp. 221–9 (p. 222).
2 Marina Warner, 'Why Angela Carter's *The Bloody Chamber* Still Bites', *Scotsman*, 15 September 2012 <https://www.scotsman.com/arts-and-culture/books/marina-warner-why-angela-carters-bloody-chamber-still-bites-2461766> [accessed 17 February 2022].
3 Angela Carter, 'The Mother Lode', first publ. 1976, repr. in *SAL*, pp. 3–19 (p. 14).
4 Angela Carter, 'Fools Are My Theme', first publ. 1982, repr. in *SAL*, pp. 39–45 (p. 39).
5 Carter, 'Fools', p. 40.
6 Angela Carter, 'Afterword to *Fireworks*', first publ. in *Fireworks* (1974), repr. in *BYB*, pp. 549–50 (p. 549).
7 Angela Carter, 'Rich life behind the cool mask', *Western Daily Press*, 19 March 1962, p. 4.
8 Paul and Angela Carter, 'Folksong and Ballad Club Manifesto', from Paul and Angela Carter's Folk Music Archive. See Appendix 1.
9 Angela Carter, *1961 Journal* (unpublished diary), BL Add MS 88899/1/86, p. 21.
10 Horesh told me in interview that Paul and Angela 'weren't at all compatible. I don't think he read any of her books', Edward Horesh and Christopher Frayling, interview with the author, 9 March 2014.
11 Christine Molan, email to author, 4 October 2015.
12 Angela Carter, 'Notes from the Front Line', first publ. 1983, repr. in *SAL*, pp. 45–53 (p. 46).
13 Angela Carter, 'A Souvenir of Japan', first publ. in *Fireworks* (1974), repr. in *BYB*, pp. 31–9 (pp. 35–6).
14 Carter, 'Souvenir', p. 36.
15 Carter, 'Notes', p. 48.
16 Sozo Araki, *Seduced by Japan: A Memoir of the Days Spent with Angela Carter*, trans. by Natsumi Ikoma (Tokyo: Eihosha, 2017), p. 45.
17 Carter, 'Notes', p. 48.
18 Lorna Sage, 'The Savage Sideshow: a profile of Angela Carter', *New Review*, 4/39–40 (1977), 51–7 (p. 53).
19 Lorna Sage, *Angela Carter*, first publ. 1994 (London: Northcote House, 2007), p. 2.
20 See Edmund Gordon, *The Invention of Angela Carter* (London: Chatto & Windus, 2016), pp. 149–50.
21 Angela Carter, *1969–72 Journal,* (unpublished diary), BL Add MS 88899/1/93, p. 68.

22 Sage, *Carter*, p. 6.
23 Carter, 'Afterword to *Fireworks*', p. 550.
24 Cecil Sharp, *English Folk-Song: Some Conclusions* (London: Novello, 1907), p. 1.
25 Angela Carter, 'Some Speculations on Possible Relationships between the Medieval Period and 20th Century Folk Song Poetry', unpublished thesis submitted to Bristol University May 1965, BL Add MS 88899/1/116, p. 29. See Chapter 2.
26 Carter, 'Speculations', pp. 13–15. See Chapter 2.
27 Angela Carter, 'Angela Carter Papers: Miscellaneous fairy tale material (1984, 1992, n.d.) Notes on Virago Fairy Tales Vol 2', BL Add MS 88899/1/82, pp. 185, 189. This idea made it in slightly truncated form into her introduction for *The Virago Book of Fairy Tales* (see p. xiv).
28 Victor Zuckerkandl, 'The Meaning of Song', in *Music, Words and Voice: A Reader*, ed. by Martin Clayton (Manchester: Manchester University Press, 2008), pp. 113–18 (p. 115).
29 Owain Jones and Joanne Garde-Hansen, 'Introduction', in *Geography and Memory: Explorations in Identity, Place and Becoming*, ed. by Owain Jones and Joanne Garde-Hansen (Basingstoke: Palgrave Macmillan, 2012), pp. 1–23 (p. 4.)
30 Jones and Garde-Hansen, 'Introduction', p. 11.
31 Angela Carter, 'Notes on the Gothic Mode', *Iowa Review*, 6/3-4 (Summer/Fall 1975), 132–4 (p. 134).
32 William Motherwell, *Minstrelsy Ancient and Modern* (Glasgow: John Wylie, 1827), p. xxvii.
33 David Atkinson, *The English Traditional Ballad: Theory, Method, and Practice* (Aldershot: Ashgate, 2002), pp. 5–6.
34 Alain Corbin, *Village Bells: Sound and Meaning in the Nineteenth Century French Countryside* (London: Macmillan, 1999), p. x.
35 David Matless, 'Sonic geography in a nature region', *Social and Cultural Geography*, 6/5 (2005), 745–66 (p. 747).
36 Matless, 'Sonic', p. 761.
37 David Matless, *In the Nature of Landscape: Cultural Geography on the Norfolk Broads* (Chichester: John Wiley, 2014), p. 69. His footnote records the source of this comment: KH Tuson, 'Cruises on the Broads', diary extract from 1923; Norfolk Heritage Centre, Millennium Library, Norwich.
38 Ginette Dunn, *The Fellowship of Song: Popular Singing Traditions in East Suffolk* (London: Croom Helm, 1980), p. 47.
39 Georgina Boyes, *The Imagined Village: Culture, Ideology and the English Folk Revival* (Manchester: Manchester University Press, 1993). Dave Harker, *Fakesong: The Manufacture of British 'folksong' 1700 to the present day* (Milton Keynes: Open University Press, 1985). Benedict Anderson, *Imagined Communities: Reflections on the Origin and Spread of Nationalism*, first publ. 1983 (London: Verso, 2006). Trish Winter and Simon Keegan-Phipps, *Performing Englishness: Identity and politics in a contemporary folk resurgence* (Manchester: Manchester University Press, 2013).
40 Winter and Keegan-Phipps, *Englishness*, p. 6.
41 Winter and Keegan-Phipps, *Englishness*, p. 12.
42 Harker, *Fakesong*, p. xii.
43 Peggy Seeger, interview with the author, 4 January 2016. See pp. 11–12, 132.
44 Iain Biggs, 'The Southdean Project and Beyond – "Essaying" Site as Memory Work', in *Geography and Memory: Explorations in Identity, Place and Becoming*, ed. by Owain Jones and Joanne Garde-Hansen (Basingstoke: Palgrave Macmillan, 2012), pp. 109–23 (p. 117).

45 Biggs, 'Southdean', pp. 120–1.
46 Martin Stokes, 'Introduction', in *Ethnicity, Identity and Music: The Musical Construction of Place*, ed. by Martin Stokes (Oxford: Berg, 1994), pp. 1–28 (pp. 3, 5).
47 Carter, 'Speculations', pp. 12, 32, 33, 36, 88–97.
48 Carter, 'Miscellaneous fairy tale material', pp. 71–8.
49 Carter, *1961 Journal*, p. 19. See p. 22.
50 Angela Carter, 'Fred Jordan – singer', *New Society*, 23 February 1967, p. 283.
51 Christine Molan, 'Authentic Magic: Angela, Folksong and Bristol', in *Strange Worlds: The Vision of Angela Carter*, ed. by Marie Mulvey-Roberts and Fiona Robinson (Bristol: Sansom & Co, 2016), pp. 29–32 (p. 31). The toy theatre Molan recalls is highly suggestive of Philip Flowers' puppet theatre in *The Magic Toyshop*.
52 Gordon, *Invention*, p. 104.
53 Angela Carter, 'Overture and Incidental Music for *A Midsummer Night's Dream*', first publ. in *Black Venus* (1985), repr. in *BYB*, pp. 326–38 (p. 330).
54 CS Lewis, *The Discarded Image* (Cambridge: Cambridge University Press, 1964), p. 9, quoted in Carter's dissertation.
55 See the greenwood's similarities to, and differences from, Agamben's 'state of exception'. Giorgio Agamben, *State of Exception*, trans. by Kevin Attell (Chicago, IL: Chicago University Press, 2005).
56 Atkinson, *Ballad*, p. 101.
57 Ian Cobain and James Ball, 'New light shed on US government's extraordinary rendition programme', *Guardian*, 22 May 2013 <https://www.theguardian.com/world/2013/may/22/us-extraordinary-rendition-programme> [accessed 14 February 2022].
58 John Burnett, 'More Stories Emerge of Rapes in Post-Katrina Chaos', *NPR*, 21 December 2005 <http://www.npr.org/templates/story/story.php?storyId=5063796> [accessed 14 February 2022].
59 Joseph Harker, 'Stop calling the Calais refugee camp the "Jungle"', *Guardian*, 7 March 2016 <http://www.theguardian.com/commentisfree/2016/mar/07/stop-calling-calais-refugee-camp-jungle-migrants-dehumanising-scare-stories> [accessed 14 February 2022].
60 Michael Symmons Roberts and Paul Farley, *Edgelands* (London: Jonathan Cape, 2011), p. 5.
61 Child, *Ballads*, Part I, p. 55.
62 Child, *Ballads*, Part II, p. 340.
63 Child, *Ballads*, Part II, p. 341.
64 Child, *Ballads*, Part II, p. 342.
65 Child, *Ballads*, Part I, p. 221.
66 Bob and Ron Copper, 'Babes in the Wood', on Bob and Ron Copper, *Traditional Songs from Rottingdean*, recorded by Peter Kennedy (EFDSS LP1002, 1963).
67 A dactyl (stressed unstressed unstressed) sounds like 'DUH-duh-duh', and resembles the sound of a cantering horse or a thumping heart. In both poetic scansion and musicological analysis, a dactyl is represented by the same diacritic schema (′ ˘ ˘). See Paul Fussell, *Poetic Meter & Poetic Form* (New York: McGraw-Hill, 1979), p. 20; Grosvenor W. Cooper and Leonard B. Meyer, *The Rhythmic Structure of Music* (Chicago, IL: University of Chicago Press, 1960), pp. 75–80.
68 Another musical prose writer, Robert Louis Stevenson, drew on this instinctive association of dactylic tetrameter with equine adventure in his poem *Windy Nights*: 'By at the gallop he goes, and then / By he comes back at the gallop again.' Robert

Louis Stevenson, *A Child's Garden of Verses* (London: John Lane, 1885), p. 15, <http://www.archive.org/stream/childsgardenofve00stev↑ge/n9/mode/2up> [accessed 16 February 2022]. Stevenson describes the 'melody of letters' in Robert Louis Stevenson, 'On Some Technical Elements of Style in Literature', first publ. 1885, repr. in *Essays in the Art of Writing*, (London: Chatto & Windus, 1905), p. 40.

69 Werner Wolf, *The Musicalization of Fiction A study in the theory and history of intermediality* (Amsterdam and Atlanta, GA: Rodopi, 1999), p. 15.
70 Geoffrey Leech, 'Music in Metre: Sprung Rhythm in Victorian Poetry', in *Language in Literature: Style and Foregrounding*, first publ. 2008 (London: Routledge, 2013), pp. 70–85 (pp. 75–6).
71 F. J. Child, *The English and Scottish Popular Ballads*, Part I, first publ. 1882 (Boston: Houghton Mifflin, 1909), p. 55, <https://archive.org/details/englishscottishp01with> [accessed 16 February 2022]. Also listen to Lisa Theriot, 'Lady Isabel and the Elf-Knight', on *A Turning of Seasons* (Raven Boy Music lisatheriot1, 2001).
72 Copper, 'Babes'.
73 Carter, 'Gothic', p. 134.
74 Carter, 'Erl-King', p. 222.
75 Angela Carter, *Heroes and Villains,* first publ. 1969 (London: Penguin, 2011), p. 26.
76 Angela Carter, 'Penetrating to the Heart of the Forest', first. publ. 1974, repr. in *BYB*, pp. 67–78 (pp. 71, 76).
77 Angela Carter, *Wise Children,* first publ. 1991 (London: Vintage, 1992), pp. 120, 124, 125.
78 Carter, *Wise,* p. 145. Presumably a reproduction of the famous Isenheim Altarpiece by the German Renaissance painter Matthias Grünewald, but through name-association Carter simultaneously evokes the dangerous locus of the anglicized 'greenwood'.
79 Carter, *Wise,* p. 121.
80 Angela Carter, *Shadow Dance*, first publ. 1966 (London: Virago, 2014), p. 68.
81 Carter, *Shadow*, p. 166.
82 Cecil Sharp, 'Chapter V: The Modes', in *English Folk-Song: Some Conclusions* (London: Novello, 1907), pp. 36–53. Percy Grainger, 'Collecting with the Phonograph', *Journal of the Folk-Song Society*, 13/12 (1908), 147–62 (p. 156). Annie G. Gilchrist, 'Note on the Modal System of Gaelic Tunes', *Journal of the Folk-Song Society*, 4/16 (1911), 150–3. B. H. Bronson, 'Folksong and the Modes', *The Musical Quarterly*, 32/1 (1946), 37–49. Harold Powers, 'IV. Modal Scales and Folksong Melodies', in *The New Grove Dictionary of Music and Musicians*, ed. Stanley Sadie, vol. 12 (London: Macmillan, 1980), pp. 418–22 (updated by James Porter 2008 <https://www.oxfordmusiconline.com/grovemusic/view/10.1093/gmo/9781561592630.001.0001/omo-9781561592630-e-0000043718> [accessed 14 February 2022]); Richard Sykes, 'The Evolution of Englishness in the English Folksong Revival, 1890–1914', *Folk Music Journal*, 6/4 (1993), 446–90 (pp. 478–9); Julia Bishop, 'Chapter 4: Our History 3: Tuning a Song' and 'Chapter 20: The Mechanics of the Music: Modes, Tune Families and Variation', both in Steve Roud, *Folk Song in England* (London: Faber, 2017), pp. 185–216, 647–67.
83 Sharp, *Conclusions*, p. viii.
84 Grainger, 'Phonograph', p. 156.
85 Sharp, *Conclusions*, pp. 63–4.
86 Sabine Baring-Gould and H. Fleetwood Sheppard, *Songs & Ballads of the West* (London: Methuen, 1891), p. xlvii. See online version <https://archive.org/details/songsballadsofwe00bari> [accessed 14 February 2022].

87 Sheppard, cited by Bishop in Roud, *England*, p. 205.
88 See a detailed analysis of Emily Portman's work in Chapter 7.
89 Emily Portman, interview with the author, 2–3 March 2019. See Chapter 7.
90 Carter, 'Gothic', p. 134.
91 A. L. Lloyd, sleeve notes to Mike Waterson, *Mike Waterson* (Topic Records 12TS332, 1977).
92 Child, *Ballads*, Part II, p. 336.
93 Nicholas Cook, *A Guide to Musical Analysis* (London: Norton, 1992), p. 19.
94 Other melodies which appear in recorded versions of this ballad are more fixed in their modal frameworks. The decorated melody Anne Briggs sings remains consistently in Aeolian mode. Anne Briggs, 'Young Tambling', on *Anne Briggs* (Topic Records 12T207, 1971). In 1956, Hamish Henderson recorded both Betsy Johnson of Glasgow and Willie Whyte of Aberdeen singing 'Tam Lin': *The Muckle Sangs: Classic Scots Ballads* (Tangent Records TNGM119/D, 1975). Their melodies present the ballad in an internally-consistent Dorian mode. Mitchell and Hamer in their 2013 version reclaim the concept of an unsettling modulation and translate it into an unexpected shift from minor to major at the end of every four-stanza cycle: Anaïs Mitchell and Jefferson Hamer, 'Tam Lin', on *The Child Ballads* (Wilderland Records WILDER002LP, 2013).
95 In Paul's notebook in the archive, I found notes taken from an essay entitled 'Physics & Music' by Martin Norgate, an undergraduate at Bristol University 1961–64.
96 Paul references d'Alembert's preface to the 1762 edition of his work *Elemens*, and Heinrich Glarean's *Dodecachordon*, published in 1547.
97 Angela Carter, 'The Smile of Winter', first publ. in *Fireworks* (1974), repr. in *BYB*, pp. 60–6 (p. 64).
98 Carter's appropriation of the affective power of mode shifts might be comparable to Virginia Woolf's use of counterpoint: as Clements observes, Woolf's 'thematic and structural material emulates simultaneous separation and correlation, as does musical counterpoint.' Elicia Clements, 'Transforming Musical Sounds into Words: Narrative Method in Virginia Woolf's *The Waves*', *Narrative*, 13/2 (May 2005), 160–81 (p. 164).
99 Carter, 'Erl-King', pp. 221–3.
100 Carter, 'Erl-King', pp. 223–9.
101 Monika Fludernik, 'Angela Carter's Pronominal Acrobatics: Language in "The Erl-King" and "The Company of Wolves"', *European Journal of English Studies*, 2/2 (1998), 215–37 (pp. 215–16).
102 Lorna Sage, *Angela Carter*, first publ. 1994 (Tavistock: Northcote, 2007), p. 57.
103 Martine Hennard Dutheil de la Rochère, *Reading, Translating, Rewriting: Angela Carter's Translational Poetics* (Detroit, MI: Wayne State University Press, 2013), p. 2.
104 See Angela Carter, 'Angela Carter Papers: "The Bloody Chamber and Other Short Stories" 2', BL Add MS 88899/1/34, and Angela Carter, *1977 Journal*, BL Add MS 88899/1/96.
105 Goethe's haunting 1782 poem *Erlkönig* was set to music by several composers including Schumann and Schubert, imbuing it with songful significance, and Carter seems at this time to have been playing not just with *Erlkönig* but with elements of Goethe's 'Mignon's song', 'Kennst du das Land, wo die Zitronen blühn', also famously set to music, which reappears in *Nights at the Circus* some years later.
106 'The Elf-king has done me harm!'

107 Hennard Dutheil de la Rochère, *Translational*, pp. 28–30. See also Marion May Campbell's links between Goethe's *Sturm und Drang* ballad *Erlkönig* and Carter's 'Erl-King' in *Poetic Revolutionaries: Intertextuality & Subversion* (Amsterdam: Rodopi, 2013), pp. 119–32.
108 Carter made extensive notes about this particular ballad in teaching notes on the Bluebeard cycle. Angela Carter, 'Angela Carter Papers: Miscellaneous fairy tale material (1984, 1992, n.d.) Notes on Virago Fairy Tales Vol. 2' (unpublished papers), BL Add MS 88899/1/82, pp. 57–8 (pp. 70–8).
109 Tolkien claims that faërie 'cannot be caught in a net of words; for it is one of its qualities to be indescribable, though not imperceptible.' J. R. R. Tolkien, 'On Fairy-Stories', in *Essays Presented to Charles Williams* (Oxford: Oxford University Press, 1947), pp. 38–89 (p. 42). The language of music in the greenwood displays a constructive ambiguity which perhaps can communicate where words fail.
110 Child, *Ballads*, Part I, p. 55.
111 Child, *Ballads*, Part I, p. 15.
112 Sarah Makem, 'The Banks of Red Roses', on LP *Sarah Makem, Ulster Ballad Singer*, recorded by Paul Carter and Sean O'Boyle in Keady, Co. Armagh, 1967 (Topic Records 12T182, 1968).
113 Child, *Ballads*, Part I, p. 216.
114 It becomes possible to conflate Paul in some ways with the Erl-King, and the greenwood as symbolic of the ensnarements of marriage. In her journals, Carter describes Paul as 'my darling husband, with his wondering brown eyes and dark fur and white face, like a badger; curled up in the Hall & Rowan chair, he looks like a nesting woodland animal.' (*1961 Journal*, entry 6 Nov 1961, BL Add MS 88899/1/86, pp. 16–17). In 1962, she writes, 'Paul was playing the recorder, and I lay with my head on his lap, pressing against his belly. And I could feel all his muscles tightening as he blew, and various pulses throbbing as he blew and quieting when he stopped to turn the page.' Angela Carter, *1961–62 Journal*, entry 10 Feb 1962, BL Add MS 88899/1/87.
115 See 'the warlike young women so familiar in folksong' Carter describes in her sleeve notes to Louis Killen's LP *Ballads and Broadsides* (Topic 12T126, 1965). Lloyd also observes 'the profusion of dauntless [...] heroines'. A. L. Lloyd, *Folk Song in England*, first publ. 1967 (Frogmore: Paladin, 1975), p. 155.
116 Dianne Dugaw, *Warrior Women and Popular Balladry, 1650–1850* (Cambridge: Cambridge University Press, 1989), p. 69.
117 Child, *Ballads*, Part I, p. 55. In the version I sing, she strangles him with his own hair, in homage to Carter.
118 Carter, 'Erl-King', p. 226.
119 For more on the significance of Ovid's myth of Philomela (the nightingale) and its relation to alternate modes of 'speaking' see Jeni Williams, *Interpreting Nightingales: Gender, Class and Histories* (London: Bloomsbury, 1997), pp. 16–25. See also Micha Lazarus, 'Birdsongs and Sonnets: Listening to Renaissance Lyric', transcript of lecture delivered at UCL, 20 November 2018. See also Chapter 6.
120 Carter, 'Erl-King', p. 228.
121 Carter, 'Erl-King', p. 228.
122 Thomas Moran, 'The Cruel Mother', on LP *The Folksongs of Britain, Vol. 4: The Child Ballads Vol. 1* (Caedmon TC1145, 1961).
123 Child, *Ballads*, Part I, p. 224.
124 Child, *Ballads*, Part II, p. 360.

125 Carter, 'Erl-King', p. 228.
126 Carter, 'Erl-King', pp. 228–9.
127 In 'The Twa Sisters', a macabre instrument fashioned from the drowned sister's body parts and strung with her hair rings out, 'O yonder is my sister that drowned mee.' (Child, *Ballads*, Part 1, p. 126). See p. 120 for more on 'The Twa Sisters'. See also the folk tale *The Juniper Tree* and the bird's call, which matches the words of this outburst (Carter, *Virago Book of Fairy Tales* (London: Virago, 1990) pp. 183–91): but crucially it is not an instrument singing out, as in 'The Twa Sisters' – so I suggest that Carter has conflated the two traditions.
128 Molan remembers how Carter 'experimented freely with narrative and the timing of beautiful, sinister ballads like "Twa Sisters", whose female protagonists are rivals in love.' Christine Molan, 'Authentic Magic', p. 32. Carter may also have been familiar with the version by John Strachan on *The Folksongs of Britain, Vol 4: The Child Ballads Vol 1* (Caedmon TC 1145, 1961). A beautiful modern version is performed by Emily Portman on, *The Glamoury* (Furrow Records FUR002, 2010).
129 Angela Carter, 'My Father's House', in *SAL*, pp. 19–24 (p. 23).
130 Simon Frith, *Performing Rites: On the Value of Popular Music* (Cambridge, MA: Harvard University Press, 1996), p. 193.
131 Carter's evocative description in her 1973 journal (cited by Gordon) of her second husband Mark creates topographical imagery to create a spatial imaginary: 'When I hold him in my arms, I hold all this country's sadness, its ineradicable poignancy, the rain, soft rain of early spring; the cold, pure weather, the fragility of the small flowers that hide themselves, the gentleness of the hills, their low lines of brown & grey, mists, mists coming down on a November afternoon, the magic silence of the wood. Your gentleness, your innocence, your sweetness, like the taste of rain & tears [...] I do not see you with my eyes but with my heart.' Gordon, *Invention*, p. 252. Note how she naturally falls into a landscape of shifting pronouns once again.
132 Angela Carter, *Omnibus: Angela Carter's Curious Room* (BBC1, 15 September 1992), cited in Gordon, *Invention*, p. xiii.
133 Gordon, *Invention*, p. 252.

5 'moving through time': folk songs, journeys and the picaresque in 'Reflections' and *The Infernal Desire Machines of Doctor Hoffman*

1 Angela Carter, *The Infernal Desire Machines of Doctor Hoffman*, first publ. 1972 (London: Penguin Classics, 2011), p. 270.
2 Lorna Sage, 'The Savage Sideshow: a profile of Angela Carter', *New Review*, 4/39–40 (1977), 51–7 (p. 56).
3 *The Satyrica* is a fictional work believed to have been written by Gaius or Titus Petronius, dating from the late first century AD. See Edward Courtney, *A Companion to Petronius* (Oxford: Oxford University Press, 2001).
4 The *Ysengrimus* is a poem written in Latin *c*. 1148, believed to be authored by Nivardus of Ghent, a Flemish priest. See *Ysengrimus: Text with Translation, Commentary and Introduction*, ed. and trans. by Jill Mann (Leiden: Brill, 1987).
5 Trouvères were individual poet-composers from northern France, such as Guy, Châtelain de Coucy. See Emma Dillon's ongoing research, 'The Romance of Song: the early trouvères and their reception, 1150–350'. <https://kclpure.kcl.ac.uk/portal/en/

projects/the-romance-of-song-the-early-trouveres-and-their-reception-11501350(3f061a7a-4387-4d67-b43e-e3b68fb4560d).html> [accessed 14 February 2022]. See also Emma Dillon, *The Sense of Sound: musical meaning in France 1260–1330* (Oxford: Oxford University Press, 2012).

6 Nicolette Zeeman, 'Imaginative Theory', in *Middle English*, ed. by Paul Strohm (Oxford: Oxford University Press, 2007), pp. 222–40.
7 William Thrall and Addison Hibbard, 'The Picaresque Novel', in *A Handbook to Literature* (New York: Odyssey Press, 1936), pp. 310–12. One of the most famous examples of the appropriation of the picaresque in English literature is Laurence Sterne's *The Life and Opinions of Tristram Shandy, Gentleman*, first publ. 1759–67 (London: Penguin Classics, 1997), which critics agree was a strong influence on Carter (see for example Dani Cavallaro, *The World of Angela Carter: A Critical Investigation* (Jefferson, NC: McFarland, 2011), p. 187). For examinations of Sterne's literary musicality, see William Freedman, *Laurence Sterne and the Origins of the Musical Novel* (Athens, GA: University of Georgia Press, 1978); Deborah M. Vlocke, 'Sterne, Descartes and the Music in *Tristram Shandy*', *Studies in English Literature, 1500–1900*, 38/3 (1998), 517–36; Peter Holman, 'Laurence Sterne the Musician', *The Viola Da Gamba Society Journal*, 2 (2008), 58–66.
8 Ulrich Wicks, 'The Nature of Picaresque Narrative: A Modal Approach', *PMLA*, 89/2 (1974), 240–9 (p. 240).
9 Thrall and Hibbard, *Handbook*, p. 310.
10 For example, The Unthanks, 'Died for Love', on *Mount the Air* (Rabble Rouser Music RRM013, 2015); Josienne Clarke & Ben Walker, 'The Banks of The Sweet Primroses', and Lisa O'Neill, 'As I Roved Out', on Various Artists, *Vision & Revision: The First 80 Years of Topic Records* (Topic Records TXLP597, 2019).
11 Thrall and Hibbard, *Handbook*, p. 310.
12 See Laurence Sterne's line illustrations of meandering narrative trajectories in *Tristram Shandy*, p. 391.
13 Cecil Sharp, *English Folk-Song: Some Conclusions* (London: Novello, 1907), p. 16.
14 Edmund Gordon, *The Invention of Angela Carter* (London: Chatto & Windus, 2016), pp. 166, 172–9.
15 Gordon, *Invention*, pp. 178–9.
16 Cornel Bonca, 'In Despair of the Old Adams: Angela Carter's *The Infernal Desire Machines of Dr Hoffman*', *Review of Contemporary Fiction*, 14/3 (1994), 56–62 (p. 61).
17 'Although desire for Albertina motivates his quest, his ambivalence renders him immune not only to Hoffman's mirages but also, at the denouement, to the image of Albertina herself' Maggie Tonkin, *Angela Carter and Decadence: Critical Fictions/Fictional Critiques* (Basingstoke: Palgrave Macmillan, 2012), p. 72.
18 For my reading of Honeybuzzard in Carter's debut novel *Shadow Dance* as a male embodiment of a version of Carter, see Chapter 3.
19 'Desiderio' is a Italo-Spanish derivation (from the Latin name 'Desiderius') of 'desiderium' which means 'a longing, ardent desire or wish, properly for something once possessed; grief, regret for the absence or loss of any thing'. *A Latin Dictionary*, ed. by Charlton T. Lewis and Charles Short (Oxford: Oxford University Press, 1879), p. 556.
20 Carter, *Hoffman*, p. 5.
21 Natsumi Ikoma, 'Her Side of the Story (Afterword by the Translator)', in Sozo Araki, *Seduced by Japan: A Memoir of the Days spent with Angela Carter*, trans. by Natsumi Ikoma (Tokyo: Eihosha, 2017), pp. 153–74 (p. 167).

22 Carter's letter to Carole Roffe, cited in Gordon, *Invention*, p. 170.
23 Caleb Sivyer, 'The Politics of Gender and the Visual in Virginia Woolf and Angela Carter' (unpublished thesis, Cardiff University, 2015), p. 223 <https://orca.cf.ac.uk/89176/1/C%20Sivyer%20PhD%20thesis.pdf> [accessed 14 February 2022].
24 I have dated the composition of this story, without any other known sources, using the following data points. Carter tells us that the stories of *Fireworks* were written between 1970–3 and that they appear in chronological order (Angela Carter, 'Afterword to *Fireworks*', first publ. 1974, repr. in *BYB*, pp. 549–50 (p. 550). Gordon tells us she began writing 'Penetrating to the Heart of the Forest' (the fifth story) just as she was leaving Japan in April 1972 (Gordon, *Invention*, p. 199). Carter talks about writing 'Reflections' in 'Notes on fiction', an essay in 'Angela Carter Papers: Working papers (1972, n.d.)', (unpublished papers), BL Add MS 88899/1/84. 'Reflections' is the seventh story.
25 'I was walking in a wood one late spring day of skimming cloud and shower-tarnished sunshine...' Angela Carter, 'Reflections', first publ. 1974, repr. in *BYB*, pp. 95–112 (p. 95). 'I left the city the next morning [...] I took the road that led north.' Carter, *Hoffman*, p. 41.
26 'She sang; and her words thrilled through me, for they seemed filled with a meaning that had no relation to meaning as I understood it.' Carter, 'Reflections', p. 95. 'Nao-Kurai rambled on in a drowsy voice, inadvertently flattening notes here and there, which subtly altered various meanings, but I continued to listen because these picturesque ancient survivals were, were they not, the orally transmitted history of my people.' Carter, *Hoffman*, p. 103.
27 'She, he, it, Tiresias, though she knitted on remorselessly, was keening over a whole dropped row of stitches, trying to repair the damage as best she could.' Carter, 'Reflections', p. 110. 'So I must gather together all that confusion of experience and arrange it in order, just as it happened, beginning at the beginning. I must unravel my life as if it were so much knitting and pick out from that tangle the single, original thread of my self, the self who was a young man who happened to become a hero and then grew old.' Carter, *Hoffman*, p. 3.
28 Carter, 'Notes on fiction', (unpublished papers), BL Add MS 88899/1/84, p. 3. The idea survives, slightly altered, in the published version, 'Notes on the Gothic Mode' *Iowa Review*, 6:3/4 (Summer–Fall 1975), 132–4 (p. 133).
29 Gordon, *Invention*, p. 175.
30 Many songs recorded in the 1950s and 1960s were performed by members of traditional travelling communities of Irish, Romani or Didikai heritage such as The Willetts, Phoebe Smith and Jeannie Robertson, whom Carter held in high esteem as artists. She noted in her dissertation the link between their travelling lifestyles and their repertoires: 'In England and Scotland, the richest tradition of both singing and songs may be found among the Didikai gypsies and their travelling relations known in Scotland as tinkers. The way of life of the travellers largely isolates them from the rest of the community, throwing them back on their own cultural resources; hence they have retained a wide repertoire of songs, many of very great antiquity. This tradition can be retained when the pattern of travelling life is disrupted, as is increasingly happening; Jeannie Robertson, the fine Scots ballad singer, who lives in a council house in Aberdeen, and various members of the Stewart family, now poultry farming in Perthshire, have ceased travelling but retain both large repertoires and a very interesting way of singing.' Paradoxically, Carter suggests, the itinerant lifestyle creates a heightened attention to the preservation of material, a kind of intentional stasis, grown from the social isolation of the travelling community in its bubble which allows

for songs to remain intact, and which perseveres even when the community settles. Angela Carter, 'Some Speculations on Possible Relationships between the Medieval Period & 20th Century Folk Song Poetry', (unpublished BA thesis), (submitted to University of Bristol, 1965), BL MS 88899/1/116, p. 4.

31 'Grenadier and Lady', in *A Dorset Book of Folk Songs*, ed. by Joan Brocklebank and Biddie Kindersley, first publ. 1948 (London: English Folk Dance and Song Society, 1966), p. 21. Paul and Angela Carter owned this book which is in the archive. This song appears on Carter's journal list of folk songs in her *1963-64 Journal*.

32 Joe Heaney, 'As I Roved Out', recorded by Ewan MacColl and Peggy Seeger in 1964, on Joe Heaney, *The Road from Connemara: Songs and Stories told and sung to Ewan MacColl and Peggy Seeger* (Topic Records TSCD518D, 2000). Listen online <https://www.joeheaney.org/ga/as-i-roved-out-1/> [accessed 14 February 2022]. This song also appears on Carter's journal list of folk songs in her *1963-1964 Journal*.

33 'Cupid the Ploughboy', in *A Dorset Book of Folk Songs*, p. 15. This song also appears on Carter's journal list of folk songs in her *1963-64 Journal*.

34 Roger Renwick, *English Folk Poetry: Structure and Meaning* (Philadelphia, PA: University of Pennsylvania Press, 1980), pp. 37-8.

35 Carter, 'Speculations', p. 47. See p. 26.

36 Carter, 'Speculations', p. 43.

37 Angela Carter, sleeve notes to 'The Banks of Sweet Primroses', on Louis Killen, *Ballads and Broadsides* (Topic Records 12T126, 1965). She cites the anonymous *chanson d'aventure* in which the narrator, riding out, encounters a girl cursing her faithless lover. See 'The Singing Maid', in *Medieval English Lyrics: A Critical Anthology*, ed. by Reginald Thorne Davies (London: Faber and Faber, 1963), pp. 77-8.

38 Anne Middleton, 'The audience and public of Piers Plowman: Middle English alliterative poetry and its literary background', in *Middle English Poetry and Its Literary Background: Seven Essays*, ed. by David Lawton (Woodbridge: DS Brewer, 1982), pp. 101-23 (pp. 114-16).

39 Zeeman, 'Imaginative Theory', p. 228.

40 Carter, 'Reflections', p. 95.

41 Carter, 'Notes on fiction', p. 3.

42 Carter, 'Reflections', p. 95.

43 Zeeman, 'Imaginative', p. 229.

44 'I never believe that I'm writing about the search for self. I've never believed that the self is like a mythical beast which has to be trapped and returned, so that you can become whole again. I'm talking about the negotiations we have to make to discover any kind of reality. I tend to think it's the world that we're looking for in the forest.' Angela Carter, *Omnibus: Angela Carter's Curious Room*, BBC1, 15 September 1992, cited in Gordon, *Invention*, p. xiii.

45 Angela Carter, 'The Flower of Sweet Strabane', recorded live at the Cheltenham Folk Song Club, 15 January 1967 © Copyright Denis Olding.

46 Paddy Tunney, *Where Songs Do Thunder: Travels in Traditional Song* (Belfast: Appletree Press Ltd, 1992), p. 58.

47 'Lucy Wan', in *The Penguin Book of English Folk Songs*, ed. by R. Vaughan Williams and A. L. Lloyd (Harmondsworth: Penguin, 1959), p. 65.

48 Carter, *Hoffman*, p. 270.

49 Angela Carter, *Expletives Deleted: Selected Writings* (London: Vintage, 1993), p. 2.

50 Heather Glen, charting the progression and persistence of mondegreens in eighteenth-century chapbooks, suggests these replacement lyrics can take on signification even in

their meaninglessness: '... the mondegreen has a strange power. It can easily become communal. It's hard not to hear one again when one has once heard it. It can, indeed [...] remain haunting the original song [...] To hear these words is to become attuned to a creative or diabolic energy whereby the song is transformed from a tissue of clichés into something stranger and wilder'. Heather Glen, 'What happens to words in songs?', transcript of paper presented at The Song Seminar, Emmanuel College, Cambridge, 7 February 2018.

51 Carter, 'Some Speculations', p. 20.
52 'The Cruel Mother', in Child, *The English and Scottish Popular Ballads*, Part 1, p. 221.
53 'Riddles Wisely Expounded', in Child, *Ballads*, Part I, pp. 3–4.
54 'The Elfin Knight', in Child, *Ballads*, Part I, p. 15.
55 Alan Lomax, Peter Kennedy and Shirley Collins, sleeve notes to 'King Orfeo', on *The Folksongs of Britain, Vol. 4: The Child Ballads Vol. 1*, ed. by A. L. Lloyd (Caedmon TC1145, 1961), pp. 16–18.
56 Walter Ong, *Orality and Literacy: The Technologizing of the Word* (London: Routledge, 2002), p. 35.
57 Angela Carter, sleeve notes to 'One May Morning', on Louis Killen, *Ballads and Broadsides* (Topic Records 12T126, 1965).
58 The first two verses of 'The Streams of Lovely Nancy', in The *Penguin Book of English Folk Songs* ed. by R. Vaughan Williams and A. L. Lloyd (Harmondsworth: Penguin, 1959), p. 98.
59 L. Broadwood and A. G. Gilchrist, 'The Streams of Lovely Nancy', in Ralph Vaughan Williams, Cecil J. Sharp, G. S. K. Butterworth, Frank Kidson, A. G. Gilchrist and Lucy E. Broadwood, 'Songs Collected from Sussex', *Journal of the Folk-Song Society*, 4/17 (January 1913), 279–324 (p. 317).
60 Broadwood and Gilchrist, 'Nancy', p. 319.
61 Carter, 'Speculations', p. 62.
62 Carter, 'Speculations', p. 62.
63 Carter arrives at a similar conclusion regarding the Corpus Christi Carol, which 'opens out like a series of Chinese boxes' (a phrase she recycles later in her short story 'The Erl-King') 'each verse growing from the proceeding verse, with a final tableau', to conclude that the meaning of the song was 'jumbled and confused over the centuries, once the key to the allegory was lost.' Carter, 'Speculations', pp. 82, 85.
64 Howard Rollin Patch, 'Some Elements in Mediæval Descriptions of the Otherworld', *PMLA*, 33/4 (1918), 601–43 (pp. 604–5).
65 Carter, 'Reflections', p. 98.
66 Carter, *Hoffman*, p. 239.
67 Angela Carter, 'The Bloody Chamber', first publ. 1979, repr. in *BYB*, pp. 131–70 (p. 138).
68 Carter, 'Speculations', p. 70.
69 'Any meaning, any abstruse religious significance, earlier forms of this song may have had is now totally lost to us; it is a puzzle to which the clues have been forgotten.' Carter, 'Speculations', p. 70.
70 '... these details would have become jumbled and confused over the centuries, once the key to the allegory was lost.' Carter, 'Speculations', p. 85.
71 Winfried Menninghaus, *In Praise of Nonsense: Kant and Bluebeard*, trans. by Henry Pickford (Stanford, CA: Stanford University Press, 1999), p. 165.
72 Menninghaus, *Nonsense*, p. 165.
73 Menninghaus, *Nonsense*, p. 165.

74 Menninghaus, *Nonsense,* pp. 207, 177.
75 I borrow the term 'material' from Carter: 'But we live in very confused, confusing and dangerous times, and fiction, which is a kind of log of these times, changes its nature and expands and sucks in *material* from all manner of places and from all manner of styles and genres to be able to adequately describe ourselves to ourselves at all kinds of levels.' [My emphasis] Angela Carter, 'Fools Are My Theme', first publ. 1982, repr. in *SAL*, pp. 39–45 (p. 45).
76 I borrow 'architecture' from an epigraph Carter used for *Hoffman*: '(Remember that we sometimes demand definitions for the sake not of the content, but of their form. Our requirement is an *architectural* one: the definition is a kind of ornamental coping that supports nothing.)' [My emphasis] Ludwig Wittgenstein, *Philosophical Investigations*, cited in Carter, *Hoffman*, p. xv.
77 *A Sailor's Songbag: An American Rebel in an English Prison 1777–1779,* ed. by George G Carey (Amherst, MA: University of Massachusetts Press, 1976), pp. 72–3.
78 Frank Kidson, *Traditional Tunes* (Oxford: Chas. Taphouse & Son, 1891), pp. 44–6.
79 *One Hundred English Folksongs,* ed. by Cecil Sharp (Boston, MA: Oliver Ditson, 1916), No. 94, pp. 220–1. <https://archive.org/details/onehundredengli00shargoog> [accessed 26 May 2020].
80 Grainger's remarkable recordings can be heard on *Unto Brigg Fair: Joseph Taylor and Other Traditional Lincolnshire Singers recorded in 1908 by Percy Grainger* (Leader LEA4050, 1972). A selection of 340 recordings, made between 1906–8, are also available to hear online in the British Library Sounds archive, including 'Died for Love'. <https://sounds.bl.uk/World-and-traditional-music/Percy-Grainger-Collection> [accessed 16 February 2022].
81 Shirley Collins, 'Died for Love', on Shirley Collins, *False True Lovers* (Folkways Records FG3564, 1959).
82 Tom Willett, 'Died for Love', on The Willett Family, *The Roving Journeymen: English Traditional Songs sung by Traditional Singers*, recorded by Paul Carter and Bill Leader at the singers' home on a caravan site near Ashford, Middlesex (Topic Records 12T84, 1962). Carter praises Tom Willett's interpretive skills: 'even with the moving sparseness of the language of this text, one must realize that it is the tune which is an elegiac, lamenting one, and the gentle unsentimental singing of the English gypsy, Tom Willett, that gives it true poetic life.' Angela Carter, 'Now is the Time for Singing', *Nonesuch*, 122 (1964), 11–15 (p. 15).
83 'Lucky for Angela he took her along on the Topic field-trips . . .' Christine Molan, email to author, 26 September 2015.
84 Angela Carter, *Several Perceptions*, first publ. 1968 (London: Virago, 1995), pp. 95–6.
85 Carter, *Perceptions*, p. 97.
86 Angela Carter, 'Alison's Giggle', first publ. 1983, repr. in *SAL*, pp. 662–76 (pp. 675–6).
87 Carter, *Hoffman*, p. 61.
88 Carter, *Hoffman*, p. 265.
89 '"He disintegrated of course", she said. "He resolved to his constituents – a test-tube of amino-acids, a tuft or two of hair."' Carter, *Hoffman*, p. 59.
90 John Haffenden, 'Angela Carter', in *Novelists in Interview* (London: Methuen, 1985), pp. 76–96 (p. 84).
91 Sarah Makem, 'Barbara Allen', on Various Artists, *As I Roved Out (Field Trip – Ireland)* (Smithsonian Folkways FW8872, 1960).

92 A. L. Lloyd, 'Fair Margaret and Sweet William', on A. L. Lloyd and Ewan MacColl, *The English and Scottish Popular Ballads, Vol. 2* (Riverside RLP 12-623/624, 1956). Listen at <https://www.youtube.com/watch?v=_OFwvmA-P1E> [accessed 14 February 2022].
93 Carter, *Hoffman*, p. 22.
94 Carter, *Hoffman*, p. 23.
95 Carter, *Hoffman*, p. 28.
96 Carter, *Hoffman*, p. 243.
97 Carter, *Hoffman*, p. 265.
98 Carter, *Several*, p. 19.
99 Angela Carter, 'Vampirella', in *The Curious Room: Collected Dramatic Works* (London: Vintage, 1997), pp. 3–32 (p. 30).
100 Carter, *Hoffman*, p. 7.
101 Carter, *Hoffman*, p. 4.
102 Carter, *Hoffman*, p. 200.
103 Carter, *Hoffman*, p. 269.
104 Carter, *Hoffman*, p. 73.
105 Freedman, *Sterne*, p. 37.
106 Carter, *Hoffman*, p. 60.
107 Carter, *Hoffman*, p. 97.
108 'The flower symbolism is sexual and may be compared with that found in such songs as "The Seeds of Love"; for instance, "rose" in verse one or Mr Willett's song clearly refers to virginity.' A. L. Lloyd, Ken Stubbs and Paul Carter, sleeve notes for 'Died for Love', on The Willett Family, *The Roving Journeymen* (Topic Records 12T84, 1962). See also George Deacon, *John Clare and the folk tradition*, first publ. 1983 (London: Francis Boutle, 2002), p. 62.
109 Carter, *Hoffman*, pp. 60–1. See other texts for Carterian roses that betray the sexual act such as 'The Snow Child' and 'The Lady of the House of Love', in *BYB*, pp. 230–1, 232–49.
110 Carter, *Hoffman*, p. 6.
111 Carter, *Hoffman*, p. 267.
112 Angela Carter, 'Notes from the Front Line', first publ. 1983, repr. in *SAL*, pp. 45–53 (pp. 49–50).
113 Susan Rubin Suleiman, 'The Fate of the Surrealist Imagination', in *Flesh and the Mirror: Essays on the Art of Angela Carter*, ed. by Lorna Sage (London: Virago, 1994), pp. 98–116.
114 Carter, *Hoffman*, p. 251.
115 Angela Carter, 'Sugar Daddy', first publ. 1983, repr. in *SAL*, pp. 24–36 (p. 35).
116 Carter, 'Reflections', p. 95.
117 'I didn't sing 'The Leaves of Life (Seven Virgins)'. I used to stay with Angela (and Paul) Carter whenever I was singing in the Bristol area. Angela and I got along well together, and we used to go for walks along the top of the Gorge, and through the local woods. As well as having a strong affiliation regarding ballads, we shared a fascination with botany.' Anne Briggs, email to David Suff, 8 November 2018.
118 Ewan MacColl and A. L. Lloyd, *Great British Ballads (Not Included in the Child Collection)* (Riverside RLP12-629, 1957).
119 Norma Waterson, 'Seven Virgins (The Leaves of Life)', on The Watersons, *Frost And Fire: A Calendar of Ritual and Magical Songs* (Topic Records 12T136, 1965). Listen at <https://youtu.be/kk6c8keJ2sA?t=510> [accessed 14 February 2022]. Carter was very taken with this album; in letters to Father Brocard Sewell, she offers to review it three

times for his *Aylesford Review*. She may have seen The Watersons perform at the Cambridge Folk Festival in 1965, which she attended with Paul. See Angela Carter, 'Letters to Father Brocard Sewell', 4 August 1965, 3 September 1965 and 11 January 1966, (unpublished letters), AYL MS.
120. McCabe, Mary Diane, 'A critical study of some traditional religious ballads' (unpublished thesis), (Durham: Durham University, 1980), pp. 168–9. <http://etheses.dur.ac.uk/7804/> [accessed 26 June 2022].
121. McCabe, p. 185.
122. A. L. Lloyd, sleeve notes to 'Seven Virgins (The Leaves of Life)', on The Watersons, *Frost And Fire* (Topic Records 12T136, 1965).
123. For more on the greenwood, see Chapter 4.
124. Carter, 'Reflections', p. 95.
125. Steven Connor, *Dumbstruck: A Cultural History of Ventriloquism* (Oxford: Oxford University Press, 2000), p. 20.
126. Carter, *Hoffman*, p. 39.
127. Carter, *Hoffman*, p. 29.
128. Carter, 'Reflections', p. 109.
129. Carter, 'Reflections', p. 112.
130. Gertrud Schiller, 'The Tree-Cross', in *Iconography of Christian Art*, Vol. 2, trans. by Janet Seligman (London: Lund Humphries, 1972), pp. 135–6.
131. Susan Sellers, *Myth and Fairy Tale in Contemporary Women's Fiction* (Basingstoke: Palgrave Macmillan, 2001), p. 109.
132. Anna Kérchy, *Body Texts in the Novels of Angela Carter: Writing from a Corporeagraphic Point of View* (Lampeter: Edwin Mellen Press, 2008), p. 95.
133. Suleiman, 'Surrealist Imagination', p. 105.
134. Carter, *Hoffman*, p. 3.
135. Carter, 'Reflections', p. 112.
136. Carter, 'Notes from the Front Line', in *SAL*, p. 47.
137. Carter, 'Now', p. 15.
138. Carter, 'Afterword to *Fireworks*', p. 550.
139. Carter, 'Afterword to *Fireworks*', p. 550.
140. Robert Coover, introduction to Angela Carter, 'Reflections', in *You've Got to Read This: Contemporary American Writers Introduce Stories that Held Them in Awe*, ed. by Ron Hansen and Jim Shepard (New York: Harper Collins, 1994), p. 120.
141. Carter, 'Speculations', p. 13.
142. '... these details would have become jumbled and confused over the centuries, once the key to the allegory was lost'. Carter, 'Speculations', p. 85.
143. 'Any meaning, any abstruse religious significance, earlier forms of this song may have had is now totally lost to us; it is a puzzle to which the clues have been forgotten.' Carter, 'Speculations' p. 70.
144. '... I believe in not wasting anything and all these years' work on folk-song and traditional verse will be a waste of time unless I can assimilate it, somehow, into my writing.' Angela Carter, 'Letter to Father Brocard Sewell', 11 January 1966 (unpublished letter), AYL MS.
145. 'Sometimes I try to get a shimmer on a text. The beginning of REFLECTIONS was trying to get a certain very specifically English shimmer, that haunted sense of immanence which is part of the spookiness of the English landscape.' Carter, 'Notes on fiction', p. 3.
146. Carter, 'Reflections', p. 95.

147 Carter, *Hoffman*, p. 74.
148 Carter, *Hoffman*, p. 79.
149 Carter, 'Tokyo Pastoral', first publ.1970, repr. in *SAL*, pp. 283–6 (p. 283).
150 Sozo Araki, *Seduced by Japan: A Memoir of the Days spent with Angela Carter*, trans. by Natsumi Ikoma (Tokyo: Eihosha, 2017), p. 37.
151 Angela Carter, *Nothing Sacred: Selected Writings* (London: Virago, 1982), p. 28.
152 Roland Barthes, *Empire of Signs*, trans. by Richard Howard (New York: Noonday Press, 1989), p. 9.
153 'Language has time as its element; all other media have space as their element. Music is the only other one that takes place in time.' Søren Kierkegaard, cited in Don Ihde, *Listening and Voice: Phenomenologies of Sound, Second Edition* (Albany, NY: State University of New York Press, 2012), p. 58.
154 Gordon, *Invention*, p. 178.
155 G. H. Gerould describes the peculiar temporality of folk songs as at once singular and yet sprawling by implication: 'Not only are all ballads stories of action, but they are stories in which the action is focused on a single episode. Sometimes, to be sure, a whole series of events in the past is revealed by the incident which is the subject of the narrative, but only by reference. [...] they are not fragments, but gain their effect of unified completeness by their concentration on one point.' G. H. Gerould, *The Ballad of Tradition* (New York: Oxford University Press, 1957), pp. 4–5.
156 Paul and Angela Carter, 'Folksong and Ballad, Bristol Manifesto', from Paul and Angela Carter's Folk Music Archive. See Appendix 1.
157 See Chapter 7.

6 'only a bird in a gilded cage': folk songs, avianthropes and the canorographic voice in 'The Erl-King' and *Nights at the Circus*

1 Angela Carter, *Nights at the Circus*, first publ. 1984 (London: Vintage, 2006), pp. 179–80.
2 Paul and Angela Carter's Folk Music Archive. At the time of writing, this archive is in private ownership.
3 Angela Carter, 'Now is the Time for Singing', *Nonesuch*, 122 (1964), 11–15 (p. 15). See Chapter 1.
4 Angela Carter, 'Letter to Father Brocard Sewell', 11 January 1966 (unpublished letter), AYL MS. See also pp. 38, 111, 134, 136.
5 Kramer's discussion of 'songfulness' centres around sung poetry, in particular Schubert's setting of Goethe's poem, 'Heidenröslein'. Lawrence Kramer, 'Beyond Words and Music: An Essay on Songfulness', in *Musical Meaning* (Berkeley, CA: University of California Press, 2002), pp. 51–67.
6 Anna Kérchy, *Body Texts in the Novels of Angela Carter: Writing from a Corporeagraphic Point of View* (Lampeter: Edwin Mellen Press, 2008), p. 8.
7 Angela Carter, 'Fools Are My Theme', in *SAL*, pp. 39–45 (pp. 43–5).
8 Elaine Jordan, 'Enthralment: Angela Carter's Speculative Fictions', in *Plotting Change: Contemporary Women's Fiction*, ed. by Linda Anderson (London: Edward Arnold, 1990), pp. 19–42; Margaret Atwood, 'Running with the Tigers', in *Flesh and the Mirror: Essays on the Art of Angela Carter*, ed. by Lorna Sage (London: Virago, 1994), pp. 117–35; Anna Kérchy, *Body Texts in the Novels of Angela Carter: Writing from a Corporeagraphic Point of View* (Lampeter: Edwin Mellen Press, 2008).

9   Angela Carter, 'The Tiger's Bride', first publ. 1979, repr. in *BYB*, pp. 183–201 (p. 201).
10 Angela Carter, *Nights at the Circus* (London: Vintage, 2006), p. 4.
11 Angela Carter, 'Penetrating to the Heart of the Forest', first publ. 1974, repr. in *BYB*, pp. 67–78 (p. 76).
12 Angela Carter, *Love,* first publ. 1971 (London: Picador, 1988), p. 104.
13 Carter compares 'The Twa Magicians' to the Ghanaian tale 'Keep Your Secrets', in Angela Carter, *The Virago Book of Fairy Tales* (London: Virago, 1990) p. 235.
14 Carter wrote about 'The Cruel Mother' in her 1960 journal: Angela Carter, *1960 Journal* (unpublished diary), BL Add MS 88899/1/100, p. 6. She returned to the ballad again in her 1965 dissertation: Angela Carter, 'Some Speculations on Possible Relationships between the Medieval Period and 20th Century Folk Song Poetry' (unpublished BA thesis, University of Bristol, 1965), BL Add MS 88899/1/116, pp. 88–97.
15 Carter wrote extensive notes about the relationship between this ballad and the Bluebeard cycle of stories in her teaching notes. See 'Angela Carter Papers: Miscellaneous fairy tale material (1984, 1992, n.d.) Notes on Virago Fairy Tales Vol 2' (unpublished papers), BL Add MS 88899/1/82, pp. 57–78, 120–6.
16 Carter includes 'Young Hunting' in her 1964 working ballad list.
17 David Atkinson, 'Motivation, Gender, and Talking Birds', in *The English Traditional Ballad: Theory, Method, and Practice* (Aldershot: Ashgate, 2002), pp. 146–84 (p. 175).
18 Barre Toelken, *Morning Dew and Roses: Nuance, Metaphor and Meaning in Folksongs* (Chicago, IL: University of Illinois Press, 1995), p. 92.
19 Stephen Benson, 'The Soul Music of "The Juniper Tree"', in *The Cambridge Companion to the Fairy Tale*, ed. by Maria Tatar (Cambridge: Cambridge University Press, 2014), pp. 166–85 (p. 179).
20 Carter, *Nights*, p. 128.
21 Gilles Deleuze and Félix Guattari, 'Becoming-Intense, Becoming-Animal, Becoming-Imperceptible', in *A Thousand Plateaus: Capitalism and Schizophrenia*, trans. by Brian Massumi (Minneapolis, MN: University of Minnesota Press, 1987), pp. 232–309 (pp. 235, 238).
22 Donna Haraway, 'A Cyborg Manifesto: science, technology and socialist-feminism in the late twentieth century', first publ. 1991, repr. in *The Cybercultures Reader*, ed. by David Bell and Barbara M. Kennedy (London: Routledge, 2001), pp. 291–324 (p. 292).
23 Mary S. Pollock, 'Angela Carter's Animal Tales: Constructing the Non-Human', *LIT: Literature Interpretation Theory*, 11/1 (2008), 35–57 (p. 51).
24 Rosemary Hill, 'Hairy Fairies', in *London Review of Books*, 34/9 (10 May 2012), pp. 15–16.
25 Angela Carter, *The Infernal Desire Machines of Doctor Hoffman,* first publ. 1972 (London: Penguin, 2011), p. 157.
26 Carter, 'Penetrating' p. 76.
27 This question of the presence of song in literature, indeed for seeing all literature as a form of song, might be posed more widely. See Chapter 8.
28 Martin Clayton, 'Introduction', in *Music, Words and Voice: A Reader*, ed. by Martin Clayton (Manchester: Manchester University Press, 2008), pp. 1–12 (p. 3).
29 Simon Frith, *Performing Rites: On the Value of Popular Music* (Cambridge, MA: Harvard University Press, 1996), p. 172.
30 Victor Zuckerkandl, 'The Meaning of Song', in *Music, Words and Voice: A Reader*, ed. by Martin Clayton (Manchester: Manchester University Press, 2008), pp. 113–18 (pp. 117–18).

31 'The so-called musicality of language is in excess of its discursive function, and this excess is sounded most forcefully in song.' Stephen Benson, 'The soul music of "The Juniper Tree"', in *The Cambridge Companion to Fairy Tales*, ed. by Maria Tatar (Cambridge: Cambridge University Press, 2014), pp. 166–85 (p. 179).
32 'Dr. Vaughan Williams once said: "The practice of re-writing a folk song is abominable, and I wouldn't trust anyone to do it except myself."' A. L. Lloyd, sleeve notes to Various Artists, *The Bird in the Bush: Traditional Songs of Love and Lust* (Topic Records 12T135, 1966).
33 In forms such as the cante-fable (spoken prose narrative interspersed with songs conveying crucial information), these elements become even more disparate within their extraordinary union.
34 Cecil Sharp famously describes processes of 'continuity, variation, and selection'. Cecil Sharp, *English Folk-Song: Some Conclusions* (London: Novello, 1907), p. 16.
35 Steve Roud, *Folk Song in England* (London: Faber, 2017), p. 13.
36 Zuckerkandl, 'Meaning', p. 115.
37 Robert Frost, 'The Hear-Say Ballad', in *The Collected Prose of Robert Frost*, ed. by Mark Richardson (Cambridge, MA: Harvard University Press, 2007), pp. 171–2.
38 Constantin Brăiloiu, 'Outline of a Method of Musical Folklore', *Ethnomusicology*, 14/3 (September 1970), 389–417 (p. 394).
39 Carter, 'Now', p. 12.
40 B. H. Bronson, 'Introduction', in *The Traditional Tunes of the Child Ballads* (Princeton, NJ: Princeton University Press, 1959), pp. xxi–xlvi (p. xxii).
41 Marina Warner, 'Why Angela Carter's *The Bloody Chamber* Still Bites', *Scotsman*, 15 September 2012 <https://www.scotsman.com/arts-and-culture/books/marina-warner-why-angela-carters-bloody-chamber-still-bites-2461766> [accessed 17 February 2022],
42 Jordan, 'Enthralment', p. 25.
43 Atwood, 'Tigers', p. 121.
44 Pollock, 'Animal', p. 48.
45 Anja Müller-Wood, 'Angela Carter, Naturalist', in *Angela Carter: New Critical Readings*, ed. by Sonya Andermahr and Lawrence Phillips (London: Bloomsbury, 2012) pp. 105–16 (p. 106).
46 Kérchy, *Body*, p. 3.
47 Kérchy, *Body*, p. 9.
48 Kérchy, *Body*, pp. 23, 160, 212.
49 Angela Carter, 'Some Speculations on Possible Relationships between the Medieval Period and 20th Century Folk Song Poetry' (unpublished thesis), (submitted May 1965, Bristol University), BL MS 88899/1/116, pp. 88–97.
50 Carter, 'Speculations', p. 91.
51 'Tam Lin', in F. J. Child, *The English and Scottish Popular Ballads*, Part 2 (New York: Houghton, Mifflin & Co, 1884), pp. 335–58.
52 'Young Tambling', on Anne Briggs, *Anne Briggs* (Topic Records 12T207, 1971). See chapter 4 for more about this song and the locus of the greenwood. 'Actually, this story started off with a record cover – cover of a record made by a wonderful girl I used to know who was a folk-singer, I hadn't seen her for years and picked up this record cover with a photograph of Anne with a dog and a gun, striding through a grove.' Angela Carter, 'Notes on Fiction', (unpublished essay), BL MS 88899/1/84. See Chapter 5 for this album cover's influence on Carter's short story 'Reflections'.

53 Child references the sources of the Scandinavian ballad in minute detail: '"Natergalen", Grundtvig, II, 168, No 57; "Den förtrollade Prinsessan", Afzelius, II, 67, No 41, Atterbom, Poetisk Kalender, 1816, p. 44; Dybeck, Runa, 1844, p. 94, No 2; Axelson, Vandring i Wermlands Elfdal, p. 21, No 3; Lindeman, Norske Fjeldmelodier, Tekstbilag til 1ste Bind, p. 3, No 10.' Child, *Ballads*, Part 2, p. 336.
54 Child, *Ballads*, Part 2, pp. 336-7.
55 Anne Briggs, *The Hazards of Love* (Topic Records TOP94, 1964). 'Polly Vaughan' is also sometimes known as 'The Swan', or 'The Shooting of His Dear'.
56 A. L. Lloyd, sleeve notes to 'Polly Vaughan', on Anne Briggs, *The Hazards of Love* (Topic Records TOP94, 1964).
57 Carter notated this from Helen Creighton, *Maritime Folk Songs* (Toronto: Ryerson Press, 1961), p. 75.
58 Carter, *Hoffman*, p. 29.
59 Angela Carter, 'Reflections', first publ. 1974, repr. in *BYB*, pp. 95-112 (p. 109).
60 Carter, 'Reflections', p. 95. Bert Lloyd also compared Briggs to a bird, but more for her nervous demeanour than her singing voice: 'Getting Anne Briggs into a recording studio is like enticing a wild bird into a cage. Nor is she best at ease when she's trapped there. Walls don't suit her as well as woods, and she's more given to stravaging than to settling.' A. L. Lloyd, sleeve notes to Anne Briggs, *Anne Briggs* (Topic Records 12T2207, 1971).
61 Steven Connor, *Dumbstruck: A Cultural History of Ventriloquism* (Oxford: Oxford University Press, 2000), p. 40.
62 Michel Chion, *Guide to Sound Objects*, trans. by John Dack & Christine North (1983) <https://monoskop.org/images/0/01/Chion_Michel_Guide_To_Sound_Objects_Pierre_Schaeffer_and_Musical_Research.pdf> [accessed 17 February 2022], p. 11.
63 Child, *Ballads*, Part 1, p. 126.
64 Angela Carter, *1963-64 Journal* (unpublished diary), BL Add MS 88899/1/89, 27 April 1964.
65 The book's title appears in a list of books inside the front cover of the journal.
66 Frank Kidson and Anne Gilchrist, 'The Story of Orange', *Journal of the Folk-Song Society*, 2/9 (1906), pp. 295-7. Carter also wrote out the song section of the cante-fable 'One Moonlight Night' in this section of her journal, which Gilchrist analyzes on the next page in the journal. Perhaps Carter owned a copy of this 1906 magazine, or perhaps she and Paul visited the library at Cecil Sharp House in London to consult back issues. Around this time, Carter probably read the Jacobs version of 'The Rose-Tree' and also the Grimm version 'The Almond/Juniper Tree', where the children's genders are inverted.
67 'Much of the singing is envisaged as very pleasant and sweet, almost seductive, and has effects which ordinary spoken prose could not have achieved. Its visual presentation on the written page cannot possibly do it justice, and we must think of it as part of an oral performance in which sung verse is felicitously used to interrupt spoken prose at appropriate points in the narrative, producing a discernible audible structure. In most folktales this device is used sparingly or not at all, thus making its occasional employment all the more startling and effective...' W. F. H. Nicolaisen, 'The Cante Fable in Occidental Folk Narrative', in *Prosimetrum: Cross-cultural Perspectives on Narrative in Prose and Verse*, ed. Joseph Harris and Karl Reichl (Cambridge: DS Brewer, 1977), pp. 183-211 (p. 194).
68 Stephen Benson, 'The soul music of "The Juniper Tree"', in *The Cambridge Companion to Fairy Tales*, ed. by Maria Tatar (Cambridge: Cambridge University Press, 2014), pp. 166-85 (p. 169).

69 Edmund Gordon, *The Invention of Angela Carter*, (London: Chatto & Windus, 2016), pp. 278–82.
70 A knowledge of Carter's folk singing praxis provides some explanation for elements of Carter's 'Erl-King' which appear not to stem from the Goethe or Grimm sources, such as the innate sexuality of Carter's Erl-King, or the redeemable aspect to this dark spirit of the woods and the capacity for Carter to see beauty and benevolence in him, despite his sharp teeth. For more on this debate, see Martine Hennard Dutheil de la Rochère, *Reading, Translating, Rewriting: Angela Carter's Translational Poetics* (Detroit, MI: Wayne State University Press, 2013), pp. 28–30; Marion May Campbell, *Poetic Revolutionaries: Intertextuality and Subversion*, (London: Rodopi, 2013) pp. 117–32; Patricia Duncker, 'Re-Imagining the Fairy Tales: Angela Carter's Bloody Chambers', *Literature and History*, 10/1 (Spring 1984), 3–14 (p. 6).
71 Angela Carter, letter to Deborah Rogers 24 August 1977, cited in Gordon, *Invention*, pp. 281–2. A 'genius loci' is a guardian spirit or god associated with a place.
72 Angela Carter, *1977 Journal* (unpublished diary), BL Add MS 88899/1/96, cited in Gordon, *Invention*, p. 274.
73 Anne Briggs, 'Young Tambling', on Anne Briggs, *Anne Briggs* (Topic Records 12T207, 1971).
74 John Stickle, 'King Orfeo', on *The Folksongs of Britain, Vol. 4: The Child Ballads Vol. 1* (Caedmon Records TC1145, 1961).
75 Ewan MacColl and Peggy Seeger, 'The Elfin Knight', *Classic Scots Ballads* (Tradition Records TLP1015, 1956).
76 Fred Jordan, 'The Outlandish Knight', on *The Folksongs of Britain, Vol. 4: The Child Ballads Vol. 1* (Caedmon Records TC1145, 1961).
77 Angela Carter, 'The Erl-King', first publ. 1979, repr. in *BYB*, pp. 221–9 (p. 222).
78 Ovid, 'Tereus and Philomela', in *Metamorphoses* (London: Penguin, 2007), pp. 146–53.
79 Carter, 'Erl-King', pp. 222, 225.
80 Albert R. Chandler, 'The Nightingale in Greek and Latin Poetry', *The Classic Journal*, 30/2 (November 1934), pp. 78–84 (p. 78).
81 Micha Lazarus, 'Birdsongs and Sonnets: Listening to Renaissance Lyric', transcript of lecture delivered at UCL, 20 November 2018, p. 1.
82 Carter, 'Erl-King', p. 222.
83 Carter, 'Erl-King', p. 224.
84 'Local humans could also appear as unselfconscious sounding fauna expressing the region, whether children singing "John Barleycorn" or adult folk song presented as local cultural essence'. David Matless, 'Sonic geography in a nature region', *Social & Cultural Geography*, 6/5 (2005), 745–66 (p. 761). See p. 66.
85 Carter, 'Erl-King', p. 224.
86 Carter, 'Erl-King', p. 226.
87 Carter, 'Erl-King', p. 225.
88 Carter, 'Erl-King', p. 227.
89 Carter cites William Blake's caged bird from the poem 'Song' whose opening line is 'How sweet I roam'd from field to field'; the poem closes with the following lines: 'He caught me in his silken net, / And shut me in his golden cage. / He loves to sit and hear me sing, / Then, laughing, sports and plays with me; / Then stretches out my golden wing, / And mocks my loss of liberty.' William Blake, *The Poetical Works of William Blake*, ed. by John Sampson (London: Oxford University Press, 1958), pp. 8–9.

90 Carter, 'Erl-King', pp. 227–8.
91 Carter, 'Erl-King', pp. 228–9.
92 Carter, 'Erl-King', p. 226.
93 Carter, 'Erl-King', p. 228.
94 Carter, 'Erl-King', p. 228.
95 Carter has used this trope of the silenced female voice as resistance before, in the figure of Aunty Margaret and her elective mutism in the face of Uncle Philip's tyrannical power in *The Magic Toyshop*. Aunty Margaret 'speaks' through the music of the flute – she 'held an ebony flute with silver keys on her lap [...] Then Auntie Margaret put the flute sideways to her lips, eagerly, as though she were thirsty for it. Another dancing tune.' Angela Carter, *The Magic Toyshop*, first publ. 1967 (London: Virago, 1992), pp. 50–1.
96 Carter called this poem variously between drafts 'Leide' and 'Liede' – in German, 'suffering', or 'songs'. Spellings across her manuscripts are unstable, so it is hard to say for certain whether this was an intentional play-on-words, or a mistake. See the handwritten version in Carter's *1972 Journal*, BL Add MS 88899/1/94 (pictured), and three undated typed manuscript versions, in 'Angela Carter Papers: Working papers (1972, n.d.)', BL Add MS 88899/1/84.
97 Carol Gilligan, 'Letter to Readers, 1993', in *In A Different Voice: Psychological Theory and Women's Development* (Cambridge, MA: Harvard University Press, 1993), pp. x–xi.
98 Carter, 'Erl-King', p. 228.
99 Angela Carter, *The Sadeian Woman: An Exercise in Cultural History*, first publ. 1979 (London: Virago, 2006), p. 88.
100 Carter, 'Erl-King', p. 229.
101 Mladen Dolar, *A Voice and Nothing More* (Cambridge, MA: MIT Press, 2006), p. 60.
102 Christine Molan, 'Authentic Magic: Angela, Folksong and Bristol', in *Strange Worlds: The Vision of Angela Carter*, ed. by Fiona Robinson and Marie Mulvey-Roberts (Bristol: Sansom & Co, 2016), p. 32.
103 Ovid, *Metamorphoses*, p. 152.
104 '... after the war, her father sent her to live with his own mother, who helped run a small brothel in the Normandy town of Bernay. The prostitutes helped look after Édith ...'. Steve Huey, *Édith Piaf*, Allmusic.com <https://www.allmusic.com/artist/mn0000150629/biography> [accessed 17 February 2022].
105 Other bird-women may have influenced Carter. In the late 1960s, Bristol singer Keith Christmas was performing 'The Fable of the Wings' in local clubs. Keith Christmas, *Fable of the Wings* (B&C Records CAS1015, 1970). In his Carrollesque ballad, a woman takes pills and grows immense wings which she then asks a surgeon to remove. It resonates with a post-war dislocation and a sense of the end of magic: the woman's suburban concern for her reputation – 'What will all the neighbours say?' – and the surgeon's drab 'suit of morning grey' is juxtaposed against the woman's 'white wonder' which fills 'the tiny room'; Fevvers endures an equally uncomfortable incongruity with her quotidian surroundings. Moreover, the rhythmic urgency of Christmas's rapid finger-picking style increases the anxiety of being viewed as a 'freak'; its repetitive insistence may have seeped into Carter's text as bullet-like alliteration: 'the notion that nobody's daughter walked across nowhere in the direction of nothing produced in her such vertigo she was forced to pause'. Carter, *Nights*, p. 332. 'So, there is a very narrow window when Angela Carter may well have heard me doing "Fable" at the Troubadour'. Keith Christmas, email to the author, 3 September 2018.
106 Carter, *Nights*, p. 3.

107 Carter, *Nights*, p. 4.
108 'Hatched; by whom, I do not know. Who *laid* me is as much a mystery to me, sir, as the nature of my conception, my father and my mother both utterly unknown to me, and, some would say, unknown to nature, what's more.' Carter, *Nights*, p. 20.
109 Carter, *Nights*, p. 171.
110 Carter, *Nights*, p. 119.
111 'The Marquis de Sade, that freest of spirits to have lived so far, had ideas of his own on the subject of woman: he wanted her to be as free as man. Out of these ideas – they will come through some day – grew a dual novel, *Justine* and *Juliette*. It was not by accident the Marquis chose heroines and not heroes. Justine is woman as she has been hitherto, enslaved, miserable and less than human; her opposite, Juliette, represents the woman whose advent he anticipated, a figure of whom minds have as yet no conception, who is arising out of mankind, who shall have wings, and who shall renew the world.' Guillaume Apollinaire, cited in Austryn Wainhouse, 'Foreword', in Marquis de Sade, *Juliette*, trans. by Austryn Wainhouse (New York: Grove Press, 1968), pp. vii–x (p. ix).
112 'Flying is woman's gesture – flying in language and making it fly. We have all learned the art of flying and its numerous techniques; for centuries we've been able to possess anything only by flying; we've lived in flight, stealing away, finding, when desired, narrow passageways, hidden crossovers. It's no accident that *voler* has a double meaning, that it plays on each of them and thus throws off the agents of sense. It's no accident: women take after birds and robbers just as robbers take after women and birds. They (*illes*) go by, fly the coop, take pleasure in jumbling the order of space, in disorienting it, in changing around the furniture, dislocating things and values, breaking them all up, emptying structures, and turning propriety upside down.' Hélène Cixous, 'The Laugh of the Medusa', trans. by Keith Cohen and Paula Cohen, *Signs*, 1/4 (Summer 1976), 875–93 (p. 887).
113 Haraway, 'Cyborg', pp. 293–4.
114 'Schenkerian analysis is in fact a kind of metaphor according to which a composition is seen as the large-scale embellishment of a simple underlying harmonic progression, or even as a massively-expanded cadence; a metaphor according to which the same analytical principles that apply to cadences in strict counterpoint can be applied, *mutatis mutandis*, to the large-scale harmonic structures of complete pieces.' Nicholas Cook, *A Guide to Musical Analysis* (London: Norton, 1987) pp. 27–66 (p. 36). I discuss in more detail the relationship between the dactyl and the greenwood in Chapter 4.
115 Carter, *Nights*, p. 3.
116 Carter, *Nights*, p. 31.
117 Carter, 'Erl-King', p. 229.
118 Carter, *Nights*, p. 37.
119 Carter, *Nights*, p. 15.
120 Carter, *Nights*, p. 17.
121 Carter, *Nights*, p. 29.
122 Carter, *Nights*, p. 16.
123 Carter, *Nights*, p. 12.
124 Carter, *Nights*, p. 62.
125 Carter, *Nights*, p. 41.
126 Carter, *Nights*, p. 45.
127 Atkinson, 'Birds', p. 178.
128 Angela Carter, 'Notes from the Front Line', first. publ. 1983, repr. in *SAL*, p. 47.

129 Carter's early engagement with the 'dark, sinuous voice' of Jean-Louis Barrault reading the poetry of Baudelaire on record was 'a critical moment in Angela's life. [...] It was after listening to it a few times that she decided she wanted to become a writer: "That record was my trigger. It was like having my skull opened with a tin opener and all its contents transformed."' Gordon, *Invention*, p. 36.
130 Carter, *Nights*, p. 42.
131 Carter, *Nights*, p. 231.
132 Roland Barthes, 'The Grain of the Voice', in *Image Music Text*, trans. by Stephen Heath (London: Fontana Press, 1977), pp. 179–89 (p. 188).
133 Stephen Benson, *Literary Music: Writing Music in Contemporary Fiction* (Aldershot: Ashgate, 2006), p. 9.
134 Don Ihde, *Listening and Voice: Phenomenologies of Sound,* first publ. 1976 (Albany NY: State University of New York Press, 2007), p. xx.
135 Carter, *Nights*, p. 47.
136 Ihde, *Listening*, p. 136.
137 Carter, *Nights*, p. 3.
138 Carter, *Nights*, p. 93.
139 Carter, *Nights*, p. 224.
140 Carter, *Nights*, p. 224.
141 Carter, *Nights*, p. 166.
142 Carter, *Nights*, p. 123.
143 Lazarus, 'Birdsongs', pp. 10, 17.
144 Carter, *Nights*, p. 47.
145 '... a rhythmic beat taken faster than the pulse seems controllable, exhilarating, and not to demand intimate sympathy; a rhythmic beat almost synchronous with the pulse seems sincere and to demand intimate sympathy; while a rhythmic beat slower than the pulse, like a funeral bell, seems portentous and uncontrollable.' William Empson, *Seven Types of Ambiguity*, first publ. 1930 (London: Pimlico, 2004), p. 30.
146 Carter, *Nights*, p. 31.
147 Carter, *Nights*, p. 35.
148 Carter, *Nights*, p. 100.
149 Carter, *Nights*, p. 103. See Kérchy, *Body Texts*, pp. 157–62.
150 Carter, *Nights*, p. 11.
151 Carter, *Nights*, p. 47.
152 'Fevvers' speech combines the highbrow, sometimes affected utterances of a cultivated perfect lady and the coarse, vulgar slang of a street girl or a rag and bone merchant.' Kérchy, *Body Texts*, pp. 157–8. 'Fevvers is a wonderful amalgam of the transcendent and the earthy'. Sarah Gamble, *Angela Carter: Writing from the Front Line* (Edinburgh: Edinburgh University Press, 1997), pp. 158–9.
153 'Do you know the land where the lemon-trees grow' or 'Kennst du das Land, wo die Zitronen blühn' is a song with lyrics by Goethe, known as 'Mignon's Song'. 'The poem is full of such delicacies of sound. It has been set by Beethoven, Schubert, Schumann, Liszt and Wolf.' Ronald Gray, *Poems of Goethe* (Cambridge: Cambridge University Press, 1966), pp. 118–19 (p. 119). Carter suggests her Mignon sings Schubert's setting (see *Nights,* pp. 180, 318). Mignon was a character in Goethe's novel, *Wilhelm Meister's Apprenticeship (Wilhelm Meisters Lehrjahre)*, who appears to have functioned rather like Petrarch's nightingale: 'she mirrors his emotions while simultaneously expressing her own state'. Anne E. Albert, *Fragments: A Psychoanalytic Reading of the Character Mignon on Her Journey Through Nineteenth Century Lieder* (unpublished thesis),

(submitted to University of North Carolina, 2009), p. 9 <http://libres.uncg.edu/ir/uncg/f/Albert_uncg_0154D_10127.pdf> [accessed 16 February 2022]
154 Schubert's song-cycle 'Winterreise'.
155 Carter, *Nights*, p. 292.
156 Carter, *Nights*, pp. 317–18.
157 Carter, *Nights*, p. 350.
158 Lorna Sage, *Angela Carter*, first publ. 1994 (Tavistock: Northcote, 2007), p. 58.
159 Kérchy, *Body Texts*, p. 12.
160 Haraway, 'Cyborg', p. 291.
161 Barthes, 'Grain', p. 184.
162 Kérchy, *Body Texts*, p. 79.
163 Larazus, 'Birdsongs', p. 17.
164 Carter, *Nights*, p. 232.
165 'Nor do people put new wine into old wineskins; if they do, the skins burst, the wine runs out, and the skins are lost. No, they put new wine into fresh skins and both are preserved.' *New Jerusalem Bible*, Matt. 9.17. 'These songs survived the centuries, being continually re-moulded to suit each new generation of country singers, but often retaining ancient features; and newly written or adapted songs were often, new wine in old bottles, cast in ancient forms.' Angela Carter, 'Some Speculations on Possible Relationships between the Medieval Period and 20th Century Folk Song Poetry', (unpublished BA thesis), (submitted to University of Bristol, 1965), BL Add MS 88899/1/116, p. 98. 'I am all for putting new wine in old bottles, especially if the pressure of the new wine makes the old bottles explode.' Angela Carter, 'Notes from the Front Line', first publ. 1983, repr. in *SAL*, pp. 45–53 (p. 46).
166 Angela Carter, sleeve notes to Peggy Seeger, *Early in the Spring* (Topic Records 73, 1962).

7 'continued threads' : Angela Carter and the folk singer Emily Portman

1 Emily Portman, interview with the author, 2–3 March 2019, tape 1.
2 'Carter had genuine muso credentials (as part of the 60s Bristol folk scene) so would be delighted that indie band Wolf Alice take their name from her story mashing up Charles Perrault and Lewis Carroll. Singer-songwriter Polly Paulusma and experimental pop outfit Let's Eat Grandma also nod to her. While she is routinely invoked, though, in reviews of leading singer-songwriters – Björk, PJ Harvey, Laura Marling – if there is an influence it's elusive: Florence Welch only bought one of her books after being compared to her, and efforts to persuade Kate Bush that she must have read her have proved unavailing.' John Dugdale, 'What We Owe to Angela Carter', *Guardian*, 16 February 2017 <https://www.theguardian.com/books/booksblog/2017/feb/16/from-fifty-shades-to-buffy-what-we-owe-to-angela-carter> [accessed 16 February 2022]
3 '... the phenomenon of the female performer persists in contemporary literature and culture [...] Madonna, PJ Harvey and Björk, all of them self-determined women artists [...] emphasize that as performers they have an independent "voice" of their own [...] the contemporary fascination with the feminine voice [is continued in] Angela Carter's *Wise Children* [placing] female performers centre stage'. Barbara Straumann, *Female Performers in British and American Fiction* (Berlin: Walter de Gruyter, 2018), p. 2.

4   'Khan's work is as informed by art and literature as it is music, combining the histrionics of Kate Bush and the psycho-sexual atmospherics of PJ Harvey with the heady imagery of writers such as Angela Carter and Susan Cooper.' Fiona Sturges, 'Bat for Lashes: Away with the fairies', *Independent*, 10 July 2009 <https://www.independent.co.uk/arts-entertainment/music/features/bat-for-lashes-away-with-the-fairies-1739707.html> [accessed 16 February 2022].
5   'My interest in folktales and fairytales largely arose from my studies in postmodern literature – writers like Angela Carter, Jorge Luis Borges, Italo Calvino, or Donald Barthelme, to name some of my favourites, who use the fairytale to reference the intertextuality central to the postmodernist conceit that all texts throughout history (and the writers writing, the readers reading) [are] interrelated and interwoven.' Stephen Mejias, 'Aidan Baker: On Music, Sound and *Already Drowning*', *Stereophile*, 30 May 2013 <https://www.stereophile.com/content/aidan-baker-music-sound-and-ialready-drowningi> [accessed 16 February 2022].
6   Laura Marling 'retains a vital sense of musical quest on her third album, and like an unholy hybrid of Angela Carter and Joni Mitchell, brings her dark, fairy tale-style lyrics even more to the fore, from the gothic-tinged nightmare "The Beast", with its lupine guitars and malignant feedback, to "Rest In The Bed", a love song that sounds as though sung from the grave.' Claire Allfree, 'Laura Marling's *A Creature I Don't Know* is a tremendous record', *Metro* 11 September 2011 <https://metro.co.uk/2011/09/11/laura-marling-a-creature-i-dont-know-album-review-145509/> [accessed 16 February 2022].
7   'When I was 16, Angela Carter's books helped me with my lyrics, especially with the language and imaginary I wanted to use. It's about reality, sexuality, desire, death and life, but it's told through a wonderful language. I think she works with very powerful metaphors. I always felt very much connected to her for giving me that first inspiration. I think she was the inspiration for changing my name to "Wolf". Music is more than just what we see here with the lights and the concrete sound: it's about finding your own world.' 'Interview with Patrick Wolf', *Disco Naïveté*, October 2009 <http://disconaivete.com/post/922048096/interview-with-patrick-wolf> [accessed 16 February 2022].
8   'Honeyblood's got a sense of voice some debut acts would be lucky to possess. "Choker", in particular, feints past platitudes and scumball-sleaze dude clichés to become something more layered; it was inspired by Angela Carter's story "The Bloody Chamber", about a bride marrying a man implied to be the Marquis de Sade, whose wedding gift is a choker of 'flashing crimson jewels round [her] throat, bright as arterial blood'; the song, accordingly, whiplashes from hooky to doomy to unnervingly placid.' Katherine St. Asaph, 'Honeyblood', *Pitchfork,* 17 July 2014 <https://pitchfork.com/reviews/albums/19589-honeyblood-honeyblood/> [accessed 16 February 2022].
9   The Blue Aeroplanes, 'Angela Carter', on *Anti-Gravity* (ArtStar/Albino Recordings ASALB001, 2011).
10 Edmund Gordon, *The Invention of Angela Carter* (London: Chatto & Windus, 2016), p. 274.
11 'When Ellie Rowsell and Joff Oddie plucked the name Wolf Alice from a collection of short stories by Angela Carter, they were a folk-pop duo armed only with acoustic instruments and a shared love of Carter's twisted fairy tales. They claim to have chosen the name they did purely because it sounded good.' Katie Presley, 'Review: Wolf Alice, *My Love is Cool*', *NPR Music*, June 2015 <https://www.npr.org/2015/06/14/412947413/first-listen-wolf-alice-my-love-is-cool> [accessed 16 February 2022].

12 'Q: What does *Wise Children* by Angela Carter have to do with Wise Children, the band? A: Well the band is named after the book. It's a book that I read and re-read many times when I was about 16 and she's definitely a writer I admire. I suppose some of Carter's imagery also appears in Wise Children lyrics – ethereal, magical, organic imagery tied up in a real life.' Lynn Roberts, 'FFS Interview: Wise Children', *For Folks Sake*, 26 June 2009 <https://www.forfolkssake.com/interviews/1678/ffs-interview-wise-children> [accessed 16 February 2022].

13 'Influences: Hank Williams, Beethoven, Elvis, Kate Bush, Schubert, The Carter Family, Arcade Fire, Clock Opera, Sigur Ros, Dolly Parton, Saloon Pianos, Music Hall, Stuart Pearson Wright, Winterreise, Angela Carter and Alice in Wonderland.' 'The Tiger's Bride – influences', Facebook post <https://www.facebook.com/pg/TheTigersBride/about/?ref=page_internal> [accessed 20 June 2020].

14 'Angela Carter has been a big influence and I love her approach to reinvigorating and subverting folk tales. Her novels have inspired songs like "Hinge of the Year" in *Hatchlings*.' Anita Awbi, 'Interview: Emily Portman', *M Magazine*, 13 December 2016 <https://www.prsformusic.com/m-magazine/features/interview-emily-portman/> [accessed 16 February 2022].

15 See Vic Gammon and Emily Portman, 'Five-Time in Traditional English Song', *Folk Music Journal,* 10/3 (2013), 319–46.

16 Trish Winter and Simon Keegan-Phipps, *Performing Englishness: Identity and politics in a contemporary folk resurgence* (Manchester: Manchester University Press, 2013), p. 11.

17 Portman, interview, tape 1.

18 See Anne B. Cohen, *Poor Pearl, Poor Girl! The Murdered-Girl Stereotype in Ballad and Newspaper* (Austin, TX: University of Texas Press, 1973); DK Wilgus, 'A Tension of Essences in Murdered-Sweetheart Ballads' in *The Ballad Image: Essays Presented to Bertrand Harris Bronson*, ed. by James Porter (Los Angeles, CA: Center for the Study of Comparative Folklore and Mythology, University of California, Los Angeles, 1983), pp. 241–56; David Atkinson, 'Magical Corpses and the Discovery of Murder', in *The English Traditional Ballad: Theory, Method, and Practice* (Aldershot: Ashgate, 2002), pp. 185–232.

19 Peggy Seeger, interview with the author, 4 January 2016.

20 Portman, interview, tape 6.

21 'These stories have only one thing in common – they all centre around a female protagonist; be she clever, or brave, or good, or silly, or cruel, or sinister, or awesomely unfortunate, she is centre stage, as large as life – sometimes, like Sermerssuaq, larger.' Angela Carter, 'Introduction', in *The Virago Book of Fairy Tales*, ed. by Angela Carter (London: Virago, 1990), pp. ix–xxii (p. xiii).

22 'About a month before she died, Angela Carter was in the Brompton Hospital in London. The manuscript of *The Second Virago Book of Fairy Tales* lay on her bed. "I'm just finishing this off for the girls," she said.' 'Publisher's Note', in *The Second Virago Book of Fairy Tales* (London: Virago, 1992), p. 210.

23 '... all these disparate women have something else in common – a certain sense of self-esteem, however tattered. They know they are worth more than that which fate has allotted them. They are prepared to plot and scheme; to snatch; to battle; to burrow away from within, in order to get their hands on that little bit extra, be it of love, or money, or vengeance, or pleasure, or respect. Even in defeat, they are not defeated...' Angela Carter, 'Introduction', in *Wayward Girls and Wicked Women: An Anthology of Stories*, ed. by Angela Carter (London: Virago Press, 1986), pp. ix–xii (p. xii).

24 'Perrault inspired Carter to delve more deeply into the origins and meanings of fairy tales, but she had to misread him or reinterpret him to make his tales more palatable to her feminist and political sensitivity.' Jack Zipes, 'Introduction' in Charles Perrault, *The Fairy Tales of Charles Perrault*, trans. by Angela Carter (London: Penguin, 2008), pp. vii–xxvii (p. xxv).
25 Angela Carter, *Journal 1963–1964* (unpublished diary), BL Add MS 88899/1/89, July 1964. See p. 33.
26 Portman, interview, tape 2.
27 See Christine Molan's comments on p. 33.
28 Christine Molan, email to the author, 28 June 2020.
29 'The Juniper Tree', in *The Virago Book of Fairy Tales*, ed. by Angela Carter (London: Virago, 1990), pp. 183–91.
30 Paul Mansfield, 'Tell tale sisters: interview with Angela Carter', *Guardian*, 25 October 1990, p. 32.
31 Portman, interview, tape 1.
32 Angela Carter, 'Now is the Time For Singing', *Nonesuch*, 122 (1964), 11–15 (p. 14).
33 Angela Carter, *Several Perceptions*, first publ. 1968 (London: Virago, 1995), p. 1.
34 Carter, letter to Fr. Brocard Sewell, 11 January 1966.
35 Portman, interview, tape 1.
36 Emily Portman, *Composition Commentary: 'Bones and Feathers'* (unpublished MA thesis), (submitted to Newcastle University 2008), p. 8.
37 Portman, *Commentary*, p. 8.
38 Portman, *Commentary*, p. 1
39 Angela Carter, 'Ashputtle, or The Mother's Ghost', in *American Ghosts and Old World Wonders* (London: Vintage, 1994), pp. 110–20.
40 John Haffenden, 'Angela Carter', in *Novelists in Interview* (London: Methuen, 1985), pp. 76–96 (p. 84).
41 'The Twelve Wild Ducks', in *The Second Virago Book of Fairy Tales*, ed. by Angela Carter (London: Virago, 1993), pp. 3–9, 211–12. 'Mossycoat', in *The Virago Book of Fairy Tales*, ed. by Angela Carter (London: Virago, 1990), pp. 48–56, 234.
42 Angela Carter, 'The Erl-King', first publ. 1979, repr. in *BYB*, pp. 221–9.
43 'I believe in not wasting anything and all these years' work on folk-song and traditional verse will be a waste of time unless I can assimilate it, somehow, into my writing.' Angela Carter, 'Letter to Fr. Brocard Sewell', 11 January 1966 (unpublished letter), AYL MS.
44 Emily Portman, 'Hinge of the Year', on *Hatchling* (Furrow Records FURR006, 2012).
45 Angela Carter, *Nights at the Circus*, first publ. 1984 (London: Vintage, 2006).
46 Carter may have named her Mr Rosencreutz after Christian Rosenkreutz, the acclaimed (and possibly allegorical) fifteenth-century founder of the mysterious Rosicrucian order.
47 Carter, *Nights*, pp. 88–9.
48 Carter, *Nights*, p. 89.
49 Emily Portman, 'Ash Girl', on *Hatchling* (Furrow Records FURR006, 2012).
50 Angela Carter, 'Ashputtle, or The Mother's Ghost', in *American Ghosts and Old World Wonders* (London: Vintage, 1994), pp. 110–20.
51 Portman, *Commentary*, p. 1.
52 Portman, interview, tape 3.
53 Portman, *Commentary*, p. 3.

54 F. J. Child alone lists thirteen versions, collected mostly in Scotland: F. J. Child, *The English and Scottish Popular Ballads*, Vol. 1 Part 1 (Boston: Houghton Mifflin, 1882), pp. 218-27. David Atkinson notes how, in Newfoundland, 'The Cruel Mother' has been 'among the most frequently collected of Child ballads'. *The English Traditional Ballad: Theory, Method, and Practice* (Aldershot: Ashgate, 2002), p. 40. Other examples include: 'The Cruel Mother', in Frank Purslow, *Marrow Bones* (London: EFDS, 1965), p. 22; 50 sets of 'The Cruel Mother' in B. H. Bronson, *The Traditional Tunes of the Child Ballads*, Vol 1. (Princeton, NJ: Princeton University Press, 1959), pp. 276-96.
55 See, for example, 'The Cruel Mother' sung by Ben Henneberry, Devil's Island, Nova Scotia: 'The more she rubbed the blood was seen'. B. H. Bronson, *The Traditional Tunes of the Child Ballads*, Vol. 1 (Princeton, NJ: Princeton University Press, 1959), pp. 289-90.
56 Angela Carter, 'Some Speculations on Possible Relationships between the Medieval Period and 20th Century Folk Song Poetry' (unpublished thesis), (submitted to Bristol University 1965), BL MS 88899/1/116, p. 91.
57 G. H. Gerould, *The Ballad of Tradition*, (Oxford: Oxford University Press, 1957), p. 152.
58 Carter, 'Speculations', p. 93.
59 'The ballad seems to be old, for it is full of primitive folklore notions such as the knife from which blood can never be washed (the instance of Lady Macbeth comes to mind). [...] Some scholars think "The Cruel Mother" may have been brought to England by invading Norsemen, since practically the same story occurs in Danish balladry [...] Verse by verse, the Danish sets of the ballad so closely resemble the English that it seems unlikely that the importation took place so long ago. More probably, it is a case of an ancient folk tale being turned into a lyrical ballad, perhaps within the last four hundred years, and spreading in various parts of Europe, possibly with the help of printed versions all deriving from a single original (whether that original was English or Danish or in some other language, our present researches do not tell us).' A. L. Lloyd, sleeve notes to A. L. Lloyd and Ewan MacColl, *English and Scottish Folk Ballads* (Topic Records 12T103, 1964).
60 Angela Carter, 'The Bloody Chamber', first publ. 1979, repr. in *BYB*, pp. 131-70 (p. 161).
61 Emily Portman, 'Little Longing', on *The Glamoury* (Furrow Records FUR002, 2010).
62 Emily Portman, '"Borrowed and Blue', on *Coracle* (FURR008, 2015).
63 Portman, *Commentary*, pp. 5-6.
64 Carter, 'Speculations', p. 98.
65 Portman, *Commentary*, p. 1.
66 Harriet Kramer Linkin, 'Isn't It Romantic? Angela Carter's Bloody Revision of the Romantic Aesthetic in "The Erl-King"', *Contemporary Literature*, 35/2 (Summer 1994), 305-23 (p. 307).
67 Portman explains that this 'baby' of sawdust and sacking was a dream she had: 'Some of them are dreams, as well. Because I was so involved, I started having some really vivid dreams during that period. A song called "Little Longing", and a song called "Pretty Skin", are both based on dreams that I had, that felt they were straight out of a fairy tale, so it felt right to write about them'. Portman, interview, tape 1.
68 See Chapter 6 for more on 'The Twa Sisters' and its influences in Carter's short story 'The Erl-King'.
69 Portman, interview, tape 1.
70 Frank Kidson, Cecil J. Sharp, A. G. Gilchrist, Lucy E. Broadwood, J. A. Fuller-Maitland and Ralph Vaughan Williams, 'Miscellaneous', *Journal of the Folk-Song Society*, 2/9 (1906), 282-99 (pp. 295-7).

71 See more on the cante-fable form on pp. 120–1.
72 Portman, interview, tape 1.
73 Portman, interview, tape 1.
74 '[Angela] experimented freely with narrative and the timing of beautiful, sinister ballads like "Twa Sisters", whose female protagonists are rivals in love.' Christine Molan, 'Authentic Magic: Angela, folk song and Bristol', in *Strange Worlds: The Vision of Angela Carter*, ed. by Marie Mulvey-Roberts and Fiona Robinson (Bristol: Sansom & Co, 2016), pp. 29–32 (p. 32).
75 *Virago Book*, pp. 48–56.
76 Angela Carter, editorial notes to 'Mossycoat', *Virago Book*, p. 234.
77 *Folktales of England*, ed. by Katharine M. Briggs and Ruth L. Tongue (London: Routledge & Kegan Paul, 1965), p. 16.
78 Carter, 'Mossycoat', *Virago Book*, p. 234.
79 Emily Portman, 'Mossy Coat', on *The Glamoury* (Furrow Records FUR002, 2010).
80 Emily Portman, *Composition Commentary 'Bones and Feathers' Appendices* (unpublished MA thesis), (submitted to Newcastle University 2008), p. 7.
81 See Francis B. Gunmere, *The Popular Ballad* (Boston, MA: Houghton Mifflin & Co, 1907), p. 91.
82 Portman, *Commentary*, p. 8.
83 Sir George Webbe Dasent, *Popular Tales from the Norse* (New York: D Appleton & Co, 1859), pp. 371–9.
84 Angela Carter, *The Second Virago Book of Fairy Tales* (London: Virago, 1992), p. 3.
85 Angela Carter, 'The Snow Child', first publ. in 1979, repr. in *BYB*, pp. 230–1 (p. 230).
86 Carter, editorial notes to 'The Twelve Wild Ducks', *Second Virago*, pp. 211–12.
87 Portman, *Commentary*, p. 4. Portman cites Marina Warner, *From the Beast to the Blonde* (London: Random House, 1995), p. 394.
88 Portman, *Appendices*, p. 2.
89 See Chapter 6 for more on the Philomel myth and the significance of avianthropes in Carter's oeuvre.
90 Emily Portman, 'Eye of Tree', on *Coracle* (Furrow Records FURR08, 2015).
91 Portman, interview, tape 2.
92 Portman, interview, tape 2. See also versions of 'Tam Lin' in B. H. Bronson's *Traditional Tunes*, Vol. 1, pp. 327–31.
93 Portman explained to me, 'Rather than being double tracked, the song features unison singing by myself and Rachel Newton. Lucy Farrell is the third voice.'
94 Angela Carter, 'The Erl-King', first publ. in 1979, repr. in *BYB*, pp. 221–9 (p. 221).
95 Emily Portman, personal compilation of 'Hind Etin', email to the author, 14 March 2019.
96 Portman, interview, tape 5.
97 Angela Carter, *1966-68 Journal* (unpublished diary), BL Add MS 88899/1/91, pp. 101, 105.
98 Angela Carter, *1977 Journal* (unpublished diary), BL Add MS 88899/1/96, cited in Gordon, *Invention*, p. 274: for the full quotation see p. 121.
99 See Walter J. Ong, *Orality and Literary: The Technologizing of the Word* (London: Routledge, 2002); *Audiobooks, Literature and Sound Studies*, ed. by Matthew Rubery (New York: Routledge, 2011), pp. 1–24; *The Sound Studies Reader*, ed. by Jonathan Sterne, (London: Routledge, 2012); Brian Kane, 'Sound studies without auditory culture: a critique of the ontological turn', *Sound Studies*, 1/1, 2–21; Gavin Steingo and Jim Sykes, *Remapping Sound Studies* (London: Duke University Press, 2019).

8 Sympathetic resonances

1. Angela Carter, 'Leide', the second of four manuscript drafts, in 'Angela Carter Papers: Working papers (1972, n.d.)', BL Add MS 88899/1/84. A fifth version appears in Carter's *1972 Journal*, BL Add MS 88899/1/94, p. 77. See p. 123. Sometimes she spells the little 'Leide' which means 'suffer', and sometimes 'Liede' which means 'song', in German. It is unclear if this is a spelling error or a more deliberate oscillation.
2. Victor Zuckerkandl, 'The Meaning of Song', in *Music, Words and Voice: A Reader*, edited by Martin Clayton (Manchester: Manchester University Press, 2008), pp. 113–18 (p. 117).
3. 'The piece about Marlene Dietrich is one of a large number of record reviews Angela wrote during this period.' Edmund Gordon, *The Invention of Angela Carter* (London: Chatto & Windus, 2016), p. 43. 'The intertextual allusiveness of *The Infernal Desire Machines of Doctor Hoffman* is so wide-ranging [...] Alison Lee identifies the composers Bach, Mozart, Beethoven, Berlioz and Wagner.' Maggie Tonkin, *Angela Carter and Decadence* (London: Palgrave Macmillan, 2012), p. 65. Benson draws attention in 'The Bloody Chamber' to 'the use [Carter] makes of music, both as atmosphere (a melodramatic touch fully in tune with the swooning desires on display) and as intertextual signifier'. Stephen Benson, '"History's Bearer": The Afterlife of "Bluebeard"', *Marvels & Tales*, 14/2 (2000), 244–67 (p. 246). '*Wise Children* has songs, too: music hall and patriotic war songs, jazz and pop.' Kate Webb, 'Shakespeare and carnival in Angela Carter's *Wise Children*', British Library website <https://www.bl.uk/20th-century-literature/articles/shakespeare-and-carnival-in-angela-carters-wise-children> [accessed 16 February 2022]. Hennard celebrates 'Carter's lifelong interest in the interplay of language and music', and indeed there are many more links between the 'songfulness' I identify and what Hennard names as Carter's 'translational poetics'; Martine Hennard, *Reading, Translating, Rewriting: Angela Carter's Translational Poetics* (Detroit, MI: Wayne State University Press, 2013), p. 15. Julie Sauvage notes the 'overall musicality of the collection'; Julie Sauvage, 'Bloody chamber melodies: painting and music in "The Bloody Chamber"', in *The Arts of Angela Carter: A cabinet of curiosities*, ed. by Marie Mulvey-Roberts (Manchester: Manchester University Press, 2019), pp. 58–79 (p. 68).
4. Carter 'had one of those magpie minds: so many things looked shiny and interesting to her.' Rachel Cooke, 'Introduction', in Angela Carter, *SAL*, pp. xi–xvii (p. xvi). 'Carter's work is nothing if not eclectic.' Mary S. Pollock, 'Angela Carter's Animal Tales: Constructing the Non-Human', *Literature Interpretation Theory*, 11/1 (2000), 35–57 (p. 40).
5. Sozo Araki, *Seduced by Japan: A Memoir of the Days Spent with Angela Carter*, trans. by Natsumi Ikoma (Tokyo: Eihosha, 2018), p. 80.
6. Gordon, *Invention*, p. 36.
7. 'I went to the opera with her...' Edward Horesh, interview with the author, 9 March 2014.
8. Angela Carter, letters to Fr. Brocard Sewell, 7 July 1965 and 4 August 1965, (unpublished letters), AYL MS.
9. Angela Carter, 'Bob Dylan on Tour', first publ. 1966, repr. in *SAL*, pp. 394–6 (p. 395).
10. Araki, *Japan*, pp. 79–80. Araki must not have known that Carter had previously performed in folk clubs.
11. Angela Carter, 'Now is the Time for Singing', *Nonesuch*, 122 (1964), 11–15 (p. 15).
12. Robert Louis Stevenson, 'On Some Technical Elements of Style in Literature', first publ. 1885, repr. in *Essays in the Art of Writing* (London: Chatto & Windus, 1905), pp. 3–43 (p. 40).

13   William H. Gass, 'The Music of Prose', in *Finding a Form: Essays* (New York: Knopf, 1996), pp. 313–26 (p. 313).
14   The neologism of 'canorography' incorporates Kramer's concepts of 'songfulness' with Stevenson's observation that 'in our canorous language rhythm is always at the door'. Stevenson, 'Style', p. 29.
15   'Open any page and a full score rises from its word-notes'; Marina Warner, 'Why Angela Carter's *The Bloody Chamber* Still Bites', *Scotsman*, 15 September 2012, <https://www.scotsman.com/arts-and-culture/books/marina-warner-why-angela-carters-bloody-chamber-still-bites-2461766> [accessed 17 February 2022].
16   Angela Carter, *Several Perceptions*, first publ. 1968 (London: Virago, 1995), p. 1.
17   'In string instruments, strings that are not played (i.e. not bowed or plucked) but nevertheless sound "in sympathy" with the same note (or one of its partials) emanating from another sounding string, generally one activated by bowing. [...] These last-mentioned strings are not bowed but vibrate sympathetically in unison with the fundamental or partial of the bowed strings, creating a silvery resonance.' David D. Boyden, 'Sympathetic strings', in *The New Grove Dictionary of Music and Musicians*, ed. Stanley Sadie, vol. 18 (London: Macmillan, 1980) pp. 427–8.
18   See, for example, its use in psychoanalysis: 'the effect of music has been explained by Daniel Webb and others as a sympathetic resonance between body and soul'. Caroline Welsh, 'Stimmung: The Emergence of a Concept and its Modifications in Psychology and Physiology', in *Travelling Concepts for the Study of Culture*, ed. by Birgit Neumann, Ansgar Nünning (Berlin: Walter de Gruyter, 2012), pp. 267–90 (p. 276).
19   Jeremy Prynne, 'Mental Ears and Poetic Work', *Chicago Review*, 55/1 (Winter 2010), 126–57 (p. 129).
20   T. S. Eliot, *The Use of Poetry and the Use of Criticism*, first publ. 1933 (London: Faber, 1948), p. 118.
21   Northrop Frye, *The Anatomy of Criticism: Four Essays*, first publ. 1957 (Princeton, NJ: Princeton University Press, 1971), p. 266.
22   Gass, 'Music', p. 323.
23   Stevenson, 'Style', p. 9.
24   Stevenson, 'Style', p. 20
25   Stevenson, 'Style', p. 10.
26   Calvin S. Brown, *Music and Literature: A Comparison of the Arts*, first publ. 1948 (Hanover, NH: University of New England Press, 1987), p. 11.
27   Werner Wolf, *The Musicalization of Fiction: A Study in the Theory and History of Intermediality* (Amsterdam and Atlanta, GA: Rodopi, 1999), p. 7.
28   Simon Frith, *Performing Rites: On The Value of Popular Music* (Cambridge, MA: Harvard University Press, 1996), p. 203.
29   'In 2020, audiobook sales revenue in the United States reached 1.3 billion U.S. dollars, continuing the upward trend which began in 2018.' Amy Watson, 'Audiobooks in the U.S. – statistics & facts', *Statista*, 29 June 2021 <https://www.statista.com/topics/3296/audiobooks/#dossierKeyfigures.> [accessed 16 February 2022].
30   See, for example, Helen Gregory, 'The quiet revolution of poetry slam: the sustainability of cultural capital in the light of changing artistic conventions', *Ethnography and Education*, 3/1 (2008), 63–80.
31   Milla Tiainen, 'Corporeal Voices, Sexual Differentiations: New Materialist Perspectives on Music, Singing and Subjectivity', in *Sonic Interventions*, ed. by Sylvia Mieszkowski, Joy Smith and Marijke de Valck (New York: Rodopi, 2007), pp. 147–68 (p. 158).
32   Emily Portman, interview with the author, 2–3 March 2019.

33 Simon Frith, *Performing Rites: On the Value of Popular Music* (Cambridge, MA: Harvard University Press, 1996), p. 193.
34 See Maurice Merlean-Ponty's Stendhal on p. 17.
35 Zuckerkandl, 'Meaning', p. 117.
36 'The experience of song as enveloping voice has not, by and large, entered into theorizations of word-music relationships, which tend to assume intelligible utterance as the sine qua non of song, at least in principle. Broadly speaking, such theorizations have tended to centre on either the musical expression of textual affect or meaning, the musical transformation (from assimilation to appropriation to deconstruction) of textual affect or meaning, or the relative independence of musical structure and expression from those of the text.' Lawrence Kramer, *Musical Meaning: Towards a Critical History* (Berkeley, CA: University of California Press, 2002), p. 52.
37 Hélène Cixous, 'The Laugh of the Medusa', *Signs*, 1/4 (Summer 1976), 875–93 (p. 882).
38 Brent Wood, 'Bring the Noise! William S. Burroughs and Music in the Expanded Field', *Postmodern Culture*, 5/2 (January 1995) <https://muse.jhu.edu/article/27514> [accessed 20 June 2020].
39 Angela Carter, 'Introduction', in *Expletives Deleted: Selected Writings* (London: Vintage, 1993), pp. 1–6 (p. 2).

Bibliography and Discography

Adorno, Theodor, 'On Tradition', *Telos – Critical Theory of the Contemporary*, 94 (1992), 75–82.

Adorno, Theodor, *Quasi Una Fantasia*, trans. by Rodney Livingston (London: Verso, 1992).

Agamben, Giorgio, *State of Exception*, trans. by Kevin Attell (Chicago, IL: Chicago University Press, 2005).

Albert, Anne E., 'Fragments: A Psychoanalytic Reading of the Character Mignon on Her Journey Through Nineteenth Century *Lieder*' (unpublished thesis), (submitted to University of North Carolina, 2009), p. 9 <http://libres.uncg.edu/ir/uncg/f/Albert_uncg_0154D_10127.pdf> [accessed 16 February 2022].

Allfree, Claire, 'Laura Marling's "A Creature I Don't Know" Is a Tremendous Record', *Metro*, 11 September 2011 <https://metro.co.uk/2011/09/11/laura-marling-a-creature-i-dont-know-album-review-145509/> [accessed 16 February 2022].

Andermahr, Sonya, and Lawrence Phillips, eds., *Angela Carter: New Critical Readings* (London: Bloomsbury Press, 2012).

Anderson, Benedict, *Imagined Communities: Reflections on the Origin and Spread of Nationalism* (London: Verso, 2006).

Anderson, Ian, email to the author, 3 September 2018.

Anonymous, 'Come-All-Ye: The Flower of Sweet Strabane', *Derry Journal* (Londonderry, 14 May 1915), Friday Morning edition, 'Come-All-Ye' column, p. 2 <http://www.britishnewspaperarchive.co.uk/viewer/bl/0001123/19150514/051/0002?_=1464951754261> [accessed 3 February 2022].

Apollinaire, Guillaume, and Marquis de Sade, 'Preface to Juliette (1949)', in *Juliette*, ed. by Austryn Wainhouse (New York: Grove Press, 1968).

Araki, Sozo, and Natsumi Ikoma, *Seduced by Japan: A Memoir of the Days Spent with Angela Carter with 'Her Side of the Story'*, trans. by Natsumi Ikoma (Tokyo: Eihosha, 2018).

Aristotle, *On Rhetoric*, trans. by George A. Kennedy (Oxford: Oxford University Press, 2007).

Aronson, Alex, *Music and the Novel* (Totowa, NJ: Rowman and Littlefield, 1980).

Artists, Various, *The Folk Songs of Britain Vol. 1: Songs of Courtship* (Caedmon Records TC1142, 1961).

Artists, Various, *The Folksongs of Britain, Vol. 2: Songs of Seduction* (Caedmon Records TC1143, 1961).

Artists, Various, *The Folksongs of Britain, Vol. 4: The Child Ballads Vol. 1* (Caedmon Records TC1145, 1961).

Artists, Various, *The Muckle Sangs: Classic Scots Ballads* (Tangent Records TNGM119/D, 1975).

Artists, Various, *Unto Brigg Fair: Joseph Taylor and Other Traditional Lincolnshire Singers Recorded in 1908 by Percy Grainger* (Leader LEA4050, 1972).

Artists, Various, *Vision and Revision: The First 80 Years of Topic Records* (Topic Records TXLP597, 2019).

Atkinson, David, *The English Traditional Ballad: Theory, Method, and Practice* (Aldershot: Ashgate, 2002).

Awbi, Anita, 'Interview with Emily Portman', *M Magazine*, 13 December 2016 <https://www.prsformusic.com/m-magazine/features/interview-emily-portman/> [accessed 16 February 2022].

Baring-Gould, Sabine, *Songs of the West: Folk Songs of Devon and Cornwall Collected from the Mouths of the People* (London: Methuen, 1905).

Baring-Gould, Sabine and H. Fleetwood Sheppard, *Songs & Ballads of the West* (London: Methuen, 1891).

Barrault, Jean-Louis, *Baudelaire et Rimbaud: Les Poètes Maudits* (Decca 105.011, 1953).

Barthes, Roland, *Empire of Signs*, trans. by Richard Howard (New York: Noonday Press, 1989).

Barthes, Roland, *Image Music Text*, trans. by Stephen Heath (London: Fontana, 1977).

Barthes, Roland, *The Responsibility of Forms: Critical Essays on Music, Art and Representation*, trans. by Richard Howard (Berkeley, CA: University of California Press, 1985).

Bayard, Samuel P., 'Prolegomena to a Study of the Principal Melodic Families of British-American Folk Song', *The Journal of American Folklore*, 63/247 (1950), 1–44.

Bean, J. P., *Singing from the Floor: A History of British Folk Clubs* (London: Faber & Faber, 2014).

'Beginners' Guide to English Folk Song', *English Folk Dance and Song Society* website <https://www.efdss.org/learning/resources/beginners-guides/52-english-folk-song/2456-efdss-themes-part1> [accessed 17 February 2022].

Benjamin, Walter, 'The Work of Art in the Age of Mechanical Reproduction', first publ. 1939 <https://www.marxists.org/reference/subject/philosophy/works/ge/benjamin.htm> [accessed 18 February 2022].

Benson, Stephen, 'Angela Carter and the Literary Märchen', first publ. in *Marvels & Tales*, 12/1 (1998), 23–51; repr. in *Angela Carter and the Fairy Tale*, ed. by Danielle M. Roemer and Cristina Bacchilega (Detroit, MI: Wayne State University Press, 2001), pp. 30–58.

Benson, Stephen, *Cycles of Influence: Fiction, Folktale, Theory* (Detroit, MI: Wayne State University Press, 2003).

Benson, Stephen, '"History's Bearer": The Afterlife of "Bluebeard"', *Marvels & Tales*, 14/2 (2000), 244–67.

Benson, Stephen, *Literary Music: Writing Music in Contemporary Fiction* (Aldershot: Ashgate, 2006).

Benson, Stephen, 'The Soul Music of "The Juniper Tree"', in *The Cambridge Companion to the Fairy Tale*, ed. by Maria Tatar (Cambridge: Cambridge University Press, 2014), pp. 166–85.

Bettelheim, Bruno, *The Uses of Enchantment: The Meaning and Importance of Fairy Tales* (London: Thames and Hudson, 1976).

Biggs, Iain, 'The Southdean Project and Beyond – "Essaying" Site as Memory Work', in *Geography and Memory: Explorations in Identity, Place and Becoming*, ed. by Owain Jones and Joanne Garde-Hansen (Basingstoke: Palgrave Macmillan, 2012), pp. 109–23.

Bishop, Julia, 'Chapter 4: Our History 3: Tuning a Song' and 'Chapter 20: The Mechanics of the Music: Modes, Tune Families and Variation', in Steve Roud, *Folk Song in England* (London: Faber, 2017), pp. 185–216, 647–57.

Blake, William, *The Poetical Works of William Blake*, ed. by John Sampson (Oxford: Oxford University Press, 1958).

Blue Aeroplanes, The, 'Angela Carter', on *Anti-Gravity* (ArtStar/Albino Recordings ASALB001, 2011).
Bonca, Cornel, 'In Despair of the Old Adams: Angela Carter's *The Infernal Desire Machines of Dr Hoffman*', *Review of Contemporary Fiction*, 14/3 (1994), 56–62.
Boyden, David D., 'Sympathetic Strings', in *The New Grove Dictionary of Music and Musicians*, ed. by Stanley Sadie (London: Macmillan, 1980), xviii, 427–8.
Boyes, Georgina, 'Introduction', in *The Singing Englishman* by Lloyd, 2004 <http://www.mustrad.org.uk/articles/tse.htm> [accessed 17 February 2022].
Boyes, Georgina, *The Imagined Village: Culture, Ideology and the English Folk Revival* (Manchester: Manchester University Press, 1993).
Brăiloiu, Constantin, 'Outline of a Method of Musical Folklore', trans. by Margaret Mooney, *Ethnomusicology*, 14/3 (1970), 389–417.
Briggs, Anne, *Anne Briggs* (Topic Records 12T207, 1971).
Briggs, Anne, email to David Suff, 8 November 2018.
Briggs, Anne, 'Polly Vaughan', from *The Hazards of Love* (Topic Records TOP94, 1964).
Briggs, Katharine M., and Ruth L. Tongue, *Folktales of England* (London: Routledge & Kegan Paul, 1965).
Britzolakis, Christina, 'Angela Carter's Fetishism', *Textual Practice*, 9/3 (1995), 459–76.
Brocken, Michael, *The British Folk Revival* (Aldershot: Ashgate, 2003).
Brocklebank, Joan, and Biddie Kindersley, eds., *A Dorset Book of Folk Songs* (London: English Folk Dance and Song Society, 1966).
Bronson, B. H., 'Folksong and the Modes', *The Musical Quarterly*, 32/1 (1946), 37–49.
Bronson, B. H., *The Singing Tradition of Child's Popular Ballads* (Princeton, NJ: Princeton University Press, 1976).
Bronson, B. H., *The Traditional Tunes of the Child Ballads* (Princeton, NJ: Princeton University Press, 1959), 4 vols.
Brown, Calvin S., *Music and Literature: A Comparison of the Arts*, first publ. 1948 (Hanover, NH: University Press of New England, 1987).
Buchan, David, *The Ballad and the Folk* (London: Routledge, 1972).
Burnett, John, 'More Stories Emerge of Rapes in Post-Katrina Chaos', *NPR*, 21 December 2005 <http://www.npr.org/templates/story/story.php?storyId=5063796> [accessed 14 February 2022].
Butler, Judith, *Gender Trouble* (London: Routledge, 1990).
Butler, Judith, 'Performative Acts and Gender Constitution: An Essay in Phenomenology and Feminist Theory', *Theatre Journal*, 40/4 (December) (1988), 519–31.
Campbell, Marion May, *Poetic Revolutionaries: Intertextuality and Subversion* (London: Rodopi, 2013).
Carey, George C., ed., *A Sailor's Songbag: An American Rebel in an English Prison 1777–1779* (Amherst, MA: University of Massachusetts Press, 1976).
Carroll, Rachel, *Transgender and the Literary Imagination: Changing Gender in Twentieth-Century Writing* (Edinburgh: Edinburgh University Press, 2017).
Carroll, Rachel and Adam Hansen, eds., *Litpop: Writing and Popular Music* (Farnham: Ashgate, 2016).
Carter, Angela, '1960 Journal' (unpublished diary), BL Add MS 88899/1/100.
Carter, Angela, '1961 Journal' (unpublished diary), BL Add MS 88899/1/86.
Carter, Angela, '1961–62 Journal' (unpublished diary), BL Add MS 88899/1/87.
Carter, Angela, '1962–63 Journal' (unpublished diary), BL Add MS 88899/1/88.
Carter, Angela, '1963–64 Journal' (unpublished diary), BL Add MS 88899/1/89.
Carter, Angela, '1965–66 Journal' (unpublished diary), BL Add MS 88899/1/90.

Carter, Angela, '1966–68 Journal' (unpublished diary), BL Add MS 88899/1/91.
Carter, Angela, '1969–72 Journal' (unpublished diary), BL Add MS 88899/1/93.
Carter, Angela, '1970 Journal' (unpublished diary), BL Add MS 88899/1/93.
Carter, Angela, '1972 Journal' (unpublished diary), BL Add MS 88899/1/94.
Carter, Angela, '1977 Journal' (unpublished diary), BL Add MS 88899/1/96.
Carter, Angela, 'A Busker (Retired)', *New Society*, 1967, 471.
Carter, Angela, 'Afterword', in *The Fairytales of Charles Perrault* (London: Penguin, 2008), pp. 71–8.
Carter, Angela, *American Ghosts and Old World Wonders* (London: Vintage, 1994).
Carter, Angela, 'Angela Carter Papers: Miscellaneous Fairy Tale Material (1984, 1992, n.d.)' (unpublished papers), BL Add MS 88899/1/82.
Carter, Angela, 'Angela Carter Papers: "The Bloody Chamber and Other Short Stories" 2 (1975–1979, n.d.)' (unpublished papers), BL Add MS 88899/1/34.
Carter, Angela, 'Angela Carter Papers: Working papers (1972, n.d.)' (unpublished papers), BL Add MS 88899/1/84.
Carter, Angela, *Burning Your Boats: Collected Short Stories* (London: Vintage, 1996).
Carter, Angela, *Expletives Deleted* (London: Vintage, 1993).
Carter, Angela, 'Fred Jordan, Singer', *New Society*, 1967, 283.
Carter, Angela, *Heroes and Villains*, first publ. 1969 (London: Penguin, 2011).
Carter, Angela, 'Letter to Deborah Rogers, 24 August 1977', Rogers, Coleridge & White Archive, cited in Edmund Gordon, *The Invention of Angela Carter* (London: Chatto & Windus, 2016), pp. 281–2.
Carter, Angela, 'Letter to Fr. Brocard Sewell, 3 September 1965' (unpublished letter), AYL MS.
Carter, Angela, 'Letter to Fr. Brocard Sewell, 4 August 1965' (unpublished letter), AYL MS.
Carter, Angela, 'Letter to Fr. Brocard Sewell, 7 July 1965' (unpublished letter), AYL MS.
Carter, Angela, 'Letter to Fr. Brocard Sewell, 11 January 1966' (unpublished letter), AYL MS.
Carter, Angela, '"Leide", Four Drafts, in "Angela Carter Papers: Working Papers (1972, n.d.)"' (unpublished papers), BL Add MS 88899/1/84).
Carter, Angela, *Love*, first publ. 1971 (London: Picador, 1988).
Carter, Angela, *Nights at the Circus*, first publ. 1984 (London: Vintage, 2006).
Carter, Angela, 'Notes on fiction' (unpublished papers), BL Add MS 88899/1/84.
Carter, Angela, 'Notes on the Gothic Mode', *Iowa Review*, 6/3–4 Summer-Fall (1975), 132–4.
Carter, Angela, *Nothing Sacred: Selected Writings* (London: Virago, 1982).
Carter, Angela, 'Now Is the Time for Singing', *Nonesuch*, 122 (1964), 11–15.
Carter, Angela, *Omnibus: Angela Carter's Curious Room* (BBC, 1992).
Carter, Angela, 'Our Author of the Month', *Storyteller*, July 1962, p. 1.
Carter, Angela, 'Preface to *Come Unto These Yellow Sands*', in Angela Carter, *The Curious Room: Plays, Film Scripts and an Opera*, ed. by Mark Bell (London: Vintage, 1997), pp. 497–502.
Carter, Angela, 'Rich Life behind the Cool Mask', *Western Daily Press*, 19 March 1962, p. 4.
Carter, Angela, *Several Perceptions*, first publ. 1968 (London: Virago Press, 1995).
Carter, Angela, *Shadow Dance*, first publ. 1966 (London: Virago, 2014).
Carter, Angela, *Shaking a Leg: Collected Journalism and Writings*, ed. by Jenny Uglow (London: Vintage, 2013).
Carter, Angela, sleeve notes to Louis Killen, *Ballads and Broadsides* (Topic Records 12T126, 1965).

Carter, Angela, sleeve notes to Peggy Seeger, *Early in the Spring* (Topic Records TOP73, 1962).
Carter, Angela, sleeve notes to Peggy Seeger, *Troubled Love* (Topic Records TOP72, 1962).
Carter, Angela, 'Some Speculations on Possible Relationships between the Medieval Period and 20th Century Folk Song Poetry' (unpublished BA thesis), (submitted to University of Bristol, 1965), BL Add MS 88899/1/116.
Carter, Angela, *The Curious Room: Collected Dramatic Works*, ed. by Mark Bell (London: Vintage, 1997).
Carter, Angela, 'The Festival Opens with Folk Music', *Western Daily Press*, 31 October 1962, p. 6.
Carter, Angela, 'The Flower of Sweet Strabane' and 'Saint Mary's and Church Street Medley', recorded live at the Cheltenham Folk Club (15 January 1967) © Copyright Denis Olding.
Carter, Angela, *The Infernal Desire Machines of Doctor Hoffman*, first publ. 1972 (London: Penguin, 2011).
Carter, Angela, *The Magic Toyshop*, first publ. 1967 (London: Virago, 1992).
Carter, Angela, *The Passion of New Eve*, first publ. 1977 (London: Virago Press, 2006).
Carter, Angela, *The Sadeian Woman: An Exercise in Cultural History*, first publ. 1978 (London: Virago, 2006).
Carter, Angela, ed., *The Second Virago Book of Fairy Tales* (London: Virago, 1992).
Carter, Angela, ed., *The Virago Book of Fairy Tales* (London: Virago, 1990).
Carter, Angela, ed., *Wayward Girls and Wicked Women* (London: Virago, 1986).
Carter, Angela, *Wise Children* (London: Vintage, 1992).
Carter, Paul, and Angela Carter, 'Paul and Angela Carter's Folk Music Archive', private archive, copyright Christine Molan.
Carver, Charlie, 'Cupid the Ploughboy', recorded at The Gardener's Arms, Tostock, Suffolk, from *The Desmond and Shelagh Herring Collection*, British Library.
Cavallaro, Dani, *The World of Angela Carter: A Critical Investigation* (Jefferson, NC: McFarland, 2011).
Chandler, Albert R., 'The Nightingale in Greek and Latin Poetry', *The Classic Journal*, 30/2 (1934), 78–84.
Child, F. J., '"Ballad Poetry", *Johnson's Universal Cyclopædia (1900)*', *Journal of Folklore Research*, 31/1-3 (1994), 214–22.
Child, F. J., *The English and Scottish Popular Ballads*, Vol. 1 Part 1 (Boston, MA: Houghton Mifflin, 1882), <https://archive.org/details/englishscottishp01with/page/54/mode/2up> [accessed 30 August 2019].
Child, F. J., *The English and Scottish Popular Ballads*, Vol. 1 Part 2 (Boston, MA: Houghton Mifflin, 1884), <https://archive.org/details/englishscottishp02with/page/n3/mode/2up> [accessed 30 August 2019].
Chion, Michel, *Guide to Sound Objects*, trans. by John Dack & Christine North (1983) <https://monoskop.org/images/0/01/Chion_Michel_Guide_To_Sound_Objects_Pierre_Schaeffer_and_Musical_Research.pdf> [accessed 17 February 2022].
Christmas, Keith, email to the author, 3 September 2018.
Christmas, Keith, *Fable of the Wings* (B&C Records CAS1015, 1970).
Cixous, Hélène, 'The Laugh of the Medusa', *Signs*, 1/4 (Summer) (1976), 875–93.
Clapp, Susannah, 'Introduction', in Angela Carter, *The Curious Room: Plays, Film Scripts and an Opera* (London: Vintage, 1997), pp. vii–x.
Clark, Robert, 'Angela Carter's Desire Machine', *Women's Studies*, 14/2 (1987), 147–61.

Clarke, Josienne, and Ben Walker, 'The Banks of Sweet Primroses', recorded 2015 for *fRoots Magazine* digital download album *fRoots 53*, physically released on *Various Artists, Vision and Revision: The First 80 Years of Topic Records* (Topic Records TXCD597, 2019).

Clayton, Martin, ed., *Music, Words and Voice: A Reader* (Manchester: Manchester University Press, 2008).

Clements, Elicia, 'Transforming Musical Sounds into Words: Narrative Method in Virginia Woolf's *The Waves*', *Narrative*, 13/2 (May 2005), 160–81.

Coates, Ian, 'Email to the author', 7 November 2017.

Cobain, Ian, and James Ball, 'New Light Shed on US Government's Extraordinary Rendition Programme', *Guardian*, 22 May 2013 <https://www.theguardian.com/world/2013/may/22/us-extraordinary-rendition-programme> [accessed 14 February 2022].

Cohen, Anne B., *Poor Pearl, Poor Girl! The Murdered-Girl Stereotype in Ballad and Newspaper* (Austin, TX: University of Texas Press, 1973).

Collins, Shirley, *False True Lovers* (Folkways Records FG3564, 1959).

Collins, Shirley, and Dolly Collins, 'The Young Girl Cut Down In Her Prime', on *Love, Death and the Lady* (EMI/Harvest SHVL771, 1970).

Cone, Edward, 'Song and Performance', first publ. 1974, repr. in *Music, Words and Voice: A Reader*, ed. Martin Clayton (Manchester: Manchester University Press, 2008), pp. 230–41.

Connor, Steven, *Dumbstruck: A Cultural History of Ventriloquism* (Oxford: Oxford University Press, 2000).

Cook, Nicholas, *A Guide to Musical Analysis* (Oxford: Oxford University Press, 1994).

Cooke, Deryck, *The Language of Music* (London: Oxford University Press, 1959).

Cooke, Rachel, 'Introduction', in Angela Carter, *Shaking A Leg: Collected Journalism and Writings* (London: Vintage, 2013), pp. xi–xvii.

Cooper, Grosvenor W., and Leonard B. Meyer, *The Rhythmic Structure of Music* (Chicago, IL: University of Chicago Press, 1960).

Coover, Robert, 'Introduction to Angela Carter, "Reflections"', in *You've Got To Read This: Contemporary American Writers Introduce Stories That Held Them In Awe*, ed. by Ron Hansen and Jim Shepard (New York: Harper Collins, 1994).

Copper, Bob, and Ron Copper, *Traditional Songs from Rottingdean* (EFDSS, 1963).

Corbin, Alain, *Village Bells: Sound and Meaning in the Nineteenth-Century French Countryside*, trans. by Martin Thom (London: Macmillan, 1999).

Courtney, Edward, *A Companion to Petronius* (Oxford: Oxford University Press, 2001).

Creighton, Helen, *Maritime Folk Songs* (Toronto: Ryerson Press, 1961).

Crofts, Charlotte, *'Anagrams of Desire': Angela Carter's Writing for Radio, Film and Television* (Manchester: Manchester University Press, 2003).

Crunelle-Vanrigh, Anny, 'The Logic of the Same and Différance: "The Courtship of Mr Lyon"', in *Angela Carter and the Fairy Tale* (Detroit, MI: Wayne State University Press, 2001), pp. 128–44.

Culler, Jonathan, *Theory of the Lyric* (Cambridge, MA: Harvard University Press, 2015).

Dasent, Sir George Webbe, *Popular Tales from the Norse* (New York: D. Appleton & Co, 1859).

Davidson, Hilda Ellis, and Anna Chaudhri, *A Companion to the Fairy Tale* (Cambridge: DS Brewer, 2003).

Deacon, George, *John Clare and the Folk Tradition*, first publ. 1983 (London: Francis Boutle, 2002).

Deleuze, Gilles, and Félix Guattari, *A Thousand Plateaus: Capitalism and Schizophrenia*, trans. by Brian Massumi (London and Minneapolis, MN: University of Minnesota Press, 1987).
Denny, Sandy, 'The False Bride', from *Alex Campbell and his Friends* (Saga Eros ERO8021, 1967).
Derrida, Jacques, *Of Grammatology*, trans. by Gayatri Chakravorty Spivak (Baltimore, MD: John Hopkins University Press, 1997).
Derrida, Jacques, *Writing and Difference*, trans. by Alan Bass (London: Routledge, 2005).
Dillon, Emma, *The Sense of Sound: Musical Meaning in France, 1260–1330* (Oxford: Oxford University Press, 2012).
Dimovitz, Scott, 'Angela Carter's Narrative Chiasmus: *The Infernal Desire Machines of Doctor Hoffman* and *The Passion of New Eve*', *Genre*, 42 (2009), 83–111.
Disco Naïveté, 'Interview with Patrick Wolf', *Disco Naïveté*, October 2009 <http://disconaivete.com/post/922048096/interview-with-patrick-wolf> [accessed 16 February 2022].
Dolar, Mladen, *A Voice and Nothing More* (Cambridge, MA: MIT Press, 2006).
Dollerup, Cay, Ivan Reventlow, and Carsten Rosenberg Hansen, 'A Case Study for Editorial Filters in Folktales: A Discussion of the Allerleirauh Tales in Grimm', *Fabula*, 27/1 (1986), 12–30.
Dugaw, Dianne, *Warrior Women and Popular Balladry, 1650–1850* (Cambridge: Cambridge University Press, 1989).
Dugdale, John, 'What We Owe to Angela Carter', *The Guardian*, 16 February 2017 <https://www.theguardian.com/books/booksblog/2017/feb/16/from-fifty-shades-to-buffy-what-we-owe-to-angela-carter> [accessed 16 February 2022].
Duncker, Patricia, 'Re-Imagining the Fairy Tales: Angela Carter's Bloody Chambers', *Literature and History*, 10.1 (1984), 3–14.
Dunn, Ginette, *The Fellowship of Song: Popular Singing Traditions in East Suffolk* (London: Croom Helm, 1980).
Eliot, T. S., *The Use of Poetry and the Use of Criticism*, first publ. 1933 (London: Faber & Faber, 1948).
Empson, William, *Seven Types of Ambiguity*, first publ. 1930 (London: Pimlico, 2004).
Fairport Convention, 'Reynardine', on *Liege & Lief* (Island Records ILPS9115, 1969).
Feld, Steven, Aaron A. Fox, Thomas Porcello, and David Samuels, 'Vocal Anthropology: From the Music of Language to the Language of Song', in *A Companion to Linguistic Anthropology*, ed. by Alessandro Duranti (Oxford: Blackwell, 2004), pp. 321–45.
Fludernik, Monika, 'Angela Carter's Pronominal Acrobatics: Language in "The Erl-King" and "The Company of Wolves"', *European Journal of English Studies*, 2/2 (1998), 215–37.
Ford, Andrew, 'Epic as Genre', in *A New Companion to Homer*, ed. by Ian Morris and Barry B. Powell (Boston, MA: Brill, 1997), pp. 396–414.
Ford, Andrew, *Homer: The Poetry of the Past* (Ithaca, NY: Cornell University Press, 1992).
Francmanis, John, 'National Music to National Redeemer: The Consolidation of a "Folk-Song" Construct in Edwardian England', *Popular Music*, 21/1 (2002), 1–25.
Freedman, William, *Laurence Sterne and the Origins of the Musical Novel* (Athens, GA: University of Georgia Press, 1978).
Freud, Sigmund, 'Remembering, Repeating and Working-Through (1914)', in *The Standard Edition of the Complete Psychological Works of Sigmund Freud*, ed. by Anna Freud, trans. by Joan Riviere (London: Hogarth Press, 1958), xii, 145–56.

Frith, Simon, *Performing Rites: On the Value of Popular Music* (Cambridge, MA: Harvard University Press, 1996).
Frost, Robert, 'The Hear-Say Ballad (1953)', in *The Collected Prose of Robert Frost*, ed. by Mark Richardson (Cambridge, MA: Harvard University Press, 2007), pp. 171–2.
Frye, Northrop, *The Anatomy of Criticism: Four Essays* (Princeton, NJ: Princeton University Press, 1973).
Fussell, Paul, *Poetic Meter & Poetic Form* (New York: McGraw-Hill, 1979).
Gamble, Sarah, *Angela Carter: Writing from the Front Line* (Edinburgh: Edinburgh University Press, 1997).
Gammon, Vic, and Emily Portman, 'Five-Time in Traditional English Song', *Folk Music Journal*, 10/3 (2013), 319–46.
Gass, William H., 'The Music of Prose', in *Finding a Form: Essays* (New York: Knopf, 1996), pp. 313–26.
Gerould, G. H., *The Ballad of Tradition* (New York: Oxford University Press, 1957).
Gilbert, Suzanne, 'Orality and the Ballad Tradition', in *The Edinburgh Companion to Scottish Women's Writing*, ed. by Glenda Norquay (Edinburgh: Edinburgh University Press, 2012), pp. 35–43.
Gilchrist, A. G., 'Note on the Modal System of Gaelic Tunes', *Journal of the Folk-Song Society*, 4/16 (1911), 150–3.
Gilchrist, A. G., 'One Moonlight Night', *Journal of the Folk-Song Society*, 2/9 (1906), 297–9.
Gilhaney, Jimmy, 'Blow the Candle Out', from *The Folksongs of Britain, Vol 2: Songs of Seduction* (Caedmon Records TC1143, 1962).
Gilligan, Carol, *In A Different Voice: Psychological Theory and Women's Development* (Cambridge, MA: Harvard University Press, 1982).
Glen, Heather, 'What Happens to Words in Songs?', transcript of paper presented at The Song Seminar, Emmanuel College, Cambridge, 7 February 2018.
Gordon, Edmund, *The Invention of Angela Carter* (London: Chatto & Windus, 2016).
Grainger, Percy, 'Collecting with the Phonograph', *Journal of the Folk-Song Society*, 3/12, 147–62.
Gray, Ronald, ed., *Poems of Goethe* (Cambridge: Cambridge University Press, 1966).
Greenhill, Pauline, '"Neither a Man nor a Maid": Sexualities and Gendered Meanings in Cross-Dressing Ballads', *Journal of American Folklore*, 108/428 (1995), 156–77.
Greenleaf, Elizabeth Bristol, and Grace Yarrow Mansfield, *Ballads and Sea Songs of Newfoundland* (Cambridge, MA: Harvard University Press, 1933).
Gregg, Melissa, and Gregory J. Seigworth, 'An Inventory of Shimmers', in *The Affect Theory Reader* (Durham, NC and London: Duke University Press, 2010), pp. 1–25.
Gregory, Helen, 'The Quiet Revolution of Poetry Slam: The Sustainability of Cultural Capital in the Light of Changing Artistic Conventions', *Ethnography and Education*, 3/1 (2008), 63–80.
Grundtvig, Svend, *Danmarks Gamle Folkeviser*, ed. by Svend Grundtvig (Copenhagen: Thieles, 1853), Vols. 1–4 and Vol. 5 Part 1.
Gumbrecht, H. U., *Our Broad Present: Time and Contemporary Culture* (New York: Columbia University Press, 2014).
Gunmere, Francis B., *The Popular Ballad* (Boston, MA: Houghton Mifflin, 1907).
Haffenden, John, 'Angela Carter', in *Novelists in Interview* (London: Methuen, 1985), pp. 76–96.
Hall, Reg, interview with the author, 5 December 2014.

Haraway, Donna, 'A Cyborg Manifesto: Science, Technology and Social-Feminism in the Late Twentieth Century', in *The Cybercultures Reader*, ed. by David Bell and Barbara M. Kennedy (New York and London: Routledge, 2000), pp. 291–324.

Harker, Dave, *Fakesong: The Manufacture of British 'Folksong' 1700 to the Present Day* (Milton Keynes: Open University Press, 1985).

Harker, Joseph, 'Stop Calling the Calais Refugee Camp the "Jungle"', *Guardian*, 7 March 2016 <http://www.theguardian.com/commentisfree/2016/mar/07/stop-calling-calais-refugee-camp-jungle-migrants-dehumanising-scare-stories> [accessed 14 February 2022].

Heaney, Joe, 'The Bonny Bunch of Roses' EP (Collector Records JEI7, 1960).

Heaney, Joe, *The Road from Connemara: Songs and Stories told and sung to Ewan MacColl and Peggy Seeger* (Topic Records TSCD518D, 2000)

Hennard Dutheil de la Rochère, Martine, 'Found in (Mis)Translation, or the Magic of Foreign Words', in *Erreurs Productives, Malentendus Constructifs* (Bielefeld: Aisthesis Verlag, 2017).

Hennard Dutheil de la Rochère, Martine, *Reading, Translating, Rewriting: Angela Carter's Translational Poetics* (Detroit, MI: Wayne State University Press, 2013).

Henry, Sam, *Sam Henry's Songs of the People*, ed. by Gale Huntington and Lani Hermann (Athens, GA: University of Georgia Press, 1990).

Herzog, George, 'Song: Folk Song and the Music of Folk Song', in *Funk & Wagnalls Standard Dictionary of Folklore, Mythology and Legend*, ed. by Maria Leach (San Francisco, CA: Harper Collins, 1984), pp. 1032–50.

Hield, Fay, 'English Folk Singing and the Construction Of Community' (unpublished thesis), (submitted to University of Sheffield, 2010).

Hill, Rosemary, 'Hairy Fairies', *London Review of Books* (London, May 2012), 34/9, pp. 15–16.

Hodgart, M. J. C., *The Ballads* (New York: Norton, 1962).

Holman, Peter, 'Laurence Sterne the Musician', *The Viola Da Gamba Society Journal*, 2 (2008), 58–66.

Homer, *The Iliad*, trans. by Martin Hammond (London: Penguin, 1987).

Horesh, Edward, and Christopher Frayling, interview with the author, 9 March 2014.

Huey, Steve, 'Édith Piaf', *AllMusic.com* <https://www.allmusic.com/artist/mn0000150629/biography> [accessed 17 February 2022].

Ihde, Don, *Listening and Voice: Phenomenologies of Sound* (Albany, NY: State University of New York Press, 2007).

Ikoma, Natsumi, 'Her Side of the Story (Afterword by the Translator)', in Sozo Araki, *Seduced by Japan: A Memoir of the Days spent with Angela Carter*, trans. by Natsumi Ikoma (Tokyo: Eihosha, 2017), pp. 153–74.

New Jerusalem Bible (London: Darton, Longman and Todd, 1985).

Johnson, James, *Scots Musical Museum*, 6 vols (Edinburgh: Johnson & Co, 1787).

Jones, Mark, *Bristol Folk: A Discographical History of Bristol Folk Music in the 1960s and 1970s* (Bristol: Bristol Folk Publications, 2009).

Jones, Owain, and Joanne Garde-Hansen, eds., *Geography and Memory: Explorations in Identity, Place and Becoming* (Basingstoke: Palgrave Macmillan, 2012).

Jordan, Fred, 'The Outlandish Knight', from *The Folksongs of Britain, Vol 4: The Child Ballads Vol 1* (Caedmon TC1145, 1961).

Jordan, Elaine, 'Enthralment: Angela Carter's Speculative Fictions', in *Plotting Change: Contemporary Women's Fiction*, ed. by Linda R. Anderson (London: Edward Arnold, 1990), pp. 19–42.

Kane, Brian, 'Sound Studies Without Auditory Culture: A Critique of the Ontological Turn', *Sound Studies*, 1/1 (2015), 2–21.

Karpeles, Maud, 'Definition of Folk Music', *Journal of the International Folk Music Council*, 7 (1955), 6–7.

Kérchy, Anna, *Body Texts in the Novels of Angela Carter: Writing from a Corporeagraphic Point of View* (Lampeter: Edwin Mellen Press, 2008).

Kidson, Frank, *Traditional Tunes* (Oxford: Chas. Taphouse & Son, 1891).

Kidson, Frank, and A. G. Gilchrist, 'The Story of Orange', *Journal of the Folk-Song Society*, 2/9 (1906), 295–7.

Kidson, Frank, Cecil J. Sharp, A. G. Gilchrist, Lucy E. Broadwood, J. A. Fuller-Maitland and Ralph Vaughan Williams, 'Miscellaneous', *Journal of the Folk-Song Society*, 2/9 (1906), 282–99.

Killen, Louis, *Ballads & Broadsides* (Topic Records 12T126, 1965).

Kim, Rina, and Claire Westall, eds., *Cross-Gendered Literary Voices: Appropriating, Resisting, Embracing* (Basingstoke: Palgrave Macmillan, 2012).

Kittler, Friedrich A., *Gramophone, Film, Typewriter*, trans. by Geoffrey Winthrop-Young and Michael Wutz (Stanford, CA: Stanford University Press, 1999).

Kramer, Lawrence, *Music and Poetry: The Nineteenth Century and After* (Berkeley, CA: University of California Press, 1992).

Kramer, Lawrence, *Musical Meaning: Toward a Critical History* (Berkeley, CA: University of California Press, 2002).

Kristeva, Julia, *The Kristeva Reader*, ed. by Toril Moi (Oxford: Blackwell, 1999).

Lazarus, Micha, 'Birdsongs and Sonnets: Listening to Renaissance Lyric', transcript of lecture delivered at UCL, 20 November 2018.

Leech, Geoffrey, 'Music in Metre: "Sprung Rhythm" in Victorian Poetry', in *Language in Literature: Style and Foregrounding* (New York and London: Routledge, 2013), pp. 70–85.

Lévi-Strauss, Claude, *The Savage Mind* (London: Weidenfeld and Nicolson, 1966).

Lévi-Strauss, Claude, 'The Structural Study of Myth', *Journal of American Folklore*, 68/270 (1955), 428–44.

Lewis, C.S., *The Discarded Image: An Introduction to Medieval and Renaissance Literature* (Cambridge: Cambridge University Press, 1964).

Lewis, Charlton C., and Charles Short, *A Latin Dictionary* (Oxford: Oxford University Press, 1879).

Linkin, Harriet Kramer, 'Isn't It Romantic?: Angela Carter's Bloody Revision of the Romantic Aesthetic in "The Erl-King"', *Contemporary Literature*, 35/2 (1994), 305–23.

Lloyd, A. L., *English Street Songs* (Riverside RLP 12-614, 1956).

Lloyd, A. L., *First Person* (Topic Records 12T118, 1966).

Lloyd, A. L., *Folk Song in England*, first publ. 1967 (Frogmore: Paladin, 1975).

Lloyd, A. L., sleeve notes to Mike Waterson, *Mike Waterson* (Topic Records 12TS332, 1977).

Lloyd, A. L., sleeve notes to Various Artists, *The Bird in the Bush: Traditional Songs of Love and Lust* (Topic Records 12T135, 1966).

Lloyd, A. L., *The Foggy Dew and Other Traditional English Love Songs* (Tradition Records TLP1016, 1956).

Lloyd, A. L., and Ewan MacColl, *English and Scottish Folk Ballads* (Topic Records 12T103, 1964).

Lloyd, A. L., and Ewan MacColl, *Great British Ballads (Not Included in the Child Collection)* (Riverside RLP 12-629, 1957).
Lloyd, A. L., and Ewan MacColl, *The English and Scottish Popular Ballads, Vol. 2* (Riverside RLP 12-623/624, 1956).
MacColl, Ewan, and Peggy Seeger, 'The Elfin Knight', *Classic Scots Ballads* (Tradition Records TLP1015, 1959).
MacKinnon, Niall, *The British Folk Scene: Musical Performance and Social Identity* (Buckingham: Open University Press, 1993).
Makem, Sarah, 'Barbara Allen', on Various Artists, *As I Roved Out (Field Trip – Ireland)* (Smithsonian Folkways FW8872, 1960).
Makem, Sarah, *Sarah Makem, Ulster Ballad Singer*, recorded by Paul Carter and Sean O'Boyle in Keady, Co. Armagh, 1967 (Topic Records 12T182, 1968).
Makem, Sarah, *The Heart Is True (The Voice of the People Series) Vol. 24*, recorded by Paul Carter and Sean O'Boyle 1967 (Topic Records TSCD674, 2012).
Mallarmé, Stéphane, 'Mystery in Literature', in *Mallarmé in Prose*, ed. by Mary Ann Caws, trans. by Malcolm Lowrie (New York: New Direction, 2001), pp. 46–51.
Mann, Jill, ed., *Ysengrimus: Text with Translation, Commentary and Introduction*, trans. by Jill Mann (Leiden: Brill, 1987).
Mansfield, Paul, 'Tell Tale Sisters: Interview with Angela Carter', *Guardian*, 25 October 1990, p. 32.
Matless, David, *In the Nature of Landscape: Cultural Geography on the Norfolk Broads* (Chichester: John Wiley, 2014).
Matless, David, 'Sonic Geography in a Nature Region', *Social and Cultural Geography*, 6/5 (2005), 745–66.
McCabe, Mary Diane, 'A Critical Study of Some Traditional Religious Ballads' (unpublished thesis), (submitted to Durham University, 1980) <http:///etheses.dur.ac.uk/7804/> [accessed 5 November 2018].
McGuire, Jerry, 'The Intelligible, the Sensible and Fictivist Thought: Angela Carter's Window on the Wolves', *New Writing*, 5/2 (2008), 126–39.
McKay, George, 'Trad jazz in 1950s Britain – protest, pleasure, politics – interviews with some of those involved', January 2010 <http://usir.salford.ac.uk/id/eprint/9306/1/trad_jazz_interviews_2001-02_PDF.pdf> [accessed 14 February 2022].
McLane, Maureen, 'Ballads and Bards: British Modern Orality', *Modern Philology*, 98/3 (2001), 423–43.
McLaughlin, Becky, 'Perverse Pleasure and Fetishized Text: The Deathly Erotics of Carter's "The Bloody Chamber"', *Style*, 29/3 (1995), 404–57.
Mejias, Stephen, 'Interview with Aidan Baker: On Music, Sound and "Already Drowning"', *Stereophile*, 30 May 2013 <https://www.stereophile.com/content/aidan-baker-music-sound-and-ialready-drowningi> [accessed 16 February 2022].
Menninghaus, Winfried, *In Praise of Nonsense: Kant and Bluebeard*, trans. by Henry Pickford (Stanford, CA: Stanford University Press, 1999).
Merleau-Ponty, Maurice, *The Prose of the World* (Evanston, IL: Northwestern University Press, 1973).
Middleton, Anne, 'The Audience and Public of *Piers Plowman*: Middle English Alliterative Poetry and Its Literary Background', in *Middle English Poetry and Its Literary Background: Seven Essays*, ed. by David Lawson (Woodbridge: DS Brewer, 1982), pp. 101–23.
Mikkonen, Kai, 'The Hoffman(n) Effect and the Sleeping Prince: Fairy Tales in Angela Carter's *The Infernal Desire Machines of Doctor Hoffman*', *Marvels & Tales*, 12/1 (1998), 155–74.

Mitchell, Anaïs and Jefferson Hamer, *The Child Ballads* (Wilderland Records WILDER002LP, 2013).

Molan, Christine, 'Angela Carter', *fRoots*, 409 (2017), 21.

Molan, Christine, 'Authentic Magic: Angela, Folksong and Bristol', in *Strange Worlds: The Vision of Angela Carter*, ed. by Marie Mulvey-Roberts and Fiona Robinson (Bristol: Sansom & Co, 2016), pp. 29–32.

Molan, Christine, email to the author, 26 September 2015.

Molan, Christine, email to the author, 4 October 2015.

Molan, Christine, email to the author, 12 May 2020.

Molan, Christine, email to the author, 23 June 2020.

Molan, Christine, email to the author, 28 June 2020.

Moray, Jim, 'Hind Etin', from *Skulk* (Niblick Is A Giraffe Records NIBL013, 2012).

Motherwell, William, *Minstrelsy Ancient and Modern* (Glasgow: John Wylie, 1827).

Moulden, John, 'The Derry Journal and the "Come-All-Ye" and "Old Come-All-Ye" Booklets', *Inishowen Song Project*, 2018 <https://s3-eu-west-1.amazonaws.com/itma.dl.printmaterial/inishowen_pdfs/derry_journal_come_all_yes_john_moulden.pdf> [accessed 4 February 2018].

Mulvey-Roberts, Marie, and Fiona Robinson, eds., *Strange Worlds: The Vision of Angela Carter* (Bristol: Sansom & Co, 2016).

Munford, Rebecca, ed., *Re-Visiting Angela Carter: Texts, Contexts, Intertexts* (Basingstoke: Palgrave Macmillan, 2006).

Munford, Rebecca, '"The Desecration of the Temple"; or, "Sexuality as Terrorism"? Angela Carter's (Post-)Feminist Gothic Heroines', *Gothic Studies*, 9/2 (2007), 58–70.

Newton Scott, Fred, 'The Scansion of Prose Rhythm', *PMLA*, 20/4 (1905), 707–28.

Nicolaisen, W. F. H., 'The Cante Fable in Occidental Folk Narrative', in *Prosimetrum: Cross-Cultural Perspectives on Narrative in Prose and Verse*, ed. by Joseph Harris and Karl Reichl (Cambridge: DS Brewer, 1977), pp. 183–211.

Onderdonk, Julian, 'Vaughan Williams and the Modes', *Folk Music Journal*, 7/5 (1999), 609–26.

Ong, Walter, *Orality and Literacy: The Technologizing of the Word*, 2nd edn (New York and London: Routledge, 2002).

Ovid, 'Tereus and Philomela', in *Metamorphoses* (London: Penguin Classics, 2007), pp. 146–53.

Palmer, Paulina, 'From "Coded Mannequin" to Bird Woman: Angela Carter's Magic Flight', in *Women Reading Women's Writing*, ed. by Sue Roe (Brighton: Harvester Press, 1987), pp. 179–205.

Patch, Howard Rollin, 'Some Elements in Mediæval Descriptions of the Otherworld', *PMLA*, 33/4 (1918), 601–43.

Paulusma, Polly, *Invisible Music: Folk Songs that Influenced Angela Carter* (Wild Sound/One Little Independent WLDSND008, 2021).

Peach, Linden, *Angela Carter*, 2nd ed. (Basingstoke and New York: Palgrave Macmillan, 2009).

Percy, Thomas, *Reliques of Ancient English Poetry*, first publ. 1765 (London: JM Dent, 1906).

Perrault, Charles, *The Fairy Tales of Charles Perrault*, trans. by Angela Carter, first publ. 1977 (London: Penguin, 2008).

Petermann, Emily, *The Musical Novel: Imitation of Structure, Performance and Reception in Contemporary Fiction* (Rochester, NY: Camden House, 2014).

Plato, *Plato: The Complete Works*, ed. by John M. Cooper (Indianapolis, IN: Hackett, 1997).
Pollock, Della, 'Performing Writing', in *The Ends of Performance*, ed. by Jill Lane and Peggy Phelan (New York: New York University Press, 1998), pp. 73–103.
Pollock, Mary S., 'Angela Carter's Animal Tales: Constructing the Non-Human', *Literature Interpretation Theory*, 11/1 (2000), 35–57.
Polwart, Karine, 'The Dowie Dens of Yarrow', on *Fairest Floo'er* (Hegri Music HEGRICD03, 2007).
Porter, James, '(Ballad-)Singing and Transformativity', in *The Stockholm Ballad Conference August 1991*, ed. by Bengt R. Jonsson (Stockholm: Svenskt Visarkiv, 1993), pp. 165–80.
Porter, James, 'Jeannie Robertson's "My Son David": A Conceptual Performance Model', *Journal of American Folklore*, 89/351 (1976).
Porter, James, and Herschel Gower, *Jeannie Robertson: Emergent Singer, Transformative Voice* (Knoxville: University of Tennessee Press, 1995).
Portman, Emily, 'Composition Commentary: "Bones and Feathers"' (unpublished MA thesis), (submitted to Newcastle University, 2008).
Portman, Emily, 'Composition Commentary: "Bones and Feathers" Appendices' (unpublished MA thesis), (submitted to Newcastle University, 2008).
Portman, Emily, *Coracle* (Furrow Records FURR008, 2015).
Portman, Emily, email to the author, 14 March 2019.
Portman, Emily, *Hatchling* (Furrow Records FURR006, 2012).
Portman, Emily, interview with the author, 13 tapes, 2–3 March 2019.
Portman, Emily, *The Glamoury* (Furrow Records FUR002, 2010).
Powers, Harold, 'IV. Modal Scales and Folksong Melodies', in *The New Grove Dictionary of Music and Musicians*, ed. by Stanley Sadie, Vol. 12 (London: Macmillan, 1980), pp. 418–22.
Presley, Katie, 'Review: Wolf Alice, *My Love is Cool*', *NPR Music*, 14 June 2015 <https://www.npr.org/2015/06/14/412947413/first-listen-wolf-alice-my-love-is-cool> [accessed 16 February 2022].
Propp, Vladimir, *Morphology of the Folktale*, ed. by Louis A. Wagner, trans. by Laurence Scott, 2nd edn (Austin, TX: University of Texas Press, 2009).
Propp, Vladimir, *Theory and History of Folklore*, ed. by Anatoly Liberman, trans. by Ariadna Y. Martin and Richard P Martin (Minneapolis, MN: University of Minnesota Press, 1984).
Prynne, Jeremy, 'Mental Ears and Poetic Work', *Chicago Review*, 55/1 (Winter 2010), 126–57.
Prynne, Jeremy, *Stars, Tigers and the Shapes of Words: The Williams Matthews Lectures 1992* (London: Birkbeck College, 1992).
Purslow, Frank, *Marrow Bones* (London: EFDS Publications, 1965).
Reeves, James, *The Everlasting Circle* (London: Heinemann, 1960).
Renwick, Roger deV, *English Folk Poetry: Structure and Meaning* (Philadelphia, PA: University of Pennsylvania Press, 1980).
Ritchie, Jean, 'One Morning in May' (a variant of 'Grenadier and Lady'), from *Jean Ritchie Singing The Traditional Songs of Her Kentucky Mountain Family* (Elektra EKLP-2, 1953).
Roberts, Lynn, 'FFS Interview: Wise Children', *For Folks Sake*, 26 June 2009 <https://www.forfolkssake.com/interviews/1678/ffs-interview-wise-children> [accessed 16 February 2022].
Robertson, Jeannie, 'My Son David', on *Scottish Ballads and Folk Songs by Jeannie Robertson World's Greatest Folk Singer* (Prestige International INT13006, 1961).

Roemer, Danielle M., and Cristina Bacchilega, eds., *Angela Carter and the Fairy Tale* (Detroit, MI: Wayne State University Press, 2001).

Roud, Steve, *Folk Song in England* (London: Faber, 2017).

Roud, Steve, 'General Introduction', in *The New Penguin Book of English Folk Songs*, ed. by Steve Roud and Julia Bishop (London: Penguin, 2012), pp. ix–xli.

Rousseau, Jean-Jacques, *Essay on The Origin of Languages and Writings Related to Music*, trans. by John T. Scott (Hanover, NH and London: Dartmouth College Press, 2009).

Rubery, Matthew, ed., *Audiobooks, Literature and Sound Studies* (New York: Routledge, 2011).

Rushdie, Salman, 'Introduction', in Angela Carter, *Burning Your Boats: Collected Stories* (London: Vintage, 1996), pp. ix–xvi.

Sade, Marquis de, *Juliette*, trans. by Austryn Wainhouse (New York: Grove Press, 1968).

Sage, Lorna, *Angela Carter*, 2nd edn (Tavistock: Northcote House, 2007).

Sage, Lorna, 'Angela Carter: The Fairy Tale', *Marvels & Tales*, 12/1 (1998), 52–69.

Sage, Lorna, ed., *Flesh and the Mirror: Essays on the Art of Angela Carter* (London: Virago Press, 1994).

Sage, Lorna, 'The Savage Sideshow: A Profile of Angela Carter', *New Review*, 4/39–40 (1977), 51–7.

Sage, Lorna, *Women in the House of Fiction: Post-War Women Novelists* (Basingstoke: Macmillan, 1992).

Sauvage, Julie, 'Bloody chamber melodies: painting and music in *The Bloody Chamber*', in *The Arts of Angela Carter: A Cabinet of Curiosities*, ed. by Marie Mulvey-Roberts (Manchester: Manchester University Press, 2019), pp. 58–79.

Schechner, Richard, *Performance Theory* (London: Routledge Classics, 2003).

Schiller, Gertrud, *Iconography of Christian Art*, trans. by Janet Seligman (London: Lund Humphries, 1972), ii.

Seeger, Peggy, *Early in the Spring* (Topic Records TOP73, 1962).

Seeger, Peggy, interview with the author, 4 January 2016.

Seeger, Peggy, *Troubled Love* (Topic Records TOP72, 1962).

Sellers, Susan, *Myth and Fairy Tale in Contemporary Women's Fiction* (Basingstoke: Palgrave Macmillan, 2001).

Sharp, Cecil, *English Folk-Song: Some Conclusions* (London: Novello, 1907).

Sharp, Cecil, Olive Campbell and Maud Karpeles, *English Folk Songs of the Southern Appalachians*, 2 vols. (London: Oxford University Press, 1932).

Sidgwick, Frank, *The Ballad* (London: Martin Secker, 1914).

Sivyer, Caleb, 'The Politics of Gender and the Visual in Virginia Woolf and Angela Carter' (unpublished thesis), (submitted to Cardiff University, 2015) <https://orca.cf.ac.uk/89176/1/C%20Sivyer%20PhD%20thesis.pdf> [accessed 14 February 2022].

Smith, Adam, and Dugald Stewart, 'Considerations Concerning the First Formation of Languages, and the Different Genius of Original and Compounded Languages', in *The Theory of Moral Sentiments and on the Origin of Languages* (London: Henry G. Bohn, 1853), pp. 505–38 <http://oll.libertyfund.org/titles/smith-the-theory-of-moral-sentiments-and-on-the-origins-of-languages-stewart-ed> [accessed 2 April 2018].

Smith, Patti, 'Gloria', from *Horses* (Arista Records AL 4066, 1975).

Smith, Phoebe, 'Higher Germany', recorded by Paul Carter and Frank Purslow 1969, on LP *Once I Had a True Love* (Topic 12T193, 1970).

Spiegel, Max, 'Lyr Req: The Flower of Sweet Strabane' <https://mudcat.org/thread.cfm?threadid=8569> [accessed 14 March 2020].

St. Asaph, Katherine, 'Honeyblood', *Pitchfork*, 2014 <https://pitchfork.com/reviews/albums/19589-honeyblood-honeyblood/> [accessed 16 February 2022].

Stalker, Angela, 'Come in, Take a Chair, Lean on It, and Sing', *Croydon Advertiser* (Croydon, London, 31 March 1961), p. 4.
Steingo, Gavin, and Jim Sykes, *Remapping Sound Studies* (London: Duke University Press, 2019).
Sterne, Jonathan, ed., *The Sound Studies Reader* (New York and London: Routledge, 2012).
Sterne, Laurence, *The Life and Opinions of Tristram Shandy, Gentleman*, first publ. 1759–67 (London: Penguin, 1997).
Stevenson, Robert Louis, *A Child's Garden of Verse* (London: John Lane, 1885) <http://www.archive.org/stream/childsgardenofve00stev#page/n9/mode/2up> [accessed 16 February 2022].
Stevenson, Robert Louis, 'On Some Technical Elements of Style in Literature', first publ. 1885, repr. in *Essays in the Art of Writing* (London: Chatto & Windus, 1905).
Stick In The Wheel, *From Here* (From Here Records SITW002, 2015) <https://stickinthewheel.bandcamp.com/album/from-here> [accessed 18 February 2022].
Stickle, John, 'King Orfeo' (fragment), from *The Folksongs of Britain, Vol 4: The Child Ballads Vol 1* (Caedmon TC 1145, 1961).
Stokes, Martin, 'Introduction', in *Ethnicity, Identity and Music: The Musical Construction of Place*, ed. by Martin Stokes (Oxford: Berg, 1994), pp. 1–28.
Straumann, Barbara, *Female Performers in British and American Fiction* (Berlin: Walter de Gruyter, 2018).
Street, John and Sara Cohen, *Popular Music*, 24/2 'Literature and Music Issue' (2005).
Sturges, Fiona, 'Bat for Lashes: Away with the Fairies', *Independent*, 10 July 2009 <https://www.independent.co.uk/arts-entertainment/music/features/bat-for-lashes-away-with-the-fairies-1739707.html> [accessed 16 February 2022].
Swann Jones, Steven, *The Fairy Tale: Magic Mirror of the Imagination* (London: Routledge, 2002).
Sykes, Richard, 'The Evolution of Englishness in the English Folksong Revival, 1890–1914', *Folk Music Journal*, 6/4 (1993), 446–90 (pp. 478–9).
Symmons Roberts, Michael, and Paul Farley, *Edgelands* (London: Jonathan Cape, 2011).
Taraz, Diane, 'The Game of Cards', from *Songs of the Revolution* (Raisin Pie Music, 2010).
Tatar, Maria, ed., *The Cambridge Companion to Fairy Tales* (Cambridge: Cambridge University Press, 2014).
Tempest, Norton R., *The Rhythm of English Prose* (Cambridge: Cambridge University Press, 1930).
Teverson, Andrew, *Fairy Tale* (Abingdon: Routledge, 2013).
Tiger's Bride, The, '"The Tiger's Bride" – Influences' <https://www.facebook.com/pg/TheTigersBride/about/?ref=page_internal> [accessed 20 June 2020].
Theriot, Lisa, 'Lady Isabel and the Elf-Knight', from *A Turning of Seasons* (Raven Boy Music, 2001).
Thompson, Stith, 'Folktale', in *Funk & Wagnalls Standard Dictionary of Folklore, Mythology and Legend*, ed. by Maria Leach (San Franscisco: Harper and Row, 1984), p. 408.
Thompson, Stith, *The Folktale* (New York: Dryden Press, 1946).
Thorne Davies, Reginald, *Medieval English Lyrics: A Critical Anthology* (Evanston, IL: Northwest, 1964).
Thrall, William Flint, and Addison Hibbard, *A Handbook to Literature* (New York: Odyssey Press, 1936).
Thrift, Nigel, and David Dewsbury, 'Dead Geographies – and How to Make Them Live', *Environment and Planning D: Society and Space*, 18 (2000), 411–32.
Tiainen, Milla, 'Corporeal Voices, Sexual Differentiations: New Materialist Perspectives on

Music, Singing and Subjectivity', in *Sonic Interventions*, ed. by Sylvia Mieszkowski (Amsterdam: Rodopi, 2007), pp. 147–68.

Todorov, Tzvetan, *The Fantastic: A Structural Approach to a Literary Genre* (Cleveland, OH, 1973).

Toelken, Barre, *Morning Dew and Roses: Nuance, Metaphor and Meaning in Folksongs* (Urbana and Chicago, IL: University of Illinois Press, 1995).

Tolkien, J. R. R., 'On Fairy-Stories', in *Essays Presented to Charles Williams* (Oxford: Oxford University Press, 1947), pp. 38–89.

Tonkin, Maggie, *Angela Carter and Decadence: Critical Fictions/Fictional Critiques* (Basingstoke: Palgrave Macmillan, 2012).

Tunney, Paddy, *A Wild Bees' Nest* (Topic Records, 1965).

Tunney, Paddy, *Where Songs Do Thunder: Travels in Traditional Song* (Belfast: Appletree Press, 1992).

Unthanks, The, *Mount The Air* (Rabble Rouser Music, 2015).

Utley, Frances Lee, 'Folk Literature: An Operational Definition', *Journal of American Folklore*, 74/293 (1961), 193–206.

Vaughan Williams, Ralph, *The Oxford Book of Carols* (Oxford: Oxford University Press, 1928).

Vaughan Williams, Ralph, and A. L. Lloyd, eds., *The Penguin Book of English Folk Songs* (Harmondsworth: Penguin, 1959).

Vaughan Williams, Ralph, Cecil Sharp, G. S. K. Butterworth, Frank Kidson, A. G. Gilchrist, and Lucy Broadwood, 'Songs Collected from Sussex', *Journal of the Folk-Song Society*, 4/17 (1913), 279–324.

Vlocke, Deborah M., 'Sterne, Descartes and the Music in Tristram Shandy', *Studies in English Literature, 1500–1900*, 38/3 (1998), 517–36.

Warner, Marina, *From the Beast to the Blonde: Fairy Tales and Their Tellers* (London: Random House, 1995).

Warner, Marina, 'Introduction', in *The Second Virago Book of Fairy Tales* (London: Virago, 1992), pp. ix–xvi.

Warner, Marina, 'The Uses of Enchantment: Lecture at the National Film Theatre, 7 February 1992', in *Cinema and the Realms of Enchantment: Lectures, Seminars and Essays by Marina Warner and Others*, ed. by Duncan Petrie, BFI Working Papers (London: British Film Institute, 1993), pp. 13–35.

Warner, Marina, 'Why Angela Carter's "The Bloody Chamber" Still Bites', *Scotsman*, 15 September 2012 <https://www.scotsman.com/arts-and-culture/books/marina-warner-why-angela-carters-bloody-chamber-still-bites-2461766> [accessed 17 February 2022].

Waterson, Norma, 'Seven Virgins' / 'The Leaves of Life', from The Watersons, *Frost & Fire: A Calendar Of Ritual And Magical Songs* (Topic Records, 1965).

Watersons, The, 'Brave Wolfe', from *The Watersons* (Topic Records, 1966).

Watson, Amy, 'Audiobooks in the U.S. – statistics & facts', *Statista*, 29 June 2021 <https://www.statista.com/topics/3296/audiobooks/#dossierKeyfigures.> [accessed 16 February 2022].

Watz Fruchard, Anna, 'Convulsive Beauty and Compulsive Desire: The Surrealist Pattern of *Shadow Dance*', in *Revisiting Angela Carter: Texts, Contexts, Intertexts*, ed. by R. Munford (Basingstoke: Palgrave Macmillan, 2006), pp. 21–41.

Webb, Kate, 'Shakespeare and Carnival in Angela Carter's *Wise Children*', British Library <https://www.bl.uk/20th-century-literature/articles/shakespeare-and-carnival-in-angela-carters-wise-children> [accessed 16 February 2022].

Welsh, Caroline, 'Stimmung: The Emergence of a Concept and Its Modifications in

Psychology and Physiology', in *Travelling Concepts for the Study of Culture*, ed. by Birgit Neumann and Ansgar Nünning (Berlin: Walter de Gruyter, 2012), pp. 267–90.

White, Enos, 'George Collins', from *The Folksongs of Britain, Vol. 4: The Child Ballads Vol. 1* (Caedmon Records TC1145, 1961).

White Stripes, The, 'Jolene', written by Dolly Parton, live music video <https://youtu.be/yXlULkwhgrc> [accessed 17 February 2022].

Wicks, Ulrich, 'The Nature of Picaresque Narrative: A Modal Approach', *PMLA*, 89/2 (1974), 240–9.

Wilgus, D. K., 'A Tension of Essences in Murdered-Sweetheart Ballads', in *The Ballad Image: Essays Presented to Bertrand Harris Bronson*, ed. by James Porter (Los Angeles, CA: Center for the Study of Comparative Folklore and Mythology, University of California, 1983), pp. 241–56.

Willett Family, The, *The Roving Journeymen: English Traditional Songs* (Topic Records 12T207, 1962).

Williams, Jeni, *Interpreting Nightingales: Gender, Class and Histories* (London: Bloomsbury Press, 1997).

Williams, Raymond, *Keywords: A Vocabulary of Culture and Society* (New York and London: Oxford University Press, 1983).

Winick, Stephen, 'A. L. Lloyd and 'Reynardine': Authenticity and Authorship in the Afterlife of a British Broadside Ballad', *Folklore*, 115/3 (2004), 286–308.

Winter, Trish, and Simon Keegan-Phipps, *Performing Englishness: Identity and Politics in a Contemporary Folk Resurgence* (Manchester: Manchester University Press, 2013).

Wolf, Werner, *The Musicalization of Fiction: A Study in the Theory and History of Intermediality* (Amsterdam and Atlanta, GA: Rodopi, 1999).

Wood, Brent, 'Bring the Noise! William S. Burroughs and Music in the Expanded Field', *Postmodern Culture*, 5/2 (1995) <https://muse.jhu.edu/article/27514> [accessed 20 June 2020].

Woods, Fred, *Folk Revival: The Rediscovery of a National Music* (Poole: Blandford Press, 1979).

Yates, Michael, 'Percy Grainger and the Impact of the Phonograph', *Folk Music Journal*, 4/3 (1982), 265–75.

Zeeman, Nicolette, 'Imaginative Theory', in *Middle English*, ed. by Paul Strohm (Oxford: Oxford University Press, 2007), pp. 222–40.

Zipes, Jack, *Breaking the Magic Spell: Radical Theories of Folk and Fairy Tales* (London: Heinemann, 1979).

Zipes, Jack, 'Introduction', in *The Fairy Tales of Charles Perrault,* trans. by Angela Carter (London: Penguin, 2008), pp. vii–xxviii.

Zipes, Jack, *The Irresistible Fairy Tale: The Cultural and Social History of a Genre* (Princeton, NJ: Princeton Univ. Press, 2012).

Zipes, Jack, *Why Fairy Tales Stick: The Evolution and Relevance of a Genre* (Abingdon: Routledge, 2006).

Zuckerkandl, Victor, 'The Meaning of Song', in *Music, Words and Voice: A Reader*, ed. by Martin Clayton (Manchester: Manchester University Press, 2008), pp. 113–18.

Index

acousmatic voice 93, 108, 111, 120–7, 134
Adorno, Theodor 10, 33, 167, 172
Almansi, Guido 5
Anderson, Ian 38
Apollinaire, Guillaume 125, 198
Araki, Sozo 63–5, 89–90, 111, 151–3, 206
Aristotle 35
Arundel Psalter, The 106–7
'As I Roved Out' 26, 88, 90–1
Atkinson, David 25, 66–8, 114, 125–6, 204
Atwood, Margaret 4, 114, 117

'Babes in the Wood' 68–71
Bacchilega, Cristina 3–6
Baker, Aidan 131, 201
'Banks of Red Roses, The' 8, 44, 82
    'Barbara Allen', *see* Child ballads
'Banks of Sweet Primroses, The' 88, 176, 187
Baring-Gould, Sabine 32, 116
Barrault, Jean-Louis 152, 199
Barthes, Roland
   Empire of Signs 111
   Image Music Text 26
     'Grain of the Voice, The' 11, 126–8, 163
   'Loving Schumann' 36
Bat for Lashes 131, 201
Baudelaire, Charles 81, 152, 174, 199
Bayard, Samuel P. 33–4
becoming-animal 114–15
Benson, Stephen
   'Angela Carter and the Literary Märchen' 3–4, 165
   Cycles of Influence 5–6
   'History's Bearer' 206
   Literary Music 126
   'The soul music of "The Juniper Tree"' 114, 121
Bettelheim, Bruno 7
Biggs, Iain 67

Bishop, Julia 75–6
Björk 131, 200
Blake, William 81, 122, 126, 196
'Blow The Candle Out' 10, 33, 48–58, 176
Blue Aeroplanes, The 131, 201
Bluebeard 30, 68, 183, 193
'Bold Wolfe' 45, 175–7
Bonca, Cornel 89
'Bonny Bunch of Roses, The' 28–9
Boyes, Georgina 34, 66
Brăiloiu, Constantin 35–6, 117
'Brewer's Daughter, The' 133, 176
Briggs, Anne 20, 92, 105, 118–20, 190, 194, 195
Britzolakis, Christina 43
Broadwood, Lucy 25, 95
Bronson, B. H. 75–8
   'Brown Girl, The', *see* Child ballads
Brown, Calvin S. 16, 154, 168
'Bushes & Briars' 133
Butler, Judith 47–8, 55

canorography 17–18, 113–18, 122–34, 150–6, 207
cante-fables 120, 134, 142, 194–5
Carter, Angela
   Afterword to 'Fireworks' 61, 64, 109–10, 186
   'Alison's Giggle' 100, 166
   'Ashputtle' 135, 138–9
   'Bloody Chamber, The' 5, 95–6, 101, 117, 140, 165, 206
   early journalism on folk song 2, 37, 61–2
   'Erl-King, The' 16–17, 30, 61–86, 113–29, 134–50, 196
   Fairy Tales of Charles Perrault, The 4, 20–1, 81, 121, 133, 203
   folk club manifesto 38, 62, 112, 157
   folk song list 33, 41, 44–51, 133–4, 175–7

'Fools Are My Theme' 25, 61, 189
Heroes and Villains 8, 42, 44, 72, 174
Infernal Desire Machines of Doctor Hoffman, The 16, 31, 59, 87–112
Japan 62–5, 89, 104, 111, 151
'Leide' / 'Liede' 123, 151, 197, 206
Love 42, 59, 114
Magic Toyshop, The 14, 42, 119, 174, 180, 197
'Mother Lode, The' 4, 20, 61
Nights at the Circus 14, 17, 55, 59, 113–29, 135–9, 165, 182
'Notes from the Front Line' 28, 41, 58
'Now is the Time for Singing' 1–2, 10, 24–5, 41, 109–17, 163–4, 176, 189
Passion of New Eve, The 5, 59
'Penetrating to the Heart of the Forest' 72–3, 114, 186
'Reflections' 16, 59, 89–97, 105–10, 120
Several Perceptions 59, 99–100, 102–3, 153
Shadow Dance 1, 14, 16, 41–59, 74, 164
'Smile of Winter, The' 80
'Snow Child, The' 121, 139, 145, 190
'Some Speculations on Possible Relationships between the Medieval Period and 20th Century Folk Song Poetry' (Carter's dissertation) 2, 16, 25–30, 41, 64, 68, 91, 95, 118, 128, 135, 139, 170, 172, 186, 193, 200
'Sugar Daddy' 5, 12, 15, 85, 105
'Tiger's Bride, The' 114, 131, 202
Vampirella 31, 103
Virago Books of Fairy Tales 3–4, 6, 11, 33, 133–5, 142–5, 184
Wayward Girls and Wicked Women 33, 133, 202
Wise Children 5, 14, 59, 73–4, 127, 131, 165, 200, 202, 206
Carter, Paul 2, 8, 19–21, 37–46, 62, 68, 75–9, 97, 119, 149, 152, 157–60, 164, 173, 176, 182–3, 189–92, 195
Carthy, Eliza 131
Carthy, Martin 131–3
Cheltenham Folk Club 19, 160

Child, F. J. 11, 12, 31, 77, 83, 106, 116, 118–19, 164, 204
Child ballads, The 116, 164
'Barbara Allen' 8, 101
'Brown Girl, The' 133, 177
'Cruel Mother, The' 8, 68–70, 83, 114, 118, 134–41, 193, 204
'Elfin Knight, The' 82, 122
'Fair Annie' 133, 177
'Fair Margaret and Sweet William' 101
'George Collins' 45, 79–80, 133
'Grey Cock, The' (or 'The Cock') 23–4
'Hind Etin' 68–9, 83, 121, 136, 147–8
'King Orfeo' 68–9, 82–5, 94, 121
'Lady Isabel and the Elf Knight' 2, 8, 30, 68–71, 82–3, 94, 114, 121
'Lord Gregory' (or 'Lass of Loch Royal') 133
'Lover's Ghost, The' 133, 177
'Lucy Wan' (or 'Lizzie Wan') 32, 45, 93, 133, 176–7
'Maid and the Palmer, The' 140
'Tam Lin' 2, 8, 67–70, 77–85, 104, 118–21, 136, 147–8, 182, 194
'Thomas Rymer' 8
'Twa Corbies, The' 22
'Twa Magicians, The' 114, 193
'Twa Sisters, The' (or 'The Two Sisters') 84, 120, 124, 142, 184, 205
'Unquiet Grave, The' 22, 68–70, 75–8, 170
'Young Hunting' 114, 133, 193
chimeras 17, 113–28
Christmas, Keith 197
Cixous, Hélène 125, 155, 198
Clapp, Susannah 3
Clark, Robert 43
Clayton, Martin 116
Collins, Shirley 46, 97
Cone, Edward 46
Connor, Steven 108, 120
Cook, Nicholas 78, 198
Coover, Robert 4, 109–10
Corbin, Alain 66
Cottle, Basil 25
Cox, Harry 29, 34–6, 91
Crofts, Charlotte 2, 5, 14

cross-dressing female warrior ballads 47, 57–8
'Cruel Mother, The', *see* Child ballads
Crunelle-Vanrigh, Anny 4
'Cupid The Ploughboy' 8, 90
Cursor Mundi 25, 95

Deleuze, Gilles and Félix Guattari 114–16
Derrida, Jacques 14, 26
Derry Journal, The 19
'Died for Love' 44–6, 69, 88, 96–105, 176, 185, 189–90
'Dowie Dens of Yarrow, The' 8, 25, 47, 177
'Down in the Meadows' 69, 177
Dugaw, Diane 47, 57, 82
Dunn, Ginette 36–7
Dylan, Bob 151–3

Eliot, T. S. 14, 122, 153
Ellis Davidson, Hilda, and Anna Chaudhri 11
Ennis, Seamus 20
'Fair Annie', *see* Child ballads

fairy tales 2–8, 11–12, 27, 33, 48, 96, 120–1, 131–44, 201–3
'False Bride, The' 44, 46
'Female Drummer, The' 133, 176
'Female Highwayman, The' 133, 176
'Flower of Sweet Strabane, The' 19, 46, 93
Fludernik, Monika 81
Freud, Sigmund 47, 71
Frith, Simon 84, 116, 154, 184
Frost, Robert 10, 35, 117
Frye, Northrop 30–1, 153

Gamble, Sarah 3–5, 41, 43, 174, 199
'Game of Cards, The' 48, 51, 133–4, 176
Gardiner, George 32
Gass, William H. 153–4
gender identity 41–59
'George Collins', *see* Child ballads
Gerould, G. H. 140, 170, 192
Gilbert, Suzanne 46
Gilchrist, Anne 25, 75, 95, 120–1, 142, 170, 195
Gilligan, Carol 124
'Gipsy Countess, The' 8, 177
'Gipsy Girl, The' 133, 177

Glen, Heather 187–8
'Grey Cock, The', or 'The Cock', *see* Child ballads
Goethe, Joseph Wolfgang von
    'Erlkönig' 81, 121, 182–3, 196
    'Heidenröslein' 13, 192
    'Kennst Du Das Land' 127, 199
Gordon, Edmund 3, 20, 42, 62, 68, 89, 152, 184, 186–7, 206
Grainger, Percy 75, 97, 189
Greenhill, Pauline 47
greenwood, the 16, 67–86, 91, 107, 118, 122, 125, 148, 180, 181, 183
'Grenadier and Lady, The' 90, 187
Grimm Brothers 7, 11–12, 121, 138, 142, 144, 195, 196

Hall, Reg 2, 8, 164
Hammond, Henry and Robert 32
Haraway, Donna 115, 125, 128
Harker, Dave 9, 66–7
Harvey, PJ 131, 200–1
Heaney, Joe 29, 34–7, 187
Hennard Dutheil de la Rochère, Martine 3, 81, 152, 196, 206
Herzog, George 10
Hesiod 35
'Higher Germany' 32, 177
Hill, Rosemary 115
'Hind Etin', *see* Child ballads
Hitchcock, Alfred 145–6
Homer 35, 122
Honeyblood 131, 201
Horesh, Edward 62, 152, 178, 206
hybrids 17, 113–18, 125, 127–9

Ihde, Don 14, 126, 128, 192
Ikoma, Natsumi 89

'Jackie Munro' 8, 45, 57, 170, 176
Jones, Owain and Joanne Garde-Hansen 65, 86
Jordan, Elaine 114, 117
'Juniper Tree, The' 120–1, 134, 142, 184, 194, 195

Karpeles, Maud 8
Kennedy, Peter 20, 49
Kérchy, Anna 109, 114–18

Kerr, Nancy 131
Kerr, Sandra 131
Kidson, Frank 120–1, 142
Killen, Louis 23–4, 28, 34–5, 94, 131, 134, 183
'King Orfeo', *see* Child ballads
Kittler, Friedrich 15
Kramer, Lawrence 10–15, 113, 155, 192, 207, 208
  'Lady Isabel and the Elf Knight', *see* Child ballads

Lady Maisery (band) 131
Lang, Andrew 7, 11
Larner, Sam 24, 34–6
Lazarus, Micha 122, 126
Leader, Bill 20
'Leaves of Life, The' 97, 105–10, 190
Lee, Sam 131
Lee Utley, Francis 11
Leech, Geoffrey 71
Lévi-Strauss, Claude 26
Lloyd, A. L.
  Carter's *Virago* dedication, their friendship 4, 27
  Folk Song in England 11, 26, 34, 44, 46–7, 183
  musicology 20, 34, 46–8
  on 'Cruel Mother, The' 140, 204
  on 'Leaves of Life, The' 106
  on 'Polly Vaughan' 119
  on 'Reynardine' 45, 48–9, 57
  on 'Tam Lin' 77
  performance 48
local fauna 66, 196
  'Lord Gregory', *see* Child ballads
  'Lover's Ghost, The', *see* Child ballads
  'Lucy Wan' (or 'Lizzie Wan'), *see* Child ballads

McCabe, Mary 106
MacColl, Ewan 20, 105
MacKinnon, Niall 34
  'Maid and the Palmer, The', *see* Child ballads
Marling, Laura 131, 200–1
Massumi, Brian 12
Matless, David 66, 196
Maynard, George 'Pop' 46

medieval literature 2, 25–7, 41, 87, 91–3, 95, 106–7, 140, 187, 200
melos 30–1, 36, 153
Menninghaus, Winfried 96
Merleau-Ponty, Maurice 17, 155
modal scales 16, 48, 75–81, 84, 153, 182
modestar 77
Molan, Christine
  Angela Carter's folk singing 19, 32–3, 84, 134, 143, 169, 175–6, 184, 205
  club activities 38, 48, 119, 157, 160
  folk music archive 1–4, 16, 20–1, 53–4, 77, 157–9, 164
  Paul Carter 62, 68, 164, 170, 173, 180, 189
mondegreens 187–8
Moray, Jim 131
Motherwell, William 66, 116
'Mr Fox' 30, 48
Müller-Wood, Anja 117
Mulvey, Laura 5
Munford, Rebecca 43

Nicolaisen, W. F. H. 120–1
nightingales 83–5, 118–28, 146, 172, 183, 199, 205
nonsense 93–6, 105, 109–11

O'Connor, Maz 131, 163
O'Day, Marc 42, 174
Ong, Walter 28, 94
Ovid, *Metamorphoses* 85, 119, 122–8, 146, 183, 205

Palmer, Paulina 42–3
Peach, Linden 43
Pearce, Mark 121, 149
Percy, Thomas 116
Perrault, Charles 4, 21, 81, 121, 133, 200, 203
Petrarch 122, 124, 199
Piaf, Edith 125
picaresque, the 16, 87–110, 185
Plato, *Cratylus* 33, 172
Pollock, Mary S. 115, 117
'Polly Oliver' 47, 57, 134, 177
'Polly Vaughan' 119–20, 195
Porter, James 46, 75

Portman, Emily 17, 35, 76, 131–50, 154, 202, 205
 'Ash Girl' 135, 138–9
 'Borrowed and Blue' 140
 'Eye of Tree' 136, 147–8, 161–2
 'Hinge of the Year' 135–9, 202
 'Little Longing' 135, 140–2, 204
 'Mossy Coat' 135, 143–4
 'Stick Stock' 134, 142
 'Tongue-Tied' 135, 143–6
 'Two Sisters, The' *see also* Child ballads 142–3, 184
Propp, Vladimir 26–7
Prynne, Jeremy 14, 153
Purslow, Frank 2, 164, 204

radio plays 2, 5, 13–14, 31, 103, 166
Rees, Eleanor 147–9
Reeves, James 2, 21, 164
Renwick, Roger 66, 91
'Reynardine' 16, 20, 45–58, 82, 88, 133, 176, 177
Robertson, Jeannie 28, 46, 186
Roemer, Danielle and Cristina Bacchilega 3–6
Rossetti, Christina 81, 141
Roud, Steve 8–11, 14, 116, 173
Rusby, Kate 131
Rushdie, Salman 4, 14

Sage, Lorna 2, 3, 14, 44, 63, 81, 87, 89, 128
Sauvage, Julie 5–6, 206
Schechner, Richard 12
Schenkerian analysis 55, 125, 177, 198
Schubert, Franz 13, 127, 182, 192, 199–200, 202
Schumann, Robert 182, 199
Seeger, Peggy 11–12, 20–8, 67, 129, 132
Sewell, Fr Brocard 38, 113, 134, 190–1, 203
Sharp, Cecil 2, 8–9, 11, 29, 32, 37, 46, 62–6, 75–6
Sheppard, Fleetwood 76
'Short Jacket and White Trousers' 133–4
Sidgwick, Frank 35
Smith, Patti 44
Smith, Phoebe 20, 32, 76, 177, 186
'Snow White' 54, 139, 144–5

songfulness 13–16, 18, 31, 86, 112–16, 121–8, 150, 153, 182, 192, 206–7
Stevenson, Robert Louis 30, 153, 154, 171, 180–1, 207
Stick in the Wheel (band) 131
Stokes, Martin 67
'Story of Orange, The' 120–1, 134, 142, 195
'Streams of Lovely Nancy, The' 25, 94–6, 106
Stubbs, Ken 20, 190
Suleiman, Susan Rubin 105, 109
Swann Jones, Steven 7
sympathetic resonance 59, 96, 134, 149, 151–6, 207

Teverson, Andrew 7
Thompson, Stith 6–11
'Three Pretty Maids' 53, 177
Thrift, Nigel and John-David Dewsbury 47
'Thomas Rymer', *see* Child ballads
Tiainen, Milla 12, 29, 36, 154
Tiger's Bride, The (band) 131, 202
Todorov, Tzvetan 41, 174
Toelken, Barre 114
Tonkin, Maggie 43, 89, 185, 206
Topic Records 2, 20, 62, 173, 189
Tunney, Paddy 19, 93, 169, 176
 'Twa Corbies, The', *see* Child ballads
 'Twa Sisters, The', *see* Child ballads
 'Unquiet Grave, The', *see* Child ballads

Warner, Marina 2–5, 11–14, 61, 117, 145–6, 153, 207
Waterson, Norma 105–6, 131, 155, 175, 190–1
Watz, Anna 41, 174
'Week Before Easter, The' (or 'The False Bride') 44–6
White, Jack 44
'Wild Colonial Boy, The' 8
Willett, Tom 20, 37, 46, 97–8, 189
Williams, Raymond 8
Winter, Trish, and Simon Keegan-Phipps 9, 66–7

Wise Children (band) 131, 202
Wittgenstein, Ludwig 189
Wolf Alice 131, 200
Wolf, Patrick 131, 201
Wolf, Werner 71, 154

'Young Girl Cut Down In Her Prime, The' 88

Zeeman, Nicolette 87, 91–2
Zipes, Jack 2, 6–7, 203
Zuckerkandl, Victor 9–10, 116–17, 151–5